PRAISE FOR

Technically Yours

"A STEM-focused romance that is as sexy as it is cozy. . . . Williams is a master at crafting relatable characters whose past traumas obstruct their road to happiness, and *Technically Yours* is no different. She writes with the precision and charm of a classic rom-com, innately knowing the code to what makes an irresistible read." —*Entertainment Weekly*

"If, like me, you love second chances, banter that snaps, and steam that fogs up your windows, do yourself a favor and put *Technically Yours* on your TBR. You'll laugh, you'll swoon, and you'll root for Pearl and Cord's happy ending."

—*New York Times*
bestselling author Carley Fortune

"*Technically Yours* is technically flawless: a second-chance romance, a workplace affair, and a love story that will keep you flipping pages until the very end. This book was such a joy to read!"

—Nisha Sharma,
author of *Tastes Like Shakkar*

"In Williams's scorching *Technically Yours*, two old flames reignite a passion that defies algorithms. Cord's magnetic charisma, Pearl's breathless yearning . . . these two are a force to be reckoned with in both the boardroom and the bedroom! This irresistible second-chance romance rewrites the code on rom-coms!"

—Nikki Payne,
author of *Sex, Lies and Sensibility*

"Williams uploads her best yet contemporary romance, full of complex characters, the highs and lows of being a Black woman in STEM, and plenty of steam. Recommend to readers who enjoyed Jasmine Guillory and Chloe Liese." —*Library Journal* (starred review)

"*Technically Yours* is a clever tech-set romance that offers insights into some of the challenges of being a woman, particularly a woman of color, in this industry."   —Bookreporter

"Realistic conflict along with searing emotion and flashbacks to Pearl and Cord's first go-round make for a uniquely terrific romance."
                                                                                      —*Booklist*

"Cord is the kind of caring and supportive hero romance readers will adore."   —*Publishers Weekly*

Praise for
Do You Take This Man

"Denise Williams is known for her swoon-worthy tales that celebrate love, and her latest rom-com follows suit!"   —*Woman's World*

"If, hypothetically, Denise Williams decided to establish an academy (let's call it the University of DW) and offered courses on how to write pent-up sexual tension, steamy banter, and enemies to lovers, I would burst into the classroom and yell, 'TAKE MY MONEY!!' The writing is unmatched, the chemistry is on fire, and *Do You Take This Man* has one of the steamiest, most addictive, most satisfyingly hard-earned happily ever afters I've read in ages!"
                                                                                   —Ali Hazelwood,
                                                     New York Times bestselling author of *Deep End*

"Denise Williams has mastered the art of writing fun, sexy banter. Smart and witty, with the perfect amount of steam, *Do You Take This Man* is a gift to romance readers."
                                                                                  —Farrah Rochon,
                                       New York Times bestselling author of *Pardon My Frenchie*

"Once again, Denise Williams masterfully blends humor and heart with the perfect amount of steam. *Do You Take This Man* is full of authentic characters with relatable issues, hilarious wedding hijinks, and swoony sexy times. Lear earns a place on my list of favorite heroes, and Williams cements her spot on my list of favorite writers."

—Falon Ballard,
author of *Change of Heart*

"This annoyances-to-lovers story is steamy like the most luxurious bubble bath! Readers are in for a beautiful ride watching the deliciously prickly RJ learn to let someone care for her body and soul. Denise Williams consistently crafts romances that are so sweetly real. Her voice shines—fullhearted and playful—through every scene."

—Rosie Danan,
USA Today bestselling author of *Fan Service*

"Denise Williams delivers again with twice the banter, twice the heat, and the best enemies-to-lovers tension. A stellar romance!"

—Jane Igharo,
author of *Where We End & Begin*

PRAISE FOR
The Fastest Way to Fall

"This entertaining read will have you sweating through your next workout." —*Good Morning America*

"Warm, fuzzy, and ridiculously cute, *The Fastest Way to Fall* is the perfect feel-good read. Britta is an absolute breath of fresh air, and Wes is everything I love in a romantic lead. It's been weeks since I read this book, and I still smile every time I think about it. If you're looking for a novel that feels like a hug, this is it!"

—Emily Henry,
#1 *New York Times* bestselling author of *Funny Story*

Just Our Luck

DENISE WILLIAMS

BERKLEY ROMANCE

NEW YORK

BERKLEY ROMANCE
Published by Berkley
An imprint of Penguin Random House LLC
1745 Broadway, New York, NY 10019
penguinrandomhouse.com

Library of Congress Cataloging-in-Publication Data

Names: Williams, Denise, 1982– author.
Title: Just our luck / Denise Williams.
Description: First edition. | New York: Berkley Romance, 2025.
Identifiers: LCCN 2024036217 (print) | LCCN 2024036218 (ebook) |
ISBN 9780593641439 (trade paperback) | ISBN 9780593641446 (ebook)
Subjects: LCGFT: Romance fiction. | Novels.
Classification: LCC PS3623.I556497 J87 2025 (print) |
LCC PS3623.I556497 (ebook) | DDC 813/.6—dc23/eng/20240816
LC record available at https://lccn.loc.gov/2024036217
LC ebook record available at https://lccn.loc.gov/2024036218

First Edition: March 2025

Printed in the United States of America
1st Printing

The authorized representative in the EU for product safety and compliance
is Penguin Random House Ireland, Morrison Chambers, 32 Nassau Street,
Dublin D02 YH68, Ireland. https://eu-contact.penguin.ie

For the people whose attention,
care, and light remind us how lucky
we are to call them friends.
This one is for Emily.

AUTHOR'S NOTE

THIS STORY IS FILLED WITH DONUTS, KISSES, AND swoony brushes of hands, but also contains references to parental abandonment and addiction, hospitalization of a grandparent, CPR intervention, and financial struggles. Along with lucky pennies, you'll also read about a character's challenges living up to family expectations while figuring out their own neurodiversity, descriptions of sexual intimacy, and discussion about what makes a dick pic really pop on-screen. Take care while reading or grab a donut or your favorite sweet treat if any content gives you pause.

Sybil

"SYBIL, IT'S ALREADY SEVEN FORTY-FIVE." MY MOM stood in the open garage door with her coffee mug in hand, waiting for me to free up her driveway. It was a little game we played every morning—me losing track of time in the shower and her tapping her foot and dressed for the occasion in her signature slacks and sweater set from Ann Taylor Loft. "We need to go. What are you doing?" Her tone was the one that communicated "you are the child who tests me" versus the one reserved for my sister, which sounded like "thank you for being exceptional, Grace." I'd really tried to be on time that morning—set an alarm and everything. It just . . . didn't work out.

"I found a penny!" I bent to wedge the coin from where I'd seen it peeking between the grass and the sidewalk under the last few layers of melting snow. My fingertips were chilled, but one didn't just leave a penny on the ground—at least, I never did. "Got it!" I held it out like a gold medal toward my mother before shoving it in my pocket.

This was a good sign. Today was going to be lucky. I rubbed my palms together against the cold, then waved through the windshield. Turning the key, I rubbed the dashboard to coax my old girl to life, and she sputtered but didn't turn over. My stepdad insisted she was a pile of junk, but I knew she just needed a soft touch. "C'mon, girl." I turned the key again and got the same result. "C'mon," I said, an edge in my voice. She *was* a pile of junk, but since I hadn't ever held on to a job for more than six months and was currently living with my parents after getting kicked out of my apartment, she was the only pile of junk I had. "It's my lucky day," I said, petting the dash again and hoping my mom didn't see me doing this dance with my car. She'd side with Paul, which would lead to a long lecture about responsibility, none of which I had time for today.

The engine roared to life, and I cheered, throwing the car into reverse and speeding toward the donut shop. Traffic was light, and I picked up my phone to dial Emi as I drove.

"It's my lucky day," I said into the phone as soon as I heard her answer, her breaths coming heavy as she talked during her run. I imagined her ponytail bouncing as she paused at a red light while we spoke. We were unlikely friends in high school— she was studious and captain of the debate team, and I was everyone's favorite invite to a party, but we discovered a shared love of gelato and the Channel 8 meteorologist we had to watch for a class project. With spoons in hand and an intensely inappropriate interest in barometric pressure, the rest was history.

"You always think it's your lucky day."

"I'm aways right." I waved at ancient Mr. Edwards, who clutched his bathrobe closed and waved his newspaper at me. Lucky again. No peek at his stretched-out briefs and everything sagging out of them this morning.

"Marcus and I are going to be at the bar tonight, so if your date is a dud and you want to hang with us . . ."

"No need." I'd been talking to Carl through the app for a few days, and he checked all the boxes. "I'll see you there, but I have total confidence he's going to be a ten. Plus, he has the most amazing eyebrows." He also had a real grown-up job in finance, liked dogs, and didn't make me cringe politically. Since I'd stretched the truth and told my mom and sister I was seeing someone kind and responsible to get them both off my back, it would be great if this worked out.

And it would.

Sure, my last several boyfriends had left a few things to be desired, and one had stolen all my forks before ghosting, but good things happened to me, and Carl was the next good thing. And if that good thing could help me convince my family I was more than just the fun sister, that I could be taken seriously, too, well, that would be a bonus. Grace had Warren, and if I could find a guy that was serious and motivated and . . . well, a little boring, I could show them they didn't have to keep worrying about me. "It's going to go great tonight," I repeated.

"Just in case. You know where we'll be."

I whipped my car into a parking spot. There were signs indicating it was backup-only parking, but I knew I'd only be a minute, and whose bright idea was backup only, anyway? With a quick glance up and down the street for parking enforcement, I closed my door. "I told my boss I'd pick up donuts for the office," I said, hurrying toward the entrance. "She ordered them from this place, and today's the day I ask to be considered for that full-time event planning job."

"Good luck," Emi said as we hung up. The bell above the door to Joe's Donuts chimed as I walked in, the scent of sugar and fried dough making me want to stop and take a longer inhale. I rolled the lucky penny in my pocket and searched for the cashier. "Hello?"

There was a crash, and a man's harried voice from the back of the store called out to give him a minute. I imagined myself surrounded by the contents of a shelf I'd bumped into in the stockroom at my last job and sent out good vibes to whoever was in the back. Everyone had those kinds of mornings, and I had a couple of minutes, so I looked around. There was a bulletin board to my left covered in thank-you notes from young kids with large, uneven handwriting and donuts colored in with crayons and markers. A couple tacked at the bottom read "Get Well Soon, Mr. Joe!" next to a flyer and a collection box for the Pennsylvania Street shelter, asking for donations to support their programming. I slid a finger along the flyer and continued my visual inspection. The drink case gave a low hum, and the coffee urns were labeled with regular and decaf on handwritten note cards.

The pink frosting and brightly colored sprinkles covering the donuts at the front of the display case made my mouth water. I imagined tapping donuts in celebration with my boss when she applauded my gusto to ask for the job and offered it to me on the spot. I grinned and glanced down at my watch. She probably wouldn't care that I was a *few* minutes late. After all, I couldn't help there being a delay at the shop. Although the donuts and pastries were for a meeting with big potential clients. I tried to peek into the back again. "Hello?"

On the counter, two pink boxes sat, labeled "Josefina." I reached for my wallet, where I'd carefully stashed the petty cash before leaving the office. The total, $36.38, was written under Josefina's name in black Sharpie, the handwriting small and blocky. "Hello?" I said again, more quietly. It was 8:05 and the meeting started at 8:30. The shop was still, save the faint voices I heard in the back of the store. I could just leave the money with a note. "Here for Josefina," I called out. "I'm just leaving the money!" I thought I heard a grunt of acknowledgment from the back, and I flashed some side-eye to the closed swinging door. We all made messes, but the clerk still hadn't returned. Customer service at this place definitely left something to be desired, but I wasn't letting it get me down. "Keep the change," I added.

I rummaged through my purse for my wallet. If I broke a few traffic laws, which, let's be honest, I was going to break anyway, I could get to the office in fifteen minutes. My fingers landed on my keys, my phone, three ChapStick tubes, and a few loose condoms, but no wallet. "Shit, shit, shit," I muttered to myself. "No, no, no." I tossed it back on the counter and looked inside. On visual inspection, there was a fourth ChapStick rolling around but no wallet. My watch brightly shone 8:07 a.m., and I looked through the door to the back, seeing no one. I searched my purse one more time, as if the wallet would magically appear, and made a snap decision.

I snatched a napkin from a stack nearby, pulled a pen from the cup next to the register, and wrote a quick note and dropped it on the counter. There was a smiley face drawn in the corner of the top box of donuts, and I imagined the owner happily packing up the treats. I traced the smiley face, glancing around for the clerk again, and debated whether I should do this. But I *would* come back with the money and I *did* need to get going. I hurried out to my car with the boxes, tossing them into my passenger seat before peeling out. This was just a speed bump. I could make it there in time. It was my lucky day, after all.

2

Kieran

"**W**HAT WERE YOU DOING ON THE STAIRS ALONE?**"
I asked, my voice sounding more panicked than intended. I looked my grandfather over for more injuries. "I would have helped you." There was a red spot on his arm, and he rubbed his thigh where I was sure a bruise would form, but I was most concerned about his head and ran my fingers across his scalp, checking for bumps or tenderness.

"Don't fuss. I'm fine." He waved off my hand and sank into the office chair.

"Granddad, you're not fine." I tipped my head to the side to check his left temple. "You just fell down the stairs."

"And lived to tell the tale," he said, offering me a wistful smile, the left side affected after his stroke, but the right the same smile I'd grown up with. "I've started my day at four in the morning for fifty years, and I'm ready to get back to work." He looked around the office, from the ancient desktop computer to the aging photos of my little sister, Lila, and me as kids.

I glanced toward the front, where I'd heard a customer call out. They'd probably left, and losing customers was the last thing this shop needed. Business hadn't been great for a while, but it was worse now. I hadn't given him the full scope of how bad things really were since I took over tending the store. He needed to heal following his stroke, and the stress would only make everything worse. I shifted so my body would block the stack of medical bills and second notices arranged on the corner of the desk, along with the letter from my medical school informing me that the deadline was nearing for me to accept or decline my deferral. Three months to make a decision and pay the outstanding bill.

I placed a hand on his shoulder. "The doctors told you that you need to rest."

"You can't run this place by yourself, and Lila's still in school. And I'm not the one who looks like he's heading for an early grave." He waved away my touch again and pointed to my face, as if he could see the evidence of my exhaustion written there. "Admittedly, you didn't like *how* I made my way down the stairs, but I'm here now. Put me to work." He stood but wobbled before straightening, and I caught his elbows as I took in the sheepish and frustrated expression on his face. "Fine," he said with resignation. "But this conversation isn't over."

"No, sir." I settled him in the chair, ran to the front, and placed the "Back in Ten Minutes" sign on the locked door. The shop was empty, so as predicted, that customer had given up on me. Jogging back to Granddad, I wondered if giving up was the right call.

I'd planned to be a doctor since I was eight years old, when I learned what it looked like for someone to make things better, for someone to have the power to see a problem and fix it. I decided then that I was a person who would fix things. Now, despite my best attempts to take care of everything, it was all still broken, and the man who raised me needed me to be better. I let out a slow breath. He was right, and I wasn't sleeping enough. If I could get a full night's sleep, I'd stop feeling sorry for myself and could figure out what seemed impossible—how to get us out of debt and how I could return to medical school.

"We hired a teenager to help a little," I reassured him as we walked. I didn't mention that Chad was unreliable, that he listened to only half the things we said, and that we couldn't afford him, but that seemed to give Granddad some comfort. "We're figuring it out." I was careful to make sure my voice sounded positive and optimistic. "We got an order from a new business client, and it's on the counter right now for pickup."

"I hate that it's all on your shoulders, son." He paused, gripping the railing and meeting my eyes. We'd lived with him and my grandmother since social services took us from our mom, so he was the closest thing I had to a parent, and I knew that look. It was the same one he'd given me when I'd quit music in high school after my grandma died and I wanted more hours to work in the shop. It was the same look he'd given me when I'd skipped parties and going out with friends in college to stay in and study, and it was the same look he'd given me when he'd woken up after his stroke and learned I'd left school to help. It was the same look I'd pretended to ignore all those other times. "I don't want that for you. Burdens can be shared."

I nodded and motioned with my chin toward the landing. "You ready to keep going?"

He nodded, and we took it one step at a time up to the apartment over the shop. "Hey," he said as I unlocked the door. He pointed a shaky finger at the dingy linoleum. "There's a penny on the ground. Why don't ya pick it up? You know, for luck."

"Sure," I said, opening the door. "I'll grab it on my way out." I helped him inside, getting him settled on the couch and making sure he had what he needed. "Tom is gonna come by later, I think," I said before leaving. His best friend was a staple in our lives, and I was glad Granddad had some company during the day. He and Tom got up to all kinds of trouble in their lives, but at least he'd have a hand down the stairs if need be.

"Don't forget the penny," he said, and I noticed how he was still breathing heavier from the exertion of the stairs. Still, he flashed me a smile, began humming "Luck Be a Lady" by Frank Sinatra, and nudged me with his elbow until I sang a line with him. "You could use the penny! And sometimes luck looks different than you thought it would."

I closed the door behind me and swiped the penny from the floor. It was hard to imagine this coin had ever been shiny and new. It looked like it had spent its life forgotten at the bottom of a garbage can. "But I *could* use a penny," I said, picturing the mounting pile of bills, the notice that property taxes were going up, and the amount due for medical school before I could reenroll. Jogging down the stairs, singing the Frank Sinatra song under my breath, I unlocked the front door and tossed the penny in the tip jar Chad would probably pilfer later in the day. I settled behind the counter, only then noticing the note scribbled on a napkin by the register. "I forgot my wallet. Will bring money later. Sorry!"

The two boxes of pastries were gone, and because Chad had taken the order, we had no phone number, last name, or credit card information, so were probably just out another thirty dollars. The audacity of someone to just take them and leave a note like this. They must have been the person who called out while I was helping Granddad after he fell. That was the kind of irresponsible, selfish thing my mom would have done, assuming it was fine as long as her needs were met.

As I stewed, it felt like the penny was taunting me from inside the jar. I pressed my thumb to the spot between my brows. Luck wasn't real—good things didn't just happen to people, at least not people like us.

3

Sybil

LOOKED AROUND THE BAR FOR CARL WITH THE GREAT eyebrows, and I scrolled through social media, looking at nothing in particular, and spun the lucky penny from that morning on the table, admiring the way it picked up the lighting overhead. He had texted he was running late, but I scanned the crowd every few minutes hoping to spot him.

"Where are the eyebrows of your dreams?" The familiar voice from behind me made me grin, and I turned to face Emi.

"Running late," I said, glancing at my smartwatch. Twenty minutes late so far. "Where's Marcus?"

Em motioned to the bar, where her roommate, a head taller than everyone else, was trying to wrestle away the bartender's attention from a pack of women who, if I had to guess, got in with fake IDs. He held two thumbs up toward us before returning to the task at hand. Em had met both her roommates randomly, and although she didn't share my thoughts on luck, we both agreed she'd hit the jackpot with Marcus. He was kind, clean, loved to cook, and would do anything for her.

"So, are we celebrating?" Emi sat in the seat next to me. "Did you ask for the job?"

I spun the lucky penny again and shook my head. I'd rushed in just in time to literally run into the clients in the lobby and drop everything on the floor, including my purse. If the ruined snacks weren't bad enough, one of the clients who was trying to help me up slipped on a wayward ChapStick tube rolling across the floor and inadvertently took a colleague down with him. As I told the story, Emi's eyes grew wider, and her hand went over her mouth. "Oh no. What happened?"

"Well, after the ambulance showed up to take care of the client who hit his head on the way down and I cleaned up the donuts, Josefina fired me."

Emi rested a hand on my arm. "Oh, Syb. I'm sorry. You were really hoping the event planning job would come through."

I'd been certain Josefina would give me the job. We'd had such good vibes! Sure, I wasn't great with details and sometimes I was a little late, but I had such good ideas, which she'd told me on multiple occasions. What I hadn't told my friend was how I'd looked into training courses and made plans for how I could learn more about the event planning field. I didn't want anyone to see me actually trying—that would make it worse if I failed. The disappointed look that followed someone noticing I'd failed was a constant reaction my whole life, usually paired with "please pay attention," "focus, Sybil," and "try to get it together." I'd try and try, but I could never quite do it. Here was one more example of trying and failing spectacularly. Luck was easier to lean on than effort—no one could fault you for luck. "Oh well," I said, brushing off Emi's concern and swallowing my disappointment. "Another temp job down, on to the next. And I still have my date with Carl."

Em looked at her phone. "Or you could hang with us since he's late."

My phone buzzed, and I saw a message. I'll be another 30 minutes. Or maybe . . . The dots bounced on his next message.

"He'll be here. Despite my getting fired, it's still my lucky day, and I like him." I held up the penny. "I know your prince charming ended up being a dud, but I don't know . . . this could really be . . . something, he's—" I clicked on the new message from Carl and stopped mid-sentence.

Filling my screen was an out-of-focus, erect, and badly framed penis. The tattoo of the Monster Energy drink logo on the pale white skin of his thigh highlighted his less-than-impressive and poorly groomed package.

CARL: . . . just meet me at my
place? 😉 🍆

I blinked at the image on the screen. "Oh."

"What?" Emi set her wineglass down on the table and stretched to peek at my screen. "Oh, you're right. That really *could* be something. I guess the landscaping stopped with his eyebrows."

Marcus chose that moment to return to the table with drinks, sliding a glass of white wine across the table for Emi. Things would have been easier for me if I could have just fallen for Marcus, the smooth-skinned, deep-voiced, damn-he-works-out sweetheart who'd moved in with my bestie. But he was young and so earnest and innocent that I couldn't bring myself to risk corrupting him. Marcus was like bizarro Deacon, her other roommate and my onetime fling, who was across the room behind the bar flirting with a trio of blondes. These were my people, and when Marcus took a seat next to Emi, he asked, "What could be something?" He followed Emi's gaze to my phone and paused, studying the screen, his expression unchanged. "Whose dick am I looking at?"

"Meet Sybil's soulmate," Emi said, bringing the wineglass to her lips. I noticed how Marcus's gaze followed the movement of her hand. Poor Marcus—nothing was ever going to happen between him and Emi, but the flash of his hound dog expression made me feel for him.

"He seemed like a good guy." I dropped my head onto the table. "We talked about politics," I defended myself.

"Guys who send unsolicited dick pics can still care about politics." Marcus's voice was as even as ever; he was always the more responsible and even-keeled of Emi's two roommates. "Given the state of the country, I think it's obvious those guys still vote."

I heaved another sigh and motioned to the phone. "Why are men like this?"

Emi reached across the table and flicked my arm. The grown-up, adult, best friend way of comforting me, I guess. "We're just kidding. Sit up. Turn off your phone. We're here."

"But it was supposed to be my lucky day." I groaned but lifted my head. "He was supposed to be a good guy."

"C'mon," Emi said, motioning to the door. "We'll take this party to our place, and you can wallow out of the public eye."

I took a gulp from Emi's glass. "But there're cocktails here," I whined. "I need cocktails."

"I can make you cocktails at our place." Marcus handed me my jacket from the back of my chair.

"And there's plenty of cock on your phone. And we haven't looked in a few minutes. Might be some tail, too." Emi finished her wine and held out her hand for me. "C'mon, lucky girl, let's go."

I leaned against Emi as we stood from the table. "All I wanted was a nice, normal guy. Someone who might convince my family I'm making good choices. Are there any guys left who don't send dick pics?"

"I don't," Marcus offered as we stepped out into the night air.

"Deac probably does," Emi mused.

I shook my head, enjoying the chilled air on my face. "Yeah, but he always asks first. And they are usually wonderful photos. He's got a real eye for it."

Emi and Marcus stopped walking and laughed as I shrugged. Deacon and I might have a slightly regrettable history, but it wasn't a secret. "I mean, they used to be wonderful photos. I haven't seen his penis in over a year," I added, focusing on the way my feet fell onto the pavement. "Or . . . well, it's at least been a few months."

Emi and I started walking again, nearing the gas station. Marcus walked on our right, hands shoved in his pockets. "What *is* the secret to a high-quality dick pic?"

Emi and I answered at the same time. She said, "When you find the right person, you can ask them what they like."

I said, "Good lighting," earning a punch to the arm from my best friend. "Or what she said," I added.

"Let's get some water," Marcus said, holding open the door. "Deac had a heavy pour tonight, and you had most of Emi's wine." His palm on my elbow was gentle.

"Your fault. You paid my tab," I mumbled, looking around

the store. A rack of Little Debbie snack cakes caught my attention. "Think how sober I'd be if left to my own money."

"Good point," he said in a way that made me think he was actually weighing out the logic of the statement. "I'll give you a liquor allowance next time."

Emi plucked three water bottles out of the case, and Marcus walked an aisle over. "You two would make pretty babies," I said wistfully, appreciating my slight buzz. "Please, just take that boy's virginity and begin a beautiful life together."

Emi shoved a bottle of water into my hand. "Me and Marcus? Not happening." We strode to the counter and met Marcus, who took my water bottle to hand to the cashier. "Too busy with work."

"Yes, yes. You with your grown-up job and lack of parking tickets. My mom would love having you as a daughter." I pointed at my friend. "How do you do that?"

"Mostly I avoid parking illegally," she said, looking at the label on a packet of mints. "But we just do things differently. Your mom is proud of you."

She wasn't, but it was easier to pretend it didn't bother me. "She certainly wouldn't have approved of Carl," I said, holding up my phone.

"Who would?" Emi tapped the screen with her fingertip.

I giggled, but my gaze snagged on the sign advertising the current jackpot amount. "That." I waved my index finger toward it. "Forget finding a responsible man and a good job. That's what I need."

"You need three hundred fifty million dollars?" Marcus raised one eyebrow.

"Yes. That's all I need! Three hundred fifty million dollars doesn't send you a picture of its dick instead of showing up for your date. Three hundred fifty million dollars is all I need to be taken seriously."

Marcus eyed the illuminated sign. "At least a third would go to taxes. Are you sure two hundred and fifty million dollars is enough to get the job done?"

I reached for my wallet—the one that I'd found in our driveway near where I'd picked up the lucky penny—and nudged him out of the way. "I can make that work. I need two hundred and fifty million dollars. And maybe a donut, too."

The cashier looked bored by our conversation, and I wondered how many times a day he heard some iteration of the same musings. In the harsh light of morning, and in a month when I wasn't jobless, apartmentless, and the consummate disappointment of my family, I might have sat longer with that question. Instead, I asked, "Do you sell donuts that replace genuine human affection and professional achievement?"

He shook his head slowly. He pointed to what could dubiously be called a bakery case, where four sad, dry donuts rested, and I leaned my head on Emi's shoulder. "Nothing is going my way. I can't even get two hundred and fifty million dollars and a donut, Em."

With a shrug, the cashier added, "There's a place down the street open late."

I tapped my phone on the card reader, ignoring the voice in the back of my head reminding me I didn't have that many more dollar bills to my name. "That's right. Thanks!" I still had the petty cash in my wallet, and I followed his motion to see Joe's Donuts down the street.

The cashier handed me the ticket. "Maybe you'll get lucky."

4

Kieran

TOM PUSHED BACK FROM THE ANCIENT COUNTER, patting the surface of the aging orange linoleum three times like he always did. "'Bout time I hit the road, kid." He scrubbed a hand over his face and downed the last of his coffee. My plan to keep the shop open late to attract people after they left parties and local bars was a bust. The only person who'd stopped by late was Tom, and his one donut and two cups of coffee wouldn't save this place.

"Your granddad is proud of you," he said, adjusting his belt and pulling his worn ball cap from his back pocket. "Bored out of his mind and annoyed you won't let him disobey doctor's orders, but proud."

Someone peeked in the door, looked around, and then ducked back out onto the street, leaving us alone in the shop again.

Tom scratched his jaw, covered in white whiskers, and looked over his shoulder at the empty shop. "Things'll pick up."

"Sure about that?"

He laughed. It was the same slightly guttural old man laugh Granddad had, and that was something I loved about Tom hanging around. Then I felt the familiar grab of panic with the reminder of how Granddad had looked right after his stroke. He'd improved bit by bit, but he wasn't ready to spend all day in the shop, and while he was sure he'd be back at work, I had my doubts. I took another glance around the empty space, and I couldn't shake the worry I was letting him down despite good intentions. "I gave up on being sure about anything years ago." He patted his pocket, pulling a Powerball ticket out and shaking it next to his face. "But sometimes you get lucky, and you have the look of someone whose luck is about to change." He gave a wave over his shoulder as he walked toward the door, slowing as he tucked the lottery ticket back in his pocket.

"Waste of money," I mumbled to myself, watching him go before glancing around my own empty shop. Tom and Granddad split a ticket every week—it was their thing, their optimism in play after working long days, Granddad in the shop and Tom at the tire plant. My reflection in the security mirror was distorted, but one thing was painfully clear. I looked nothing like someone whose luck was about to change. I looked like someone who had fucked it all up—and I wasn't a person who fucked things up. At least, I never had been. I was the person who put things in order. I'd never had any other choice. Ironically, that Frank Sinatra song had been stuck in my head all day, like a catchy, cruel joke, and I sang to myself as I prepared to close.

The bell over the door chimed as three people walked in. One of them was laughing as they entered, her wild curls obscuring her face. She called out, her voice echoing through the empty shop. "Are you still open?"

"We're open," I said, wiping the already spotless counter. "What can I get you?"

She strode farther into the shop, pushing her hair off her forehead, revealing a face that made it hard to look away because each new feature I noticed—her full lips; her wide, dark eyes; the dimples in her cheeks—made me want to keep looking at her. My gaze dipped, and I took in her tight jeans, reminding me how long it had been since I was near enough to a woman to feel the way denim stretched over their thighs. The hours I kept with the shop and taking care of Granddad made dating kind of impossible, and Tom wasn't my type.

When she reached the counter, her short red nails clicked against the smooth surface as she eyed the display case. "Hi," she said with a wide smile.

Mine. The voice in my head was startling. I didn't think about possessing women, let alone strangers, and I wasn't someone who was taken in by a pretty smile and a tempting body, but the voice persisted. *I want her.*

The two people who trailed behind her eyed the case with less interest. "Hey. Can we get . . ." The two exchanged a look, then back to me. "An apple fritter and a glazed cake donut?" The man reached for his wallet. "Sybil, what do you want?"

I glanced at the woman again, taking in her curvy body and the way her lips pursed as she considered her options. She had really great lips, and my attention kept landing on them, imagining how they'd look kiss-swollen.

"Give me a minute. This is a big decision." Her words were a reminder she was a customer here to get donuts, not to be objectified by someone like me.

"Take your time," I said, intentionally looking away from her and denying my desire to glance at her lips again.

The two others exchanged a wary glance, and the woman chimed in. "It's just a donut, Syb."

She held up a hand. "No, this is *the* donut."

I followed the tip of her finger as she slid it over the glass when she looked away to say something to her friends before returning the intensity of her focus to me.

"I'm replacing men and a dream job with two hundred and fifty million dollars and a donut, and since winning the lottery is a long shot, it has to be a really good donut just in case that's all I get." She didn't look up from the display, and I glanced at the two people behind her, who rolled their eyes good-naturedly.

"C'mon, girl. Decide so we can get going." The woman tapped Sybil's arm as a loud group of couples pushed through the door, their voices echoing off the walls. "Remember? Cocktails at our place?"

I'd normally be overjoyed at having a large group of customers, all ordering the Sober-Up Special: water, two donuts, and a single dose of Advil, all for sixteen dollars plus tax. I felt guilty charging that much but got over it once the group started talking, with one woman exclaiming, "Ooh! Let's take a selfie with the donut guy! If he had money, I'd totally enjoy some glazed holes with him!" All the while, I monitored the strangely captivating woman still looking between the display case and her friends. She motioned for the group to go ahead of her, but I caught the tail end of their conversation as I handed a credit card back to a customer.

"Go ahead; I'll hang here for a while and then grab a ride back to my sister's place. I have a standing invite to their guest room."

My ears perked up listening to her shoo away her friends, and I wondered about their story. "Go home," she said. "I know it's past both your bedtimes. You wouldn't last through cocktails, anyway."

"We can wait with you," the guy offered, covering a yawn.

I wanted to get a jump on prep so my little sister didn't have as much to do when she came in to help, but I also kind of hoped this woman would stay. She seemed different from the customers I usually interacted with, and my days had become so similar it was hard to tell one apart from another.

She gave her friend a pointed look with her hip cocked and her arms folded. "You both have work early in the morning. I'll be fine. It's not like I haven't been here before."

I stole another surreptitious glance, wondering why I didn't recognize her if she'd been in the shop before.

"Fine. You're right." The woman covered her own yawn and leaned to hug Sybil. "Text me when you get home?"

When the two of them headed for the door, Sybil turned back to me. "Okay."

"Okay," I said, leaning forward on the counter and noticing how she glanced at my arms. I wondered when she'd been in before, because I was shocked I didn't remember her. Interesting. "Decide on something?"

She mirrored my pose, and I caught a whiff of something sweet like vanilla as she shifted positions. I took another quick breath to get more of the intoxicating scent. "Which one is best?"

"Which donut is worth millions of dollars?" I rubbed the back of my neck. "Not sure we've got anything like that."

"No. Which donut, when *paired* with two hundred and fifty million dollars, will help me avoid finding a meaningful career and forget all about men? Bonus points if that donut could also go to my sister's wedding with me." Her eyes flashed while she awaited my answer, and it felt like a challenge and an invitation.

She made me want to flirt back, except my flirting skills were beyond rusty, and I mentally prepared myself to loosen up. And who knew? Maybe Tom was right about something. If I was going to be broke, exhausted, and stuck in my hometown, maybe my luck would change for a few hours with this woman. "Well, that depends on what you like."

She arched an eyebrow and brought one manicured finger to her plump lower lip. "Do you really want to know?"

"Definitely." I nodded, glancing left and right. The other group were happily chatting at the tables, ignoring us, but it was kind of hard to remember there were other customers with the woman in front of me capturing all of my attention. "Let me guess. Chocolate?"

"Mm . . . yes. Or glazed."

I swallowed and leaned forward on the counter. "Filled?" The blatant euphemism was clumsy, but she kept tapping her lip with that red fingernail, and fighting how much I wanted her was a losing battle.

"Filled is good," she said. "Filled to overflowing with . . ." She leaned forward and lowered her voice, the words raspy, just above a whisper, and so fucking sexy that it took my brain a moment to register she was saying something else. "Lemon curd."

I paused, unsure what was happening until her serious expression cracked into a giggle. Actually, she kind of snorted. "I'm sorry, that's the one I want and I was trying to sound sexy, but it just isn't a sexy flavor."

Her face lit up when she laughed, her smile wide and genuine, and I couldn't help sharing her laughter. "No, it's the least sexy filling, but it's good." I stepped to the side to get the filled donut dusted with powdered sugar. I handed it to her in waxed paper. "This one has blueberry, too."

"Thanks," she said, eyes growing wide in a way that had me guessing she was a woman who never hid her joy. "But sexy or not, this is amazing."

"On the house." I scrubbed my hand over the back of my neck, hoping I didn't smear powdered sugar over my skin. Not that it would matter. I spent so much time in the shop, the smell of the dough and the fryer seemed to take up residence in my pores. "And, for the record, it was still very sexy."

"I didn't peg you for a curdy talk guy." She bit into the donut, powered sugar falling onto her black shirt and dusting the tops of her breasts, followed by a blob of lemon filling, which landed just above her neckline, my gaze tripping on its slow progression over her smooth skin. "Because—" She stopped mid-sentence, drawing my eyes back to her face, her expression annoyed.

"Seriously? You couldn't keep your eyes on my face while I finished my sentence? What is wrong with me? I pick these guys who suck. This is why I needed the donut." She huffed, blowing a curl off her face, her eyes narrowed.

I stammered a reply, floundering with how to backtrack. The other group of customers interrupted me, stumbling toward the counter. "Sorry, but can I get a box of assorted donuts before we go?" The woman's voice, grating and loud, hung between Sybil and me. I wanted to tell her I was busy helping another customer, though said customer thought I was a lecherous asshole.

"Cute top," she said. "You spilled stuff all over your boobs, though." She checked out Sybil's chest, as I had, before handing me cash and taking the box.

"That's what I was, um, looking at," I said. "But I'm sorry."

The click of the door closing as the crowd left, followed by sudden silence, punctuated my sentence.

Her expression softened and she looked down, seeing the mess. "Oops," she said, grabbing a napkin from the counter. It didn't clear the mess so much as spread it across the swell of her breasts. "I might have overreacted."

I didn't know what to say, so I just handed her another napkin. "Nah."

She laughed, dabbing at the lemon. "I didn't think I was drunk, but clearly I'm making a mess. Should get your Sober-Up Special. Does it work?"

I shook my head. "Your body metabolizes roughly one drink per hour, and alcohol causes an increase in insulin so you crave carbs and sugar with the low blood sugar. It doesn't actually sober you up."

She looked at me critically, mouth slightly agape, and I glanced away.

"I was premed in college," I added in explanation, not mentioning the two years of medical school and mountain of student loan debt I hadn't begun to make sense of yet.

"I think you're kind of interesting, Joe." She took another bite of her donut.

"It's actually Kieran." I felt buoyed until I remembered she was drunk. Though her pupils looked normal, and her eye movements were smooth.

She held out her hand. "Sybil." She scanned the shop. "I will try not to snap at you for looking at my boobs."

We shook and she smiled, putting my mind at ease further. Her hands were soft. "I'll try not to look."

She winked. "Well, I didn't say that. Just wait until I finish my sentence before looking?"

"Feels wrong to admire your curves while you're drunk," I said, instead letting my gaze fall on her lips.

"I was playing it up a little earlier. I actually only had two drinks." She touched her index fingers to her nose. "So I'm sober enough to give you consent to look once my sentence is done."

I let my eyes drop cautiously. "So I should stare at your body while I respond?" I flicked my gaze back to her face, taking in the way her dimples popped on her cheeks when she smiled. "Then I'd never know if what I said made you smile."

Sybil grinned wider, and I held her gaze for a moment longer before she slid a fingertip along her lower lip, catching a drop of the lemon curd, and unlocked a turn-on I didn't know I had. "Okay, Donut Man has some good lines."

I coughed into my hand. "And the Donut Man is my Granddad. You can just call me Kieran."

"His name is Joe?" she said, finishing the donut, and I definitely didn't notice the smattering of powdered sugar dusting her soft-looking skin.

I nodded. "He's in poor health, so I'm just trying to keep things afloat." That was so much simpler than it seemed. I had given up on "afloat" a year earlier, and now I was just shooting for drowning with dignity. I couldn't give up, though. This place was Granddad's pride and joy. He'd built it from the ground up, and if I could just get things back to even ground before going back to school, then it might be okay.

"Sorry to hear that." Her smile faded. "Premed to a donut shop must have been a change."

"Medical school, actually. I'd just finished my second year."

She whistled, a long, drawn-out twee sound. "Medical school. Damn. That's impressive. Too bad I can't date you." She dabbed at the spot where she'd spilled the lemon curd, studying her chest. "But I've already decided on two hundred and fifty million dollars and the donut."

A silence fell between us, and I glanced at the clock. "This is normally the time I lock up."

"Oh God. Sorry. I'll order a ride and get out of here so you can close." She wiped her hands on her thighs, and my brain tripped.

"You could stay," I said in a rush. I'd been fine being alone my whole life, but I didn't want to be alone right then. I'd hoped she'd give me more of her smiles and stories and make me forget how much of my life felt full of frowns and grim prognoses. "I'll just be cleaning."

She eyed me, biting her full lower lip. "Okay," she said with a slow smile. "Think you could manage more curdy talk while you do it?"

I tipped my hat backward, leaning forward to get cleaning supplies. I was already in over my head with this woman, but so what? Maybe for one night I could be a different person with a different life. "Yeah, I think curdy talk can be on the menu."

5

Sybil

"S O, WHY DO YOU NEED DONUTS TO REPLACE MEN?"
Kieran opened the display case and began moving the leftover donuts from the trays into a bag. He was cute—tall with black hair and a sharp jaw. I couldn't quite take my eyes off his arms, with their defined, corded muscles that looked like they came from work in this kitchen and not the gym. I'd never had a thing for men in uniform, but the apron was kind of doing it for me. I followed the lines of his torso as he twisted, and he handed me a donut covered in sprinkles when he caught me looking.

"Donuts *and* two hundred and fifty million dollars," I corrected him, and took a bite of my second donut. "Well, two hundred and fifty million after taxes. I'm giving up on men, not trying to run afoul of the IRS."

"Okay, why do you need donuts *and* two hundred and fifty million dollars to replace men?" He set one bag aside and began packing another. He must have caught my expression, and he shrugged. "There's a shelter nearby. I drop them off."

My face warmed and I wanted to say something, but my mouth was full, so I tried to grin with my eyes. I remembered seeing the flyer on the bulletin board earlier in the day, and knew I needed to fess up about taking the donuts that morning, but this felt like the moment my luck was kicking in, and I didn't want to interrupt fate quite yet.

"It's not a big deal." He answered my silent response with humility and another shrug, those well-developed shoulders lifting toward that damn backward hat. *Oh boy.* "So, the story?"

"I found a lucky penny this morning." I held it up, the light catching on its shiny surface. I admired it before setting it back on the counter. "But the day hasn't really gone how I planned. I messed something up this morning, I got fired, and I was really excited about this guy I was talking to. It felt like maybe something was going right for me, and I might finally have a date who made me look serious to my family. Then, tonight, he was late for our date and sent this photo." The store had long since emptied and, in one of my less well-reasoned decisions, I'd stayed and sat on the counter, legs dangling off the side while he cleaned.

"And it was such a sad little picture." I held out my phone, Carl's image on the screen.

"Let's see this." He dropped the bag of day-old donuts on the counter next to me and reached for my phone, his muscled forearms once again distracting me. I wanted to trace my finger along the lines of his veins.

I watched his expression turn from "I'm curious" to "I just drank expired milk" in a matter of moments. "You could have warned me it was a dick pic." He turned the phone over and slid it across the counter, his arm grazing my thigh and pausing centimeters from my leg.

"I wanted you to get the full experience."

"I definitely didn't need that experience." He was standing almost in front of me now, our eyes level, a smirk on his face. "And why is it lit so badly?"

"That's what I said!" I laughed, taking the phone back. "Welcome to my world."

His arm inched closer on the counter, so his elbow was just barely touching the outside of my thigh. He met my gaze. "I hate that your world is . . ." He motioned to my phone. "Like that."

I shrugged. "A glimpse into the life of the modern single woman. The donuts helped, though." I held up the last bite and two sprinkles fell from my hand, landing next to me. "Even though I'm a mess."

He slid his hand over the countertop and pressed his finger over the sprinkles, then lifted it to show me the blue and orange sugar sticking to his skin. "You are a very intriguing mess." His eyes flicked to mine and I waited, hoping he might lick the sprinkle from his own fingers, because, I'd decided, I would be into that.

Heat blossomed low in my belly at the thought of his long fingers. Suddenly, the donut wasn't cutting it anymore, because losing my job and having to move in with my mom had meant very little privacy.

"You still haven't explained why you're replacing men." He abandoned his cleanup duties and leaned one forearm on the counter, bending forward. "I mean, I get why you're replacing *that* guy." He pointed to my still-overturned phone. "But why all of us?"

I rested my hand on his shoulder to angle myself in his direction, and he flexed at my touch, his body responsive under my fingers. "That's how it goes. You like a guy, imagine something more, and become certain your family might approve of him, and then you get a dick pic." I grazed my thumb over his shoulder, appreciating how soft the worn cotton felt under my fingertips. "Donuts like this will always be delicious. And two hundred and fifty million dollars is reliable."

"But surely your family doesn't only plan to respect you based on the guy." The backs of his fingers trailed a slow path over my knee, but his eyes didn't leave mine. "And you'd be kind of lonely. Donuts are great, but they make lousy partners."

"I wouldn't be lonely." I licked a bit of frosting from the corner of my lip. "I'd still have plenty of sex."

He laughed, his head tipping back and his hand closing over my knee. I tightened my grip on his shoulder and admired the scruff on his jaw.

"It's true," I insisted. "I can give up on a meaningful connection with a serious person without giving up on toe-curling orgasms."

"Donuts won't give you toe-curling orgasms, either."

"I don't know." I licked the last bit of chocolate off my fingers. "Yours were pretty good."

He followed my finger to my lips, something I'd noticed him doing earlier, and his eyebrow quirked. "Have you been having toe-curling orgasms this whole time without me knowing?"

"You'd know. I'm not subtle, plus life is too short to stay quiet." I dropped my hand to his. "My sister thinks I'm sad that I can't find a nice, reliable guy to love, but at this point I'd be happy with a nice guy to fuck me up against a wall with the fervor and gusto I deserve."

His expression was hooded, and his fingers moved in small circles over my thighs. "Oh yeah?"

"Yeah." I glanced at his long fingers and traced the lines of his body up his forearms. My palm rested on the hard wall of his chest, and his heart thudded under my hand. That made me smile, knowing he was excited, maybe nervous. "Are you a nice guy?"

"That's not usually how people describe me." He met my eyes again, hands still resting on my hips. "But sometimes, on special occasions . . ."

I held on to his shoulders and scooted toward the edge of the counter, settling him between my legs and taking the feel of him against me. "This feels like a special occasion."

"You know, I found a lucky penny this morning, too. Maybe it was a sign." His breath came fast at my touch. "I don't usually believe in luck, though."

I ran my nails through his hair, enjoying the way his eyelids closed as I gently dragged my nails along his scalp. "Will you make me a donut after?"

Edging closer, his lips dropping to my neck, he kissed and lapped at the spot just below my ear. "After?" The word vibrated against my skin, and his hands slid up my waistline with aching deliberation, fingers stretching up my sides as his lips trailed down my throat.

I let out a raspy breath when his thumbs stroked under my breasts. "After."

"I can do that." He pulled me to the edge of the counter, his fingertips digging into my hips. "My office," he said on an exhale before dropping a heated kiss to my lips before his mouth trailed down my neck.

We crashed through a door into a cramped office and his

tongue played over my lips, teasing before taking my mouth with an almost bruising intensity. The shy guy I thought I'd seen was gone, and his body crowded against me, backing me into the space until the backs of my knees hit his chair and I collapsed into it. "This isn't a wall."

He dropped to his knees in front of me. "What if we changed the plan?"

My stomach flipped in a delicious way as he stroked my stomach over the waist of my jeans. "You promised."

"You got a donut. I want a treat, too." He circled his thumb over the button of my jeans until I nodded for him to keep going, then his lips brushed across my stomach, sending a wave of anticipation to the tips of my toes.

Oh wow. I raised my hips as he pulled my jeans down. "You're not playing around."

"I take things seriously." His lips returned to the inside of my knee. "And you wanted gusto." He dragged the back of his finger along the wet fabric between my thighs, back and forth with slightly more pressure each time. "I think you mentioned fervor," he murmured, sliding his fingers under the elastic of my underwear. "I want to know what you taste like."

I nodded, my breath hitching. "This is good fervor." The sudden absence of his hand was jarring, but he settled between my legs, and his mouth worked toward where I wanted him. This was officially the best impetuous decision I'd ever made.

"No time to waste." He pressed my thighs farther apart and ran his finger through my slick folds before dropping his mouth to me.

I stared at him, disbelief wrestling with the wave of sensation from his tongue and lips on my sensitive skin, kissing and licking my thighs before edging closer. My head swirled with the turn the night had taken. Here I was with my legs spread in a donut shop with a hot baker on his knees. I was no virgin, but it had been a while since someone made me feel like that, like I was moments from lifting off from the first touch, like I was seconds from combusting. I sought more pressure against his finger, begging for him to slide inside. Maybe my plan would work—no need to keep looking for love when I could enjoy things like this, even if I stayed broke. At least it seemed like a sign that good things could happen to me. I moaned and ran my fingers over his hat, pushing it off his head, guiding him until it was the right pressure from his finger, the perfect speed of his tongue and . . . yes. "There, right there!"

I closed my eyes and gripped his hair as my body rose, the wave cresting until delicious heat washed through me. "Yes! Yes! Yes!" My words ricocheted around the small space as I rode the wave, my cries fading to murmurs as he pulled away from me, licking his fingers and then wiping his mouth with the back of his hand.

"Dear God," I said, catching my breath, my body still pinging. I'd never had someone go down on me with that much energy and enthusiasm, and definitely not with those skills. "A-plus gusto. World-class fervor." I pressed my hand to my chest and sucked in a breath. "I am officially thankful for your fervor."

He kissed my thigh and grinned. "You're right about not being quiet. I would have noticed that. I—"

A knock sounded, and then a woman's voice came through the door. "Kieran? Are you back here?"

His eyes widened. "Oh fuck."

6

LILA KNOCKED AGAIN AND THEN CALLED THROUGH the door. "Sweetie, when you're done in there, let your *guest* know their purse is outside the door." She was poorly disguising that she was fucking with me, but Sybil didn't know that, and her eyes widened and she squirmed under me. The body that had been so languid and open under my touch a moment before snapped tight in an instant.

"What the hell?" She pushed me back and pulled her pants up while I mourned the loss of her soft skin. "Are you married?"

"No," I said, rising to my feet, running a hand through my hair. "It's my sister. She's just being . . . weird. I lost track of time, and she's here to prep for tomorrow. I thought we had time." Lila was early for once in her damn life. Damn it. "Stay here. I'll convince her a customer left the purse and we can . . ."

Sybil searched the floor, casting a doubtful glance in my direction as I trailed off, my frustration rising.

"Kier?" Another knock at the door left me flustered, and

Sybil hadn't responded, but I turned the handle to slip out after adjusting myself.

"Please, just wait. I'll send her home. Don't go yet."

On the other side of the door, Sybil's purse rested near the wall, and my cheeks heated as I set it inside before looking for my little sister. The back of the shop wasn't cavernous, so I had to only peek around the corner to find her setting up supplies. My younger sister was helping me with the shop while she finished her accounting degree and decided which of the multiple companies courting her she wanted to go with. She'd decided to stretch her last semester into two so she could help, and she took the overnight shift, prepping everything for the next morning while studying for her CPA exam. I hated that she was putting off graduation and starting her life, but I was always glad to see her, to have someone to share this place with. Well, I was *almost* always glad to see her. In that moment, I wanted her to get the hell out and leave me with the prep, because a sleepless night would be worth it to have more time with the woman in my office.

When she spotted me, she smirked without losing her place, measuring out ingredients for the cake donuts. "How's it going? Catching up on some *paperwork* in there?"

I tucked my hands in my pockets and glanced over my shoulder at the closed door to my office. "Drop it."

"What?" She pulled the mixer and ingredients she needed off the shelf, her movements efficient and practiced. "I am truly impressed, even though hearing it from my brother is a big ick."

I heard Sybil moving around inside the office, and I had a feeling the night would not end as I'd hoped. "Why don't you go home, and I'll prep for tomorrow," I offered hurriedly.

Ignoring me, Lila poured the mixture into the ancient industrial mixer that whirred to life. "It sounds like you looked up how to find and really work the G-spot."

"Sex advice from my little sister is not something I need," I gritted out. "And I went to medical school. I'm familiar with anatomy."

"So many men think they're familiar." Lila pushed past me toward her bag, slung on a hook across the room. "I have earbuds. Don't worry. Carry on.

"And please," she said with an eye roll, counting out eggs and arranging them in rows on the counter. "You'd fall asleep halfway through prep, and you know one of us has night owl genes and it's not you." Lila flashed a sweet smile. "Maybe take your guest home, though, if you can avoid waking Granddad?"

I glowered, her smart-ass smirk pushing my panic into annoyance. "Can you give me a break? Just . . . I don't know. Give me a few minutes to get out of here."

"If it only takes a minute, I feel bad for that poor girl. You can do better than that, Kier. Put your back into it!" She laughed, pouring the flour into the batter. "Besides, I'm positive you need to wash your hands before stepping anywhere near this kitchen."

That was my sweet baby sister. It had been me and her against the world, until she broke her arm on the playground at school and neither the school nor the hospital could find our mom, who'd been gone for a few days by then. I remembered the doctor setting Lila's arm and then looking me in the eye to talk to me, to tell me they were going to get help for us. That's when we were placed with my grandparents. We were both tough, but I'd turned to type A tendencies to avoid dealing with emotions, while she'd figured out how to make hers charming. She was quick with a joke and gave me more shit than anyone else I knew. I glanced at the closed door again. My heart was still racing from the encounter, being interrupted, and—God, how Sybil had tasted. How she'd sounded. I shook my head again. "Lila, please."

She straightened her smirk and tilted her head. "Fine. I'll make sure the front is cleaned up and give you a few—"

The crank-crank-clank sound of the mixer's rotating blade becoming detached from the apparatus distracted us at the same time. We both lunged for the machine, but it was too late, and we both shielded our faces from the flying mixture. The ancient machine had been on borrowed time for two decades. I'd fixed this problem a few times, but the banging grew louder and the mess bigger as we wrestled with the machine to turn it off without breaking the bones in our hands. When I could finally pull the plug from the wall, the sound of the bell on the front door and the subsequent slam broke through the silence. The office door was open, but there was no one inside.

"Fuck." I pushed off the wall and sprinted to the front of the shop. Outside, a car was pulling away from the curb, and I could vaguely make out the outline of Sybil's curls in shadow under the streetlights. I watched the lights disappear up the street with an oddly consuming sadness. Yeah, I'd wanted to sleep with her—she was hot and funny—but there was something else, something I hadn't experienced in a long time. When I was with her, I'd forgotten how much I wanted to go back to my old life. I turned slowly back to the kitchen, where Lila had begun to clean up. *I guess that's why distractions are dangerous.*

"Damn it," I muttered, surveying the mess. "I'll get the toolbox. I can try to fix it."

"You need to buy a new one," she said, wiping flour and egg from the nearby wall.

"I know." It wasn't happening anytime soon, though. Industrial mixers were expensive, and there was no way I could afford it with all the bills mounting faster than I could pay them. In my office, I slumped into the chair where Sybil had sat, legs gloriously spread. It was just a desk chair now, and I glanced around and spotted a scrap of paper on my desk. It was a lottery ticket on top of two twenty-dollar bills. I picked it up, the curls of her loopy handwriting betraying the message. "Thanks for the donuts and the orgasm," I read. "For the boxes I sort of shoplifted this morning—the ones for Josefina. Sorry!" The scent of her lingered in my office, and I could still taste her on my tongue. I'd spent just enough time with her to hear her voice forming those words in my head perfectly.

I reread the note and flipped over the ticket. Confusion swamped me, followed by bewilderment as I held up the two twenties. She'd been the one to take the donuts that morning, and now she was tipping me . . . with a lottery ticket?

I slumped back in the chair, still fully dusted with flour. This was my life. It was already midnight, I'd be cleaning and doing repairs for at least an hour, and the woman I'd lost my mind over thought my sexual services were worth the long-shot chance at $350 million and a quickly scribbled thank-you note. "Two hundred and fifty million after taxes," I muttered, tossing the ticket and the twenties on top of the ancient keyboard. This *lucky day* had turned out exactly the way I'd thought it would.

7

Sybil

RISE AND SHINE!" THE VOICE CUT THROUGH MY HEAD like a shard of glass, and I cracked one eye open to see my sister standing over me in her guest room. She had the annoying habit of being not only the perfect, high-achieving, career-driven daughter, but also a morning person. Based on the off-key singing emanating from the kitchen, her fiancé, Warren, shared this trait. They had met at the dental office where she was a dentist and he an orthodontist. She said it was in a staff meeting, but I always imagined their eyes meeting over somebody's root canal and sparks flying. She'd reminded me multiple times that root canals were not romantic and that an orthodontist wouldn't be present during one, but I liked my version better than the real one. The story of Warren and Grace (Sybil's version).

"Go away," I grumbled, turning my face into the pillow and stroking my finger along the high-thread-count fabric under my cheek. "These are really nice," I said. "And are these feather pillows?"

"It's time to get up." She sat on the bed next to me, and I heard ceramic against wood on my nightstand. Well, her nightstand.

"I'm an adult," I said, swatting at her hand as she tried to coax me from my cotton cocoon.

"Could have fooled me."

The smell of coffee luring me, I turned slowly to look at my sister. I'd managed to get my own apartment after dropping out of school, but between jobs I couldn't quite hold on to and, admittedly, bad money management habits, it didn't last long. The worst part had been how no one was particularly surprised when I'd moved back in with my mom. I'd overheard her telling a friend it was "classic Sybil." It hadn't been cruel, derisive, or even sarcastic . . . just resigned. Her friend Janice had replied, "That girl couldn't find good luck or good sense at a luck-and-sense sidewalk sale."

On top of that joke not even making sense, *Janice*, I'd eagerly awaited my mom's rebuff, because no one talked about Mary's babies, but she hadn't corrected the friend. I'd heard silence before they moved on, but the idea of her nodding in agreement was imprinted on my mind. It was the way she agreed when Janice talked about my dad or her own ex-husband.

"You look awful," Grace said, handing me the coffee and interrupting my stewing.

"Didn't you use to be nicer?"

Grace smiled. "I'm still nice. I brought you coffee and let you crash in my guest room." She patted the bed and stood. "Get up!"

I sipped the coffee and leaned back against the headboard. I hadn't had enough to drink the night before to have a real hangover, but the lack of sleep made me feel like I had. I could probably thank the donuts and bottles of water from the night before for my relatively clear head, though.

The night before.

I dragged a finger absently over my neck, remembering the donut shop and Kieran's kisses landing there. It had been amazing until it was mortifying. Thank God something distracted him so I could sneak out. Once my panties were securely back in place, I couldn't imagine the level of awkwardness that would come with facing him to admit I'd been the donut thief that morning, so I'd scribbled a note, and my ride was blessedly nearby. Shame I couldn't ever go back there. The donuts were really good. He was really good. I settled back against the wood, and the mug warmed my hands as I allowed myself a few memories of him and the night before. Really good.

My fantasy was interrupted by my sister's impatient knock on the door frame. "Sybil. C'mon! Mom is expecting us in an hour."

I slumped back into bed. "Do I have to go?"

"Well, you live there. So, yes, it's not optional." She shot me a bored and lovingly disappointed look that only an older sister could give. I half expected her to drop in a "my house, my rules" line, but she didn't, she just leveled me with a stare. "What time did you get here last night?"

I'd crept in the front door with my shoes off using the key she'd given me. Everyone was gloriously asleep. I'd walked in more than once to hear my sister and her fiancé still at it, and I had been in no mood for that. I mean, all the flowers to my sister for scoring someone with so much stamina and, based on what I overheard, creativity, but is anyone ever in the right headspace to hear a mild-mannered orthodontist tell their sister she's a good girl after several loud spanks? "Late. I hung out for a while at a donut shop."

"A donut shop?" Grace's disappointed expression faded, and she stepped into the room, leaning against the dresser. "Why?"

"The . . . donuts?" I sipped my coffee and didn't meet her eyes. She wasn't a prude or anything, but she'd have thoughts on me hooking up with a random baker after a bad day and a few drinks. I guessed most people would have thoughts about that, but in my defense, he was hot. And sweet. And that tongue . . . I pulled myself from the memory and met Grace's gaze again.

She surprised me sometimes, and a giddy smile crossed her face as an eyebrow went up. "Was your guy there?"

I'd told them I met someone without thinking it through. How I planned to casually continue seeing the imaginary man and then also take him to my sister's wedding, I had no clue. We'd been sitting around the table, Grace with Warren, and Mom with Paul, everyone talking about their jobs and careers, and there I was, shoving food in my mouth with nothing to contribute. I couldn't manifest a career from the ether, so when the conversation turned to me, I blurted out that I'd met someone and we were taking it very slow. Very slow indeed, considering I forgot about the lie most of the time and it had been two months. Clearly Carl wasn't going to be the saving grace. "Uh, yeah, he was there for a while."

Grace waggled her eyebrows. "I can't believe you won't tell me anything about him. What does he do? Did you say he looks like that hot actor you pointed out last week?"

Warren poked his head in the door. "Would we call that guy hot?"

"Theo James?" I grinned because Kieran looked nothing

like him, but he had those brown eyes and corded muscles. Warren was waiting for a response, and I almost forgot who I was talking about. "He is objectively hot."

"Absolutely," Grace said, without looking away from me.

"Fair enough." Warren shrugged and leaned in to kiss her on the cheek. "Leave in twenty minutes?" He would be sure to be on time—our mother loved this buttoned-up orthodontist as much as either of her actual children. When he stepped back out, Grace's gaze landed back on me.

She nudged me again. "I was surprised you didn't stay over at his place," she said once Warren was out of earshot.

My face heated, and the dull ache in my head made itself known. I mumbled into my mug, "It didn't get that far. We, uh, we talked for a long time." And fooled around, though "fooled around" was underselling what had happened. Only by three thousand percent, but still. I squeezed my thighs together instinctively at the memory of Kieran's mouth. "He's more traditional than guys I normally see." Traditionally handsome. Traditionally educated. Traditionally eager to go down on me. "No sleepovers. We're taking things slow."

"Really?"

"Yeah," I agreed, looking away and wishing I hadn't lied myself into this corner and put my hopes on Carl.

"That's so unlike you, but great! I hope we can meet him soon."

"He's really smart. In medical school, actually." If I'd had more to drink the night before, I could blame my lie on that, but she'd never meet my donut shop one-night stand, so it really didn't matter.

"Always good to have another doctor around," she said, patting my arm. "I'm proud of you for taking your time." She playfully elbowed me. "And I want to make sure he's not some kind of serial killer."

"Wow," I said with a yawn. "You really don't have much faith in my choice of men."

"Well," she said, tipping her head back and forth. "You have a track record."

"And he hasn't murdered me yet." Well, I might have died for a minute or two there at the end, actually. *La petite mort.* I settled on the bed, taking another sip of coffee. "Besides, if he took me out, you'd never wake up to find your sister in your guest room again."

"True. But then, the inevitable trial, true-crime interviews, and Netflix special would eat up a lot of time I need to put toward wedding planning." Grace slid her long index and middle fingers to drag along her eyebrow, the diamond on her hand catching the light and casting multicolored spots onto the nearby wall. She grinned at me. "But I'm glad you're taking this one slowly. It'll be good for you. Change of pace from your normal of going all in right away. But get up. I'll hear about it all day if we're late to Mom's again, and I'm bringing cobbler."

"You're not my keeper," I grumbled, pushing the covers aside and grabbing my phone from the nightstand.

"Tell Mom that!" Grace called over her shoulder, walking back down the hall. My phone chimed, and I saw the group chat light up with a message.

EMI: You're safe?

MARCUS: And $250 million richer?

SYBIL: Safe! No hangover so the
lucky penny came through. And I
lost the ticket. No one ever wins,
anyway. It was stupid to drop
money on it.

Sighing, I swung my legs over the side of the bed and glanced at the screen. Overnight, two other messages from Carl had come through. One with just another question mark and the second calling me a tease and a bitch. I hit delete with more force than necessary and blocked him. "Screw that guy," I muttered.

Sure, all I'd ended up with after finding a lucky penny was the donuts, but they were really fantastic donuts. Something else would fall into place soon. It always did.

8

Kieran

'D ONLY GOTTEN A FEW HOURS OF SLEEP, BUT IF I HIT snooze a second time, what little sleep Granddad would get in the morning would be interrupted, so I'd dragged myself out of bed. There was only one other unit in our building, and our neighbor, Mrs. Nguyen, had a hard time getting up and down the stairs, so I didn't mind helping her out. I heard the low whine from the other side of the door and used my key to crack it and let her dog out into the hall. I checked my watch, and I was already a little late, but I did this every morning to save her one trip on the stairs. Penny wagged her tail, her whole body vibrating until I laid a hand on her head and scratched behind her ears. The dog was probably ten years old but still acted like a puppy, and I led her down the stairs to the small patch of grass behind the building, pulling on the back door to the shop as I walked by, just to make sure it was still locked.

The morning was still and frigid, and I breathed into my

cupped hands as I waited for Penny to make seven laps of the space to find her perfect spot, her brown and black ears perking up when, on lap eight, all was revealed. "Good dog," I said, seeing my breath puff in front of me. Traffic was beginning to buzz on the interstate nearby, but otherwise the street was quiet. In that space alone, I let my mind wander. I was the only one awake with the exception of Penny, and I imagined starting the day I wanted to have. I thought about going back inside my own place and not to the cramped quarters of my childhood bedroom in Granddad's apartment, imagined looking ahead to a long shift at the hospital, and a date after with a woman, maybe a fellow doctor. I rubbed my hands together, waiting for Penny to finish her business. That life would not include a late night with a would-be thief who left me a lottery ticket after sex. My body reacted to the memory, even as I shuddered remembering the moment of realization. The sweet taste of her kiss had lingered on my lips, but the familiar, sinking disappointment at learning she'd been the one to walk off with the donuts that morning was more lasting. That was a red flag I wouldn't ignore, but I didn't have time to spare her any more thought.

I clapped twice, beckoning the dog back inside. The sun wouldn't be up for another hour, but the sky was hinting at shifting from night to the first brush of azure in the sky. The alley smelled like fried dough this morning. Another morning in my real life, and not that fictional version I'd imagined. I checked my phone as the dog started making her way toward me. I had three notifications from Lila the night before.

LILA: Three thousand dollars for a
new mixer.

LILA: And that's for a used one in
not great shape. Anything decent
is closer to five.

I couldn't believe she'd been coherent enough to search. We were both exhausted after staying up until all hours cleaning and attempting to fix the mixer. I covered the yawn that fell from my mouth. The mixer was working, but just barely, and it made noises that let me know it would not hang on for much longer.

LILA: And we need to think about
replacing the fryer.

I clapped again, and Penny came bounding toward me, tongue lolling out the side of her mouth, waiting expectantly at my feet for another scratch behind the ears with all the energy of a dog half her age. I was fairly certain I'd let her back into their apartment and she'd sleep all day. Still, I scratched her behind the ears, giving her a few extra pets before jogging up the stairs. Even in the cold February morning, the dog looked up at me like I had the answers to all her problems, and that was easier than thinking about Lila's messages.

As soon as Mrs. Nguyen's door closed and I turned the key to lock it, our door opened and Granddad stepped out, his cane in one hand.

"Don't even try to stop me." He held up a palm, his voice hushed. "I'll be careful, but I'm going to work."

I opened my mouth to speak. It had been only the day before when he'd fallen down the stairs.

"I need this, son," he said more quietly, meeting my eyes. "I know you understand needing to work and be productive more than anyone."

I did. Every day, all I wanted to do was get back to school. I held out my hand without another word. "Okay," I said. "Slow, though. And hold on to my arm."

"And I'm working the front," he said, the humor I'd known my whole life coming back into his voice as the stairs creaked under our feet. "You and Lila got all the brains in the family, but let's face it. I'm better looking and everyone knows sex sells." He laughed as we reached the landing, and I unlocked the back door to the shop.

"I think I do all right," I returned, enjoying the familiarity of this. Joking with Granddad used to be part of my day. Singing along to the music piping through the speakers in the shop was normal, and on some level, I'd missed that.

The shop was cold, and I didn't catch the next thing Granddad said, already thinking about what the heat going out would mean for business, though Granddad continued. "All that schooling and they never taught you to keep the best-looking employee out front. I—" The rest of his observation froze in the air as we both stopped short. The heat wasn't the issue; the front door was open, and the cold February air rushed in over the landscape of broken glass and upturned tables, and across the bulletin board, where someone had ripped down most of the notes from the third-grade class. I looked left and right trying to take it all in while cursing myself for sleeping too heavily the night before. The front case was bashed in, and the donuts I'd planned to walk to the shelter the night before were scattered on the floor under the mangled cash register, the drawer open and empty.

"What the hell happened?" Lila approached the front door, eyes wide, with her backpack slung over her shoulder. I wasn't sure when my sister found time to sleep—she'd been in the shop later than me.

I kept looking around, trying to make a plan, but I had no plan, and I kept gulping in air.

"We were robbed," Granddad said, leaning against the wall. "Call the police." The sigh in his voice erased all the previous humor. "How much was in the register?"

"But I locked up," I said uselessly, crossing the shop and inspecting the door. "Before the mixer went haywire, I locked up."

"The mixer?" Granddad eyed me with a look between skepticism and confusion.

"Little issue last night," I said, skirting his question. "But I swear I locked the door . . ." I studied it again, realization dawning. Sybil had run out the front door while I was distracted, and then I'd never checked it again. "Oh, God," I said to myself, running my fingers through my hair. "Oh, God. This is my fault."

Lila was already on the phone with the police, and I wandered back across the room. "I'm sorry, Granddad. This is my fault."

He patted my arm. "You didn't destroy the shop. Only ones to blame are those to blame," he said, though his gaze swept over the mess as well. I imagined him totaling the hours he'd spent making that shop like a home in the community, and the way it was all but destroyed when he'd had to leave me in charge.

"They're sending a car," Lila said. "Whoever broke in didn't seem to get into the office. Computer is still there, and nothing looked out of place. I even found this." She held up a piece of paper and two twenties.

It took me a moment to piece together what she had in her hand, and I lunged for it, not wanting to explain the note on the back or that my one-night stand had been the one to take an order without paying the day before. "Set it down. We need to start sweeping up all this glass."

She turned away, pulling the ticket from my grasp, and I followed her gaze between her phone and what she had resting on the desk near her elbow. I recognized the corner of the logo I saw at the top and the bleed-through of the blue ink.

"Why are you messing with your phone? The shop is destroyed."

Lila dragged her eyes from her phone to me, her pupils wide. "Did Tom leave this here?"

I rolled my eyes and made a grab for the ticket. "Focus," I said, motioning to the room. "A customer left it." She blocked me again. "It doesn't matter."

"A customer?"

I made another grab for the ticket, my body tense with the memory of finding it. "A customer. Give it to me. It's trash."

Lila held the ticket to her chest, twisting away from me. Sybil's curly handwriting was visible on the back. "Then why was it in the office?"

The last two days pushed against my back suddenly, the exhaustion and frustration and stress, but instead of crushing me, it just decimated my patience. "It doesn't matter. Why are you on this? Who cares?"

"Kier, this matters." She held out the ticket, looking at the front of it again before pulling it against her chest when I tried to grab it from her hand. "Stop it," she said, her voice reminding me of when she was younger, of when I would tease her or Granddad would ask her about her boyfriends or girlfriends. But before I could tell her she was acting like a kid, or better yet walk away and let her draw her own conclusions, she held out a hand and clutched my arm. "Kieran, this is a winning ticket."

Her words bounced back and forth like a Ping-Pong ball. "No, it's not. Stop fucking with me," I said, walking to the other side of the tiny office. "It was hers, okay? Are you happy? You got it out of me and solved the mystery."

"The woman who was back here with you last night?" Lila hadn't let go of the ticket, but she looked closer at the hand-writing on the back and then stifled a giggle.

"I'm glad I could amuse you," I said, pushing past her toward the corner where we kept the broom. "It's good to laugh after the shop was ransacked."

"Seriously. This is a winner," she hissed, following me. She pitched her voice low so Granddad couldn't hear. "Kieran, you won the *lottery*."

"No one actually wins. The odds of you getting struck by lightning while fighting a bear are better."

"People win," she exclaimed, following me into the kitchen. "*You* won, dummy. Or your guest won, and since you have her ticket . . ."

"You probably read the numbers wrong. Granddad does that all the time."

"Granddad has cataracts and still calls the internet 'America Online.'" She waved the ticket in front of me. "I have twenty-twenty vision and a degree in accounting, and I double-checked the winning numbers from last night." She handed me the ticket after studying my face and deciding I wasn't going to tear it in two. "Oh my God. You won the *lottery!*"

I stared at the ticket between us, the blue ink of Sybil's scribbled note in sharp contrast to the crumpled white of the paper. "No."

Lila's smile widened. "This could solve everything!" Her voice rose, eyes wide. "The medical bills, the shop, your school bill, Granddad's living costs . . ." She looked over my shoulder as if tallying. "This would solve it all."

"No, it won't." I handed the ticket back to her. I studied the loop on the *h* in "thanks," the way the ink curved in a careless way. "Not for us. We can't keep this."

9

Sybil

MORE MACARONI AND CHEESE, WARREN?" MY plate was empty, too, but Mom held out the serving spoon to her future son-in-law at the other end of the table.

"I couldn't. I'm training for that triathlon, but you know I loved it, Mary. Almost as much as the dressing and ham."

She beamed at him, then her gaze swept to Grace. "A triathlon. I can't believe your level of dedication. And that you two are doing it together!"

Grace had been the put-together daughter her whole life. Her Barbie dolls always ended the day tucked into their sleeping quarters next to tidy and color-coded closets. Mine usually had half their hair colored purple, and at least one would be missing a leg that I'd used as an impromptu knife when I got bored with playing house and decided to play assassin with my stuffed animals. It carried over into adulthood. She was the carbon copy of our mom's personality, while I was my dad's girl. How my parents had ended up together was still a mystery to me. I wondered if my dad would have turned the conversation to add how proud he was of my commitment to exploring different career options like office temp, stationery store clerk, and trampoline park attendant. He'd bounced from job to job most of his life, so I figured he would have, if he'd stuck around.

"I'm just so proud of you two," Mom continued, looking between Warren and Grace. It wasn't a dig at me—I mean, it probably wasn't—but it felt like one, since there was no afterthought to include her youngest as she returned the spoon to the bowl.

"I'd love some more, Mom," I said.

She huffed but spooned some onto my plate. "I bet you would, seeing as it's good for hangovers."

"I'm not really hungover. I'm just tired." I thought about reciting what Kieran had said the night before about alcohol and insulin and carbs, but then I remembered I'd gathered that tidbit while tipsy and with my pants down in a donut shop. Activities Mama Mary rarely approved of. I opened my mouth to speak, but she gave me one of her pointed mom looks, and I shut my mouth.

"That's what I thought. Aren't you too old for things like that? Partying and carrying on? It's no way to get back on your feet." I curled my toes into the carpet, wishing I could burrow my way into the basement. The lecture that was about to begin was why I didn't want to come home. Mom pulled no punches, and she had me in her crosshairs. "Especially now that you're seeing this new guy. He's not out all night drinking, too, is he? Because—"

"Mom," Grace interrupted, changing the direction of the conversation on my behalf. "We got some good news." God bless my sister, who ran interference like a pro. "I talked to the seamstress, and she'll be able to make the adjustments to Great-Grandma's wedding dress in time. She's a specialist in vintage clothing."

I shot Grace a thankful look for diverting the conversation and distracting our mother. Her mom's dress had been in the family for generations and passed down, but Grace had been concerned about the age of the fabric and whether the alterations would be safe to make. Grace for the win again.

"And . . . tell her the rest," Warren prompted, his beaming smile hiding nothing. I'd known forever Grace would knock it out of the park as a parent and be a lot like our own—loving but firm. Warren would be the cheerleader parent on the sidelines of every game, but no one was going to be as fun as Aunt Sybil. I'd always known I would be a fun aunt.

Grace grinned at me. "Since there is so much fabric on the train that the dress can't structurally support anymore, she said there will be enough to make that into Sybil's dress, too." Grace met my eyes kindly. "So we'll both get to wear some of her dress."

Tears immediately filled Mom's eyes, and she grabbed her chest, resting another hand on Paul's arm. My annoyance with her lecturing faded to nothing immediately, and she held out her arms to hug Grace and then clasp my hand. "I can't wait to see both my girls in that dress. That means so much. We'll take a hundred photos." She wiped a tear away from her eye, and I reminded myself she meant well. My stepdad grinned and patted her back.

Later, I helped Mom clear the table and began scrubbing plates in the kitchen.

"I can't believe it. Grandma's dress." Mom repeated that for the fifteenth time. "I just want to twirl. It would mean so much to her that one of you girls was getting married in her dress."

She grinned ear to ear, and it was contagious. When Mom was happy, she kind of sparkled, which I'd always admired. "And I knew it wouldn't be you. You told her at her eightieth birthday you thought it was ugly and you would never get married if you had to wear a dress like that." Mom laughed, the dish towel waving in the air. It was one of her favorite stories, repeated over and over whenever the wedding came up.

"Yeah, well . . . I was seven."

"Oh, my sweet girl," she said, wrapping an arm around my waist. "You were the same girl at seven that you are now."

I wasn't sure how to take what I knew she meant to be loving, and I tried to ignore the growing sense of disappointment that fell on me like a cloak when I walked into this house. "That's me," I said, drying a serving dish and tucking it into the cupboard. "Lucky you've got one daughter who didn't let you down."

"Oh, stop that."

Water sloshed as I scrubbed out a well-used pot, and I waited for more, but she pivoted away from me.

"Sorry to interrupt," Grace said, and I mouthed "Thank you" to her. She gave a conspiratorial eyebrow raise and started scooping leftover ham into a glass storage container. "I wanted to add one more person to the guest list for the bachelorette party weekend. Do you have any extra save-the-date cards?"

"I haven't actually mailed them yet," I said, a sinking feeling tugging at me as I put a plate in the drying rack. "So, good news! Easy to add another person."

"Oh, honey. It's in two months. Those should have gone out a month ago, especially since some people will be flying." Mom helped Grace pack up the food, the two working side by side.

"Yeah. Just need to confirm the hotel," I said, speaking into the sink and hoping the water would swallow up my words, because I also needed to call the hotel and, before I did that, pick a hotel.

"If it's too much, I can just do it myself," Grace offered, and there was only kindness in her tone, which was much worse. "I know you're busy and things are stressful."

"No, I'm your maid of honor. I can do it!" I added cheer to my voice. "You shouldn't have to plan your own bachelorette party." I scrubbed the pot in my hands with an intensity I'd never before shown for dishes. "I'll take care of everything."

In the silence, I peeked over my shoulder to see Grace and Mom share a look. A "how do we tell her?" look that made me want to curl up into a ball. They didn't think I could take care of it. And I didn't want to ruin Grace's wedding. She deserved to have a hiccup-free, well-planned event. "Or maybe Shelby can help. She's so organized," I said with the same false chipperness, referring to her oldest friend and bridesmaid.

"Great idea," Grace said, and Mom agreed. "She'll be happy to, and it'll take the burden off your plate," Grace added, and the two of them shifted into conversation about the dress, leaving me able to escape unnoticed.

I hurriedly dried my hands and slipped out of the kitchen. I slid a hand along the familiar sideboard covered in family photos. The one in the back in a purple frame was my favorite. I was six or seven with missing front teeth, and Dad had snuck me onto a roller coaster I wasn't tall enough to ride. He'd snapped the selfie while we were loading into the car and told me first not to tell Mom he let me break the rules. He was always saying things like that, and I loved how free I always felt with him. In elementary school, I'd been working hard on a science fair project, tending to my plants and checking how the different additives to water influenced their growth. Grace did so well in school, and I'd wanted to do the same, so I'd spent all my time and energy making sure it went well, and then my best friend introduced me to a new video game two weeks before it was due, and I kind of forgot about the plants. In the end, my project titled "How Long Can Plants Go Without Water?" earned a ribbon, and Dad said some people did better with luck than work and I was one of those people.

I smiled and traced a finger over the frame. I'd told my mom immediately about the roller coaster because I had a big mouth, but he was right. Things like forgetting to water plants or mail invitations were normal for me my whole life. Luck worked better for me than trying only to end up failing. Dad called sometimes, and we saw him every couple of years after he moved across the country to chase his dreams of opening a skate park, but he was a footnote in our lives. I had his eyes and his nose and his laugh. I knew that if one day my luck ran out, I might end up as a footnote, too. That's why it was best to let Grace hand planning to her friend. I could still share the notebook full of ideas I had. I set the photo back down, tracing my and my dad's matching smiles.

In a little white basket at the end of the sideboard, my mail was stacked, the top three envelopes stamped with "past due," "final notice," and "open immediately." I thumbed through them, hoping for something more fun, or at least less ominous, but the best thing in the pile was my invitation to Grace's wedding. "Ms. Sybil Sweet" was in an elegant script across the envelope.

"Your mom insisted yours be mailed like everyone else's," Warren said from behind me, glancing over my shoulder. "Said it was more special."

"Waste of money," I said, studying the cream-colored envelope and graceful slope of the calligraphy.

"I don't disagree, but I've learned to not quibble over the small things with your mother." His brow creased at the stack of bills in front of me. "That doesn't seem promising," he said, pointing to the basket that could have doubled as a colorful bouquet with the amount of red text and pink envelopes.

"Yeah, my student loan provider wanted me to feel special, too."

I chuckled, but Warren's expression remained unchanged. "Do you need to borrow some money?"

I had seventeen dollars in my checking account and five more bills waiting in my email inbox, the ones that hadn't turned to my physical mailing address yet. "No," I said, shoving the mail into the pocket of my hoodie. "It's okay—I'm good. I'll actually be moving out soon. A few things are panning out." I tried on the false chipper tone that had worked with my Mom and Grace. "I'm sure Mom and Paul will be ready to have their house back," I joked, giving him a good-natured punch in the arm.

I wasn't sure why I'd said it. I had nowhere to go except the couch in the small house my three best friends shared with their ancient pit bull, Cupcake. Grace would have seen through this half-assed, very obvious lie, but Warren was from a family where they spoke honestly to one another and didn't hide their fuckups if they ever happened, so he didn't get it yet, and his face cracked into a smile.

"That's great, Sybil!" He raised his hand for a high five, which was adorably clueless enough to give my panic a moment of respite.

"Yeah," I said, returning his high five while the weight of the impressive collection of failure in my hoodie's front pocket shifted. "Great."

Warren flashed another smile and patted my arm awkwardly before walking toward the kitchen. After a moment, I heard my mom ask, "She is?" I pulled the phone from my pocket.

> SYBIL: Is Cupcake looking for a nighttime snuggle buddy?

MARCUS: Well, yes . . . but Cupcake's farts are currently room clearing.

> SYBIL: Don't tempt me with a good time.

EMI: She's on some new medication. But if you need to stay here, you can!

DEACON: You can share my bed 😏

I chuckled and posted a heart reaction to Deacon. I looked back at my dad's photo and then to the stack of bills. I knew I could crash at Emi's and go back to the temp agency. I considered returning to the donut shop to get another lemon-curd-filled treat—something sweet always helped me whenever I had to make a decision—but even if I needed the sugar boost, it was clear I could never show my face there again.

10

Kieran

THE OFFICER CLOSED HIS NOTEBOOK AND HANDED me his card, sharing there'd been similar break-ins and vandalism across town and they'd be in touch if there was more information. Feeling numb from the cold still blowing in through the shop and the number of complications this added, I thanked him and tugged the door shut as much as I could—whoever had destroyed the shop had taken a few hits at the door frame, presumably for fun, and it was warped and dented.

"We should make a list," I said, approaching the counter. "There's insurance, getting the door frame fixed, replacing the case . . ." I searched the counter for a pen and noticed a single penny still shining at the bottom of the overturned tip jar.

"And you're a multimillionaire who could hire someone to do all of that," Lila said, eyes wide.

"Let's take a minute to celebrate," Granddad said, clasping my forearm.

"There's nothing to celebrate," I said. "It's not mine."

"Holy hell!" Tom's voice filled the shop as he pushed through the door. "Everyone okay?" He gave Lila a side hug on his way to the counter and stepped over broken glass.

"No one's hurt," Granddad said. "But big news!" His smile was wide for his friend, and I rolled my eyes.

"It's not good news," I said, but he ignored me, and I heard him telling Tom about the ticket as Lila dragged me into the back.

"What is wrong with you? Why are you blowing this off?"

"I'm not," I said. I stretched my neck from side to side, the stress sliding up my spine like a slowly moving fog rolling in. "If she comes back, we'll give her the ticket." And I'd get to see her again and maybe get a second chance to impress her. No. I shook my head and fought the urge to check if she'd somehow sauntered back into the shop. She was everything I didn't need. A tornado of distraction, and I didn't have to look any farther than the shop to see that.

"She might not come back. How would she even know to come back? I have never had sex so good that I'd go back after a situation like this." She lowered her voice. "If a woman I didn't know interrupted my orgasm and then a mixer exploded outside the door . . ." Lila looked up and to the left in thought. "Well," she said. "I mean, if my partner—"

"Lila, I swear to God. Today has already been seven years long. Please. I'm begging you. Do not finish that sentence."

Lila laughed, her face softening, almost pushing me to smile through my exhaustion. "Fine. Fine, but I don't think she's coming back," she said. "And you don't have a way to find her, so why are you being stubborn?"

I pulled the apron over my head and hung it on a hook. "I'm not being stubborn. I'm being ethical. It's not mine."

"I think there's legal grounding here—she effectively signed it over to you. Look," she said, pointing to where Sybil had scribbled her name at the bottom, ironically almost exactly over the space for a winner's signature.

"Not sure 'thanks for the orgasm' would stand up in court," I muttered, stacking the papers sitting on the corner of the desk, eager to get moving.

"Can you imagine how much great press we'd get for the shop if you shared that?"

"Shared that my sexual favors were up for sale at the cost of one lottery ticket? Yeah," I said, rolling my eyes. "Not sure that's the press I want." I pushed through the swinging door leading back into the shop, where Tom and Granddad spoke excitedly, and I heard a few more voices. "I'm serious," Lila said from behind me, standing in the door frame, her expression no longer playful.

"Drop it." Even to my own ears, my tone sounded cold and like I was at a breaking point. And I was. The sleepless nights were getting to me.

"No, seriously." Lila pushed forward and joined me behind the counter. "If you won't claim the ticket . . ." She let her sentence trail off.

"Which I won't."

"Then use it to get some good press. My old roommate works for Channel Thirteen, and Stewie has a huge follower count. You could go public with the story—it's a win-win."

The coffee machine gurgled behind me, and I watched a jogging couple move toward the store before turning the other way at the light. "What's your definition of winning? I'd be humiliating myself."

"It would be a fun human-interest story, plus . . ." She

leaned forward and poured herself coffee in a disposable cup. "How else are you going to find her to give her back her ticket? She already signed it, so it's not like someone else could claim it."

"What Stewie finds interesting isn't how I want to save Granddad's shop." Stewie, as far as I knew, had been Lila's friend with benefits all through college, something I tried not to think about.

"Well, here's some cold, hard truth. Pretty soon, it won't matter what we do, and Granddad's shop will be gone. I know you're the smartest in the family, and I know you gave up a lot to be here and you've done everything to try to keep this place afloat." She met my gaze, our dark eyes like mirror images, only hers were lined in black.

I glanced away, her words hitting me in the chest in a way I didn't expect.

"But we're still sinking, and this might be the last lifeboat coming." Her words hung in the air between us alongside the sounds of the coffee brewing. Each drip was a soft punctuation mark on her points, but before I could answer, the bells over the door chimed, bells our grandmother had hung before we were born, and two business owners from down the street walked in with questions for Granddad.

"So?" Lila was back to questioning me as soon as the door closed behind the two women.

I inhaled the surrounding scents that were so familiar. She was right. The bills hung over me constantly, the looming threat of shutting down. My pride was the only thing in my way. I couldn't stand it if I was the one who let Granddad's business slip away from us. I caught my reflection in the security mirror nearby. The distorted image of me was just as accurate as reality—I was a barely recognizable version of the person I'd planned to be. A shadow of the person I'd imagined that morning outside with the dog. What did my pride matter at this point?

"Fine. You can call Stewie." At least this charade would stop conversation about me claiming the ticket for myself.

Her eyes sparkled, and her expression turned into one I knew so well. "I knew you'd cave. He'll be here in an hour."

"We're doing this now?" It bugged me that my first concern was how my hair was out of control and I probably looked like someone who hadn't slept in days. And that was what Sybil would see again, but this time in the light of day.

"No time like the present!" Lila gave me a quick hug and disappeared into the back, her fingers moving over her phone. "All you need to do is figure out what you're going to say. If you sound like you're lovestruck, all the better."

I rolled my eyes, avoiding the security mirror and wondering if there was any chance this could possibly work—both the publicity angle and if Sybil would actually see it and come back. "I will not sound lovestruck. I'm going to be annoyed. Am I the only one who remembers we were robbed a few hours ago?"

"You're always annoyed." She was tapping furiously at her phone. "Just fake it."

11

Sybil

EMI NODDED TOWARD THEIR TINY GARAGE UP THE street, her regular signal for "let's sprint the rest of the way." My best friend had missed the memo that Des Moines, Iowa, in February was too damn cold to be running outside.

As a gust of wind kicked up, forcing me to close my eyes against the blistering cold, I shook my head. "It's too cold. I'm stopping here." I sucked in a breath. "I can make a new home here. My legs are on strike."

She would scold me about my whining if she could hear it over the music streaming through her earbuds. Anyone passing us might assume the petite, chipper-looking Emi was listening to Top 40 or show tunes. She looked like a person whose Spotify Wrapped would definitely include Taylor Swift and Disney-based bops in a one-to-one ratio. I knew she was humming along to the loudest, angriest metal I'd ever heard. Except for the music and flatulent pit bull, Emi's life was a study in politeness, organization, and order.

"Come on, slowpoke," she teased, her pace keeping time with whatever song had come up next on her playlist.

"Fine," I said, my acquiescence lost to the gusts of wind as we hustled toward the tiny bungalow my three best friends shared on the east side of the city. Around the sagging porch, they'd strung white lights that we'd never taken down after Christmas.

"Welcome back, you masochists." Marcus was at the stove when we pushed through the back door, Emi wiping her brow and me resting my hands on my knees, debating whether breathing again was my number one priority or if keeling over was the inevitable end to this early morning. He held a spatula in his hand and glanced between us. "How was the run?"

"It's so cold," I huffed.

"It's not that cold," Emi said over her shoulder, hanging up her coat on the hook by the door before stretching. "It's over zero."

Marcus shot me a knowing look and handed me a plate of French toast and eggs. If I wasn't one hundred percent certain he was half in love with Emi, I would have married him just for the breakfasts.

"Dear God," I said, taking a bite, my cheeks flushing at the realization of how I'd said the same thing in the donut shop before being interrupted. The eggs were so good, though, that I worked through the embarrassment. "Marcus, you should be paid for these cooking skills." I thought back to my meager checking account. "Not by me, of course," I added, savoring another bite before moving on to the French toast. "But by the world at large."

"That's what I keep telling him," Emi said, grabbing fruit to make a smoothie. Much like he assumed I'd want a plate, he knew she was going straight for the healthy green options. "Everyone will want him."

I caught the longing on his face, just for a flash. Sadly, Emi was not counted among the everyone who would want him, but I held up my fork in salute to him. He was a good-looking guy, and I wished he'd find someone else to shower with this attention that was lost on Emi.

Marcus laughed, joining me at the table with his own plate. "That's fine, but no one is hiring someone with zero experience."

"Is this lemon?" I took another bite of the French toast.

"Not to change the subject," Emi said, approaching the table where we sat with a dark, purple-colored concoction in her hands. "But what was with your text last night?"

An embarrassment that wasn't so easy to erase with eggs warmed my face, and I looked down at my plate. We were all struggling somehow—none of my friends were living large yet. Hell, most of us were gazing longingly into the distance toward medium, but if there was a ranking for these things, I was clearly in last place. Marcus dreamed of cooking but worked in an office job that provided health insurance. Emi had engineering and design degrees with a goal of designing high-end watches but was in a manufacturing job she hated. I watched her swipe a piece of spinach from her cup and pop it in her mouth. And then there was Deacon, who bounced from bartending job to cater-waiter position and driving for Uber to whatever other job he could find and charm his way into. He never talked about his time in the military, but he had started a psychology program in January with his GI Bill benefits. And then there was me.

"Things are bad at your mom's place?" Marcus chewed after asking, some flavor combination being evaluated.

"Lemon, right?" I ran a finger along the side of the plate, where the remnants of the syrup were begging to be finished, and I thought about the lemon and blueberry donut Kieran had handed me.

"Stop changing the subject," Emi demanded. "But let me taste." She swiped a finger over my plate before I could blink. "Oh, yeah. Definitely lemon. That so good."

Reprieve! I reminded myself of yet another reason to marry Marcus—excellent eggs and subject-changing homemade syrup with hints of lemon.

"So . . ." Marcus ignored our praise as always. "Something going on with your mom?"

"No," I said with a sigh. "But it's like I can't ever get things together, and she and Paul always seem to notice. Do you know my whole family was convinced I'd bring someone re-grettable to Grace's wedding? Like, they're already planning on that being a joke. They told story after story of my dating screwups until I told them I was seeing someone." I made a swirling pattern in the syrup. "Sometimes it feels like my whole life is a joke."

"Oh, honey," Emi said, wrapping an arm around my shoul-der. "Your sense of humor is mid, at best. There's no way you're a joke."

We both laughed, the sides of our heads together, and Mar-cus cleared our dishes. Reason number three.

"But I get it," Emi added. "And you can crash here, but there's not much room. Are you sure you want to move out of your mom's place, where you kind of have your own little suite?"

I didn't. Well, my first choice would be to have my own place again, but landlords like getting rent paid on time, and the electric company got all in their feels about that, too. "I got flustered and told Warren I was moving out, so I kind of backed myself into a corner because I can't afford a security deposit." I paused my fork midway to my mouth. "I'll kick in for rent and it won't be for long," I added.

"Works for me." Marcus nodded and gave an added hum of acknowledgment. "Wouldn't life be easy if we could all just win the lottery?"

I laughed but dropped my head into my hands. "I should buy another ticket."

Marcus spoke over his shoulder. "You'd look good as a millionaire. Any idea where you lost it?"

The memory of Kieran on his knees, my fingers in his hair, and the scent of the donut shop washed over me. "I don't know. Probably on the street or something."

I was saved from having to explain further when the screen door crashed open, earning half a bark from Cupcake, who lost interest almost immediately when she saw it was Deacon, whose face was red from the cold and who was, inexplicably, wearing shorts. "Why aren't any of you answering my texts?" He ran what had to be a frozen hand through his long hair. I'd seen photos of him in the air force. His hair buzzed and jawline visible. That had been abandoned almost immediately.

"Did you see it?" Deacon stood between Emi and me at the table, holding out his phone. "This is everywhere! I couldn't believe it, but it's about you, Syb. It was posted last night."

Deacon hit play on the video, inching up the volume. I recognized the influencer who had shared the video—he was a minor celebrity in town, connected everywhere and always in the thick of things. Briefly, I'd looked into that influencer life for myself, but I'd given up on it quickly. It wasn't Stewie Haynes on the screen, though, when I looked back a few seconds later. It was Kieran. Donut Kieran. My Kieran.

He looked uncomfortable in front of the camera but still somehow so at ease with himself, the apron hanging from his neck and the baseball cap, the same one from the other night, sitting backward on his head. He glanced off camera for a moment before staring into the phone. "Our family business was robbed and vandalized last night," he said, looking around. "My grandfather opened Joe's Donuts on Grand Avenue forty years ago and, uh, he's been ill, so this comes at a really bad time."

I remembered, running out that night, I'd flipped the lock open on the front door. The blood drained from my face as I watched. Surely he'd locked it behind me. Right? I searched my memory for some indication he knew I was leaving. I missed the next thing he said on the video, but on the screen, he held up a piece of paper.

"The thieves missed a few things, though, and I found this winning ticket," he said without preamble, "but it's not mine."

I stared at the screen, immediately recognizing the blue ink bleeding through the back of the paper.

"A girl . . ." He glanced off-screen for a moment. "A woman left it here last night. She signed it and everything but left it here. I hope she'll . . . come back in to see me, I mean, see us." He looked adorably flustered; his ears were pink, or maybe they were just reflecting the donut poster behind him. "I want to find her to give her the ticket." He held it up again. "Her name is Sybil and she's about this tall," he said, holding his hand to his shoulder. I thought about how he could estimate my height because we'd been pressed up against each other, and I flushed.

Stewie turned the phone to himself. "Three things. One, it's a great time of year to shop locally. Once Joe's Donuts re-opens, come in. I also started a crowdfunding page to help them. We're a strong community and need to support our local businesses. Check the link in my bio. But finally," he said, turning the camera back to Kieran. "Tell us more about the woman who left the ticket."

"Um, she has curly hair, big brown eyes, and she was really . . ." He looked to the side again. "She had a great smile. She smiled a lot, and it was the kind of smile that made you . . . you know, made you want to smile, too. Like a sunny day. She made the shop feel brighter. She's beautiful. I think that's the best way to describe her. Really . . . beautiful. She said she was a lucky person, and I guess she was right. So, if you know a Sybil who fits that description . . . please have her come back to see me."

He glanced away, maybe at the person holding the phone, but then back into the camera, so it felt like his eyes were right on me. "I hope she comes back. I'd love to see her again."

The video ended, and I looked up at my three best friends, all staring wide-eyed at me, the words coming out of our mouths at the same time.

"Holy shit."

12

Kieran

"SORRY FOR THE WAIT," I SAID FOR WHAT WAS PROBA-
bly the hundredth time.

Next to me, Lila had been saying the same thing over and
over again, that and "not yet," when they asked if she'd come
in yet.

It had been two days since the video, and we'd been
slammed with a line around the block, despite the boarded-up
window and display case. Stewie, true to Lila's word, had delivered an audience, and the city had turned out to find out
what happened and to get a chance to witness the reunion
dotted with dollar signs. The local news had even picked it up,
and though I never would have agreed to starting it, the crowdfunding site Stewie shared had already brought in enough to
make the repairs. I was uneasy about all of this and kept waiting for the other shoe to drop.

Tom was behind the counter filling orders, and Granddad
was at the cash register. He'd told me more than once to stop

fussing over him, but I couldn't help but worry this exertion and excitement would be bad for him. You wouldn't know it to look his way, though. Every hour or so, he'd clap me on the back and shake his head, repeating "I just can't believe it" with the widest grin on his face.

I handed the woman in front of me her coffee and a cruller. "Your speech." She rested her hand on top of mine. "I have to tell you it was so sweet and so romantic. I hope she comes to find you," she said with a kind smile. "I could hear in your voice how much it will mean to you for her to come back."

In reality, Lila had taken one look at what I planned to say on the video and ripped it up, telling me it lacked heart. When I told her heart had nothing to do with this, she rolled her eyes and told me to keep the apron on while she made quick cue cards. In the end, I couldn't read the sappy lies she'd scripted for me, so I'd just said what I thought women might want to hear. That was the only explanation for how I'd gone on about her smile. That wasn't like me, even though it was true.

"Did she come back yet?" the trio of teenagers asked before ordering, and I shook my head.

The crowd didn't thin as the day went on, and I'd stopped recognizing individual faces as people kept coming and coming just like the day before. I escaped the front of the shop to get receipt tape from the office and took a moment to regroup. The ticket was locked in a desk drawer, and I eyed its resting place, wondering what I would actually do if she never came back, if she lived somewhere else, or if she wasn't connected on social media like me. I'd told Lila there was no way I would claim it, and I couldn't now, but the crowds out front were my first glimmer of hope that we might be able to keep Joe's open long enough for me to go back to school. The lightness in my chest was unfamiliar, and I reminded myself to stomp down that hope—this was all still unlikely to work.

"Kier? You back here?" Lila leaned against the doorjamb, studying me.

"Yeah. Let's get back out there." I swiped the receipt tape from the shelf and tried to push past her, but she didn't move.

"I'm just waiting for you to admit I was right," she said, crossing her arms over her chest. "Need cue cards? They'd read, 'I should listen to you more often, little sister.'" She laughed at her own joke, clearly amused by blocking my path, but I looked over her shoulder at Tom, who leaned in close behind Lila, making her jump.

"I think she's here," he hissed, his eyes sparkling. "Beautiful woman with big brown eyes and a smile like sunshine just got in line!"

"Tom," I sighed. "That description didn't even make any sense. Eighty percent of people in the world have brown eyes." That was why I added her sense of humor and how charming she was. It wasn't because those things had been living rent-free in my head.

"Yeah, but all those women aren't beautiful like this," he said. "Just come out and see for yourself. It's what you wanted, right?"

Lila and I exchanged a glance, because I wasn't sure either one of us had thought this all the way through. If Sybil showed up to get the ticket, the mystery was solved. No more human-interest story, no matter how well Stewie had convinced people they needed to be here to witness something special.

Tom ignored our silence. "Of course it's what you wanted. C'mon." He walked back out to the front, where two friends of Lila's were covering the counter with him, and we followed. I scanned the space, looking at each face in search of Sybil's, my heart rate rising. It wasn't because of the attraction to her—it was just nerves about this boost in business drying up, and it wasn't eagerness to be closer to her again, it was just wanting a redo of last time, only with no interruptions.

Tom unsubtly pointed to the back of the line near the door, where a tall, thin, redheaded woman chatted with a middle-aged man in front of her. I'd always hated the saying because it seemed overdramatic in addition to being physically impossible, but in that moment my heart really *did* feel like it was sinking down into my stomach, and I didn't expect the disappointment to hit me so hard.

"That her?" Granddad's voice carried and, in an instant, the entire store was looking around, the volume rising as they tried to figure out who she was.

"Who?" "Where?" "She's here?" "Who?" The questions flew from every corner of the store.

"Not her," I said, directing my words at Tom, but it was too late and the redhead he'd been pointing out was looking around like everyone else.

"It's not her," I called out. "She's not here," I said again, trying to raise my voice over the crowd without success.

"Hey!" Lila had climbed onto a back counter, clapping her hands together the way our grandmother had. It was a louder clap than I'd ever heard anyone outside our family create, and the crowd quieted. "False alarm, she's not here yet." Lila's voice carried over everyone, filling all the corners of the store, and then there was a moment of silence as the crowd reset from their frenzy of curiosity.

The moment of quiet lasted long enough for everyone to hear the chime on the door as someone else entered, and it was like the entire store turned as one to look.

13

MARCUS LEANED IN CLOSE AFTER THE BELLS ABOVE
the door to the donut shop chimed, and the space
full of people grew silent all at once. "Why is everyone staring
at us?"

"I . . . don't know," I said. "Do they know?"

Marcus shrugged, but the crowd looked away from us and
returned to a normal volume. "Maybe they were admiring my
jacket." He slid his palms down the front of the bright orange
nineties-throwback windbreaker he'd found at a thrift store.
"But who could blame them?"

"You look good in retro," I said, distracted by how being
back in the shop reminded me of Kieran's voice, his corded
muscles, and how he'd gathered the donuts to donate to a shelter. And his eyes. I didn't remember the exact color, just that
they were dark and something about them made me want to
just stare at him, to sink into his gaze. And when he'd looked
at me . . . my body reacted to that memory, too. That's why I'd

waited two days to come in, despite Deacon's near constant reminders and Marcus checking hourly to make sure the search for me was still on.

"I look good in every color. It's the skin tone," Marcus added, but I stopped paying attention because those dark eyes that had given me all the feels the other night were on me from behind the counter. Everyone around us was talking to one another, on their phones, or who knew what else, but his eyes were locked on me from across the room. The moment stretched out, but it was probably only a few seconds before he held his fingers to his lips and nodded to the left, where I knew the office was located.

"That's him?" Marcus followed my gaze to where Kieran stood, now talking animatedly with a woman who looked a lot like him. I liked the tattoos running up her arm, and I nodded.

"You ready to go get the ticket and confront the guy whose heart you stole?" Marcus held his fist to his chest and batted his eyes.

"I didn't steal his heart." I mean, maybe his dignity when I ran out, but not his heart. I'd watched that video a hundred times, and it made sense this crowd had gathered like this. What he said made what we shared seem like the start of an epic love story and not just an epic orgasm.

He walked toward the office, the woman following, and I tried to casually circumvent the line. Luckily, no one was paying attention to me. Marcus was on my heels gathering a few looks, but mostly because his jacket was impossible to ignore. "You want me to go in with you as, like, muscle?"

I snort-laughed. "Muscle?"

"I've got some muscle," he said as we approached the short hallway leading to the office. "And you're going to walk out of here with a winning lottery ticket. It might not be safe for you to be alone."

"Cover my six," I joked while wrapping an arm around his waist. He was right, and I was pretty sure he knew I knew he was right, but he had the decency and kind heart not to make me eat my words. The office was smaller and more cramped than I remembered, though in fairness, this time I wasn't about to get laid, so I took in more of my surroundings. Kieran was crouched next to the desk, unlocking a drawer, his arm muscles bunched under his T-shirt. I'd never been an arm girl before, but damn if I couldn't stop remembering how they felt wrapped tight around me again.

"Hi," the woman standing next to him said, stretching out her hand to shake. She had a wide smile and the gem in her nose piercing caught the fluorescent light, giving her a sparkly effect. "We didn't get to actually meet the other night, but I'm Lila."

Lila's hand was soft and small in mine, and I waited for her to lob a barb my way for running out or having a one-night stand with her brother, but her gaze had drifted to Marcus. "Hi," she added in his direction, flashing a smile.

Marcus had already dropped the tough guy stance he'd taken up and extended his hand, too. I couldn't help but notice how his gaze dropped to the sleeve of tattoos up her arm. "Marcus—I'm a friend of Syb's."

"Here it is," Kieran said, standing and handing over the ticket, ignoring the vibes between Marcus and Lila. He held it out, the blue ink dotting the paper's edges.

"Hi," I said, because "You gave me the strongest orgasm of my life in this office" seemed a little too familiar given the circumstances.

"Hi," he returned, glancing down at the ticket, his voice more clipped than I remembered. "I'm glad you came back to get it."

"Wow," I said, brushing my fingers over the edge of the paper, but not taking it from him yet. "I can't believe it's a winning ticket."

"Three hundred and fifty million dollars," Marcus said with a whistle from behind me.

My finger grazed Kieran's, the back of my forefinger sliding against his, the contact sending goose bumps up my arm as we both said, "Two hundred and fifty after taxes." My eyes shot to his at the end of the sentence, and I couldn't help but smile.

"Jinx," I said. "You owe me a Coke." Our dad played that game with Grace and me as kids, and I smiled, but Kieran's expression didn't change, though Marcus and Lila both chuckled.

Awkward.

"I owe you, I guess," he said, finally moving the ticket toward my hand again. "It's already signed, so you should be able to run with it."

I held the ticket loosely in my hand. "Ironic, since I ran without it last time." I gave him another smile, but this time only Lila laughed. I was beginning a new list of reasons to marry *her* alongside Marcus. Laughing at my jokes was top of the list.

"Yeah," Kieran said, stepping back, the contact from our fingers slipping farther and farther away. "I guess so."

"Well," Lila said, clapping her hands together and interrupting this uncomfortable AF exchange. Another plus on the list for Lila. "Should we give you two a moment?" She exchanged a look with Marcus, who nodded, gaze skating up her arm again.

"That okay, Syb?" He said it with his hand on the door, I guess forgetting he'd agreed to be my bodyguard.

"Sure," I said, tucking the ticket in my pocket, sliding it gently into the denim. "I think I can handle him."

Lila was asking about Marcus's jacket as they stepped outside and the door closed, leaving me with Mr. Talkative, who was now leaning against the desk, one long leg slung over the other. "Pretty sure I handled you last time," he finally said, and I looked from his worn shoes to his face, where his lips tipped up in a tiny smile.

"Ah," I said awkwardly, trying to figure out what to do with my hands. "Yes. You definitely did." The chair where he had indeed handled me sat behind him. "And I'm so sorry I left the door unlocked when I ran off and didn't say anything . . ."

"You did leave a note," he said with a tip of his head and the rise of one of his shoulders.

"Oh my God," I said, pulling the ticket from my pocket. "Do you think they'll accept this with 'thanks for the orgasm' written on the back?" I studied my writing and he stood straighter, taking a step closer to me.

"I guess that's better than 'thanks for the lack of orgasm.'" Kieran smelled like donuts and coffee and, underneath it, something minty.

"Look who's got jokes," I said, letting my body relax and ignoring the way his scent and proximity made me want to ask for a repeat of last Friday.

"Look who's a millionaire," he said, raising his hand like he might brush my arm, but he ran it through his hair under his hat.

"We should split it," I said, holding it up. I could picture Grace and Mom seeing this moment play out and lecturing me about not consulting lawyers and financial planners first. The truth was, I couldn't imagine that much money and I didn't want to think about the kinds of decisions I'd have to make to manage it. I glanced around and down at Kieran's shoes again. "I mean, finders keepers, right? You could have kept it all for yourself."

Next to me, Kieran stiffened. "I wouldn't do that." He stepped back and that cool expression fell from his face. "If you gave me money, that would be like you paying me for sex. Or giving me charity in exchange for sex."

"That's a stretch," I reasoned. "And no one would have to know the circumstances."

"I'd know." He shook his head. "I don't want your money."

"C'mon," I said. Even split in two, that jackpot could change everything. "It was accidental sex work, at most."

"It's yours."

"You're being irrational," I said, pushing the ticket back into my pocket. "You realize you're turning down millions of dollars for your pride."

"Better irrational than impetuous. It's your money. Don't you think you'd regret giving half to a complete stranger?"

"You're not a complete stranger," I said, hearing my family's voices in his words, hearing the constant reminders to think before I acted. My hackles were up, and I was ready to do something even more impetuous, like kiss him or storm out to google what to do with a winning lottery ticket, but I looked him over again, my eyes once more landing on his worn shoes. I wondered what the real reason was that he would refuse the offer. Was it truly pride?

"I mean, I know you a little. Tell me your last name and

we'll be one step closer since we already . . ." I waved my hands in front of my jeans.

"I remember."

My hands were still motioning in front of me, and I gave up on erotic charades and let them fall. "Until we got caught. That's why I ran out."

"That makes sense." He nodded once, posture still stick straight. "But I'm still not taking your money."

"Ugh," I breathed out, frustrated. "I can't leave you with nothing."

Kieran motioned to the store. "We got a lot of press and customers the last few days. That helped."

I saw the familiar red print on some envelopes on the edge of the desk behind him and remembered a few references he'd made on Friday when the store was mostly empty. I noticed the logo from a nearby hospital on several of the envelopes, and he'd said in the video his grandfather had health troubles. "Did it help enough?"

He saw me looking and pushed them aside and out of my line of sight. I knew that trick, and I studied his face. "It helped."

I gave a hum and turned, taking in the family photos on the walls between documents. One caught my eye—it was an older one with a little boy and little girl in front of the same Ferris wheel in the photo of me with my dad. "Is this you?" I pointed, and Kieran shifted behind me.

"Yeah. With my granddad."

As I traced a finger over the side of the photo, his stories about his grandfather came back to me from that night we shared eating donuts together. The similarity to my photo with my dad, the realization of both of us being in that place and standing here now . . . the ideas were a tornado in my head. Next to it was a photo of Kieran and the same old man at a graduation ceremony, and one of Kieran standing by a sign for medical school.

"What if you took just enough to pay off your bills?"

He bristled. I saw it in the tensing of his shoulders. "You don't need to share your winnings with us."

"I know," I said, placing my hands on my hips. "But it's partly my fault you were robbed, and I know what it feels like to have bills hanging over your head. Can't you just accept a bit of good fortune?"

He paused for a moment and then shook his head. "No, I'll figure out a way to take care of the bills. Getting something for nothing isn't . . ." He began to explain further but clamped his mouth shut. "It's not something I can do. I've always made my own way."

"No offense," I said, my own posture tensing. "But that's the dumbest thing I've ever heard. Take the money and pay your bills. Can you imagine having no debt at all? I honestly can't, but it's going to be amazing!" I held up the ticket as if he'd forgotten I had it. "Let me at least do that for you."

I wondered if Kieran had taken some vow of poverty or just really enjoyed interacting with debt collectors, because his resistance made no sense. No sense unless his only reason was that I was the one offering the money. I'd taken the donuts and only left a note; I'd run out on him, leaving the door unlocked. Maybe it wasn't so much pride as not wanting to engage with me.

"Is that your grandfather out there behind the counter?"

He nodded.

"I should just offer him the money," I said, crossing my arms. "Since you're being unreasonable. Would be just as good."

I thought I saw the glimmer of a smirk. "His knees are bad. Wouldn't be *just* as good." With Kieran's dry delivery, I almost missed the joke that made me want to throttle and kiss him, but I landed on a grin. He was smart, and not just because he'd been in medical school; he was witty, and I remembered him talking about taking donuts to the shelter and how it seemed like he cared about the community. He was the kind of guy who my family would think was a good choice.

"If you won't take the money straight up, we could arrange a deal."

"What kind of deal?"

"You take enough to pay off your bills," I said, and I held up a palm, sensing the argument I was about to get. "I know what it looks like being deep in debt," I added. "And you are."

"I don't want your—"

"Let me finish!" I held his gaze for a moment before continuing. "You take enough to pay off your bills, and in return, you keep up this charade that you're into me, and we pretend we're a couple through my sister's wedding in three months."

"You want to pretend to date me? Why?"

I stepped closer to him, within arm's reach in the tight space. "Everyone thinks this is a romance. What if we just pretend it is?"

"People don't fake relationships."

"Sure they do!" I paced, the ideas coming too quickly. "I mean, celebrities, right?"

"Yeah, but not normal people."

"Hate to break it to you, Donut Man, your little video went viral. This is your fifteen minutes of fame."

"I don't want fame," he grumbled. "Anyway, I told the world I didn't know your last name or anything about you. Who would believe we were dating?"

I considered reminding him he knew how to describe my eyes and that I brightened things up, but the fact that I'd watched the video enough times to memorize his description was a little embarrassing.

"Think about it. People might stay interested if they think this is real, if this whole wild situation started a love story. Not forever, just . . . you know, for a little while, to help your shop."

"Why would they continue to care?"

I shrugged and stopped my pacing. "We're hot. I'm funny. Plus, money and donuts. I don't know . . . seems like the kind of thing we could get a month or two of interest in. Would a couple months of good business help save the shop?"

Kieran looked uncomfortable, scratching the back of his neck, a skeptical look on his face. "We'd be lying."

"I'm a great liar," I joked, trying unsuccessfully to put him at ease. "We'd use creative truth telling," I said when my joke didn't work, stepping into his space and resting a hand on his biceps, his warm, solid biceps. "We met in the shop. We'll just . . . I don't know. Make it sound more romantic." Truth was, I'd thought that night was pretty romantic until his sister had interrupted things. It had felt like Kieran was about to surprise me that whole night, and in a way that would make me feel lucky to see it. "Please let me help you—it's the least I can do if you won't take half."

His face jerked to mine at the touch, but he didn't move away as our eyes met, his gaze assessing.

"I know we don't know each other well, but I know this place matters to you, and you had the chance to look out for yourself and instead you looked for me." I brushed my palm down the length of his arm, the muscles flexing under my hand. "And people say I'm usually selfish," I said, parroting what I'd heard my whole life, "so if you say no, you're really robbing me of the rare chance to do something nice for someone else."

"So this is really about you?" His grin tipped up. The one I remembered from that night, the one that reminded me why it had been so tempting to kiss him.

"Yeah." My hand slid back up his arm. "You're catching on. And I'd benefit, too. My family thinks I'm seeing a nice soon-to-be doctor, and you'd fit the bill."

"I don't know," he said. "What would we have to do?"

I had no idea, but I was confident I could figure it out. "I think we'd need to . . . well, look like we're into each other in a few Instagram posts. Maybe tell people I've been in a couple times, but never told you my name, which is technically true. If we look like we want to tear each other's clothes off, I bet people will believe it," I added, letting in too much honesty. Everything in my life was on shaky ground, and as much as money would solve a lot of problems, it made me just as unsteady. But Kieran was solid, like if I leaned against him, he'd stay put. "You'll meet my family a few times and be a nice almost doctor, but they're busy with getting ready for my sister's wedding, so it won't be a big deal, and . . . you could go with me to the wedding as my date."

He studied my face, his expression so serious and unmoving. "A couple of social media posts and family dinners and a wedding and then just . . . let people believe what they want to believe?"

"Look, if it doesn't work, I'll still give you the money."

"I don't like the idea of accepting this big a gift. We'd need at least three hundred thousand dollars to pay everything off."

"I've been told I'm a lot. You'll earn it," I joked. "And would spending time with me be such a terrible thing?" I flashed what I knew was a flirty smile. "As I mentioned, I'm hot and funny."

Kieran stilled for a moment, eyes on my face. He'd said he wanted to be a doctor. I couldn't imagine having a doctor who looked like him, and I wondered if he'd turn me down again and send me on my way. I didn't want him to. I'd enjoyed him as a solid surface on this unsteady ground.

He studied my face intently and finally nodded, extending his hand to shake. "Okay. It's a deal." When our palms met, his grip was firm and warm, and I tried my best to ignore the tingles moving through my body at his touch. I felt really good about this—maybe with a guy like Kieran next to me, and hundreds of millions of dollars in the bank, I could finally get my family to take me seriously. He seemed perfect on paper, even if a real relationship between us would never work. "It will be great doing business with you," I said, releasing his hand and holding up the lottery ticket with my handwritten note for him to see. "Just don't go falling in love with me along the way."

"Believe me," he said, hand on the doorknob. "Everything about the situation makes me certain that won't happen."

14

Kieran

I LOOKED UP THE STREET TO THE ADMINISTRATIVE building, where I spotted Stewie's signature blue hair as his head tipped down while he did something on his phone.

"Hey," I said as I approached, my breath visible in the cold.

"Salutations!" Stewie took a moment to look up from his phone. "Wow! You cleaned up a bit," he said. "Your ladylove here yet?" He scanned the street, and I shook my head.

"Not yet." I shoved my hands in my pockets. "Thanks for doing this," I added, realizing too late I'd never had a conversation with Stewie without Lila, and I felt old and deeply uninteresting standing next to him.

"Are you kidding? People love this story—my views and engagement are off the charts. Great for my bottom line, too."

That was comforting and troubling in equal measure, and I tugged on my collar, scanning the area for Sybil. I'd expected the office to be in a high-rise, but the building was tucked away in the suburbs, a modern-looking two-story building with natural landscaping and wooden beams crisscrossing the front. The area wasn't crowded, but I was anxious for this thing to begin. It had been a miracle we hadn't been found out in the shop and Sybil had slipped out through the crowd with no one noticing. Even with my head in overdrive about what I'd agreed to do, I marveled that anyone could take one look at her and not see what I'd described in the video—someone who lit up the room.

I shuffled from foot to foot in the cold. "So, how does this work?"

Stewie looked at me quizzically. "Not much to it. We'll snap a photo and a quick video of you two. You don't have to say much—the story has taken off, but if you look like you're half as into her as you looked in the first video, it'll go well."

"Sure," I said, seeing Sybil walking toward us. She'd changed and wore a flowy dress that hugged her upper body and blew in the chilly breeze. The outfit was completely impractical for the cold weather, but my gaze snagged on her legs as the dress blew around her, before taking in her red-painted lips. Her coat was open, and the afternoon sunshine made her skin appear kind of golden.

"Just like that," Stewie said.

"What?" He was still holding up his phone when I turned. "Did you just take my picture?"

He laughed and was already tapping on his phone. "Your face when you saw her—it was perfect. Captioning it with 'Guess who just showed up?'" He chuckled again, holding the phone away from me. "Don't worry. People will be all over this."

My stomach lurched at the idea of the attention and how little control we had over any of it.

"Hi, again." Sybil held out her hand but then leaned in for

an awkward hug, something I picked up on a second too late, so we kind of collided, with my hand nudging her side and her forehead knocking my chin.

I shot a glance at Stewie, who was tapping the screen of his phone. "Don't worry. Deleting that one." He turned to Sybil. "Hey, I'm Stewie. I posted the original video."

"I know who you are," she said with a wide smile, leaning in for a hug. It annoyed me because it looked so much more natural with Stewie than it had with me. "Your Des Moines Fails posts are everything."

Stewie beamed, and I wondered if Sybil made everyone feel like that—she'd certainly made me feel that way, but maybe that was just how she was. "I'll just get a couple of pics and maybe a video we can post later."

"Did your friend come with you this time?" I looked around for the big guy who'd come to the shop with her, the one I'd been immediately jealous of, especially when Sybil had casually wrapped her arm around him. Lila told me she liked him—by the time we'd come out, the two of them had been behind the counter and he'd been talking about baking and obscure bands with her. The jealousy had lingered, though.

"Nah. He was in the middle of a complicated-looking meal that involved a lot of chopping and whisking, and I told him you'd protect me." She moved to my side, remembering we were supposed to be smitten.

"I'm protecting you?" I followed her toward the door, Stewie saying he'd catch up in a few minutes.

"Well, sure. I assume letting me get kidnapped would put a damper on this publicity stunt."

"Yeah, but then I would have to lead the charge to get you back."

"That might be better press. Well, better press for you . . . it would definitely suck for me."

My posture eased slightly as I opened the door for her to walk in. "I guess so. I'll just try my best to protect you." We crossed the sunny lobby. "Did your family not want to come?"

Sybil avoided my gaze. "I . . . haven't told them about winning the lottery yet."

I let her enter the elevator ahead of me, my gaze dropping to the curve of her butt on instinct, but, damn winter, her coat blocked my view. "Must be hard to keep that secret."

"I wanted to turn in the ticket first," she said, pulling it from the small bag in her hand. Her voice was lower and just a little less bright when she spoke again. "Just in case something goes wrong. I have a reputation for mistakes in our family, so if I messed up this big and it really wasn't a winner or something . . . well, I'd rather just be sure first."

I nodded, watching the numbers tick slowly as the elevator ascended. "If it helps, we did double- and triple-check," I said. "The ticket, I mean. It's the winning numbers."

She nodded. "I know. I checked it a hundred times." She placed a palm over her chest and took a deep breath.

"Are you nervous?"

She laughed, the bark kind of escaping, as if without permission. "Well, yeah." The elevator doors dinged and opened, revealing the lobby. "I mean, what am I supposed to do with this much money? I can't even hold down a temp job."

"Well, those are temporary. I don't think you're supposed to hold them down."

She narrowed her eyes for a second, but then I could see her wheels spinning again. "I don't even have my own place." Her face fell again, something else behind her words I couldn't place, but she was visibly anxious, breaths coming faster and her eyes darting left and right. "I've never once dated a decent guy who treated me well, and now I've got you and no one will believe it." She sucked in a ragged breath. "This whole thing is going to blow up."

"You'll be fine," I said, trying to keep my eyes ahead. "It's fine."

"I'm gonna screw this up. I know I will." Her breathing sped and she started talking faster, the words tumbling out. "And so many people will see it. There are so many things I have to do, but I don't know what they are. Do I take a lump sum or payments, and what about taxes?" She looked up into my eyes, her irises catching the light in the room, and her voice was a whisper. "What if I screw it up?" She was panicking, and a drop of sweat slid down her neck, leaving a trail along her throat, where I saw her pulse.

I fought the urge to touch her there, to wipe away the evidence of her anxiety, but instead I took her hand in mine, earning a startled expression as we waited in the elevator vestibule.

"Breathe," I said, squeezing her hand. "That's the only thing you have to do right now. In and out."

She clutched my hand, chest expanding as she inhaled. Her eyelids fell as she exhaled, lashes casting shadows on her cheeks from the harsh overhead lighting before she looked at me again, expectant.

"Good," I said. "Again. Nice and slow." I modeled for her, our breathing in sync, and she kept her eyes with mine, the sensation of breathing together oddly comforting for me, too. "One more time."

I lifted her hand, rotating her wrist so her palm was up.

"There's a pressure point on your wrist," I said, gliding two fingers down her thumb to the place I wanted. "Here," I said, pressing my fingers gently but firmly into her skin, ignoring the jump in my chest when touching her. "It's said it can relieve physical signs of anxiety." Sybil stepped closer, watching me work my fingers over the spot.

"Does it actually work?"

"Do you feel better?" I circled the spot on her wrist, taking in the smoothness of her skin and inhaling the scent of her.

"Yeah, I think I do," she said, moving her gaze from our joined hands to my face, and I listened to her breaths slowing. "That might just be you talking to me, though."

I kept talking, seeing how my voice was calming her and ignoring how good that felt. "Acupressure has been part of Chinese medicine for centuries. Western medicine is catching up," I said. I had a mentor in school who taught me some things. "This is called the Great Abyss point." I turned her hand, pressing my thumb into the connection between her index finger and thumb. "Hegu point," I said, ignoring the way her eyes fluttered closed at the pressure. "You'll figure it out. It will be fine," I added. "You're lucky like that, right?"

She nodded, the corners of her lips tipping up. "I am," she said, eyes on mine, that hint of a smile. "I am lucky."

"Perfect!"

We both startled apart at Stewie's voice. I hadn't even noticed the elevator open again as he came up behind us, but I dropped her hand and we stepped apart. "What's perfect?" Sybil was holding the hand I'd dropped, and my gaze snagged on how she skirted her thumb over the spot I'd rubbed.

"The lottery sign was in the background, and you two

looked all intense with your hands together. Great photo. You want to see?" He held his phone forward, but the receptionist returned to us just then, interrupting.

"Can I help you?"

Sybil's eyes widened, and she pulled the ticket from her purse again, but she didn't say anything.

"Um, yes. She has a winning ticket," I said, nudging Sybil forward with my hand at the dip of her lower back.

"Congratulations," the receptionist said, tapping on her keyboard. Sybil approached as if the woman was typing on a boa constrictor and not a keyboard, and held the ticket out for inspection. The receptionist nodded, taking the ticket and typing in something until her fingers froze and she made an O with her mouth as she checked the ticket again. "You won big," she said, finally handing the ticket back to Sybil, who looked like she was going to vibrate out of her skin. I couldn't very well give her another hand massage, but I lowered my hand to brush hers, and she linked her fingers with mine, squeezing. The gesture surprised me, and I tried to remember the last woman to hold my hand.

The receptionist was about to say something else, but her gaze snagged on me, and she slapped the desk. "Oh my gosh! You're the guy from the donut video!"

My face heated—I had not planned to be part of this other than for Stewie's documentation.

"Gail! Come out here!" Another woman strode from behind a partition. "It's the guy from that video. He found her. It's them!"

"Love and donuts!" Gail looked from Sybil to me. "My daughter showed me that video. How sweet!"

"Um, that's us," Sybil said, squeezing my hand tighter. It wasn't a romantic move, it was a grip of panic that I interpreted as "If I'm going down, you're coming with me."

"This is just the sweetest thing," the receptionist added with a warm smile. "I love stories like this," she said. "You sit tight for a minute while I get our manager, who will take you from here."

"So," Gail said, a fist resting under her chin. "Was it just sparks and romance at first sight? Was there a reason you never told him your full name, sweetie?"

I looked over at Sybil, whose panic didn't seem to extend to making things up on the spot, because she looked more relaxed than she had since we'd met in the parking lot. And I guessed Gail was going to be the first to know about our fictional relationship.

"It all happened so fast," Sybil deflected. "I can't even put words together yet." I gave her a mental high five. "But I'm glad we found each other again," she said, looking up at me with a grin. "And he's here with me."

Gail said something else, but I was focused on Sybil's quick wink, and then a tall man came around the corner. "Sybil Sweet?" He extended his hand. "Congratulations," he said, motioning to an office nearby. "Are you ready for your life to change?"

She looked up at me again, and I returned her vise grip.

"Yep," she said, looking back at him. "Let's go change our lives."

15

Sybil

MOM? YOU HERE?"

I dropped my purse on the kitchen table after using my key to let myself in. I'd been somewhere between a tornado of anxiety and a fog of disbelief for hours. Really, the only time I'd felt calm was with Kieran, helping me focus on my breathing and holding my wrist. I traced my fingers over the spot he'd rubbed and wondered if that was just his professionalism, his method of calming patients. *Or maybe that was just for me.* I shook my head at the silly thought and looked around the corner. "Mom?" The house was quiet. I should have called ahead, but when you're given millions of dollars and pick up a fake boyfriend all in the same day, it's easy to lose track of your manners.

Kieran had sat next to me through the whole thing, only dropping my hand when I had to sign documents and take a photo with the big cardboard check. He'd been sweet and kind and more like the man I'd met before I ran out on him than the grumpy one I'd encountered in the store that morning. He was going to be the perfect guy for this charade, I could feel it in my bones.

"Sybil!" Mom said, pushing through the door loaded down with bags. "You scared me." Grace was behind her, carrying shopping bags. "What are you doing here? Your car was blocking my spot. I've asked you a hundred times not to do that."

She hustled past, dropping the bags in the living room and circling back to me, wrapping an arm around my shoulders for a squeeze. "What's wrong?"

"Nothing, just wanted to share some news."

Mom squealed, an actual squeal, as she fell into the other chair at the small table. "You got a full-time job?" Her face was bright and her smile hopeful. I wondered if she knew her hands were clasped as if in prayer.

"No, not a job. I haven't started looking yet."

"Oh," she said, that hopeful smile falling. "I thought for sure it would be a job after I put you in touch with my friend's uncle in real estate. Did you call him yet? You really need to stop being lazy about this and get moving."

"Um, no, I haven't called him yet," I said, not even remembering her giving me any contact information and trying not to let her reference to me being lazy hurt, though it did. It always had. Instead, I turned on a forced brightness. "But that sounds interesting. I'll check into it."

"Oh good," she said, patting my arm. "I just want you to land somewhere. You're so talented at so many things." Mom stood and pulled a glass from the cupboard. "So, what is the news? Are you finally ready to tell us more about this guy you've been seeing?"

"No. I mean, well . . . kind of."

Mom looked over her shoulder as she approached the sink to fill her glass. "What does that mean?"

"Well, remember Friday night, how I told you I hung out at the donut place?" This time I spoke to Grace. I hadn't thought this would be so hard to get out, and I also wasn't sure why I was burying a pretty significant lede with the millions of dollars, but I continued.

Grace nodded. "Sure. You went out there with the guy."

"Kind of." Technically, we hadn't so much gone out as gone down the last time, but Mom didn't really need those details. "It's a wild story, actually. But we weren't exactly seeing each other before, just, you know, flirting and spending time together."

"Oh no. Honey . . ." Mom turned from the faucet. "You didn't do something regrettable, did you? I just don't know if I can handle another romantic storm from you. You're not pregnant, are you? In trouble with drugs?"

I dug my fingernails into my palm to stifle the hurt response that triggered, the one deep down in my chest. "No! God, Mom."

"Mom, just let her finish," Grace urged.

"The guy actually owns the place, or his family does, and I've been going in there but I . . . well, I never told him my name. I wanted it to stay casual." I'd worked out what I was going to tell them in the car, but to my own ears, this lie was cockeyed. "Not casual like casual sex, but like . . . slow and mysterious and romantic."

"Oh, Sybil . . ." Mom's face fell. "You're going to bring a guy you're just sleeping with to your sister's wedding? Please, no."

I rethought my lie. It wasn't pregnancy or drugs, so she'd mentally skipped the part where I'd claimed a relationship with someone who didn't know my name. "It's not that. I like him, but I was afraid of getting hurt, but we like each other, so we're really dating now." That was a lie on so many levels that I held my breath.

Mom pulled me into a hug, her voice immediately softening. "It's hard to open up our hearts, honey."

I froze at her sudden shift. This was going better than I thought.

"That's great," Grace encouraged. "Can't wait to meet him."

"You'd like him," I offered. "He cares about the community, and he's running his family business. He's even going back to medical school as soon as his grandfather's health is better!"

"I don't know why you lied to us," Mom said, releasing me and walking toward the kitchen. "Or made me think the worst. Bring him by. I want to meet him."

"Well, there's more. I left something at the shop on Friday, and since he didn't know my name yet, he didn't have a way to get it back to me." I glossed over the finer points about why I'd left it there and also decided not to sprinkle in how much fun I'd had with Kieran. That felt almost more intimate than what we'd done later. I waited for Mom to interrupt, but she was sipping her water patiently. "Well, thing is, he tried to find me to give it back, and there was a video online that kind of blew up."

"Why was he so adamant about finding you?" Mom asked from the kitchen before taking a sip of water. "Didn't he assume you'd be back if you've been *flirting*?" She put emphasis on the word, implying flirting might still mean casual sex and perhaps a little light meth distribution.

"Well, that's where it gets wild . . ."

"Wild how?" Grace asked. "What did you leave there?"

"Um," I said, speaking with my chin tucked to my chest the way I had as a kid. "It was a lottery ticket."

"Oh, Sybil," Mom said, returning to her task with an eye roll. I didn't need to see her face to know it was there. "That's such a waste of money!"

"Yes, but not this time, because the ticket was a winner. Three-hundred-and-fifty-million-dollar jackpot."

Grace screamed and Mom's glass crashed to the ground, shattering into hundreds of pieces, the shards and water catching the overhead light like a kind of violently beautiful glitter.

Grace hugged me, her face a mask of shock, and Mom stood stone still in the middle of the glass. "Mom!" we both said, getting to our feet to clean the glass.

"Sybil, you won the lottery? You won the actual lottery?" She didn't seem to notice the glass, and she was pale as a ghost, her hand shaking over her mouth. She kept repeating the question before I could answer. "Just, I'm sorry, you won the lottery?"

Grace grabbed the dustpan, and I scooped paper towels from the counter to clean up the glass. "Don't move yet, Mom—there are shards all around you." Grace began a circle around her to clean, but Mom didn't seem to notice.

"Sybil Marie Sweet. You actually won the lottery? Like, you're a millionaire?" Mom usually only used my middle name when I was in trouble, so this was a new context.

I slid a paper towel over the floor to catch glass and water. "Ouch!" I cried out when several shards made it through. It was the first time in my life Mom hadn't lectured me about taking my time with cleaning broken glass. No matter, though; Grace was making quick work of it, and Mom was vibrating to get out of her circle of danger.

She finally screamed the way Grace had, and I grinned, joining her in the scream. "I know!"

Grace swept the last of the glass into the trash, and Mom leaped forward, wrapping me in her arms. "I can't believe it!"

"This is unbelievable, Sybil!" Grace joined in, adding to the hug. "I have to tell Warren."

"Do you want us to go to the lottery office with you?" Mom's hands slid up and down my arms as if checking to make sure I was still actually there and this wasn't a dream.

"I actually went this afternoon," I said, and she froze, as did Grace.

"Alone? Honey! That's not safe!"

"When did you get the ticket from the donut shop guy?" Grace motioned to my hand, where there were tiny trickles of blood from the run-in with the glass. In typical older sister fashion, she interrogated me while tending to my injuries.

"It all happened really fast. And I wasn't alone, Mom." I gave them the rundown, from the video to Marcus being my muscle to seeing Kieran again. That's where I stumbled. I couldn't tell them we were pretending to date, but I didn't know how else to explain him. "We'd had such a connection when we talked, and I know it sounds wild, but when we saw each other again, it was there still. It's . . . it might be something special, and I didn't want to go alone, so he went with me to the office."

Grace and Mom shared a look, their faces sporting matching creases between their brows.

"What?"

"It's just a little convenient, right? That he's interested in you and this connection blossoms the day you win the lottery?"

Grace dabbed at my hand with a wet paper towel. "You're being careful, right?"

"Yeah, it's not like that. He doesn't want money from me." I bit my cheek at the lie. I knew it would be worth it.

"Things are different now, baby. How do you know this boy isn't trying to scam you?"

Oh, Mom. If you only knew. "He's a really nice guy. He's a lot like Grace, actually."

She gave a harrumph. "Don't give him any money." She left it there and then began writing down a laundry list of things I needed to take care of.

We were still at the kitchen table together thirty minutes later, and they'd moved on to a third page. I tried to breathe the way Kieran had told me to at the lottery office instead of admitting to the hives that list gave me. When Mom ran down the hall to grab another notepad, I pushed the list to the side. "Grace, I was thinking, I know I dropped the ball on the bachelorette party weekend and I was late for the appointment with the cake guy and I lost your wedding bands for a few hours when I picked them up for you, but I could pay for the whole wedding now!" My smile grew as I said it, feeling good about being able to contribute something. "And for your honeymoon, too."

I expected another round of screaming, but Grace placed her hand on mine. "That's way too generous," she said. "You don't need to spend your money on us. You can figure out what *you* really want. We've got this." She hugged me, and the familiar scent of her perfume wrapped around me. "Thank you for the offer, though."

"Sure," I said, trying to ignore that niggling self-doubt. I'd been excited to contribute something to her wedding, to be able to be the hero, but now I felt that same old shame at trying to do something and failing.

After Mom returned, I stepped into the hallway, feigning a need for the bathroom, and pulled my phone from my pocket. I shook off my disappointment at Grace turning down my offer and opened the group chat with my friends.

> SYBIL: Update.

> EMI: ?

> MARCUS: ?

> DEACON: You had a sex dream
> about me?

> SYBIL: Are you sitting down?

Emi sent a selfie of the three of them together at their kitchen table with a delicious-looking dinner in front of them, no doubt prepared by my muscle, who really did need to be a chef.

> SYBIL: Don't freak out

> EMI: Just say it!

> MARCUS: Are you okay?

> DEACON: Did the dream start with
> me sitting down?

SYBIL: I'm pretending to date the donut guy, who is actually going to be a doctor, to impress my family and get good press for the shop. As far as you know, it was love at first sight, okay?

EMI: I have questions, but we got you.

MARCUS: 👍

DEACON: Was he in the dream, too? I'm just saying, I'm game.

I chuckled and tucked my phone away, bracing myself for a return to the kitchen table and the inevitable fourth page they'd moved on to in my absence. I rolled my shoulders back and took a step forward but paused when I heard their low voices.

"I don't know why you're worried," Grace said in a hushed tone. "You're always concerned about her keeping a job, and now she doesn't have to. She's going to be set." I leaned against the wall and angled my ear to them.

"She'll have plenty of money, but . . ." Mom paused, and I imagined Grace tilting her head to the side and welcoming part two without comment. In my head, I was already saying, "But what?" Mom sucked in a breath. "She doesn't commit to anything. She never follows through. I was hoping that was on the horizon, and now she has no reason to."

I stiffened at her observation and awaited Grace's rebuttal, but Mom kept going. "And now this new guy she barely knows . . . I don't know. I hope I'm wrong, but I think she's going to keep flitting from thing to thing with no motivation to *do* anything or *build* anything. She's always said she's letting luck drive her, and now this . . ." The pause hung in the air for a moment. "I think this lucky break is going to ruin what little drive she had to find and do something meaningful."

I covered my mouth to stop from sucking in an audible breath at Mom's assessment. Hearing the words so plainly was like experiencing a long, slow paper cut. I knew I was the disappointing daughter, but I didn't realize she'd already decided I was such a lost cause.

"Syb is so talented," Grace said, voice pitched low. "She's got so much potential."

"She does. She always has, but she never sticks with anything or anyone long enough to realize it." Mom let out a heavy sigh. "Now, with all this money, I worry she's going to keep flying in circles until she crashes, and if he's actually a good guy, which I don't believe yet, she's going to crash into this boy and his small business." She flipped the list in front of her, the paper rustling.

"Okay," Grace said slowly. "But can you imagine how great she'd be if she found the right thing and stuck with it?"

I couldn't hear my mom's response, but my eyes stung with the impending tears at the plain prediction. This was perhaps the luckiest day of my life, and I was pressed against a wall listening to my own mother describe how I had no hope of being a serious person living a meaningful life.

If I ever wanted to, I had a sense this was the time. Blowing off things with Kieran and the shop wasn't an option—it would just further cement that nothing had changed. I wiped away the tears and walked toward the bathroom in the hall to splash water on my face. I'd show them I was serious about this, that I could commit, that I was doing something meaningful, that I could make a real difference, even if the thing with Kieran was fake. I looked at myself in the mirror. "Time to show them I found the right thing."

16

Kieran

FLIPPED THE SIGN IN THE SHOP WINDOW TO THE SIDE
reading "Closed" and heaved a sigh as I double-
checked the lock on the door. The bell hanging above it had
been constantly ringing since we'd opened. I'd had to grudgingly admit to Lila that this wasn't the worst idea, even though
the lie still ate at me.

"Probably feels a little strange to close up so early after your
late-night-donut experiment, huh?" Tom was perched in his
normal spot at the counter across from Granddad, who'd decided medical advice no longer applied to him. He was keeping
his promise to stay seated by the register, though I suspected
when I ran off to let out Mrs. Nguyen's dog, he'd get into the
kitchen. Behind him now, the trays, our only storage until the
display case was replaced, were empty. The last two crullers
had been snapped up by two people on their way to the bar
across the street after work. "You might just have to get your-

self a life, kid!" Tom's deep laugh was as familiar to me as the sound of the coffee brewing, and I gave him a wan smile.

"I think I'd like to see that," Granddad said, folding his arms over his chest and nodding to his best friend. "Tom was never so considerate about overnight guests when the two of us were roommates years ago," he added with a chuckle.

"Wait. Considerate like he's quiet or considerate like he's alone?" Tom smacked the counter at his own joke, and the two laughed at me again. Truthfully, it was good to see Granddad laugh again, even if it was at my expense. "Never mind, Joe. I don't even need to ask. This kid is alone. But maybe that's about to change with this new woman in his life . . ." Tom waggled his eyebrows suggestively, a move that, when delivered by a seventy-six-year-old man with bushy eyebrows and a matching white mustache, was anything but sexy.

"My nightlife aside . . ." I joined them at the counter. "This rush of people won't last, but after the break-in and everything with the ticket, it has been nice to get steady business." I hadn't heard from Sybil since we went to the lottery office a couple of days earlier, but Stewie had posted the photo he took when I was trying to calm her, and every third customer had mentioned it. Tom and Granddad brought it up enough on their own that their eyes basically had hearts over them. "Don't worry about me abandoning you to go clubbing anytime soon," I reassured them.

"I can't imagine you'd know what to do in a club," Granddad mused, finishing his coffee.

"Probably ask 'em to turn down the music." Tom laughed at his admittedly solid dig. "Hopefully your new lady will make sure they turn it back up. You need a bit of bump and grind if you ask me." Tom did an exaggerated body roll, smacking the back of his old Levi's, earning a belly laugh from Granddad.

"I really don't need to hear either of your thoughts on bumping and grinding." I pulled the cleaning supplies from behind the counter, scanning the tables for trash before starting the process. "Granddad, you want a hand getting upstairs?"

He shook his head and nodded to Tom. "What good's an old friend if he can't help you up the stairs?" He clapped Tom on the back and walked to the bathroom off the right side of the shop, leaving Tom and me alone.

I topped off his mug before dumping out the rest of the pot. "You know I'm right. I always am," he mused, pointing to the empty display case and front door, where the bell had stopped its incessant ringing. "I told you your luck was about to change, after all." He smacked his flat palm onto the counter, repeating what he'd been saying for days.

"I guess it did," I said, pulling a broom from the small cabinet near the register. I hated lying to Tom, but the worst of it was over. We hadn't taken any more photos, so Sybil had nothing left to post. As I swept along the edge of the counter, I thought about her perched there that first night, her legs swinging. She'd been like a breath of fresh air after being stuck inside all day. I'd had lots of days that all ran together during my semesters of med school, and working in the shop had started to blur into a routine that I could do half asleep. Every one was a prelude to more and more of the same. Until that night. Until Sybil breezed into my world and threw everything into chaos and vivid color. Of course, I'd never admit that to Tom or anyone else. It sounded like I believed this whole love story.

"Just can't believe it," Tom said for the fifteenth time.

"Three hundred and fifty million dollars." He took a contemplative sip of his coffee. "Don't that beat all."

"I didn't win it, though," I reminded him.

"Yeah, that pretty girl you found did." Tom raised his cup of coffee, obviously waiting for the tea, but I just nodded while sweeping. "Aw, you're no fun," he said, downing the rest of his coffee. "I don't come here for this swill, boy. I need stories." He set his cup aside. "You decide when you're going back to school?"

I swept more aggressively. I'd earned scholarships all through college, and that helped, but my student loan debt would probably be my longest-lasting relationship, and I'd be taking out more when I got back to school. I bent to use the dustpan, Tom's words at my back. "Not yet," I said. "I've got a little time to decide." When I gave Sybil that total of three hundred thousand, it only included the bills I had yet to pay, not the many that would come after. If I could take care of the medical bills and get the shop back on track, I would be okay with more loans. The school had called earlier that day to confirm I knew the deadline to accept. I didn't have a lot of time to figure everything out.

"I think what you did—coming home and all, I mean— well, it shows how good a man you are, but your granddad doesn't want you putting your life on hold," Tom said, pitching his voice low. "Not for him."

I nodded as I heard Granddad come out of the bathroom and approach us, his steps still slow and heavy. "It's not on hold, it's just . . . you know. It's life. It's family." I coughed into my hand. "It's what you do."

Granddad leaned against the counter by Tom. "Are you still harassing my grandson about his social life?"

"Of course," Tom said, giving me a knowing look. "Just making sure he doesn't mess things up with his new lady friend."

There was a knock at the door, and Tom hustled from his spot to open it for Sybil. "Speak of the lovely devil," he said as he motioned her toward the counter with a flourish.

Sybil wore jeans that hugged her hips and thighs, and her coat hung open, revealing a shirt that showed off a sliver of the stomach I knew was soft and inviting. "Devil?" Sybil placed her index fingers on either side of her head and curled them into horns. "Who told?"

Tom smacked the counter again, letting out a loud belly laugh. "Damn, I like this one," he said. "I'm Tom, Kieran's favorite old man next to Joe."

When Sybil leaned in and kissed him on the cheek, there I was, suddenly jealous of the attention Tom was getting, a counter between us and me debating hopping it to get to her. "Sybil," she said.

"His favorite young woman," Granddad added, taking her hand in both of his.

"You gonna greet your girl or let us have all the fun, kid?" Tom knocked his shoulder against Sybil's.

"Yeah, Kieran. I might have to pick a new guy," she said, resting an arm on his shoulder. "You single, Tom?"

"He can't bake," I said, setting the broom aside and leaning on the counter. "Aren't copious amounts of donuts part of your master plan?"

Sybil gently pushed Tom away. "He's right." She mirrored my stance, leaning forward on the counter, which brought our faces near each other, close enough that our noses brushed for half a second. "I gotta serve my sweet tooth." She widened her eyes at me like we were in on a joke, and she leaned in at the same time I leaned in, and though I expected our mouths to collide again, her lips landed on the tip of my nose, grazing toward the left.

We both fumbled as she pulled back. "Hi," I said again, watching Sybil slide back down the counter. I hadn't expected to see her tonight, and I definitely hadn't expected my heart to beat faster when I did. "What are you doing here?"

"Nice to see you, too," she said in an exasperated tone, her eyebrow cocked. She must have heard it in her voice, because she shot a quick glance at Granddad and Tom and changed her smile. "I wanted to see you," she said, not very convincingly.

"I think we can take a hint," Tom said, standing. "Let's leave these kids to it, Joe. I'll make sure you don't tumble down the stairs again."

"Sybil, it was a pleasure. I've known this one a long time," he said, motioning to me with his thumb. "I think you just might be the one to loosen him up." He held out his wide palm to shake her hand. "And I'm hoping a bit of your luck will rub off." They set off for the back of the shop.

Granddad called over his shoulder, "Night, kids."

"So . . ." I tucked the broom back into the cupboard and faced Sybil again, using every bit of willpower to keep my eyes on her expression, one filled with relief now that we were alone. "What's up? I thought we didn't need to do anything for a while after that picture."

"We don't," she said. She sank her teeth into the corner of her lower lip in a way that made me want to kiss away the pain of that bite, before I reminded myself this woman was off-limits, and for good reason. "I realized I never got your phone number," she said, looking around the shop.

"Oh, okay." I accepted her phone and typed in my number. "That's all you needed?"

"I was just in the area." She tapped her fingers on the counter the way she'd done the night we met. "Can't a girl stop in to see her fake boyfriend on the fly?" She accepted the phone back and tapped out a text to me. "Now you have mine so we can exchange flirty texts," she said. She looked like she wanted to say something, nervous energy rolling off her in waves as I walked around her to lock the front door and flip the sign to "Closed."

"I'm not really a flirty text guy," I said, straightening behind the counter.

"You know," she said, tapping something out on her phone, "that doesn't surprise me."

My phone buzzed, and her text flashed across my screen. I'll show you how I like it done. 😼

The text sent my mind in a very specific direction, but I put the phone back in my pocket, ignoring her suggestion. "I'm just closing up, and then I was going to head home for the night. Was there anything else you needed?" Lila would have thrown something at me and told me that was rude, but I didn't know the rules here, and time and again I'd let myself get distracted when Sybil was nearby. I'd recognized the pattern, so now I could interrupt it.

"There is something else," she said, ducking her head. In my brief experiences with this woman, I had no idea how to interpret her body language. It could have meant she wanted a cup of coffee, that she'd inadvertently stolen all the money from the cash register, or that she wanted a second crack at hooking up in the office. As tempting as that last option was, the second seemed more likely. "There wasn't anything after that photo, and I meant to get in touch with you earlier today, but I didn't have your number and then the day got away from me . . ."

"What is it?"

Her words spilled out fast, like water from a tap. "Channel Thirteen wants to have us on to talk about what happened, you know, tell our story, and I thought it would be good press and a good way to convince everyone it was real, so I agreed."

"On live TV?"

"Yeah," she said, "but we can figure out what we'll say in advance. It'll be fine!" Her blue T-shirt stretched across her breasts and read "Yes, there are Black people in Iowa" in blocky letters, and she smiled sheepishly. "I probably should have asked you first," she said. "I hoped you'd be fine with it since it would be a good chance to promote the shop."

I sighed because she was right. We could never afford a TV commercial, or any ads really, and it would be good exposure, but I hated everything about going on TV to prove this lie was real. We'd have to spend time figuring out what we were going to say and how to say it, and I had no free time to dedicate to this. "When is it? Next week?" I could figure out a way to squeeze in some preparation time with her.

"Um." She looked down at her nails and then sank her teeth into her lower lip again before meeting my eyes. "Tomorrow morning," she said with eyebrows raised. "But not until nine, so we have time to prepare."

I looked at the clock on the wall over the door. I'd hoped to use the free hours to do laundry and stare at the letter from school outlining the process to come back. But now this. "That's fourteen hours away." I studied Sybil, whose expression was hopeful. It felt like something practiced, like she'd spent most of her life doing things like this and having people give in to what she wanted because her smile was so sweet. The fact that my first instinct was to do the same annoyed me. "We know next to nothing about each other."

"I know . . ." She tucked a curl behind her ear, the glittery pink of her fingernails catching the overhead lighting. "I really did mean to get here earlier to run it by you. I just thought it would be helpful for the shop. And it's not like we'd need to know *everything* about each other. They're not going to quiz us."

"They're going to interview us." I heard the annoyance in my voice and sighed, running my fingers through my hair. She was right about it being good for the shop, and she was still looking at me with that sweet expression. "Fine."

"It might be fun," she exclaimed.

Lying on live TV with no time to prepare was not my idea of fun. It sounded as far away from fun as I could imagine and as far away from my normal life as I could imagine. Somehow Sybil kept talking me into things that should have been second nature for me to refuse. But I took in the way she bounced with excitement, and, just for a moment, wondered if far away from normal wouldn't be so bad.

17

Sybil

SMACKED MY PALMS DOWN ON THE STEERING WHEEL as I was forced to circle the block for a third time. My confidence in my ability to find the address was waning, and Siri kept guiding me to a gas station. I'd ended up on the wrong side of town in a suburb, with only ten minutes to get back across town to the studio for our interview. Kieran had texted three times, but while making U-turns and cursing at other drivers for not being in the same hurry I was, I hadn't been able to message him back. "Damn it, damn it, damn it," I said, going up the same street again, trying to find what I thought would be an easily identifiable building. My little Honda Civic, the one I'd been driving since high school, was holding on, but it would be just my luck if it crapped out on the street in front of the building I couldn't find. Letting out a frustrated growl in my car solved nothing, but it felt good, so I did it again.

The phone screen illuminated with a text on the seat next

to me, since my car was too old and broken to have anything like Bluetooth connections.

KIERAN: Is that you driving up and
down the street?

"Yes! How to do I get to the damn entrance?" I yelled into the car, figuring out too late he couldn't actually hear me, but he texted again right after.

KIERAN: Go left at the stop sign,
then an immediate left into the lot.

I slammed on the brakes as that stop sign came up a little faster than I was expecting. Sure enough, Kieran stood—well, more like paced—at the corner, glancing at his watch and then at me before pacing again. He knew which car was mine after watching me cruise up and down the street for ten minutes. Plus, I waved at him, but he looked at his watch again instead of directly at me.

"Sorry," I called out, hustling across the lot. "I overslept and then got lost and then I couldn't find the building."

"We're fifteen minutes late," he said flatly.

"I know." I channeled positive energy, despite being exhausted after we'd studied until midnight. "But I'm here. It'll be fine."

He muttered something under his breath, and I bristled. "Look, I'm sorry, but I'm here now. What else can I do?"

"Leaving earlier might have been a start," he replied curtly as we walked toward the building, his long strides forcing me to almost jog to keep up with him. The night before had had the possibility to be a fun, flirty, get-to-know-you session. In reality, it had been me asking question after question and getting short, clipped responses, making me wonder if he had a secret, sexy, fun twin whom I'd met that first night. Fake-dating the sexy twin might be easier.

"I said I'm sorry. What else can I do? I'm here now."

"I hate being late," he said, opening the door for me to walk in ahead of him.

An all-too-familiar guilt at letting someone down crept along my spine. I'd heard that tone of voice my whole life, the "do better" tone, but I'd tried to get out the door on time. I'd changed at the last minute because I thought if I wore a dress the color of the Joe's Donuts logo, it might be catchier on camera, and maybe a good anecdote. The teal-colored dress was a close match, but I'd had to swing by my mom's place to get it. "I just wanted to get my look right."

"What did I expect?" he mumbled under his breath as we neared the receptionist.

I turned on my sweetest voice to greet the woman, ignoring the jab from my new boyfriend. "We're running just a little behind to be on a segment about the lottery for *Good Morning, Des Moines*?"

"They're expecting you," she said, returning my warmth and smile. *Take that, Kieran. People like me.* "Have a seat, and someone will be out to grab you shortly."

We both crossed to a bright yellow couch, and I leaned close to Kieran so the receptionist couldn't hear me. "What do you mean, 'what did I expect'?"

"Running late, running from thing to thing, running out." He glanced at his watch again, his body stiff. "It's your whole vibe."

"You don't know my whole vibe yet," I hissed, his point hitting far too close to home not to hurt, because maybe he did know me. "And you're making me think your vibe is uptight asshole."

His gaze flashed to mine, but we were in this now.

"We're doing this to help *your* shop, so back off, okay?"

I held his stare and he didn't look away, the moment reminiscent of a staring contest, except that I noticed the way his lip shifted. Against my will, I remembered the intensity of his kiss, the way those same lips had almost demanded I melt against him.

"Sybil and Kieran?" Our standoff was interrupted by a woman with a clipboard, and we both stood. I smoothed a hand down the front of my wrap dress, centering myself with a smile for the woman and an invisible middle finger to Kieran. "We're about ready for you—follow me."

We followed the production assistant through the hallways of the local news affiliate studio, and I tapped my fingers against my thigh, realizing too late I was supposed to be really into the guy next to me and maybe should have been holding his hand or something. One glance in his direction disabused me of that notion—Kieran looked like he'd rather be anywhere else.

"Okay, you two. You'll wait here in the greenroom, and I'll come to get you a few minutes before your segment with Maria." She pointed out the mini fridge in the room and flashed us a bright smile.

"Well, this should be fun. I've never been on the news for anything positive before," I said, hoping to ease the tension, but Kieran sat at the edge of the seat, tapping the toes of his shoes on the tiled floor. "That was a joke," I added.

He looked up, his brow pinched, like he hadn't heard me. "What?"

"Never mind." I sat on the other couch, avoiding eye contact. "It's admittedly a little late to ask, but are you okay doing this?"

"I don't think we should be lying like this on TV."

"It's not really different from when it was on social media," I reasoned.

"It's still a big deal." His toe tapping grew faster, and I worried he might actually bolt. "Plus, we're both pissed off with each other."

"Are you pissed off?" I pressed my palm over his knee to stop the tapping.

"Yes, I'm pissed off. And I didn't get any sleep worrying about how this would go."

"Let's do this so we can help your business and I can look like a responsible member of my family," I hissed, hearing the click of heels on the tile signaling the return of the production assistant. "Just smile like you like me."

"Fake smiles all around," he said, stretching his mouth into a wide, distorted grin. "This is why we work so well together, right?"

I narrowed my eyes at him, then flashed my own wide grin. "It *is* why we work so well together. Aren't you and the shop lucky to have me?"

"Okay, folks." The assistant had pushed through the glass door and was now holding a clipboard. "You ready to share your love story with our viewers?"

"We're ready," I said, reaching out my hand for Kieran's and hoping he'd take it. He let it hang there for a moment too long, and I worried the production assistant would see through it, but he finally took it in his, standing so close to me it was like he'd learned everything he knew about PDA from a pamphlet in a doctor's waiting room. I whispered near Kieran's ear, "You don't think she heard us, do you?"

The studio was smaller than I expected, the set looking like a nicely appointed den with only two walls and a green screen for a view. The host, who the PA introduced as Maria, wore a gorgeous purple dress, and I admired the way it made her body look on the monitor as we watched the current segment finish up. I slid a hand over my hips and stomach to adjust my dress, imagining how I'd sit on camera.

"What are you doing?" Kieran's voice was low in my ear as we stood side by side, watching the current guest talk about an upcoming fundraiser for a youth basketball program.

"Just figuring out how to sit so I look okay on camera," I said, angling left as I imagined I might when it was our turn. "Don't worry, it won't keep me from being on time to walk across the room," I added, needing him to know he'd crossed me.

"You'll look fine on camera," he said gruffly. "You always look good."

I stared at his profile, waiting for this man to realize he had just paid me a compliment in the middle of a fight, but he was intently watching the cameras ahead of us like they might burst into flames at any moment.

"Thank you." I slid a palm over my stomach, but this time because of nerves, as the former segment wrapped up and they went to commercial while we swapped places. The PA fitted us both with microphones and guided us to the couch opposite Maria, who greeted us warmly before conferring with the PA.

Kieran's toe was still tapping incessantly, and I thought

about crashing my heel down on top of it but reached for his hand instead, squeezing a little too hard. "It'll be fine. Stop looking so nervous," I whispered in his ear, cognizant of the microphones clipped to our chests.

"You were the one thinking through how to sit."

I flashed him a smile that loosely translated to "I know where you live" and squeezed his hand forcefully.

"Aren't you two sweet!" the host exclaimed. "We'll show a clip of the video, I'll introduce you, and then we'll have a little Q and A, okay? You've made quite the splash the last few days!"

Kieran squeezed my hand back, and I smiled and nodded to the host, not wanting to give him the satisfaction of a reaction.

"Welcome back. You may have met my next guest first on social media. Kieran Anderson, whose family owns Joe's Donuts in the East Village, went viral when he tried to return a lost item to a customer. A winning lottery ticket." The video from Instagram began to play, Kieran's voice filling the studio.

"She had a great smile. She smiled a lot, and it was the kind of smile that made you . . . you know, made you want to smile, too. Like a sunny day. She made the shop feel brighter. She's beautiful. I think that's the best way to describe her. Really . . . beautiful." Kieran's hand relaxed slightly, and even though I'd watched the video a ton of times, it never stopped surprising me when he described me that way. "So, if you know a Sybil who fits that description . . . please have her come back to see me."

"And as some of you know, she did come back to see him. Kieran and Sybil, we're happy to have you on the show, and congratulations!"

"Thank you," I said. "This whole thing has been a whirlwind."

The host looked between us. "Sybil, what was it like seeing that video?"

I glanced at Kieran, who still looked nervous, a muscle in his jaw twitching, and my anger receded by a few centimeters. "It was surreal," I said. "Obviously that my ticket was a winner is unbelievable, but also . . ." I waited for Kieran to meet my gaze before continuing. "I'd met this sweet, good-looking, funny guy one night, and then he was telling the world I was beautiful." My face heated, even though I knew this wasn't really a love story. "That's the stuff of fairy tales or romance novels, right?"

Maria grinned. "Absolutely. And I guess the stuff of donut shops. Kieran, you returned a winning lottery ticket. Many might have kept it. What made you go looking for Sybil?"

I hadn't realized Kieran was still looking at me until he turned to the host. "It was the right thing to do," he said. "It was her ticket."

"Anything else?" she prodded.

"And . . . well, like she said, we met in the shop. And I didn't know if I'd see her again, but she's . . . well, I said it in the video . . ."

She pressed her hand to her heart. "Like a sunny day?" She looked from us to the camera. "I hope some viewers are taking notes on how to describe a partner and make them and everyone else swoon at the same time."

Kieran fidgeted but kept his expression unmoving. "I'm glad she came back to get the ticket."

The host smiled at his follow-up, and I smiled, too. "And we're glad you two are together now. What a great how-we-met story. Sybil, Kieran mentioned you didn't share your name with him at first. Why is that?"

Kieran's hand tightened around mine, and I glanced at his face, willing him to relax. "Honestly," I said, looking back at the host, "I didn't think he'd end up being someone important to me. I did what lots of people do, and I kept myself protected. Kept myself anonymous in a way. I've been burned before, and that makes you not trust it when you feel the spark."

"And you experienced a spark when you met Kieran?"

I smoothed my fingertips over the skirt of my dress and remembered how his hands felt on me when there was a spark versus the grip of his hand when I wanted to wring his neck for being a judgmental jerk. I pasted on what I hoped was a convincing smile. "Absolutely."

"And what about you, Kieran? You felt the spark immediately?"

He stiffened behind me, and I squeezed his hand hard after he'd been silent for half a second too long. "I've never believed in sparks," he said, squeezing my hand back. "But it's hard to ignore how you feel about someone like her. And, yeah, there was a spark."

I sent a silent cheer of relief into the studio at his response and opened my mouth to move things on, but Kieran kept talking.

"I learn more about her every day," he said. "Like that she likes running."

Running late, running from thing to thing, running out. I squeezed his hand again, hard. "He's so perceptive," I said, wishing I had a quicker response.

"And we heard you're working together! How wonderful. At the donut shop?"

Silence. The PA had heard us, but not the fight, just our stupid sniping about working well together. We both were frozen like we were muted as the host looked at us expectantly, and I realized it would be up to me to deftly field this one, but before I could speak, Kieran jumped in. "We're short-staffed and she offered to help."

He was going to push me in front of a bus for making him do this interview, I just knew it, so I didn't look over my shoulder. "It's a really wonderful place for the community and it's important to him, so . . . I want to be there while I figure out my next steps."

"Well, you two certainly are an adorable couple. We're so glad you found each other, and it seems you can't stay apart."

"It's hard not to just tackle him to the ground every time he speaks," I said sweetly.

Kieran jumped in. "I think what she means is that since everything happened so fast, and our connection was so strong, it's strange to be apart, or not touching."

I normally raged when a man started a sentence with "I think what she means," but he'd said it better. I smiled at him and then back at her. "Or not kissing."

"We frown on tackling in this station, but don't let me stand in the way of a kiss between two people fated to be together." The host looked at us expectantly.

Oh shit. I hadn't thought that one through, and Kieran and I hadn't talked about PDA or kissing in public, let alone on television. He looked at me, eyes wide, and I returned the look, very aware we were on camera until his fingers slid to the back of my neck, his warm touch immediately distracting, and I shifted closer to him. I raised my eyebrows, and then his lips were on mine. I expected a soft peck, and I planned to return my attention to the host, making some joke about keeping things appropriate for all viewers. The spark at the tip of his tongue grazing my lower lip sent a shot of lightning through the core of me. The kiss lasted only a moment, and it must have looked family friendly, but it felt like something completely different.

"Well," Maria said, looking at the camera as we pulled apart. "We love a good love story, and this one has a million reasons for you to keep an eye on this couple. Stop into Joe's Donuts on Grand Avenue in the East Village to experience a little of this sweetness for yourself."

The impression of Kieran's kiss lingered on my lips, similar to the way his fingers lingered at my hairline, grazing as if he'd never touched me before and couldn't quite bring himself to break the contact. In fifteen minutes, I'd gone from wanting to mow this man down with my car to wanting to pull him into my arms. I wondered if he felt anything close to that, too.

18

Kieran

THE STUDIO LIGHTS HAD COME BACK INTO FOCUS, and my lips still tingled after our kiss. For a moment, I'd forgotten everything, not just where we were but the mounting bills, my plans for medical school that had been put on hold, and how absolutely everything about Sybil drove me nuts, and I'd only thought of her lips and her skin and the way she smelled like springtime. Sybil opened her eyes, lids rising slowly to reveal a slightly dazed expression.

"Thank you for joining us, Sybil and Kieran," Maria said, looking into the camera while I looked at Sybil. Her gaze was soft, her skin soft, her whole presence was soft, and heat rose on my face, something between embarrassment about kissing her live on camera and knowing how easy it was to forget everything else when I had the chance to get closer to her.

"Up next, winter salads to enjoy on these blustery days and what to look forward to this weekend around the metro area. Stay tuned."

One of the crew announced we were clear, and the host thanked us, shaking both our hands and inviting us back for a follow-up.

Sybil linked her fingers with mine as the PA led us through the studio toward the exit.

"Okay," she said, once we were outside and we pulled our hands apart. "That went well."

Both our cars were on the other side of the lot, and we walked ahead, the wind blowing against us. "Thank God we don't have to do that again." My phone buzzed in my pocket, and I had missed texts from Lila, Tom, and Granddad.

LILA: 🔥 🔥 🔥

TOM: Well done, boy!

GRANDDAD: Wow?

GRANDDAD: I mean wpw!

GRANDDAD: I mean wowo

GRANDDAD: dammit.

"It wasn't so bad." She glanced over her shoulder and winked. "I think that kiss added some believability. Will you tell me who taught you to kiss so I can send them a thank-you note? Or buy them a thank-you Tesla?"

I rolled my eyes, even though the joke wasn't bad. My phone buzzed again, a reminder that my granddad and Tom thought this was real. "It was humiliating, and who knows how large their audience is? No more of this on video, right?"

She stopped walking for a moment, and I saw the way her face fell, her smile faltering, an honest disappointment shading her expression. "Sure." She nodded resolutely as if to underline the promise. "No more kissing in public."

We walked again toward our cars in silence, something that didn't feel right with Sybil beside me. "And thank you." I pulled my keys from my pocket. "I know I can be a jerk, and I do appreciate the help with promoting the shop, but no more public appearances, right?" I was adding more before I realized what I was saying and how much I was admitting. "It just makes me feel really anxious, and I don't want to mess it up."

She nodded. "No more TV—you told them I was working at the shop, though."

I blanched. Perhaps a testament to that kiss, because I'd forgotten all about it—the PA overhearing us, getting questioned about it; and it wasn't Sybil who'd let something slip, it was me.

"I actually kind of like the idea," she said, the lightness returning to her voice. "I don't have a job, and I guess now I don't need one, but I don't know what to do with my time." She looked at her hands. "And I'm free labor!"

I studied her, unable to ignore the way her expression changed when admitting she was kind of bored. "Have you ever worked in food service?"

Sybil laughed, not a light tinkle of a giggle but a hearty one that sounded like it started deep in her belly. "I've done it all, baby." She ticked off on her fingers. "I was a waitress at Mama Puccini's, I worked at Tastee-Freez, served at Hogtied Pizza and Barbecue, and three stints at fast-food places. I'm actually overqualified to volunteer in your shop."

I narrowed my gaze. "Did you last more than three weeks in any of those jobs?"

She grinned, reading the joke in my tone, which made the corners of my lips tip up, too. "Shut up," she said. "I didn't need to look responsible and grounded when I held any of those jobs. No motivation, and no one was watching."

"Okay," I said, holding out my hand for a shake. "But when you want to quit, there's nothing tying you to it. You can do it for a week and then move on."

She reached for my hand. "We've only been in love for a few days. Are you trying to get rid of me already?"

Over her shoulder, I saw the PA walking across the lot and approaching us. *Shit.* I clasped Sybil's outstretched hand and tugged her to me, my hand resting on her waist. Sybil yelped, and I ducked my lips to her ear. "We have an audience," I whispered, hand sliding under her coat as she shifted to hear me, and my lip grazed her ear. "The PA is walking toward us."

"Oh," she murmured, relaxing against me and dragging her palm up my biceps to my shoulder. "And you wanted to give her another show?"

We were chest to chest, and her breath ran opposite mine, giving a push-and-pull effect between us when I tipped my head back to look at her. "I didn't think a handshake sold the love story."

Sybil's lip quirked. "No, I guess not. Handshakes are really only appropriate immediately following one-night stands."

"I didn't get a handshake," I said, my fingers against the smooth fabric of her dress under her coat as I fought the urge to stroke her back.

"I guess I always knew you'd be so much more than a one-night stand." She tickled her fingers along the nape of my neck, and my body didn't care if we were in public. She always touched me like we were on the precipice of something. "Is she gone?"

"Not yet," I said. I couldn't place Sybil's scent—it was floral and sweet, but the only other word I could use to describe it would be "playful." I'd never smelled anything like it before, and I dipped my lips to her ear again, taking the chance to inhale her intoxicating scent once more. "And it was Hannah Carson in the tenth grade after choir practice," I said, tucking a curl that tickled my face behind her ear. "My first kiss."

Sybil leaned back this time with a smile spreading across her lips like a flower blooming. "There's so much to unpack there, starting with you in a choir. You sing? Will you serenade me?"

A gust of cold wind blew around us, and I pulled her closer without thinking. "No."

"Please?"

I shook my head, shifting us so my body could block some of the wind for her. I'd joined the choir at my grandmother's insistence and thought it would look good when I applied to college. While I was racking up the extracurricular hours, I'd fallen in love with it, but I'd dropped out after she died and I needed to spend more time studying and at the shop. "I regret telling you this."

"Fine. What color Tesla do you think Hannah Carson would want?"

"Well, she kissed Bryan Jakonski the next day at rehearsal. Said he was cuter and she wasn't going to kiss such a loser again."

Sybil traced a finger over my neck again, and goose bumps ran down my right side. "What a cunt. Just a thank-you Kia, then. And a used one." She grinned, and I had that feeling again, the one that felt like getting lost in a daydream.

"Is she still looking?"

In my periphery, I saw the PA looking right at us, phone in hand. "Just snapped a photo," I said.

"It's what we wanted." She dropped her arm and rested a palm on my chest.

"You two are so cute!" the PA yelled across the parking lot before waving and climbing into her car.

"We're cute," Sybil said, eyebrow cocked as I heard the car behind us. "I told you this would work."

No one was watching, but I still lifted her hand to my lips and brushed a kiss across her knuckles, because I lost my grasp on what I *should* do whenever I was in her orbit. "I am very much looking forward to breaking up with you, Sybil."

19

Sybil

MY FIRST DAY AT JOE'S DONUTS AS THEIR NEWEST staff member was not going great, and I puffed my cheeks and blew out a slow breath. Pink and chocolate sprinkles fell to the counter when I swiped the back of my hand across my forehead and felt smears of dried icing. I'd arrived on time in the wake of taking Emi's advice and starting a morning routine, and having something to leave the house for was great. Emi and I had driven downtown together, and Marcus had even made me lunch (reason number five I should want to marry him). It had felt like the first day of school. I'd even taken time to lay out the perfect outfit the night before. I'd greeted Kieran at the front door, realizing too late his grandfather was with him, leading to a sloppy, awkward half kiss with my fake boyfriend. But that spark from our TV spot? Gone. The parking lot embrace seemed like years and a few bouts of amnesia ago.

"Tomorrow will be better," Joe reassured me from his perch

by the cash register, a cash register that was $12.15 too empty because I'd offered to cover it and counted back someone's change incorrectly. By the time I realized my mistake, Joe was back and wouldn't let me replace the money myself. Not that I could have. No one ever tells you that when you win the lottery, you stay broke for a few more weeks until the money actually arrives. That big cardboard check isn't exchangeable for cash. I'd asked.

"I don't think Kieran is going to let me back in the kitchen," I said, leaning on the counter. "I was not great at frosting donuts," I added, checking my face for more frosting.

"He wasn't good at it at first, either." Joe leaned toward me conspiratorially. "The first time he helped me, he was dunking them in, and when I looked over, his whole arm was covered in chocolate icing." He laughed, the lines around his eyes deepening with the joke. I'd never seen Kieran crack up, but I imagined it looked like that. Joe smacked his own leg, letting out one last chuckle. "He learned quick after that, though. He's always been good at studying and learning. Always was. I'm sure you see how smart he is. Lila's the same way. Both of 'em A students."

I gathered the fallen bits of frosting to brush into my hand. "I was more like a C student," I said. "Guess I got lucky scoring a guy like him."

Kieran walked in from the back, where he and Lila had been unloading boxes of supplies that had been delivered. He'd taken off his apron, and his T-shirt stretched across his chest and showed off his toned arms. He replaced the hat on his head, turning it backward in a way that was so unexpectedly sexy.

"You both got lucky finding each other," Joe said, patting

my arm. "And if memory serves, I got Cs, too, and look how good I turned out!" He chuckled again, coughing at the end, the two sounds mingling.

Kieran's posture stiffened the way it did anytime his grandfather coughed, had to grasp for a word, or got up to walk with his cane. I'd seen the hesitation when the delivery arrived and he realized he'd have to leave me alone with his grandfather, probably concerned I'd inadvertently sell him to someone who ordered a large coffee. I couldn't exactly blame Kieran—he'd spent a good chunk of the day cleaning up my messes. Kieran motioned to my neck. "You've got a little there," he said, and I swiped at the spot under my ear.

Joe accepted the cup of water from me before taking a deep breath. "Anyway, son, you can't just tell someone to do something like that, you gotta teach 'em. Not everyone learns by hearing instructions like you do."

My face flushed. I *had* listened carefully, wanting to do a good job, but once I started doing it myself, it all went to hell. I waved Joe's words off with a laugh, preferring that to the conversation. "Some of us are unteachable. And after that I got to hang out with you."

"That's baloney. Everyone is teachable. We just need the right kind of teaching!"

Kieran looked uncertain but nodded, studying his grandfather again until the bell over the door chimed and I jumped at the sight of my parents. "Mom!" I ran a hand down the front of my shirt. "What are you doing here?"

"Paul thought it would be nice for us to see where you're working," she said with a brightness I knew tasted like vinegar in her mouth, and I was certain Paul had made her do this to be supportive. "And meet your new . . . gentleman friend."

"You make it sound like we're on the set of *Downton Abbey*, honey," Paul said, reaching his hand out to Joe. "I assume you're Sybil's new boyfriend."

Joe laughed and took Paul's hand. "Don't it beat all? She turned me down in favor of my grandson."

My mom studied Kieran intently as if to spot a secret birthmark or freckle that would give him away as a gold digger, but gave an unconvincing smile when he held out his hand, which was smeared with something black and dusty, probably from the boxes they'd been unloading in the back.

"Mrs. Waters," he said, smoothly stepping forward, earning another wide-eyed stare from me because he hadn't realized his hand was dirty. "It's nice to meet you. Welcome to Joe's."

Mom pulled her hand back and gave a little wave instead of shaking, her assessing gaze never waning. "Nice to meet you as well."

Kieran shot me a confused look, and before I could stop him, he dragged his hand over his jaw.

"You've got a little something here," Paul said, motioning to his face.

"Shit," Kieran said, looking around for a napkin. He turned to the counter, not finding one, and muttered under his breath, "Fuck!"

This wasn't exactly the first impression I imagined—they needed to see how polite and kind and smart he was, and now Mom and Paul were exchanging looks. Blessedly, Lila handed him a napkin she'd run under the faucet.

"I imagine you two are worried about my boy here taking advantage of Sybil's winning, huh?" Joe, God bless him, cut through the bullshit with a hot knife. "I would be, too, but he's a good boy, and usually not quite so dusty." He smiled at

Kieran, who was still scrubbing his face, before looking back at my mom. "Which I'm sure you'll see for yourself. Plus, I'd take him to task if he ever hurt this girl, who I've grown kind of fond of." He patted me twice on the shoulder, his heavy hand comforting me.

"We all look out for our kids," Paul said, wrapping an arm around Mom's shoulders. "Kieran, we'd love to have you over for dinner. We're out of town the next two weeks, but maybe after that?"

Kieran nodded and tossed the napkin aside. "That would be nice." From the set of his jaw and his stiff posture under my mother's still-assessing gaze, I interpreted the nod to mean he'd rather lick up the frosting I'd spilled on the floor than subject himself to what would be an interrogation.

Mom finally concluded her inspection when they had to leave a few minutes later and she lost her ability to physically see him.

"Nice folks," Joe said, standing slowly from his seat.

"Yeah," Lila said, slipping from the back. "Kieran made a *great* first impression."

"Her bark is worse than her bite," I said, holding out my arm for Joe to steady himself against. "She's just a little tough at first, and she probably didn't even notice the dirt on your face."

Kieran looked flustered, and I gave him a smile I hoped was supportive, but he glanced away when Lila said something to him we couldn't hear that made his brow furrow.

"C'mon, Granddad. Let's give these two kids a little time alone. I'll help you upstairs." She nodded toward the back stairs and took my spot next to him.

Once they'd left, Kieran began cleaning again, before remembering his hands and checking them front and back.

"What did Lila say?"

"She reminded me I was supposed to be impressing your family." He wiped his hands, scrubbing away the last smears of grime. "Very helpful."

"They'll be impressed once they get to know you and see us together more." I looked around the shop and noticed the sign on the door, which must have been printed on both sides announcing Joe's Donuts would be closed the next day because of a local festival they'd be attending as a vendor. He and Lila had been preparing all day when not cleaning up my mess. That was why they'd been hauling the delivery in, plus getting things from the basement. "They'll see we're spending more time together and they'll trust it's real."

"Yeah," he said skeptically. "How are we supposed to do that? You're already working here, and your mom didn't seem impressed by that."

"I'll go with you to the festival tomorrow—that looks relationshippy, right? Plus, it gives us a chance to get people to buy your donuts. They're great. People should be wild about this place for that alone."

"It's an all-day thing," he said, shaking his head. "We'll be working the whole time. I won't have time to—"

"I can help!" I interrupted, holding out my hands, palms up. "I promise I won't mess anything up."

"We couldn't pay you," he said, and I gave him what I hoped was a look that communicated how ridiculous that statement was.

"Lottery winner, remember? I think I'll be okay. It's the

perfect solution—you guys could use help, it looks natural, and people might stop by to see if it's legit or not and stay to buy some donuts."

"I'm not a good actor," he said. "You saw on the TV segment. We look like strangers when we try to fake it."

I paused my pacing. "I don't think we'll have to act much. You said it yourself, right? It'll be busy."

He looked doubtful. "We have to be there at seven in the morning."

I bristled at the fact that he thought waking up early would be a sticking point for me. I mean, it usually would have been, but I was in a motivated place today and embracing it. "I have an alarm on my phone, and I was on time today."

He cocked his head to the side and his lip twitched.

"On time–ish," I said. "There's a seven-minute window for on time."

"I'm not sure. Plus, Lila will be there."

"She knows the deal." I leaned on the counter. "It won't be that hard, and it'll work." I stretched my arm across the counter. "It's worth a shot, right?"

"I guess," he said, eyes skating across my face before looking away.

"Can't be that bad, can it?"

20

Kieran

LILA HURRIED IN FROM THE BACK, PULLING HER HAIR into a ponytail. "What do we have left to do?" She tugged an apron off the hook and began tying it around her waist. "Sybil still here? Do you need a few more minutes to make use of the office?"

"Shut up," I grumbled, studying the list. "She left, but she's going to join us tomorrow." I'd begrudgingly agreed to Sybil's plan to help the next day, only there wasn't a lot of actual grudging if I was being honest with myself.

Lila didn't respond, and when I looked up, she was moving her hand in a circle, waiting for me to continue. "Oh?"

"She thought we should be seen together. As you so aptly pointed out, we looked unimpressive when her parents stopped by," I said, pointing to the back, where we had been preparing earlier, but we still had a long night ahead.

Lila followed me to the back of the shop. "And you're okay with this?"

"I guess." I pulled the rack from the proofing oven and set it on the counter near the fryer. "It makes sense. And I don't want Granddad out there for the whole day."

"You say that, but you hate working the festival, and really anything related to peopling. It's actually shocking to me that you think you'll enjoy talking to patients one day. I can't imagine you agreeing to put on a romantic show on top of that."

"I don't hate people," I said, nudging my sister out of the way.

"No. Just interacting with them."

"The only thing I hate is small talk." There was nothing worse than talking about the weather repeatedly while someone searched for a five-dollar bill in their wallet or couldn't get the chip on their card to read. *Do they think their thoughts on humidity make the technology work faster?*

"Hate to break it to you, but that's peopling." I took an elbow from Lila at that as she pushed me out of the way to gather bags of coffee cups to take with us in the morning. "But it will be nice to have another set of hands to help." Lila handed me an armful of sleeves so I could take them to the van. "And she's right—it might get more people to stop by the stand. I'll post something on Instagram in the morning."

I grumbled again but let it go, and we worked mostly in silence gathering the rest of the supplies, not needing to say much as we worked side by side. Running Joe's was never my plan, but I'd grown up in this kitchen, and there was a comfort to the normal rhythm of it. Every tool, every recipe, every corner of the shop felt pulled from my DNA, and with Lila humming along next to me, her earbuds in and our movements around each other so cohesive they felt choreographed, I was free to let my mind wander. It wandered where it always did these days, and I pictured the look of shock and horror on Sybil's face when the bowl of strawberry frosting had toppled to the floor, splattering everywhere. With her eyes wide and her lips forming an O, my first reaction had been to pull her to me and kiss that O away, telling her it was okay. I'd imagined how she'd feel in my arms and the sweet way she'd look at me when we cleaned it together. I'd ignored that instinct, though, and asked her to just go out front while I cleaned. I was learning I was safer being annoyed with Sybil than enamored of her, and I kept bringing myself back to that as we worked.

Lila planned to start making donuts while I got a few hours of sleep, and I climbed the stairs to Granddad's place. The apartment above the shop was small, but the familiarity of my cramped space always felt right after a long day. Peeling off my clothes and tossing them into the hamper, I walked toward the shower. I wanted to wash off the smell of the shop, even though it never fully disappeared, but I also wanted Sybil's scent off me. The hot water beat down, and I'd intended to go through the checklist in my head one more time to make sure we were prepared for the food festival, but Sybil's grin and the way her curls brushed her shoulder kept sneaking back into my head. I remembered how those curls felt when my fingers moved through them, and I imagined her sitting in the chair, legs gloriously spread for me, and gave myself permission to forget my smart plan to deny my attraction to her while I was under the spray.

My hand slipped lower to stroke my dick, hard at the memory, her scent still living in my head along with how she'd mewled when I kissed her, the way she'd melted under my touch. That I'd been able to do that to her had my hand moving faster, the bodywash making the slide of my palm mimic what I imagined she'd feel like—hot and slick.

And I remembered her gasps and how her stomach tightened right before she came. The water beat down on my shoulders and I gave in, imagining what might have happened next, imagined earning that wide-eyed playful expression when I slid into her, when she was pinned under me. Imagining how good it would be between us if I let myself lose control.

I shuddered at my release, spilling over my hand. I rolled my head from side to side. "Fuck," I muttered, rinsing my hand under the spray. I'd stopped myself from imagining that more times than I could count the last week, forcing my mind to forget her and let this attraction go, but now that I'd given in to the memories, they kept circling. If I was honest, they'd never stopped.

I cursed myself again and shut off the water, wrapping a towel around my waist before walking the short distance into the bedroom.

My phone sat on the bed where I'd tossed it, and two notifications flashed. A voicemail from my best friend in Texas and a text message from Sybil. I hit play on the voicemail and pulled a pair of boxer shorts from my dresser.

"Hey, man. It's been forever!" I hadn't heard Miles's voice in over a year, though we'd exchanged a few texts. We'd lost touch the way you do when you no longer have anything in common day to day. "Sorry I didn't call, but third year has been kicking my ass. Clinical rotations are no joke, but it's amazing. You wouldn't believe how real shit gets. I got to scrub in to observe a coronary artery bypass. Man, I was, like, in there! All I was doing was holding a retractor, but I was in there!" He sounded the same, and I missed drinking a beer with him after class and complaining and imagining being done with school and practicing medicine. "Anyway, we are going to have a room in our apartment next year. Philips is dropping out. Are you coming back? Spot is yours if so, we just need to know by end of March. We miss you, man!"

The message ended, and I pulled a T-shirt over my head. I'd missed year three with my cohort, the year we went from the classroom to hospitals and clinics. Everyone said we'd love it or hate it because of the hands-on experience and the harried pace, plus the constant expectation to learn more as we explored specialties. There was a hollow sensation in my chest at knowing I'd missed it all, missed the next step. My class had been moving forward while I was standing still. The letter from the school was on my nightstand like a ticking clock for making the decision. I read it over and set it down before climbing into bed. I had every word and every digit of the amount due memorized anyway.

I'd be a year behind my cohort, but I'd do my own rotations and be back on my way toward graduation, residency, and my future. A future that would include financial stability and the opportunity to fix things like that doctor years ago had done for us. I didn't blame anyone for my decision to come home—I owed Granddad and Grandma Rosie everything, but lately I'd been disconnected from myself. Needing to be a doctor, to reach the goal I'd set for myself when I put the pieces together of my role in our family, was all I'd worked for, and without it, I was floundering. I just had to let this thing with Sybil take its course, and if I could keep reminding myself her constant energy and the dimples that popped on her cheeks when she smiled were annoying and not sexy as hell, I'd be fine. I tapped on her text message before setting my phone aside.

SYBIL: Alarm is set.

SYBIL: See you in the morning.

SYBIL: 😘 😘 😘

My thumb hovered over the message, touching the screen the way I wanted to touch her. I pictured the way her tongue was probably peeking out between her teeth because she thought she was embarrassing me or annoying me with the emojis. I navigated to the menu, toying with the idea of sending one back, of sending something that might make her smile in that way that made her dimple pop on her cheek. I selected the same icon she'd used and typed Sweet dreams, beautiful.

"What am I doing?" I held down the delete key until the regrettable reply was gone. This was exactly the kind of thing I needed to avoid. I sent a thumbs-up and tossed my phone aside, vowing to keep myself in a thumbs-up headspace the next day. There was no room for kissing-face emojis.

21

Sybil

AT THE SOUND OF THE BLARING ALARM ON MY phone, I rolled over, groggily slamming my finger against the screen until the noise stopped, but by the time it did, my brain had caught up to my body and the joyful, sleepy haze was gone. It was five thirty in the morning on a Saturday, and I wanted to reject this new reality. I glanced at the screen on my phone.

> SYBIL: Why do you all get up this early on the regular?

EMI: Good time to run.

MARCUS: Just how my body clock works.

DEACON: I got home from my date
twenty minutes ago.

EMI: Why are you up this early?

I pulled the blankets over my head and muttered against the fabric, "I have no idea."

The phone chimed again with my reminder to get up early to make it across town by six thirty for the food festival. The night before, it had seemed like such an ideal time for Kieran and me to be seen while I helped staff their booth, but in the cold light of morning (or rather, the lack of light since the sun wasn't up yet), I had regrets.

SYBIL: Because I make bad
decisions

EMI: I'm guessing Deacon's date is
thinking the same thing.

DEACON: My date made excellent
decisions. You might say she
made several rounds of good
decisions. 🍆 😏

I groaned against the mattress and rolled out, stumbling down the hall to shower. I'd asked Grace if I could crash in their guest room since it was much closer to the festival than Emi's place.

"Hey there," Warren said when we ran into each other in the hall. He was dressed head to toe in spandex with wrap-around sunglasses perched atop a bright orange beanie. "Grace and I are getting in a quick ten-mile run before the day gets going. What are you doing up so early?"

"I'm helping my . . ." Boyfriend? Lover? Fake and slightly fraudulent life partner? "Helping Kieran at a food festival."

He saluted, holding two fingers to his temple. "Will leave you to it!" I loved that about Warren—there would be no follow-up questions. Grace or Mom or any of my friends would have made me explain more about my decision to help, to work at the donut shop, or to get up hours ahead of my normal wake-up time, but Warren took the world at face value. I was glad he'd be joining the family.

By the time I made it across town to the food festival and found parking, I was only fifteen minutes late, which I considered a win, and by then, Kieran was too busy getting the booth ready to give me any real side-eye.

"Hey!" Lila greeted me with a smile, her piercings catching the morning light, and handed me a bright blue T-shirt matching her own. "Kieran hates it, but Granddad always said it helped if we were matching. We didn't have any extra, so I brought you one of mine. Hopefully that's okay."

I accepted it and stripped out of my T-shirt, revealing a thin tank top that left very little to anyone's imagination. I caught Kieran's eyes skirting over my chest before I pulled on the T-shirt. *Still got it.* Though "it" in this case was a T-shirt that was vaguely pornographic in how tightly it clung to my boobs.

"Sorry," Lila said sheepishly. "I know it's a little small."

"No worries. Put me to work. Where can I help?"

Kieran looked frazzled, flicking his gaze at his watch every few minutes. The booth was fun—we were in a corner, and they'd loaded trays of donuts into a portable cart with a mini version of the store's display case lit on the counter. "Can you keep the case stocked and help with boxes?" He motioned to the mountain of cardboard in the corner, the boxes the same blue as our shirts.

"Sure thing, boss." I searched the counter for rubber gloves, making note of the donuts and also wondering how inappropriate it would be for me to have one, since I'd skipped breakfast in my effort to be just barely not on time.

"I'm not the boss," he grumbled, checking the iPad and a small cashbox.

"Sure you are," Lila said.

"O Captain! my Captain!" I exclaimed, earning a laugh from Lila.

"It's too early for the two of you together," Kieran said, eyeing the door.

"Oh, sweetie," I said, wrapping my arms around his waist from behind. I didn't expect the firm muscle of his abs under my touch when I squeezed. "But is it too early for the two of us alone?" Lila giggled again, but Kieran tensed under my touch, long enough that I was certain this ruse of ours was not going to work out. No one would believe we were into each other. Hell, at this rate, no one would believe he even liked me, but just when I was about to pull away and embarrassment at the rejection began to take over, he spoke.

"It's never too early for you." He paused before adding "muffin" in a voice so robotic, I questioned if he'd learned the word from a Speak and Spell, but still, he played along.

Lila doubled over in laughter, and I could only imagine the expression on her brother's face. "I'm sorry," she said, wiping her eyes. "But, Kieran . . . you look like you're doing calculus in your head. Loosen up."

"What else do you want? I called her muffin," he said, shrugging out of the embrace. "You two ready?"

I gave a thumbs-up that earned me a tight nod.

"HEY, YOU'RE THE guy from that video!" One woman pulled her phone from her pocket and held it out for her friend after a few clicks. "May, this is the guy I told you about! With the lottery ticket and the donuts."

I watched the back of Kieran's head, which was pretty much all I'd seen of him for the previous hour, even though the festival had started slowly. The few people who had mentioned the video had been met with what I imagined felt like a cool acknowledgment. And these two seemed to be no different. Kieran gave a quick nod and then asked them what they wanted, moving them briskly to order two donuts before walking away.

"I'll be back," Lila said, pointing toward the restrooms and leaving Kieran and me alone in the tight space.

"Can I say something?" I asked, stepping up to the table where Lila had been occupied with the iPad and money box.

"Would it matter if I said no?" He reluctantly turned away from the nonexistent line and seemed to really see me for the first time, his eyes dipping quickly to the Joe's Donuts logo stretched across my chest.

"You're right," I said, stepping close so we wouldn't be overheard. "You know we're doing this thing to get business for your shop, right?"

I'd have bet money Kieran wanted to roll his eyes at that moment, but he just nodded. "Yep."

"Well," I said, inhaling the scent of his bodywash, a scent that mingled really perfectly with the smells of baking and the booth around us. "That might be easier if you didn't immediately shut down any interest in the lottery and donut thing."

"I didn't shut them down," he whispered, looking around. "I acknowledged they were correct and then sold them donuts. It's what I'm here to do."

"Yeah, but . . ." I raised my hands in exasperation. "Have you ever studied sales?"

"Yeah, lots of sales classes offered in medical school," he said.

"Sarcasm." I was wondering again if the playful and earnest guy I'd met the first night was an illusion. "Shocking." This tense, kind-of-pretentious guy was less fun and much more common. Two other women with a young child in tow approached us, looking between us and the phone.

"Can you let me?"

"Let you what?"

"Hi," I said brightly, nudging Kieran out of the way with my hip as they approached. "What a pretty pink dress!" I made eye contact first with the little girl, who twirled and then used her hand to make a chopping motion, the pink fabric twirling around her, giggling. "I'm a princess and a warrior," she said.

"Good morning," I said to the adults. "What can we get for you?"

I saw Kieran's hand twitch in my periphery, certainly ready to reclaim control of this interaction.

The two women conferred while the little girl stepped forward to identify six or seven donuts she wanted, earning laugher from the women. "Well," I said. "That might be too many donuts for a princess warrior—how would you carry them all and fight the bad guys?"

The little girl nodded sagely. "Lady, I am the bad guy."

This girl was my hero.

"Bad guys get one donut," one of the women said. "We'll take one of those." She pointed to a pink frosted cake donut. Kieran pulled it from the case and handed it to the woman in a waxed paper sheet while we talked. The woman handed it to the little girl, asking, "Aren't you two the couple from that video?"

"Is there anything else I can get you?" Kieran said, and I'd never wanted to side-eye anyone harder in my life. I settled for letting my foot fall on top of his.

"Yes," I said, tapping on the screen of the iPad without hitting the total button. "We are. He's a charmer, but the real draw was the donuts," I joked, resting a palm on his forearm.

Both women giggled, and the second studied the case. "That video was so romantic," she said. "Can you convince my husband to say something like that about me?"

Kieran gave a flat smile, and I poked him in the side, urging him to give a genuine human response. "I'm sure he already does," Kieran finally added. "We're not always good at voicing it. But I bet he thinks it every day." The response surprised me—it didn't sound sarcastic, and the woman's face flushed as her grin widened.

"You know what? Give us a dozen. We'll take them home for him and the other kids. Maybe that will remind him to say loving things out loud once in a while," she said to her friend, cheeks still pink as Kieran loaded a box with assorted options from the tray, and I rang up the purchase. "You know," she said, leaning in, "he's really very sweet, isn't he?" She tapped her credit card on the screen.

I glanced at Kieran, who was listening patiently to the little girl explain the expectations of princess warriors, particularly that you had to seem to be only a princess at first. Then they wouldn't expect the attack, because people think girls can't fight. "Are you going to fight me?" Kieran asked her, handing the box to the two women.

"Nah. You seem all right," she said with a wave to Kieran. "But don't forget, sometimes beautiful princesses are dangerous."

He nodded and looked at me dramatically. "Believe me, I know."

The woman gave me another grin. "He's sweet. And he's cute, too," she mouthed as they walked away. "What a keeper."

I waited until they'd moved on to another booth before crossing my arms over my chest and looking at Kieran. "Did you see the difference?"

He grumbled under his breath and restocked the case, replacing the donuts he'd pulled for the box. "I've never been good at that kind of thing." He worked for another moment, and I admired the stiff set of his shoulders until they relaxed. "I would worry I'd lose the sale with small talk, and we need every sale we can get." His movements didn't slow. I studied the muscles across his back as he moved, and latched on to what felt like honesty in his words. Maybe he wasn't intentionally grumpy and shadowy, but just unsure how to be bright.

"Hm," I said. "I was born for small talk." Teachers constantly told me to stop talking, and my mom reminded me basically daily not to speak to strangers. The warnings never worked. I still did it. It was probably the reason I was standing here now. "I'll help. Trust me."

"What if you're one of those beautiful princesses who are dangerous?"

"Beautiful, huh?" I didn't get a chance to tease him any further before his sister returned.

"Did I miss anything good?" Lila settled back behind the table, rearranging the iPad how she'd had it before her brother took her spot.

"Just figuring out how to work as a team," I said. I couldn't shake the shift in his voice, the earnestness when he talked about losing sales. It made me want to make sure this was the most popular booth at the festival. When Kieran turned and our eyes met, I held up my palm. "Dream team, right?" His gaze paused on my hand, and I worried he'd leave me hanging.

"Oh my gosh," a high-pitched voice exclaimed as a group moved to us from the neighboring booth. "It's them!"

I grinned, wiggling my fingers, now even more worried he was going to leave me hanging, but his palm met mine, firm and warm. It was surely just the tight T-shirt causing the butterflies that swooped in my stomach.

"Dream team," he said back before turning to the group, voice lighter than before, if not completely natural. "You're right. It's us," he said, giving me a small smile. "Welcome. What can we get you?"

22

Kieran

BY FOUR IN THE AFTERNOON THE FESTIVAL WAS coming to a close, the other vendors beginning to pack up and the last few stragglers making their way toward the exit. For the first time, we were almost sold out of everything. Lila had already made a run to the shop to take a load of empty trays and supplies and make more donuts, leaving Sybil and me alone again. Not that we'd been alone. The booth had been packed all day, and I begrudgingly had to admit that Sybil and Lila had both been right about public interest in our story. At a certain point in the afternoon, it had almost felt natural when Sybil touched me or smiled at me. Of course, the touching and smiling stopped when the customer turned their back, like it should have.

The older woman standing with us now leaned over the almost empty case and spoke to Sybil conspiratorially. "Was it love at first sight?"

"Love at first sight? I don't know, but there was a connection." She motioned to the box in her hands. "Oh, do you want to try a few flavors of the cake donuts?"

The woman nodded, and I admired the easy way Sybil did this. Letting her take the lead had been my best decision of the day, and not just because standing behind her meant I had the opportunity to drink in her thick thighs under those tight jeans.

"A connection," the woman said, her voice sounding wistful. "And you knew she was the one?" Her eyes swung to me, inspecting me as if to catch the lie, but before I could answer, I had an elbow nudging at my ribs.

"Of course he did," Sybil joked, smiling widely so that her dimples popped on her cheeks. "That's seven," she said. "Want me to grab five more so you make it a full dozen?" I kept waiting for a customer to catch on to her pattern—skirting their questions and then selling them more donuts. No one did, though, and this woman nodded like so many others had, pulling her wallet from inside a massive purple purse before handing over cash, saying she'd take them to her book club.

"You knew as soon as you saw her?" She pressed a palm to her heart and then saved me from having to answer by answering her own question. "Oh, I know you did. Look at how you look at her." The woman glanced over her shoulder at a man loaded down with reusable bags standing about ten feet back. "My George used to look at me that way. You did know as soon as you saw her, huh?"

I hadn't realized I'd been looking at Sybil until the woman's comment, but my face heated and I glanced away. "I knew she was something special," I said.

"Baby," Sybil said, shooting me a sweet smile. "You're embarrassing me."

Sybil had been at this all day, and I knew I wasn't even coming close to embarrassing her.

"Anything else for you?" She handed the box to the woman and leaned away from me. "Don't tell him, but I added an extra cinnamon roll to your box. No charge. They're my new favorite, and there's only one left. I bet George will love it."

"What if George has diabetes or can't have gluten?" I posed the question once the woman walked away after giving Sybil and me a few more encouraging comments about our love.

"Then he won't eat it," she said, rolling her eyes. "Must you always be so pessimistic?"

The man who must have been George greeted the woman with a smile across the room, and we caught the two of them looking back at us. I leaned in toward Sybil until my lips were close to her ear. "I'm told pessimism is part of my charm."

"I promise you," she said in a soft voice, batting her lashes for the world to see us in love. Sybil's lips grazed the tip of my nose in a soft peck. "It's not."

"I can't leave you two alone for a second," Lila said, brushing her pink hair from her face. "I swear there's always a fifty-fifty chance I'll return to you either bickering or screwing under the table."

Sybil pulled away and pointed at me with her thumb. "This one would raise concerns of food safety if that happened."

"I would *rightfully* raise concerns about food safety if that happened." I looked around for what needed to be packed and ignored both women and my own hypocrisy, because I hadn't been worried about any kind of safety when we'd crashed into my office that first night. Also, the thought of reliving that with her had an effect on me I didn't like.

I expected an immediate response from either woman, but none came for once. I saw them exchange shrugs out of the corner of my eye, and Sybil finally said, "I guess that's fair."

"I think we can manage this." Lila spoke to Sybil behind me as I boxed up what was left of the donuts. "If you want to take off."

"I can help," Sybil said, the honey in her voice blotting out the last of the annoyance I wanted to hold on to.

I set two boxes aside, the last of the inventory. "You don't have to," I added. I was certain she had places to go and fun to have. I imagined Saturdays were a minefield of fun for someone like Sybil, and she was working harder at pretending to be in love than me, so probably ready to give it a rest.

"I don't mind," she said, helping Lila load a few totes onto our cart. "Want me to take this out to the van?" She was still ignoring me and spoke to Lila, the two discussing a few instructions before Sybil walked toward the exit, the cart in tow.

"You could be a little nicer to her," Lila commented, stacking the unused boxes and beginning to fold up our banner, the faded one Granddad had purchased in the early nineties with big cartoon donuts surrounding the text.

"I'm nice."

"She helped us all day," she added. "And we sold a lot more than usual. Even you have to admit that."

"I know." I checked the cashbox and powered down the iPad before tucking both away. "But this was dishonest."

"We didn't cheat anyone," she said, resting a hand on my arm. "There was no price gouging. And I was here all day— you two never once brought it up. She just talked to people if they brought it up. And," Lila said, shifting from the comforting palm on my arm to a finger tapping my forehead, "we sold a ton." She motioned to the two boxes that were left. "I even cleared out what we had back at the shop."

"But we're not dating. That's a lie."

"Then go on a date," she said, exasperated. "I don't know what else to tell you. We're in this thing now, and we're in it with her." Lila hoisted the last case into her arms. "Why don't I take the van back to the shop and begin unloading?"

"Am I just walking home?"

Sybil returned, twirling the van keys around her finger before tossing them to Lila.

Lila grinned. "Would you give Kieran a ride back, if you don't mind? I know you two lovebirds could use more time together." With that, she sauntered off, and I cut my gaze to Sybil's confused expression.

"I'm sorry for my sister," I bit out. "I can figure out a way to get home. Don't worry about it."

"I can take you."

"I want to drop these off at the shelter on the way." I picked up the box I'd packed for the shelter between this location and the shop. "It's not much, but it's something."

"I don't mind. There isn't anything else I need to do today." She nodded toward the exit, pulling on the hem of the tight shirt that had snagged my attention more than once during the festival.

Her car was a block or two away, and we walked side by side in silence, the streets near the festival relatively quiet. "I'm surprised you don't have plans," I said, climbing into the passenger seat of her compact car, my knees scrunched against the dashboard.

Sybil shrugged, turning the key in the ignition and getting

a grinding sound from under the hood. She turned the key again, whispering, "C'mon, girl."

"Do you need me to take a look?"

Sybil shook her head, her stare intent on the steering wheel. "She's just a little grumpy at first. Kinda like you." She cooed to the car again, and the engine finally roared to life. Sybil's grin widened and she looked at me. "She just needs a little love and tenderness to warm her up."

"Sounds like she needs a new starter," I said as Sybil pulled from the lot.

"Maybe that, too," she said with a laugh. "But I was being cute and suggestive."

"You don't have to do that when we're alone."

She mimicked my tone from earlier. "I'm told it's part of my charm."

We were immediately stopped at a red light, and she drummed her fingers on the steering wheel. "And why are you shocked I don't have plans? Do you have plans?"

"Of course not." I looked up and down the street, but the row of nondescript office parks nearby didn't provide much distraction. "My plans are only ever work. I just figured you would because you're . . . I don't know. Fun."

"Honestly, if I go to my friends' place where I'm crashing, I'll be by myself. My sister is busy with wedding planning, and if I go to my mom's, she'll just be on me about figuring things out for my life." Sybil's car lurched forward when she tapped the gas as the light turned green. "So why not drive around with someone who kind of tolerates me?"

She smiled, but not as widely, and I immediately felt bad. Lila was right—she'd been with us all day and had been a huge help, and she didn't have to do any of that.

"I don't just tolerate you."

"You endure me? Suffer my presence? Bear my proximity for the greater good?" She tapped her finger on the turn signal, and I noticed a tiny chip in the color on her ring finger.

"Endure is probably closest." I paused, waiting for her gaze to snap up and worried she'd take me seriously, but her eyes kind of sparkled, and the smile was genuine. She got my sarcasm, and like the sight of her in that tight T-shirt, that smile evoked feelings in me I didn't want to think about.

"I've always thought you were funny, Kieran."

"It's a few blocks up and then take a right." I motioned to the stretch of surface road in front of us. We drove with a comfortable quiet between us until we approached a yellow light. "And thank you," I added. "For today. You were great. We appreciated it. I know I'm not always easy to work with."

"I endure you," she said, hitting the gas again. "And you're welcome. I just wish you'd loosen up a little."

The business parks gave way to more industrial real estate, a corner of town that was probably next in the spread of gentrification but had yet to be touched. I pointed out the corner where we'd take a right. "Maybe I'm just like you—I don't want to deal with not having my life together, so I keep my head down." I hadn't expected that bit of honesty to slip out, and I looked back out the window, holding the two boxes of donuts steady from the lurching of the car mixed with the uneven pavement. Ahead, I saw the shelter, a line already forming for the night. "I volunteer here," I said, wanting to move past that blurted-out truth. "When I can. It's run by a friend of my grandfather's, and when it was just us and my mom when I was little, we'd spend time here."

Sybil hadn't responded to either statement, and she looked deep in thought while taking in the surroundings.

"I'll just run these in and be right back," I said, pointing to a metered spot on the street.

"I'll go with you," she said after a moment of drumming her fingers on the steering wheel and looking around. She joined me on the sidewalk leading up to the building, and her hand brushed mine as we walked. "It will be easier to loosen up if we're in a place you're comfortable." She linked her hand with mine, squeezing.

When I didn't respond, she laughed self-consciously. "Or you can just endure my presence for a few additional minutes and we'll fool a few more people. I'm good either way."

She pulled her hand away, but I squeezed her fingers with mine, keeping them linked. Maybe she was right. Or maybe I just liked her hand in mine more than was healthy for me to admit. Either way, we didn't let go.

23

Sybil

KIERAN AND I WALKED OUT OF THE SHELTER FIFTEEN minutes later. The director, a woman he said was friends with his grandfather, had shooed us out, telling Kieran there was no need for him to stay and that they were set for volunteers for the night. Aside from anything having to do with me, I'd never seen Kieran uncertain—he seemed to move through most things with self-assurance, but when she'd told him to go, his eyes had snapped around the space. The crease in his brow made me assume he was taking in everything that needed to be done, things that he could do.

"If you want to stay, that's okay," I said when we stepped out onto the crumbling concrete.

"Nah. She said they're staffed."

I yanked my door handle up, my grunt earning a sideways glance from Kieran. "What? It sticks."

I felt his stare on my fingers, and I turned the key, whispering for the car to start up, which it luckily did after two attempts.

"Guess you'll probably get a new car soon with your winnings, huh?"

I looked over my shoulder, since the passenger mirror wasn't exactly usable. The idea of money had been distant all day. At the festival, I could focus on the donuts and ignore the existential dread of everything I could possibly want being at my fingertips. I ignored his question. "The money posted to my account today, actually," I admitted. "I got the notification when we were packing up."

I thought I would jump for joy or scream when I saw that message, but I'd just stared at it, rereading the text three or four times and letting it sink in. I didn't know how to be a rich person, and it felt completely bizarre to have so much money available to me. I'd logged out of my account feeling overwhelmed instead of looking at the numbers any longer.

"That's exciting. What will you buy first?"

I scanned the road. "I don't know." Walking through the shelter with Kieran had me thinking I should donate some of it to a good cause. I knew my mom would be proud of that, but more than that, I'd seen how many people needed support, needed people with money to care. I'd always known that, but it was just hitting me that now I was one of those people with money. I'd stood back while Kieran and the director, Maggie, talked to two men they knew, and thought back on my own life. I'd been allowed to rely on luck knowing I had a safety net whenever the next lucky break didn't pan out. Not everyone had that. "I should see how I can use the money to help those who are unhoused or hungry," I said.

"There are a lot of people to help," he said.

"And I could give you your portion now if you want," I said. "I trust you'll follow through on our deal."

He nodded and looked out the window. "We'll see," he said, facing the window. "I should finish our deal first." I'd had a feeling he'd say that, and I wished I'd just given Joe the check to begin with.

We drove in silence, and perhaps he was thinking it through or just tired of talking to me, but I couldn't take the quiet any longer. "What do you like to do for fun, Kieran? I mean, I know you pretty much just work, but if you had time, what would you do?"

"I still study every night when I can. Making sure I stay sharp."

"And what else? I know I'm the love of your life on Instagram, but there are a lot more girls who could use kissing after choir practice. When was the last time you went on a date?"

"I don't sing anymore, and we spent the evening before the TV spot together. That counts as a date."

"That doesn't count!" My exclamation was louder than I planned, but that answer couldn't stand. "That was a strategy session, and it was at your place of work. An actual date. One that starts with butterflies in your stomach and ends with a great, if awkward, first kiss."

When he chuckled, it caught me off guard, and I didn't expect how that low rumble would make me feel something unexpected, like that first night. "When was the last time you went on a date like that? I seem to remember that you'd given up on men in favor of donuts and cash. Something about a poorly lit dick pic?"

"Well," I said, hitting the gas to make it through another yellow light before his white-knuckle hold on the door tightened. "You don't have to grip the handle like that," I said. "I'm an excellent driver."

"You know yellow doesn't mean speed up, right?"

"That is a matter of opinion." I waved him off. Grace drove like my mom—careful, cautious, deferent to other drivers. Although he'd long since taken off and my mom was the one who'd taught me, I drove like my dad, taking every additional mile per hour as a point of pride. "Yellow is a challenge, like a moment when you can do or die."

"'Die' being the operative word," Kieran said, but he loosened his grip and relaxed into the seat, his hand resting on his thigh. "You didn't answer my question about the date," he added finally. His voice was casual, but the reminder came out of nowhere as we slowed behind a semi.

"It's been a while since I went on a good date." I flipped my blinker as I shifted to the left lane, catching Kieran's grip tightening again in my periphery. "Do *you* want to drive?"

"Yes," he said, not loosening his grip on the handle. "How do you still have a license?"

I reached out to swat him on the arm, intending to lay into him about overreacting about my driving, but we swerved just a little when I moved my hand, and the blaring horn from the car next to us left me pulling back my defense. I gripped the wheel with two hands and let out a slow exhalation before saying under my breath, "I guess it's just one more thing about me that's kind of a mess."

The sounds of the road filled the air between us, and deep down, I was hoping he'd fight me on my comment and tell me I wasn't a mess, but he just looked out the window. I noticed his grip loosening again, though. "You just do it differently from me," he said. "I'm not used to it."

"It's okay," I said. "Maybe that's our thing and I'll make fun of how slow you drive when you're behind the wheel."

"How do you know I'm a slow driver?" He chuckled at my raised eyebrow. "Fine. It's a deal, but for the record, I drive the speed limit." I saw him grin out of the corner of my eye. "Why did you ask if I date?"

"We're trying to convince everyone we're in love. It seemed relevant." I looked and then double-checked my mirrors before merging toward the exit for the East Village and Kieran's apartment. "Maybe it doesn't matter."

He nodded, looking back out the window, and I wondered if I'd made a huge mistake. It was feeling more and more like this was going to blow up in our faces very publicly and I'd be even more of a joke to my family than I already was.

"We should practice," he said. His hand jerked toward the handle as I hit the brakes, maybe a little hard, but I noticed him pull his hand back and rest it on his thigh. "Today it felt awkward every time you touched me. Other people probably noticed that, right?"

I was pretty sure they hadn't. I'd lost track of the number of people, almost always older women in patterned sweaters, who had oohed and aahed at us with hearts in their eyes. This felt like progress, though, so I didn't commit to an answer. "You did seem a little stiff."

He chuckled to himself, finally looking away from the window and at me. "Sybil, I think you're planning on making a joke about me being stiff, and I'm begging you not to."

"Okay," I said as I flipped my blinker to turn down his street. "But you're making it really hard," I tossed back, risking a glance at his face and being rewarded with his set expression unfolding into a laugh.

"Glad we could avoid that sticky situation," he said.

"Kieran, you made a dick joke." I said a prayer that I wouldn't have to parallel park as we neared the building. "And it was a marginally good one."

"I'm not always as rigid as I seem," he said, unbuckling after I found a mercifully well-spaced-out spot so I didn't have to experience the trauma of parallel parking while someone watched.

"I mean, from what I remember . . ."

He held up his hand. "Must we?"

I laughed and leaned back in my seat. "Okay. Okay. Continue."

"It just takes a while for me to feel comfortable with someone. I can't do casual intimacy, at least not convincingly." His sobered voice hit a nerve in me, and I looked up at his apartment. "I was a total wreck on that TV show."

"That makes sense. Well, we can practice or whatever, in private so you're more comfortable next time we're in public." I fingered my seat belt, ignoring my phone vibrating in the cup holder, my mom's name flashing on the screen.

"You're popular," he said, motioning to the phone.

"My mom has been sending me the names of financial planners all day and reminding me to make a plan." I picked it up and silenced it after catching the most recent message. "And reminding me to invite you over to meet her. I'll get back to her later. What are you doing tomorrow?"

"You're not sick of me yet after a whole day?"

"Who can resist someone so effervescent?"

He laughed this time, and it sounded to me like a pity laugh, but at least I'd gotten behind that tough exterior. "I'll be trying to get some sleep. Lila is going to a concert, so I'm on prep tomorrow night at the shop. We have a big order to fill."

"Oh," I said, still toying with the seat belt clasp. "Must be a lot of work to keep everything going. I could keep you company?"

"I can't ask you to do that."

"Well, you didn't ask. I offered." I reached for his hand, and he tensed under my touch. "It's private, and we could practice looking natural as a couple. Plus, who doesn't like someone to keep them company? And if you want, you can feed me donuts. It'll be like a throwback to our first night."

His eyes widened, and his hand twitched under my fingers. "Without the phenomenal oral sex. We'll be all business." I patted his hand and then pulled mine back. Him tensing under my touch gave me a weird combination of feeling ashamed at being too forward and turned on at the idea of practicing. "Scout's honor," I said, holding up three fingers, the one thing I'd held on to from my stint as a Brownie.

"Okay," he said, looking down at his hand as if I might have marked him. "If you're sure."

"Positive."

We made a plan to meet at the shop the next night, and he hopped out of the car. I'd had a fun day, even if I was bone tired.

My phone buzzed again in the cup holder, this time a call from Mom, and I tapped the ignore icon. Muting the reminders of everything I needed to figure out all day had been freeing, and I wanted to put them off a little longer, staying in this happy bubble from my day with Kieran. It seemed like each time we hung out, I saw a little more sweetness from him, so I wondered what practicing intimacy would be like.

24

Kieran

"YOU'RE SURE YOU CAN HANDLE THIS ON YOUR OWN?"
Lila asked from her perch in the doorway of the tiny office. "It's a big one." She motioned behind her to the boxes readied for the large catering order for a corporate retreat the next day. We'd been so slammed during the day, there hadn't been time for me to get some sleep, and it was going to be a long night.

"I got it. I don't want you to miss the concert."

"Yeah. It's a lot of work, though—I could come back after the show." She rested one shoulder against the peeling paint of the door frame. It used to be a stark white against the yellow walls, but over the years, the colors had morphed closer and closer together. The black of her top was a study in contrast. "I hate to leave you all alone to handle it."

"I won't be alone," I said, closing the window I'd had open to review our sales numbers. "Sybil is coming over to help." I'd been compiling our receipts from the festival and the last few days. We had done even better than I'd thought, and I pictured Sybil's quick smile, the one she'd flashed over her shoulder at me a hundred times that day. I knew I had an "I told you so" coming, but she'd smile when she said it. The smile I'd started to anticipate and hope I'd get to see again. I tried not to give that away, though, and I studied the screen and keyboard to avoid my sister's expression, one I knew would be two parts "well, well, well" and one part crass euphemism. I finally gave in after the moment of silence and looked at her.

"Sybil, huh?"

I corrected myself. It was three parts "well, well, well," and I expected that the crass euphemism would just be vocalized.

"She offered to help, and it wouldn't hurt for us to get used to being near each other and looking natural." I nudged past her and out into the kitchen, the weight of her raised eyebrow on the back of my head. "Why are you looking at me like that?"

"You like her," she said in a singsong voice that made her sound much younger and sweeter than she actually was.

"She's kind," I admitted, checking on our baking supplies. "And less . . . annoying than I thought she might be."

"And she makes you laugh." Lila pushed away from the door frame and sauntered past me.

"I chuckle at most," I said.

"And she's hot," Lila commented casually.

Hot was an understatement. Every time I closed my eyes, I pictured the way her thighs and hips took shape under her jeans and how distracting her chest had been under that tight shirt. And her smile . . . The wattage of her smile, the way it made my face relax and my heart beat faster, was the most persistent image in my head. I coughed into my fist and looked intently in a box. The way she looked was distracting, but I didn't want to give it a voice. "She's single, if you think so," I said. "Shoot your shot."

"She's dating you, brother." Lila bopped my nose with the tip of her finger, something she knew I hated. "Very publicly. And do you plan to spend time together in your *original* way? Just deciding how far I need to steer clear of the shop tonight."

"We're going to make donuts and talk. I'm having dinner with her family soon, so we need to prepare." I motioned her toward the back exit. "That's it. It's strictly business. Go away."

"Kieran and Sybil sitting in a tree, K-I-S—"

I interrupted her song with the creak of the back door as I held it open. I dug into my pocket and fished out three twenty-dollar bills. "If you're done," I said, "here. I wish it was more, but I appreciate you helping so much more lately on top of school."

Lila's expression softened, and she took the bills from my hand, looking from them to me. "You don't have to thank me. I know the shop fell to you to run as the oldest, but he is my granddad, too," she said, leaning in to kiss my cheek. "For what it's worth, I appreciate everything you're doing to save it." She took a few steps toward her car, knowing I'd wait at the door until she climbed in. "And also for what it's worth, I think Sybil likes you, too."

I shook my head and waved again, wanting her gone before Sybil arrived so I didn't need to consider her assessment. "I never said I liked her," I added, too late.

"You didn't have to. Have fun with your girlfriend," Lila said, the teasing tone back before she closed the door and drove away. The sky was fading from the glow of the Des Moines skyline into the indigo of night, the stars beginning to appear over the old neon Travelers insurance sign.

"Hey!" A familiar voice carried through the alley behind the store, and Sybil rounded the corner. She wore a black puffy coat over jeans and a pink T-shirt cropped to reveal a sliver of her belly. I loved those shirts and that peek at her skin. "I wasn't sure if I could park back here or not," she said, walking across the uneven pavement.

"Just as well," I said, motioning her inside and hanging her coat on a hook by the door. "The odds were decent that you'd crash your car through our back wall."

"Funny," she said, sliding past me through the open door. The tight fit of the T-shirt meant the entire side of her body grazed mine, and I stifled the urge to reach for the small of her back, realizing too late that that was exactly what we were meant to be getting used to doing. "You're funny."

She spun in a slow circle, and my vision snagged on the way her jeans tapered down her thighs, thighs I remembered more than was good for me. I was distracted enough to forget the door, and it slammed behind me, making us both jump.

"Sorry," I said, shooting my eyes to her face. "One more thing that needs fixing."

Sybil had changed her hair, and it was in two braids along the side of her head and tucked behind her ears. "You really don't have to help," I added, pulling an apron from a hook on the wall and sliding the strap over my head.

"Take full advantage of me," she said, holding out her hand for the other apron, and the glint in her eyes made me think it was a challenge to take or ignore her double entendre.

I ignored it, knowing my brain would remind me of the shape of those words leaving her mouth later. "You'll need to cover your hair," I said, our fingers brushing when I handed

over the apron. Her skin was so soft, which I knew from earlier, but that still seemed to surprise me every time.

"I came prepared," she said, snatching a bandanna from her
back pocket. "I know I look good in whatever I wear and that
this is all fake, but I couldn't do a hairnet on a first date, even
if it's for show." Her fingers worked over her hairline as she
spoke and tied the bright blue bandanna over her hair. "But
don't let me stop you from making it look good." She smiled,
her arms still raised as she tied a knot in the bandanna.

I pulled my hat from the hook and pulled it on over my
hair, the bill facing backward. "No net for me, either."

"Nice," she said, guiding the apron over her head. It was a
relief and a disappointment to lose the view of her body under
her tight clothes but a friendly reminder to get my head back
on straight.

"Okay," I said, stepping around her and pointing to a white-
board where I'd outlined what we needed for the next day.
"They've ordered twenty-seven dozen for a conference happening in the morning, so objectives for the night are to prepare
yeast, cake, and buttermilk donuts."

"And to get you used to being around me." Sybil's hands
were on my sides, her delicate fingers resting over my obliques.

"To get used to each other," I corrected, gritting my teeth. Her
hands on me, even in that simple way, felt so damn good.

Sybil didn't move. She actually stepped closer behind me,
the warmth of her presence and the swell of her curves against
my back making me tense all over as her fingers wiggled at my
sides. "Relax," she said, her voice like a purr.

"Ordering me to relax doesn't relax me," I said, though I
wasn't tensing under her touch because I was uncomfortable. I

was fighting the urge to pin her against a wall with that fervor and gusto she'd wanted so badly.

"Pretend to relax, then. Pretend you've known me for years and I've touched you like this a thousand times. Like it's just what we do." Her left palm slipped, and her fingers grazed the waist of my jeans, sending a shot of electricity through me. "Pretend I've touched you like this in the shower, or after you've explored every inch of my body, or when you'd been gone for a long time and I missed you."

I closed my eyes against the sensation and the image forming in my head of her touching me in the shower, willing my body to calm down. "That's better!" she exclaimed, and let her hands fall away. "But I promise not to surprise you again," she said, a sheepish expression on her face that convinced me she'd read my reaction very wrong. "You should know I'm a toucher, but I'll try to give you more warning next time."

"It's doubtful you'll ever stop surprising me." I pointed at the donut mixes and began explaining the different doughs and how we'd start with the yeast donuts. *Do not think of Sybil in the shower. Do not think of Sybil in the shower.*

"Lila and I made the first batch of dough already, and it's in the proofer." When I motioned to the expanding dough behind the glass, my gaze snagged on Sybil's expression.

"Ooh! I used to love rolling out dough baking with my mom as a kid. Can I do that part?" She studied the equipment, her eyes lighting up with curiosity, and I bit back a grin. I had no intention of smiling like a lovesick puppy just because she was happy, just because her face lit up when she was interested, so I turned away and grunted a "sure" over my shoulder.

"You know," she said, watching me haul the dough from

the proofing oven to the counter, "direct and targeted marketing to local companies might increase your catering business. I bet you could scale back the late-night hours—there are so many local businesses that might be good customers." She chuckled and walked toward me. "I should know—I've temped everywhere, and I started looking into it. I read a bunch of articles and then I found this YouTube channel and watched, like, twenty videos in a row on strategies."

I sank my hands into the dough, the familiar burn in my forearms more pronounced with her eyes on me. "That's actually a really good idea," I replied, thinking through what she'd said.

"Yeah, and you could have a section on the website with deals for bulk orders." She spoke faster as she got excited. "Oh my gosh! What if we took samples to places downtown and pitched to them in person?"

I grinned to myself, my back to her. "We?" I tried to ignore the way heat prickled on the back of my neck, and I tipped the dough onto the counter the way Granddad had taught me. The scent mingled with whatever Sybil was wearing, and it took all my energy to focus my attention on the dough rather than the way her voice seemed to wrap around my body as I separated the dough with the same blade we'd used for decades.

"Of course, we." Sybil placed a palm on my back and leaned around me to watch me work. "You're horrible at small talk, and we're a team, remember?"

I paused my movements and glanced over my shoulder, and she held out her palm for a high five. "I guess we are." I motioned to the roller behind Sybil. The long cylinder was heavy, and I watched the line of her biceps as she walked it over, examining the wood. "If your arms get tired, I can take over." I guided her to take my place in front of the dough atop the counter.

"I have excellent upper-body strength." Sybil met my gaze over her shoulder. "Have you seen me in this shirt?"

"That shirt shows off your excellent upper body," I said without thinking. "Not sure about the strength."

"I swear to God, Kieran, it's like you can't help but flirt with me despite your best efforts to put up this grumpy front." She positioned her hands on the roller and rolled out the dough, her giggle fading away, and I couldn't see her face, but I imagined her concentrating, focused on how the dough spread.

I ignored her comment about me flirting with her. "Start in the middle and roll out. You'll want it evenly thick," I said.

"Thickness is a personal interest," she said without looking back at me and then paused her rolling. "See, jokes like that are how I get everyone besides you to like me."

She rolled her shoulders and flexed her fingers before beginning to roll the dough again, and I knew the burn she was feeling in her muscles. I kind of liked her having that in common with me, but I didn't like how resigned she'd sounded in that last statement.

"Let me help," I said, stepping behind her. I placed my hands next to hers on the roller, stepping into her space. "May I?"

She nodded and her fingers grazed mine. "I guess I was a little overconfident in my upper-body strength," she said.

"Like this." I guided her, our arms moving together, my chest against her back. "Let the roller do the work," I added, lowering my voice since I was so close to her ear.

"Okay." Sybil sounded breathless, probably from how much

effort she'd put into rolling out the dough, but I wanted it to be something else, so much that I stayed there, helping her roll slowly, our bodies pressed close together.

"You know, you don't always have to have a dirty joke at the ready. For the record, there are lots of reasons people like you." I inhaled the scent of her hair product as we moved in tandem. "I'm sure I'm not the only one who sees that."

"You like me?"

I grunted in the affirmative. There was no other sound to make, because I was putting all my energy into not getting an erection while rolling dough out with her. "Not the jokes," I added. "But there are a lot of reasons to like you. You're really creative and you think about possibilities. Like the direct marketing to local businesses—that's a really good idea. You don't always have to be the comic relief is what I mean."

She was quiet, going back to her work. "You really think so?"

"Yeah," I said. "I do." I wasn't sure what else to say, so I didn't say anything, but studied the length of her arms and the side of her neck.

"How's this?" she said, voice still breathless, and I stepped in to her to peer over her shoulder, regretting the movement right away because it put me against her ass.

"This is good," I said, stepping back immediately. I motioned to the dough and handed her one of the donut cutters hanging on hooks above the counter. She turned the tool in her hands, eyes lighting as she examined it.

"A cookie cutter? Er, donut cutter?"

I grinned, grabbing the other cutter from over her shoulder. "You just thought we all shaped them by hand and kept them the same size?"

"I guess I never thought about it," she said. "You're such a precise guy. It's not like it's out of the realm of possibility. That's probably why you liked medicine, huh? Science is precise."

I showed her how close together to make the shapes and watched her work, positioning each piece of dough to get it just right. "What I really like is answering questions that will ultimately help people. There are so many unanswered questions about our bodies and minds," I said, guiding her hand an inch to the right, really for the excuse to touch her. "I enjoy the precision of medicine."

"Speaking of precision, check out these beautiful donuts!" Sybil pressed her palms together over her heart. "Even the holes are perfect!"

"They're beautiful holes," I said, pointing to her tray and ignoring her raised eyebrows. "And that one was for you."

Her grin lit up her face—hell, it lit up the room, and I returned her smile this time before I could stop myself.

"Thank you," she said. "It was an elegantly constructed joke." She finished arranging the dough to fill the baking sheet.

"Not really a joke," I added, beginning to gather the scraps together.

"Close enough," she said, bopping me on the nose with her flour-covered finger.

"What was that for?" I wiped my nose, brushing the flour away with my forearm.

She touched my face again, this time dragging flour along my chin. "For 'not really a joke.'" She reached for my nose again, but I intercepted her, my fingers at her wrist.

"It wasn't a joke, mostly just . . . wordplay." With her wrist still in my hand, I returned her gesture, spattering her nose with flour.

"Hey!" She yelped and wriggled under my grasp, but I held her tight enough to get a long swipe along her cheek in. "No fair."

"All's fair in love and donuts." I tried to get her once more, but she slid out of my grip. We'd have to change our gloves and rewash our hands, but I liked how she felt in my grip, and her energy was contagious somehow. How else to explain why I was in the shop kitchen circling with this woman, both of our faces sprinkled with flour? "I've been doing this a lot longer than you, Syb," I taunted. "I'll come out on top."

"I don't believe for a minute you've been acting a fool in a kitchen longer than me," she said, reaching for me but missing entirely. "Next swipe wins, and you're going down."

The first thought was on the tip of my tongue. *I've gone down before, and I haven't stopped thinking about it since.* I swallowed that, though. "Wins what?"

"First warm donut," she said, sliding her hands along the counter, picking up more flour.

"Deal." I mirrored her action and stepped closer.

"You called me Syb," she said, shifting from left to right with a bounce in her step that had my gaze slipping to her chest.

"Is that okay?"

She circled me, stepping forward and back as if we were boxing. "I like it. You've just never done that before. Does that mean you're beginning to like me?"

I dropped my hands. "I never didn't like you." Lila's taunting rang in my head. "I don't want you to think—"

She moved fast before I could finish my sentence. "Victory!" Her finger slid the length of my cheek, ending at the corner of my lip.

Sybil stood so close, I could see the tiny freckles dotted across the bridge of her nose, and I let my hand fall, my fingertips skimming her arm. "You got me," I said. "Was this a ploy to get me comfortable with you touching me?"

"No." Sybil tapped my chin with her index finger. "I'm not that strategic. But did it work?" She slid her palm down my biceps, and goose bumps rose all along my skin.

"Yeah," I said, resting my hand at her waist. "But, Syb?"

When I used the nickname, she got the same light in her eyes, like her face brightened. "Yeah?" She tipped her chin up, and it would have been so easy to kiss her, but I dragged my thumb across her dark red lower lip instead, smearing flour over it. "Rematch begins now."

25

Sybil

"THIS IS MY LAST CHOCOLATE ONE." I LEANED A HIP against the counter and popped the final bite into my mouth. "I didn't think it was possible for me to get tired of these," I said, taking in the tray of frosted chocolate donuts, some with sprinkles and coconut, and one notably missing from the neat and even rows.

"I don't believe you *are* sick of chocolate," he said, finishing his rotation, cleaning everything. "You just ate a third one."

"Two and one-third. That middle one was small and kind of deformed, so it didn't count." I grinned, crossing one ankle over the other. "And I didn't say I was sick of all donuts. I'm just saying I'll have a different kind next time."

"That makes more sense." Kieran laughed to himself, something he'd done a lot that night. He had a nice laugh, like it was a secret he was slowly revealing. "And you can have all the donuts you want."

"I've been waiting for you to say that. It's all I've ever wanted any man to say to me." I touched the spot on my lip where he'd brushed flour earlier. I didn't even notice I was doing it until I caught him following my movement, and I let my fingers fall away. "I guess you're the guy I've always been looking for." I leaned against him in a faux swoon.

Kieran's hands rested against my arms, holding me. "I'm sure that's not true." His voice was more gravelly than I expected. I looked up, our gazes meeting, and took in the way his eyelashes framed his dark eyes, making me want to argue, but he coughed into one hand and helped to right me with the other. "That's what we need everyone to believe."

His hand hovered near my forearm until I regained my balance. The ghost of his touch had me in my feelings, and I smoothed my palms down the front of my shirt for something to distract myself. "On second thought, I might pass on that next donut. I'm feeling wired after all this sugar."

Kieran's movement in the corner of my vision caught my eye. He stretched, raising his arms over his head. "Thanks for your help." He still had a swipe of flour along the side of his face and a bit on the tip of his nose. I didn't even want to guess what I looked like, because he'd been a fiercer competitor than I thought he would be.

"You know," I said, brushing the back of my hand along my forehead, finding it smeared with flour when I pulled it away, "that was fun."

"Yeah." He paused his movements and ripped a paper towel from the roll near him, running it under the tap in the sink for a moment. He motioned for me to stand between his spread knees and placed two fingers under my chin. "You missed like . . ." His eyes roamed my face. "Like seven spots. May I?"

I nodded as he dabbed the paper towel against my skin.

He'd used hot water, and each drag felt a little like a kiss. "I'm surprised you played along," I commented, letting my eyelids fall closed as he slid the wet towel along my cheekbone.

"I am, too." He wiped across my eyebrow and then down along the skin in front of my ear. The paper tickled when he reached the edge of my jaw. "It's been a long time since I played. I guess you bring it out in me."

I opened my eyes, taking in the shape of his brows and the furrow between them as he cleaned flour off my face. "I'm glad," I said, carefully resting a palm over his heart. "Sometimes I think you're so serious, you'll get sick of me and my shenanigans, you know?"

His gaze snapped to mine. "No." He dabbed at the space between my nose and mouth. "I mean, you are . . . something, but I like having you around." He tossed the paper towel aside but kept his hand against my jaw. "Shenanigans weren't part of my life before you."

I swiped two fingers over his forehead to erase the smear of flour there. "Why is that?" The flour was gone, but I stroked the spot between his brows again anyway.

I thought he might step away, clam up, or start working again, but when my finger slid down his nose, he closed his eyes, the gesture showing a side of him I hadn't seen before. He had softened.

"My mom was always chasing the next big thing, the next relationship, the next big high . . ." He blinked a few times, and I stroked his face again, tracing his cheekbones. "There wasn't really time to play, because I had to look out for Lila while Mom played, and then school took all my focus and there wasn't any time left over."

I dragged my fingertips down the column of his throat,

over his Adam's apple. "Oh," I said, continuing my path toward the roundness of his shoulder under an impossibly soft and worn-in shirt. "So is school fun for you?"

Kieran's eyes closed again, and I stroked a finger over his brow. "It's not fun, but it's . . ." He seemed to search for the right word. "It's a step forward. When I finish and do my residency, I can have fun. I can do research. I can take care of my family. So . . ." He trailed off, and I pulled my hand away as he opened his eyes. "I've been putting fun off until later."

"We still have to practice getting comfortable with each other for real. Like, touching each other," I added, realizing I'd been bringing my finger to my lips again. "That could be fun."

His expression was unchanged, though. "Yeah."

"Don't sound so excited. Pretending you want in my pants shouldn't be *that* challenging."

"No, it won't be." His posture relaxed, and he rolled the stool closer to me, his gaze flicking down to my tight T-shirt and back up. "You're . . . well, you know what you look like."

His direct answer took me by surprise, but before I could respond, he added, "That's not intimacy, though. Not convincing intimacy, anyway." As if in slow motion, he extended his hand, sliding a fingertip down my arm, making goose bumps rise as he trailed down my forearm, past my wrist, and to my own fingertip before crooking his finger into the belt loop of my jeans and tugging me forward to the space between his spread knees. "If we're going to keep this up, it should seem like I want into your heart," he said, slowly raising his palm to my hip, where it settled.

I leaned in to where his finger was tucked into the belt loop and nodded, swallowing back a stammer. "My heart and not my pants."

His palm moved from my hip up to my side, fingers slipping under the shirt, tracing tiny rivers on the map of my skin. "Your heart *and* your pants, Syb."

"How do we do that?" I gave a sharp inhale as his fingers neared the underside of my bra and then slid back to move down my side. "I'm . . . pretty clear on the pants part. But how do we fake the heart side?"

"I don't know." His gaze was on my face, chin tipped up as he stroked my side. "Like this, I guess."

I dragged the tip of my tongue along my lower lip. "By letting me talk you into shenanigans?"

"Pretty sure pretending to date is a shenanigan, and you already talked me into that." His fingers flexed at my waist.

"I'm convincing." I barely recognized my voice, which was breathy and close to a whisper, and I stepped forward into his arms.

"You make me feel . . ." His fingertips grazed my side as he spoke, and I held my breath. He searched my face like he'd find the right word scribbled somewhere on my features, and when his gaze fell to my lips, I slid my tongue over them again. I tipped my chin up, waiting. This was the moment of anticipation before a perfect kiss—the energy pulsing between us as I swiped a fingertip along his chin, catching the last bit of flour. Then his face dipped toward mine, and I waited to sink into this moment.

"Still here?" Lila's voice carried ahead of the squealing of the door, and we leaped apart. "Wanted to see if you two still needed help."

I stumbled over my own feet and fell, my body hitting the linoleum hard after I'd let go of Kieran. His sister had a real knack for finding the worst moment to show up.

"Are you okay?" Kieran stretched out his hand to help me off the floor, which might have been romantic and a cute opportunity to end up back in his arms, save the way I'd slightly rolled my ankle before crashing into the floor, elbows first. I'd let out a string of curses set to the tune of a high-pitched wail.

I pressed my fingers to my ankle gingerly. "Peachy keen."

"Peachy keen?" He crouched down. "You just let out a stream of expletives so creative, I don't think I know what all those words mean. Peachy keen?"

Lila hurried to the freezer and retrieved an ice pack, rushing back over.

Kieran reached for my ankle. "Can I see?"

I pulled my leg back. "Nah. I'm fine." I brushed his hand away, knowing nothing good would come of him touching me again. "I should go."

"Let me keep ice on it." He reached for my elbow. "To stop the swelling."

I struggled to my feet, keeping my ankle up. "I look good with swelling." I fumbled around for my purse, which was luckily within reach on a nearby chair.

"That doesn't make any sense." He tried to guide me to the chair, but I flashed a big smile, blinking back the multiple layers of cringe from the fall and the almost kiss between us.

"You'll learn I rarely make sense. It's part of why people like me so much."

"That's not true." His palm moved up and down my forearm, and his voice dipped low. "You're only not making sense in this instance. I told you, you don't always have to make yourself the joke."

"I didn't park far away." I took a limping step toward the door. I pulled on it, stumbling back at the weight, and then pulled again. The door was jammed hard into the frame. "Damn it."

"I got it," he said from behind me, his chest pressed to my back as he reached around me to grip the door's ancient handle and yanked. He called to Lila over his shoulder, and Kieran's body was still pressed to mine as the cool air blew in. The juxtaposition of sensations was jarring but pulled me out of my lust haze.

"I had fun," I said. "Making the donuts and the other shenanigans with you."

He grabbed something from behind the door and stepped with me out into the cool air, shoving keys in his pocket and shrugging into a jacket. "Let me walk you to your car. It's past two."

The nearby streetlight cast his face in shadows, even standing close to me, and I admired the way his brows moved as he searched my face again. "Thank you." I dug in my purse for my keys, pawing past what felt like three ChapStick tubes—were they multiplying?—and what I knew was a month's worth of receipts I'd shoved in there. "And thank you for saying what you said, about me not being a joke." I pulled the keys from the very bottom of the purse—always a mystery to me how they wound up there, since they were the last thing to be tossed on top. That kind of compliment from Kieran was like someone giving a speech about my talents. I hadn't known him long, but I knew he didn't say things he didn't believe. "It means a lot."

His cheeks pinked, visible even in the dark, and I grinned.

"You seem much more comfortable when we're touching, too," I said, brushing my fingertips over his hand. "I'm glad we sorted that out. But we probably shouldn't . . ."

"Yeah," he said. "We almost . . ."

"I blame the donuts entirely." I grinned, knowing he'd felt it, too, that electricity of a kiss about to happen. "But we shouldn't let things get out of hand. Just pretend out of hand," I said with a smile, squeezing his hand and then stepping into my car. "We've got two more months. So maybe just think of me as a cousin until then. Unfuckable."

His eyes widened at my terminology, but after a moment, he saluted and stepped back, closing my door for me and waiting on the sidewalk. Thank God the car cooperated this time and started on the first attempt. "Put ice on that when you get home, and elevate it. And take some ibuprofen." He pointed into the car, and for a split second, I thought he was pointing to the apex of my thighs, where I'd definitely needed cooling earlier—the twisted ankle was really battling with the melty feelings I'd been enjoying before Lila arrived. It felt very responsible and very disappointing to agree nothing else should happen with Kieran. "Hey," I said. "Before Lila came in, you said being with me made you feel something, but you never finished your sentence." I waited for the heat to kick in. "Feel what?"

"I don't remember." He shoved his hands in his pockets and shifted his weight from foot to foot. "It's not important."

"You sure?" I tossed the car into reverse, and he stepped back with a nod, watching me pull off before starting the short walk back to the store. He was lying. I caught him in my rearview mirror as I stopped at the corner, and admired the way his silhouette moved in the dim light, how his legs and arms looked in shadow, and I thought back to how they'd felt wrapped around me earlier in the night. Which was a good way to ignore my throbbing ankle, because that made other areas tingle in direct opposition to how I'd asked him to think of me like a cousin.

Mainly, though, I imagined how he planned to end that sentence. For a while there tonight, I'd seen something new in Kieran, and I got the sense most people didn't get to see him open up like that. And it felt important that he was so comfortable around me. So why had my honest, ethical-to-a-fault, and new-to-shenanigans man lied to me just now?

26

Kieran

THE EVENING SKY OUTSIDE WAS APRICOT COLORED from the sinking sun, and rays of purple streaked through the twilight. The door was locked, but we were all perched around the seating area where Sybil, Granddad, Tom, and Lila were playing poker. Tom eyed Sybil after her bold five-nickel bet. I watched her tongue peek out to touch the corner of her lip, the pink of it in contrast with her dark red lipstick. She wasn't bluffing this hand, but I still followed the path of that tongue during her standoff with Tom. Since that night in the shop the week earlier, it had been easier to be around her in that we'd seemed to figure out how to touch and talk in a way that felt natural. It had also been exponentially harder, because every time I walked into the kitchen, I flashed back to her in my arms, the moment when I should have kissed her, and how I'd been just about to confess that she made me feel lucky. I hadn't said it out loud, regretting the notion of oversharing immediately. Still, seven days later, it was more difficult every day not to bring it back up.

"I'm out," Lila said, dropping her cards.

Granddad eyed his hand and then studied Sybil before tossing his hand to the table. "Too rich for my blood."

I'd run upstairs to let Penny outside since Mrs. Nguyen was sick with a cold, and came back to the game in progress, the four of them around the table. They invited me to join, but I'd preferred to watch. Sybil fit in so well here with us, laughing with Lila and calling out Granddad for cheating. I imagined walking up behind Sybil and rubbing her shoulders, sharing secrets about Tom's tells as an excuse to whisper in her ear.

"I'll call." Tom kept a serious expression, eyeing Sybil. "What you got, girl?"

"That's Ms. Sweet to you, old man," she said, laying out her cards. "Full house, queens and threes, baby!" Her grin widened as she grabbed the pot from the middle of the table. "I told you I'm lucky!" She giggled, stacking her coins and listening to Tom's good-natured grumbling.

"She's a shark," Granddad said, shuffling the cards. "You better watch out, son."

I nodded, earning a smile from Sybil. "Why do you think I refused to play? I'm saving my loose change to pay for school."

Lila held up a palm. "That's it for me," she said, glancing at her phone. "There's a new food truck I'm going to check out with Marcus."

"My Marcus?" Sybil asked. "He finds the best places to eat."

"You're dating her roommate?" I slid from my perch and took a few steps toward the table.

"Leave her alone," Sybil said, stretching her arm around my

waist. The gesture was so casual, so easy, and the way she pulled me closer was innocent, but the sensation rippled through my body. "They're just hitting up a food truck."

"He's always way too protective," Lila said, nudging my shoulder as she grabbed her bag from the chair.

"Good." Tom knocked on the surface of the table. "Always important for an older brother to look out for his siblings."

Granddad chuckled. "I don't know . . . I think my Lila Bean takes care of herself pretty well." He'd used the nickname for Lila since she was small, and she dropped a kiss on his cheek.

"That's right," she said. "Kieran is way more likely to need looking out for."

"True," Sybil said, slipping her fingers into my pocket. "You really dropped the ball with me."

Lila shot me a quick look, her eyebrows raised before she glanced at our linked fingers. "I don't know," she said, pushing open the front door. "I think my record of success is still intact."

Granddad pushed back from the table. "Always a pleasure, Sybil," he said, swiping his small stack of pennies from the table. He bent to kiss Sybil's cheek and clapped a palm on her shoulder. "We'll get ya next time."

"I'll be ready." She let go of me to stand and give him a hug. He'd already told me how good for me he thought she was and how happy he was to see us together. It hurt to hear that, to know it was all a lie. "And I'm onto your cheating now," she called after him, and he laughed with a wave.

He and Tom were on their way to dinner at the pho place a few doors down, and I watched Granddad's movements, encouraged by how he was getting stronger and steadier every day. Just a month earlier, it had seemed impossible that he was ready to take the shop back over, but now, it felt safe to hope. Returning to school was within reach, only I hadn't called them yet about my reenrollment. I'd been having fun lately with Sybil, but I had no choice but to go back. School wasn't supposed to be fun, so why did I keep hesitating? I was building something for my future by attending medical school. There was no real choice facing me; still, I just hadn't called.

I flipped the lock on the door now that Sybil and I were alone. "How'd you do?"

When she spread her pennies out in front of her to count them, the urge to step behind her hit me again. Maybe to drop kisses along her nape as she counted, seeing if I could throw her off.

I let go of the door and picked up the cards from the table. Having something to do with my hands was helpful in pushing thoughts of Sybil's neck from the front of my mind.

"Forty-six cents," she said. "Not too shabby."

I walked behind the counter where we kept the cards for slow days, not that we'd had many lately. "You *are* a shark," I said. "Should I be concerned?"

She dropped her handful of change into the tip jar, the coins clinking against the side of the glass. "Probably." She crossed her arms on the counter and leaned forward, the motion pushing her breasts out and giving a tempting—way too tempting—view down the V-neck of her shirt as she slid a fingertip along the pattern in the countertop. "I'm pretty good at bluffing."

"I could figure you out," I said, dragging my gaze back to her face before she caught me admiring the freckles that spread up from her sternum.

"Bet I can read you better," she challenged, one eyebrow cocked. "That's probably why you didn't want to play." She waved her index finger between us. "You knew I could read you like a book."

I made a grab for her fingers, wrapping my hand around hers. Her hand looked small in mine, and she gently curled her finger against my hand. "You're cocky, Sweet."

"It's not being cocky when it's true." She cupped her palm over mine. "For example," she said, "I know you were just checking out my boobs when you thought I wasn't looking. A total tit scan. Official TTS behavior."

I placed my other palm over hers, like we were a team about to leave the dugout. "I was looking at your freckles," I admitted. "Not your tits."

"My freckles?" She tipped her head to the side and slid her hands away, brushing the bridge of her nose. "Nice try. You were definitely looking at my chest."

"Not those freckles. Here," I said, pointing to the spot I'd been inspecting, and regretting the motion immediately because it was hell to have my finger hover so close but to not trace the constellation on her skin. "You have five right here."

She looked at my finger and then at her chest. She traced the path I would have, and I followed her fingertip's movement from left to right. "How have I never noticed that?"

I swallowed and pulled my hand back, leaning on the counter. "I guess some things are easier for other people to see," I said, letting my gaze dip to where her finger traced again and listening to her little "hm" of amusement.

"Like how I can see how much fun you are secretly," she said with an impish grin, hoisting herself onto the counter and tucking one leg under her knee.

"Lies."

She laughed, and I heard her phone buzz in her pocket.

"Don't mind me if you need to get that."

She let out a breath, puffing her cheeks. "It's my mom. She's been on me about you coming for dinner tomorrow."

I'd agreed to a meal with her family after they'd stopped by the shop, but that felt like eons ago, when I figured it would all be easy—truthfully, now I felt nervous. "She's been on you about how I'm probably a scam artist?"

"That, food allergies, your astrological sign, how serious we are, what kind of medicine you plan to practice, how you feel about retirement planning, and if you've ever been interested in skate parks." She held up her phone for me, where the notification read nine unread messages from Mama Mary. "Oh, and if you have any aliases, because she didn't find any outstanding warrants on you but wants to be sure."

"No allergies," I said, running through the list of questions in my head. "I'm a Virgo." I noticed a loose thread hanging from the pocket of her jeans. "And I want to be a neurosurgeon—the human brain is fascinating, and I've always had really steady hands." I snagged the thread and rolled it between my finger and thumb. "No aliases or warrants, outstanding or otherwise, and I'd feel better about retirement planning if I had more income, but I'm all for it."

I pulled gently on the thread, and instead of giving, it tugged Sybil's leg closer to me. I liked the tether between us and how it felt comforting to tell her things and for her to know me, even in those small ways. "Why did she ask about skate parks?"

"When I was a kid, my dad left us and opened a skate park in Connecticut," she said. "I guess she's just making sure history doesn't repeat."

"Is there a big market for skate parks in Connecticut?"

"No idea. I hope so—it made him happy. He used to visit, and then it was only calls. We don't hear from him very often now. I kinda thought he'd call when I won, but I'm sure he'll check in at some point. He's honestly kind of a footnote in our lives now. Grace didn't invite him to her wedding." She shrugged one shoulder. "Irony is that I'm much more likely than you to run off and open a skate park."

I saw the shrug for what it was—another of her attempts to make herself the joke, and I pulled on the thread again, harder this time, in hopes of pulling her out of where she was going with her explanation. "You'd be cute in a helmet and elbow pads, but you'd never abandon your family. You're not built like that. And you're too memorable to be a footnote." I moved the pad of my thumb up and down the thread. "But to your question, I've never even been to a skate park, nor do I have plans to own one."

"She's really going to love you," Sybil said, looking down at where I held the fabric. "Once she understands you're not scamming me."

"That I want into your heart," I added, parroting the agreement from the night in the shop.

"And my pants if you don't pull them apart before tomorrow." She swatted at my fingers tugging on the thread until I let it go.

Reminded that I shouldn't be pulling on the seams of her clothes just to create a connection, I looked for something to do behind the counter and began stacking receipts. "You're right. I'll keep my hands to myself."

Sybil gave a small, distracted laugh. "My sister and her fiancé, Warren, will be there. And you met Mom and Paul.

They're cool, but probably there shouldn't be a lot of PDA in front of them. I think more serious probably looks better, like . . . I don't know. Professional?" She was staring at her hands when I looked up.

No PDA and acting professional were what I would have wanted a few weeks ago—it was the closest thing to not lying. Except I'd been looking forward to the excuse to touch her more away from the shop. "Sounds good. Hands off and keep it focused."

"Just . . . you know. They think I'm the wild one, so someone like you who's so focused and serious . . . and if I look that way, too, it'll be good."

"Definitely," I said. "Sounds good." I placed the neat stack of receipts back where it belonged, everything lined up and in order, because she was right: I was serious and focused, and I could put things, like my too-vivid imagination, in order. "That will be easy."

27

Sybil

"S YBIL."

I focused on drying the drops of water from the plate I'd pulled from the dishwasher, intent on clearing them one by one. I'd heard my mother, and I'd come over early with the express intent to help her cook and soften her up, but I'd made a critical error. Mom didn't soften up with conversation, she homed in.

"Sybil Marie!"

I winced, knowing number three was coming.

"Sybil Marie Sweet!"

There it is. "It's okay, Mom," I said, placing the dish on the counter. "It's not a big deal."

"It most certainly is!" Mom paced back and forth across the kitchen floor, a wooden spoon in one hand and a tomato in the other. "You're moving home again."

"No, she's not," my stepdad said from behind his newspaper.

Characteristically, Mom ignored him, continuing her pacing. "You did not tell us when you moved out you were going to be sleeping on a couch. I thought you at least had a room there."

"She's an adult, honey."

"She's not acting like it," Mom said, returning the tomato to the cutting board. In my humble opinion, she was dicing it a little aggressively while still lecturing. "You could get a place of your own. I'm not saying live here forever, but you shouldn't be staying on a couch in that neighborhood!"

I'd let it slip that I was crashing at Emi's place in what I could only describe as a haze of carelessness. I blamed the home brew Paul had handed me when I arrived. While Mom had continued her exploration of the joys of nagging her children, he'd been tinkering with making and bottling his own creations in the basement for years. "The neighborhood is fine," I said finally. "And I'm living with a veteran and a black belt." I swiped a finger full of frosting off the side of the bowl and held it up. "Plus, Marcus is a great cook, so I'm eating my vegetables!"

She gave a harrumph. "You have money. You have so much money. I just don't understand." She continued to chop, moving from a tomato to an onion. "Why are you standing still? You could be making progress on so many things."

"I'm just getting things figured out. But I'm happy, and I'm not always staying there. Sometimes I'm over at Kieran's place in the East Village. Who knows? Maybe we'll move in together eventually."

I knew immediately I'd played that wrong. Her chopping paused, the blade suspended in the air, and Paul winced before sliding back behind his paper. "The donut man."

"Kieran," I repeated, handing her a cucumber. "We've been really busy. You know . . . new love."

"Yes," she said, slicing again, the sound of metal against vegetable in a steady rhythm. "And I do hope I'm wrong, honey." She paused her slicing but this time set the knife down to let me know she was serious. "But this whole thing is strange to me. And I saw you two together at the donut shop—it looked like he'd never met you before. Janice said she saw you at the Downtown Food Festival and said the same thing. I just worry you're seeing love and he's seeing dollar signs." She let out a sigh and glanced at Paul. I suspected she'd agreed not to say that to me in their premeal planning and she'd thrown an audible. "And even if not dollar signs, it looked a lot like you were far more into this than he was, and I don't want you to get hurt."

I popped a crouton in my mouth to avoid having to respond right away. Because what could I say? "Mom, you saw us before we practiced intimacy, and trust me, he was into it way before the money"? I'd never in my life until that moment considered telling Mom about good sex I'd had, but if knowing Kieran's prior enthusiasm would stop her from going down this rabbit hole . . . If she wasn't still studying my face, I might have laughed at the idea, but I was saved by the doorbell. "I'll get it!" Scampering would have had more dignity than faking left to dodge my mom before sprinting to the front door, but in a fight between elegance and escape, I chose escape. If it was Grace, she'd help me run interference. That was the only reason I'd agreed to bring Kieran in the first place—my sister would be a buffer between Mom's questions and me. If it wasn't her at the door, it would be Kieran, and my stomach fluttered at the thought of seeing him, something I tried to deny, even to myself, because we had a plan. I clipped the edge of an end table on my sprint to the door, gripping my thigh with one hand and mumbling "Shit, shit, shit" before throwing open the door.

It wasn't Kieran smiling back at me, nor was it my sister, ready to go into battle for me.

"Where's Grace?" I looked around Warren to see if she was traipsing up from the car—unlikely, since they were the hand-holding, "where you go, I go" kind of couple, but a girl could hope.

"She got pulled into an emergency procedure for one of her patients." Warren held up a bottle of wine and stepped inside, giving me a side hug. "She'll get here soon."

"Warren!" Mom hurried in behind me, taking a little more time, thus circumventing the end table. She wrapped two arms around him as if he'd been away at war, and Paul sauntered in to shake hands with him in a very familiar and, I thought, old-school manly way. "Come in. Come in."

I looked out the open door helplessly. No Grace meant no buffer. No Kieran meant I had no distraction.

"Have you met Sybil's friend? Because she's keeping something from us about him."

"I am not," I said.

Warren looked between us and gave me a kind Warren smile that I'd normally appreciate. "Haven't met him yet, but he's coming today, right?"

"Supposedly," Mom said, giving me a raised eyebrow and looking at her watch. "But he's not here yet, and it's already almost five."

I looked at the clock above the fireplace. "Mom, it's four thirty-five."

Warren laughed. "Gotta agree. Give him a chance, Mary."

Paul chuckled. "Let it go, dear."

Warren gave me a reassuring smile, and for a moment I thought she'd drop it and we'd have a nice dinner, but my luck wasn't that good. "I'm sure he's a nice guy," Warren said as the doorbell rang again. "Grace said he'll be going back to medical school soon, right? Will you move with him?"

This was why I needed Grace. Sweet, trusting Warren didn't realize that question was an entire jar of pythons set free in Mom's brain. "Oh, I don't know," I said, trying to remember what I'd told Grace the last time we talked. The lies were catching up with me. "I really like him, so maybe."

"You *are* moving in together?" To call Mom's voice a screech would be kind, and since my hand was on the door handle, Kieran's finger was still hovering over the bell when I opened it.

"Hi," he said, holding up a tray of pastries. He glanced over my shoulder at the scene—Paul's magazine held in front of him, Mom's mouth wide, and Warren's smile dissipating based on her reaction.

"Let's talk out here for a minute," I said, pushing him backward onto the porch, underneath the glow of the porch lights in the cloudy weather. The door slammed behind me, blocking out my family.

"What's . . ."

I held up my palms and whisper hissed, "There's no time." My mom was approaching the front door. "We're deeply in love and thinking about moving in together, okay? And we can't keep our hands off each other."

"Wait. What? I thought the plan was professional?"

"Things went a little . . . sideways today," I said in a hushed voice. "Just . . . please be madly in love with me?"

I heard the doorknob turn and stood on my tiptoes. "Can I kiss you?" I pressed my palms to his chest, my lips inches from his.

"I'm confused," he said, an adorable crease between his brows, but his hand rested at my waist.

"I'll explain later, but please?" I worried he'd refuse, because that was the logical thing to do and Kieran was a logical guy. We'd agreed to professional, and my mind began to spiral, because what if he didn't want to kiss me the way I imagined kissing him? My family would see it, and this whole thing would be for nothing.

"Syb—" my mom called from behind the partially closed door, but the end of her sentence was lost to me as Kieran's lips crashed into mine, his hand tightening at my waist, pulling me to him. The breeze swirled around us and grazed the back of my bare calves as Kieran's tongue stroked mine, the dual sensations heating me through my core. I'd hoped for one kiss, a single demonstration of his interest, but as I pulled back, he stole another, his grip around my middle firm and unyielding as he demanded another taste from my lips. Kieran had never demanded anything from me, and my whole body tingled with the pull to give him everything he asked for.

"Ahem," Mom said from behind us. "It's nice to see you again, Kieran."

Kieran broke the kiss and took a step to the side. "Sorry, she's just so . . ." He looked at me, voice flustered and his expression somewhat dazed. "So irresistible."

"I'm sure." Mom held out her hand, shaking his briskly, like he was there to sell her encyclopedias. "Please come in if you're done making out with my daughter in front of the neighbors." She turned on her heel, walking back into the living room.

Kieran gave me a wide-eyed WTF stare, but I couldn't explain with the door wide open. "Thank you. And I'll explain later," I whispered, taking his hand. I was trying to school my own dazed expression. I'd kissed Kieran before, I'd even kissed him when we were faking it before, but this time felt as dizzying as the first two, and maybe even more so. "And thank you, Hannah Carson," I added under my breath. I didn't plan for Kieran to hear that, but he squeezed my hand, and the corner of his lips turned up before he winked at me. We were in sync tonight. We were a real team.

"Kieran," Paul said, setting his magazine aside and greeting him. "Despite what my wife probably implied, we're glad you're joining us."

"Thank you." Kieran shot me another look of uncertainty. "I brought these," he said, handing over the plate, and I noticed the chocolate-dipped donut holes I loved, plus the ones filled with lemon and blueberries. "They're one of Sybil's favorites, so I thought everyone might like some."

"Well, isn't that nice. Mary? Isn't that nice?" God bless Paul, who was taking over for Grace in her absence.

Mom was unimpressed, but I knew she'd change her tune when she tried one, something I was about to mention when she gave Kieran a laser-like stare. "Are you scamming my daughter?" Her arms remained crossed over her chest. "Because you're not getting her money, no matter how taken in she is by you or how kind your grandfather seems."

"Mom!"

Warren still sat on the couch like a fish out of water with our family. He motioned to his phone. "I . . . better check in with the office and make sure Grace doesn't need another set of hands," he said.

"C'mon, son. You can call from the kitchen," Paul said, nodding to the doorway. He called over his shoulder, "If you survive this inquisition, you're welcome to join us, Kieran."

So much for my Grace substitution. "Mom, you're being rude," I said again.

"I'm not being rude. I'm protecting you." She cut her gaze to Kieran again. "So, tell the truth. What kind of scam are you running?"

I opened my mouth to protest again. Kieran didn't deserve this, and I wanted to just get him out of there, but he spoke first. "If I was in your shoes, I wouldn't trust me, either. I mean, everything between us happened when your daughter won the lottery."

Mom nodded, letting him continue.

"But Sybil is smart. She's an excellent judge of people."

Carl's dick pic might have weakened his argument, but for once I kept my mouth shut.

"And she trusts me." His fingers linked with mine, and he raised them to his lips to drop a soft, sweet kiss on my knuckles. "I'm falling in love with your daughter. I'm falling in love with her more and more every day, and I don't want her money or anything other than to make her smile and to get to be next to her when she does something truly amazing." He looked into my eyes, and my knees felt weak. "Because I know she will."

My heart jumped into my chest, and I'd never wanted a lie to be true so much in my life. Kieran's fingers were in mine, and even when he looked back at my mom, I felt the heat of his stare on my cheeks and all down my neck. He'd said he was in love with me, and the words sounded so good, but they weren't real. I knew I couldn't trust my reaction.

My mom's stance relaxed incrementally, but she said, "I think she will, too."

"Well, that's one thing we agree on, Mrs. Waters," Kieran said, holding out his hand for her to shake.

"Mary," she finally said, still keeping him at a distance. "But one nice speech doesn't mean you're good enough for my daughter."

"Mom!" Mortification didn't even begin to describe this situation.

"It doesn't," Kieran said, unflapped. "But what I feel for your daughter can't fit in a single speech. She's so full of life and energy and creativity . . ." He glanced at me, the emotion in his eyes so convincing, even I believed it. "So maybe you'll think me more worthy after a couple more hours of assessment."

Despite his use of the word "assessment" and glowing critique of her daughter, she didn't seem convinced yet.

Things were still tense, but Paul's voice floating in from the kitchen broke the verbal stalemate. "My God! Mary, try these." He walked in, holding out one of the donut holes Kieran had brought.

"I don't think—" Mom protested, but Paul pushed it into her hand anyway.

"Trust me."

She reluctantly took a bite, and I saw it, that tiny crack in her facade when she realized how good they were, when her defenses melted.

Paul clapped Kieran on the back. "She's actually a hopeless romantic. Don't let her scare you off."

"No, sir. I won't," Kieran said, giving me a quick glance before following Paul into the kitchen.

"Sorry I'm late!" Grace pushed through the door, still in her dark blue scrubs. She pulled me into a quick hug, and then Mom. "What did I miss? Is Sybil's boyfriend still standing?" She gave me a wink and, God, I loved my sister. "Mom get him in the interrogation room yet?"

"She tried her best to run him off, but he's in the kitchen with Paul and Warren."

Mom took another bite of the donut. "Well, he *seems* like a nice boy," she said, brushing crumbs from her hands before walking toward the kitchen. "And any man who sees how great you are, well . . ." She studied her hand for any more offending crumbs. "He's worth giving a chance, I suppose."

Grace gave me a wide-eyed stare behind Mom's back. "Is that the most support she's ever given a guy you brought home?"

"He seems like a nice boy." I parroted Mom's words, and Grace giggled, lowering her voice.

"Um, girl, that's a nice *man*. Why didn't you tell me he looked like that?" She took my elbow, and we went after Mom into the kitchen, following the sounds of Paul's laughter and the scent of roasting garlic. This was working just like I had hoped.

28

Kieran

So then," Paul said, after taking a sip of his wine, "we find Sybil in line for the butter cow, because she wanted to see it again to decide if she could make one with the butter that was at home." He laughed, finishing the story of how he and Mary had met while looking for a lost ten-year-old Sybil, who'd wandered off at the Iowa State Fair.

"I was out of my mind with worry," Mary said, placing her palm on Paul's arm. "But there she was, safe and sound."

"And she only grounded me for two weeks," Sybil said, holding up her wine. "Banned me from touching the butter in the fridge."

"I thought the punishment fit the crime," her mom said, but the smile on her face was good-natured, and she seemed to be warming to me. "But we were lucky Paul was there to help look, and that's how we met."

Grace sat across from me and seemed to have Sybil's same

kindness and warmth but without the sometimes frenetic energy. I liked her. I liked the whole family, and Sybil's worry that she was the outcast seemed unfounded to me. "We're all lucky in love, I guess." Grace dropped a hand on Warren's knee under the table, and his arm draped around her chair. I studied their movements with a quick glance before draping my own arm across the back of Sybil's chair, my fingertips grazing her shoulder.

"We are," Sybil said, and she glanced up at me. "But I'm sad I never got to replicate the butter cow." It was odd, but I had no trouble picturing Sybil with stacks of butter attempting to sculpt an animal out of them. Even weirder, I could imagine helping her with it.

"You could make a donut cow," Paul offered. "Is she allowed into the kitchen yet, Kieran?"

"Watch out if she is," her mom said. "She set our microwave on fire last year." She looked at the appliance. "Forgot to add water to a microwavable rice bowl, and poof!"

Sybil stiffened against my fingers, making me want to stroke her skin again until she relaxed.

"I just misread the directions," she said, and I saw the color rise on her cheeks. "The microwave survived." She smiled, but it didn't reach her eyes.

"And that time she mixed up salt and sugar when making those cookies you sent Grace when she was in dental school?" Sybil's mom and Paul laughed, and it took a moment, but Grace covered her mouth to stifle a giggle.

"It's not my fault the salt and sugar are stored in containers that look exactly the same," Sybil defended herself. "Don't listen to them," she said, that same not-quite-real smile on her lips. "I will not burn down your kitchen." I thought of the way

I'd gotten annoyed that first day she'd helped in the shop, and felt guilty. I knew Sybil well enough to see this was the moment when she saw herself as the other in her family, like the joke.

I didn't like the way her expression dimmed with their teasing, and I remembered her asking me to pretend we were in love on the porch, before that kiss. It was my job to stand up for her, but the urge to defend her was real. "I trust you in my kitchen," I said, pulling her toward me and dropping a kiss on her forehead. She smelled sweet, and I squeezed her shoulder, taking in the way her body lined up against mine. "Sybil's been a huge help at the shop. The customers love her and she's had some great ideas. She actually designed an entire catering outreach campaign to local businesses and researched implementation strategies, and the response has been amazing."

"That's wonderful," Paul said. "Getting a real jump on things. But have you figured out what you want to do next? I mean, when Kieran goes back to school, you'll probably do something else, right?"

An uncomfortable knot formed in my stomach. All I'd been trying to do was return to school, but if I imagined the shop without Sybil in it, without me in it, even though it had functioned that way for years, it still felt wrong somehow.

"Not sure yet," Sybil said, squirming away from me and the question. "Oh! I brought some things for everyone!" She tossed her napkin on the table and jogged to the other room, leaving her family staring at me.

"When do you plan to go back to school, Kieran?" Sybil's mom took a delicate bite from her plate. "Sybil mentioned she was thinking of possibly going with you, but I would hope that would be a ways off."

I hoped for my girl, my fake girl, to rush back in at that moment with one of her off-the-cuff tales, but I heard her moving in the other room. "Um, the fall, I hope. They don't usually allow people to step out like I did, so trying to get back as fast as I can." As to part two, Sybil's idea that we'd considered her coming with me, I had no idea what to say. "Details are still . . . up in the air."

Sybil's mom and sister opened their mouths to speak, no doubt to ask for more information on my BS response, but that's when Sybil breezed back in, her hands full of gift bags she began passing out. "I brought presents!" She stretched in front of me to hand her mom and sister matching brown bags with the logo of a local jewelry store on them. Her breast grazed my hand resting on the table as she leaned away. "Sorry," she mouthed.

"What's this?" Her mom held up the bag, inspecting it.

Sybil brightened. "Open it!" She pulled two green boxes from another bag and handed one each to Paul and Warren. "What good is winning the lottery if you can't surprise your family?" She settled back in her chair and looked from person to person, all of whom were inspecting the gifts at the table. "I was going to wait until after dinner, but I'm so excited!"

"Well, thank you," Paul said, breaking the silence, opening the box in front of him, and holding up a watch that, based on my limited understanding of fashion, looked expensive. "Oh, wow," he said as he studied the timepiece, the gold accents on it catching the light.

"My friend Emi knows everything there is to know about watches, and she recommended that one," Sybil said, leaning forward, forearms on the table. "And, Warren, yours is water resistant. I thought it could be good for the triathlon."

"Thanks, Sybil," he said, taking it from the box. A smile spread on his face. "They were just talking about this one on a training podcast I listen to. It's one of the best brands you can get."

"That's so generous, honey," her mom said, thumbing the ribbon on the bag in her hands. "I hope you didn't spend too much on us." Her voice was careful, and she pulled a jewelry box from the bag, clicking it open and inhaling sharply.

"I thought it looked like the one of Janice's that you like, only bigger." Sybil bounced in her seat despite the quiet around the table.

Her mom turned the box to show everyone else. "It's a diamond bracelet."

"That's definitely bigger than Janice's," Paul said with an awkward chuckle. "I'm fairly certain Janice's is plastic, too."

"Grace, yours has sapphires. It could maybe be your something blue."

Grace was just opening the box when her mom gasped again, but this time while holding a receipt. "Sybil, this is too much!"

"I didn't mean to leave that in there." Sybil made a grab for the paper, but her mom held it to her chest.

"I know you won lots of money, but you have to be smart about it. I don't need a fifteen-thousand-dollar bracelet." She said the last part low, as if the media might be listening from outside the window. "This is too much, honey."

"I wanted to do it," Sybil said. I noticed her bouncing energy had dissipated, and she sank into the chair at her mom's admonishment. "And I can afford it."

"I know, but money is finite, and you have to make good choices." The diamonds caught the overhead light and cast what looked like prism-colored raindrops across her face and splashed up onto the wall. "You know you have a long history of making bad choices with money."

Sybil's shoulders slumped, and she nodded along with her mom's words. I noticed the same fake smile begin to curve her lips. The one that didn't make the skin around her eyes crinkle. "She's been thinking about philanthropy and supporting needs in the community," I said, wanting to offset this narrative that was pulling her down. She'd mentioned donating a few times over the last few weeks since we'd stopped into the shelter. "Tell them about it, Syb," I said, resting a palm on the middle on her upper back.

At my use of her nickname, she shot me a quick glance, and I squeezed the back of her neck gently, feeling like I was letting her down if I couldn't change the flow of this conversation.

"Now, that's really great," Grace said. "There are so many people to help. So many good causes."

Sybil bit back a grin, but it was a real one this time, and every muscle in my body pulled me to kiss that bottom lip, where her teeth rested. "Yeah, Kieran helps with a shelter near the shop, and it got me thinking about food and housing insecurity, and I think I want to make a difference if I can." She started talking about reading she'd been doing on the issues locally and nationally, citing studies and sharing statistics, and I had no idea she'd been gathering that much information. "So I've been talking with some people about it."

Her mom beamed, and I knew it was the right way to interrupt the conversation, which quickly turned to causes everyone believed in or volunteered with, and it was like Sybil blossomed right there at the table, sharing all the ideas she had, ones I'd had no idea about. She'd gone ten steps beyond writing a check in her mind, and I didn't know her family, but they seemed proud and excited. I realized I was grinning, too. I was proud of her and indulged every excuse I found to touch her—to squeeze her neck again or wrap my arm around her shoulder to show I was cheering her on.

"Well," her mom said as I helped her clear the table and followed her into the kitchen. "This is all still fast, but you might just be a great influence on her."

I heard Sybil laugh from the other room, a loud, free sound I recognized as the laugh she had when something struck her as truly funny, and I could picture exactly how she must look. "I think it's the other way around, ma'am. She's the best person to come into my life, maybe ever," I replied, and though I might have thought to say that while pretending, I said it because I meant it.

29

Sybil

MY HERO," I SAID ONCE WE CLIMBED INTO HIS truck. "You saved me from a lecture about proper car maintenance. I kind of let mine run low on gas." It had sputtered into the driveway on my way over, and I figured I could fill it from a gas canister once no one was home. I ran my finger along the dashboard of Kieran's truck—it was spotless, not even a speck of dust. "So thank you for rescuing me."

"Part of the job, right? Fake boyfriend and all." He did that thing that was so inexplicably sexy as he backed out of the driveway, putting his hand on my headrest and looking over his shoulder, his body precious inches closer to mine.

"No." I dragged my finger down the pattern on his shirt while I had the chance, and it drew his eyes to me. "That would mean you were pretending to save me. You actually do it."

"I guess I'm a sucker for a smile." His gaze flicked to my lips, just for a moment, and my face heated before he finished backing out and put the car in gear. Heat rose in my body at the attention. And I smiled. Could anyone hear a compliment about their smile and not immediately grin? I couldn't.

"So, I could get you to do just about anything, huh?"

He chuckled, the sound low in his throat. "What did you have in mind?"

"Well," I said, looking around. "Do you have to get back to the shop?"

"No." He slowed as we neared a stop sign on the corner, easing the car to a careful and full stop. "Chad is closing."

I chuckled. "Are you expecting to walk into chaos tomorrow?"

Kieran's laugh was easy and filled the car. "Probably, but I didn't want to have to abandon you if things with your family went long."

"See," I said, settling back in my seat. "My hero." We pulled to a red light, and I noticed the way Kieran tapped his fingers on the gearshift. There was a pattern where he tapped each finger in order and then just the middle three. He had long fingers and neat nails, and I had a flash of how he'd stroked the back of my neck during dinner, giving encouragement, and how they'd felt sliding into me in the cramped back office of the donut shop. The latter had me squirming in my seat and reminding myself he'd been acting at dinner, and the first night had been something different. Still, I settled my fingers over the top of his. "Nervous habit?"

He looked at my fingers on his, confusion coloring his face. "I'm not nervous," he said, but he tensed when I slid my fingertips along his. "Should I be nervous? Did you have something in mind you wanted to do?"

"I have one thing we could do," I said, fiddling with my necklace and sliding the pendant back and forth on the chain.

He nodded and scanned the road before dragging his gaze to mine. "Sure." The single word hit me like a full monologue, and I bounced in my seat with surprise. "I'm not ready to go home yet." His watch caught the light of the streetlamp when he rested his forearm on the steering wheel at the intersection.

"Yay!" I clapped and earned a laugh from him. "I have this silly tradition. My dad and I used to throw a coin in the river from the bridge by the amphitheater when things went well, kind of like a reward for having such good luck, and today was such a good day." I nibbled my lower lip, thinking about those trips with my dad when he was still around. He'd lift me up so I could rest my elbows on the concrete ledge overlooking the water and the city lights beyond. He'd whisper in my ear, "Make a wish for one more good thing," and I'd squeeze my eyes shut to think of what I wanted most.

"You want me to take you?" His gaze moved from my fingers to my face and paused, his dark eyes on mine.

"Well, yeah. The good day was because of you. We both deserve rewards." I dragged my index finger along his pinky, and he curled it against mine. "If that's okay."

"Of course," he said. Kieran's expression softened sometimes when he put all his attention on me—the full weight of his focus always seemed soothing, like I was in a warm bath. I had that feeling now, until a long honk from the car behind us broke the spell and Kieran's gaze whipped to the road and the green light in front of us. He hit the gas, flustered and raising a hand of apology to the person behind us.

"How can I make fun of your overly careful driving if you're getting honked at?" I teased my fingers over his knee. "What happened to our deal?"

"You're rubbing off on me."

I opened my mouth, but his laugh stopped me from jumping in with the joke. He was still chuckling when he said, "There should be some coins in the center console for meters." His attention was back on the road as we merged onto the interstate toward downtown. I looked out the window and toyed with my own fingers until he spoke. "Were you happy with how things went with your family?"

"They really liked you," I said. My mom had pulled me aside to tell me she thought he was a good influence. "And thanks for saying what you did."

"It's true," he said, catching my eye for a moment when he looked around me to merge into the other lane. "Can I ask, have you ever told them it bothers you when they tell those stories of you messing something up?"

"How did you know?" I looked out the window at a passing semi. "It's just how they are. I try not to let it bother me."

He gave a "hm" and flipped his blinker for the exit. "It seemed like it made you sad. Your expression dimmed each time it happened."

I thought about it, the stories they loved to tell. They were usually funny, and I'd laugh with everyone else, but I'd struggled to find the humor in Paul's story about meeting my mom while searching for me at the state fair, or any of the others. "I don't usually mind, but yeah, the best stories in the family are about me fucking something up." I hadn't been sad, though; I'd been embarrassed hearing story after story. I thought having him next to me might inspire them to tell different stories, but once they started, I'd kept stealing glances at Kieran to see if he was laughing, too. And he never was.

"The stories weren't *that* good," he said dismissively as we cruised toward the river. Traffic was still light, and he passed people on their way to restaurants or clubs. "I'd share different stories." He paused to wait for a car to pull out. The tick-tick-tick of his blinker filled the silence.

"What stories would you share?" I crossed my arms over my chest, angling my body in the car toward him as we waited for the spot to open. "How I sort of robbed you the day we met? How I spilled pink icing all over your kitchen? It looked like a Tarantino film took place in the Barbie Dreamhouse. Which, okay, is kind of funny."

He huffed, and I braced for him to agree. "That teenager who sits out on the corner every weekend because they don't want to go home to their transphobic family. You've taken them donuts and slipped them cash when you've visited with them the last few weeks. They came in the other day looking for you to tell you they got into college and to thank you for encouraging them." He wasn't looking at me; his focus was on parallel parking, angling his body to check the mirrors and cranking the steering wheel at the right moment. "I'd tell that story."

"Alex," I said. "Their name is Alex."

Kieran nodded. "Or how you ask Tom about his grandkids, and he lights up because you listen and ask questions and want to see photos when he's done." Kieran put the car in park and cut the engine. The car dinged when he opened his door, and the interior light flicked on. "And I might tell the pink frosting story, but only because it starts with you helping out my family's business, and I like remembering your face sprinkled with pink frosting. You looked surprised and kind of . . . adorable."

"I didn't know you were paying attention when I did those things," I said.

"I was." He darted his eyes to me, lingering on my face for a moment before looking away. "I always pay attention to you."

I waited for him to say more, but he pressed his lips together, the next sentence contained before he stepped into the street. Kieran's door closed behind him, and he left me in the car, dumbfounded and watching him walk around to my side as if he hadn't just bowled me over with his observations. I hadn't even undone my seat belt yet, and the night sky reflected off the water beyond the edge of the bridge. I had no idea Kieran had been paying attention when I'd done those things, the frosting excluded, and knowing he had should have been creepy, but instead I felt noticed. I felt seen.

He knocked on the window, and I jerked my head to the side to take in his face. "Are you going to make your wish from in the car?"

The night air was cooler than I expected, since this March had been on the warm side, and I leaned against the concrete railing after he pulled me from my dazed state. The sound of cars moving through downtown and the hum of voices filled the space around us, and I looked at the water.

"What's your wish?" He stood next to me, hands in his pockets. "Or is this a don't-tell-or-it-won't-come-true situation?"

I grinned and toyed with the coin in my hand. "Every wish is a don't-tell-or-it-won't-come-true situation. Are you new?"

Kieran chuckled and joined me in leaning on the ledge, his forearms making a V and his hands clasped. "That's a universal rule?"

"Absolutely," I said, clutching the coin. Kieran smelled like sandalwood, and I wondered if I had any more luck in my future or if I'd used it up with one big lottery win. Him charming the pants off my family, more than I could have hoped for, was certainly a bonus, and it was greedy to want more, but I did. I looked over my shoulder. "So don't ask me what I'm hoping will come true."

I examined the coin—a nickel I'd taken from Kieran's car console—and raised my arm to throw it into the river, but before I could launch it, a gust of wind kicked up, and I shivered. The thin material of my dress was a poor choice for early spring, and the bottom began to lift up. I dropped my hand to keep my skirt down, but Kieran was already there, his body pressed behind mine and his palms moving up and down my bare biceps. He wasn't grinding against me, but the wall of him behind me felt like being caged in the best possible way. "There goes that rescuing behavior again."

"You were about to flash Locust Street." He let a hand fall down the side of my skirt, the warmth of his skin coming through the fabric as he settled it back to his hip.

"It wouldn't be the first time." I leaned back, wanting him closer behind me, and pictured him rolling his eyes in the way he did when he wanted me to think he was annoyed, but the corner of his mouth would twitch and give the hint of a smile. "Or even the third time, really."

"You looked cold," he said, continuing his movements up and down my arm even though the wind had died down. I was the opposite of cold with his body pressed to mine. I felt like a match was struck deep in me and the warmth was working its way toward my skin. "It's supposed to rain tonight," he added. "Figure out your wish yet?"

"You want me to hurry up so we can go?"

"No." Kieran's hands still slid up and down my arm. "I don't need to be anywhere else."

The only way Kieran and I would work for real was divine intervention. We were too different. I was too chaotic and he too ordered; I had nowhere to be, and he had plans to get back to medical school, and without $300,000 on the line, none of this would be happening anyway. I flicked the coin into the river below because sometimes magic happened. It wouldn't hurt to wish.

"Are you going to make one?" I pulled the second coin from my pocket and held it, palm out, for him to grab.

"I don't make wishes." He wrapped his fingers around mine and closed them around the coin. "I stopped doing that a long time ago."

"That's sad." I opened my palm again. "Why did you stop?"

I figured he'd back away—it was what usually happened when I pushed—but he seemed to shift closer, and while one hand dropped to flatten my skirt against the wind again, his other slid to the ledge next to mine. "I learned young that good things don't just happen to me, and when they do, they don't last. Better not to hope." His voice wrapped around me the way his arms felt, steady. "For me," he added. "But I like that you make wishes and believe in lucky pennies."

I turned to face him, my back grazing the ledge and our bodies a few breaths apart. "I think something good is going to last for you soon." I reached for his jeans pocket and slid my fingertips inside to let the coin fall in. "I really do." I kept my hand at his waist as another gust of cold wind cut through the air. "When you get back to medical school, good things will start happening."

He sucked in a ragged breath at my mention of medical school, and his hand moved up my arm, over my shoulder, and then cupped the back of my head. Kieran's gaze was intense, and I could tell he wanted to say something, needed to say something. It could have been to tell me I was wrong or to share something about his hopes and dreams, but the heat behind his piercing gaze looked like something else. It looked like gusto and fervor and kisses under the night sky that went on forever, and I couldn't take the anticipation.

"Are you going to kiss me?"

His fingers shifted against my hair. "No one is watching."

"Someone might be," I said, tipping my chin up. "There are all kinds of voyeuristic people out this time of night."

He chuckled, but I noticed how his gaze fell to my mouth. "You should wish for fewer voyeurs, then." Kieran's fingers stroked along the nape of my neck.

"Good idea, but I already made my wish."

"Then you're right." His thumb slid along the shell of my ear. "Maybe someone is watching."

I swallowed, feeling my heartbeat throughout my body, the apex of my thighs pulsing. "Might be someone important. We should make it look good." The ledge was firm against my back as I settled my hand at his side, guiding him toward me.

Kieran's face lowered, and I let my eyes drift closed, but he didn't make contact with my lips. Instead, his kiss grazed my jaw, lips working over the sensitive skin where my neck and jaw met. Tingles radiated from the spot he'd kissed, and I let out a moan that was lost in the gust of wind. He'd heard it, though, and stepped closer, his thigh nestled between my legs, and he surrounded me on all sides. "Is this convincing them?"

I groaned as he kissed my neck, his hand still supporting my head, fingers tangled in my curls. It was impossible to feel his leg between mine and not shift against it. "Convincing who?"

He chuckled against my neck and pulled back to meet my gaze. "The strangers watching us." Kieran's gaze was heated, and he was hard against my stomach, which made my whole body hot despite the cold wind, but when he looked at me, it was almost playful. This was Kieran relaxed, and it looked so good on him. "The reason we're so . . . intertwined."

"I have a confession." I took the opportunity to lean forward, kissing the base of his neck and sliding my hand up his chest, over his pecs, and down. "I don't actually think anyone is watching."

"Probably not." He didn't step away from me. "But I liked this story."

"The story of us making out on the bridge?"

He dropped his lips to my neck again, finding the same spot that made my knees feel like jelly. "Is it making out if we haven't kissed yet?"

"Easy way to fix that," I murmured, tipping my head to the side to give him better access to my neck. I ran my fingers through his hair, savoring the softness of his strands. "Kiss me again," I said. "Just because you want to. Just for tonight."

He paused his movements, stilled completely for a minute, and I listened intently, trying to hear beyond my own beating heart to the sigh slowly escaping his lips.

"It doesn't have to mean anything," I added, grazing a finger along his hairline. I wasn't sure I could kiss Kieran here and have it mean nothing, but I knew I could hold on to that and keep it to myself like a little secret. "We could scratch an itch and lose control, just a little."

He dropped another peck on my jaw, but instead of moving to my lips, he stepped back, sliding his hand from my hair but still grazing two fingers along the hem of my skirt. "I really want to lose control with you, but I know too many good stories about you," he said, taking another step back, the distance between us allowing the wind to cut through the gap. "I think it's too late for meaningless and one night."

I opened my mouth to respond, but my words were drowned out by a crack of thunder that shook the ground and a lightning strike near enough that it lit the sky. I screeched as the rain began all at once, the downpour soaking our clothes and drowning out the words hanging in the air. We scurried toward his truck to get out of the rain, and by the time we were inside, all the reasons I'd planned to tell him he was my wish felt less clear in my head. He was going back to school in another state, and I was paying him to help make me look responsible to my family. It was working. Kisses in the rain didn't fit into that plan, no matter how hard I wished for them.

I looked out the window as he edged out of the tight parking spot. He was right—it was too late for meaningless. I didn't need the next story in my family's arsenal to be about how I fell for the guy I was paying to date me.

30

Kieran

THE PARKING GARAGE WAS PACKED, AND WE strolled from the spot we'd snagged on the top floor. The midday sun made it feel like spring, and Sybil unzipped her jacket to reveal her Joe's Donuts T-shirt. We'd gotten one made for her that actually fit, but I missed the way the first one hugged her body. "There will be a lot of people there in addition to my mom," she said, pointing to the Science Center of Iowa, where rivers of kids moved through the front door. "Think of it as guerilla marketing."

"When you said your mom wanted us to stop by her workplace, this is not what I imagined." I'd assumed we'd be dropping by some kind of corporate office, which hadn't made me more comfortable, but Sybil had asked, and it was harder and harder to tell her no, so here we were. "And I don't think that's what guerilla marketing is. I think it's just you liking how good you look in that T-shirt."

She was looking at me with an incredulous expression, the

one where her eyes narrowed slightly and that plump lower lip dropped open, without it being clear if what was coming next was going to be a laugh or a cutting remark. Without over-thinking it, I touched my fingertip to her lower lip, feeling the give. That was a mistake, because it only reminded me how much I'd wanted to kiss those lips that night on the bridge. How I'd replayed the moment in my head a hundred times. She'd melted when I kissed her neck, and I'd wanted nothing more than to stay there all night. Now, at my touch, she pulled that lip into her mouth, her front teeth sinking down, and then there was her smile, that grin that seemed to always make me second-guess everything. She giggled. "I do look good in this. My boobs are amazing." She held open the jacket and studied her own chest. "Even though you can't see my freckles."

"No comment," I said, gripping the door handle and look-ing the other way with an almost superhuman strength. "But I still know they're there."

"Such a horndog!" She laughed and swatted at my back.

"It is a weird place for a date, I'll admit," she said, motion-ing to the Science Center across the street as a stream of kids filed through the glass double doors. "Isn't it for kids?"

I shrugged, pulling my hand back to avoid reaching for her again. "I guess science is for everyone."

Sybil gave me a light laugh, the sound filling my car. "Mom wants us to see the new exhibit she's been working on," she said, reaching for her own door handle. "And we can get freeze-dried ice cream! When we did field trips here as a kid, I always remember getting some."

I stepped out of the car, too, our eyes meeting over the roof. "Anything for you, baby," I joked, letting my voice go deep in the way that always made her smile.

"It's a lot of families." Sybil leaned in close as we waited at the counter to pay for our admission. "Do you think anyone will recognize us here? It might be kind of nice if they didn't."

The scent of her perfume tickled my nose, and I lowered my lips to her ear. "Sybil Sweet is tired of attention?"

She chuckled, swatting at my stomach. "If you tell anyone, I'll deny it." She leaned against me, her body molding to mine. "It's just nice to not have to pretend in real time. Our last few selfies blew up." She'd taken one of us in the shop with Grand-dad between us. He'd taken credit for the popularity of the photo, going so far as to create an Instagram account so he could track the engagement and reply to comments. She'd also snapped one after we left the bridge, both of us soaking wet from the torrential rain, and it had been physically painful to stand close to her, her dress soaked and clinging to every curve, and not lose control again.

Really, this was the best possible location if we needed to be seen in public. No one would expect us to keep close contact in a place filled with so many screaming kids, and I'd meant what I said to Sybil on the bridge. I liked her too much to lose control for one night, and every time our hands brushed or I thought about kissing her, I wanted more. More that wasn't possible. So this place would be safe.

"So, you just want me for my selfie potential now?"

"You're twisting my words." She swatted me again, though this time I caught her hand. "I'm also using you for your truck." Her grin was playful and wide as she jumped out of my grip, laughing at her own joke.

I reached into my back pocket for my wallet as we neared the front. "Are you finally going to cave and buy a new car?"

"Kieran! I haven't seen you in years." Before Sybil could answer, we both whipped around to see a woman approaching with three small children in tow, one of them perched on her hip. "I thought that was you!"

It took a moment for my brain to place her, to go back to high school. "Erin," I said, stepping forward to greet my old friend. "Hi."

She brushed her hair off her face, blocking the toddler's grasping fingers a moment before they took hold of her glasses. "I haven't seen you in years, and now you're on the news. Wild. How are you?" Without her eyes leaving mine, she reached for the arm of a little girl, pulling her to her side.

"I'm good." I glanced from child to child and back to her. "You?"

"Busy!" The third kid, whose face looked like a map of chocolate bars, was reaching up for Sybil. "Percy, no!" Erin hurried past me to pick up the sticky child. "Sorry," she said.

"No problem. I thought he might know where the best chocolate was around here," Sybil said, giving the little boy a smile and then holding out her hand to shake Erin's. "I'm Sybil. You're Kieran's friend?"

She took a step closer to me, linking her arm around my waist. We were pretending after all, but she was doing a good impression of possessiveness.

"We went to high school together," I supplied, still marveling that Erin Akers had three kids. Because of our last names, we'd sat next to each other in every honors class for years, and the idea of dating her had been the only thing that came close to my laser focus on getting into college and medical school.

"And we were friends," she chided. "We volunteered

together with Pennsylvania Street Shelter. Gosh, it's been so long." The little girl tugged on her hand and said something about the dinosaurs.

"I took Sybil there with me to volunteer the other day. I still try to help when I can."

Erin smiled—she still had a pleasant smile, but there were none of the butterflies it had evoked when I was seventeen. "I never have time. We're those people who throw in money and not time now." She looked wistfully at her kids. "Long way away from my parents, huh?"

I nodded, remembering the long talks we'd shared about our families while getting to know each other, and I warmed under the collar of my polo. That had more to do with Sybil's inquisitive stare than memories of my high school crush on Erin.

"Anyway, it's great to see you. If I don't get these three inside soon, there will be a riot, but we could have coffee sometime and catch up?"

Sybil tensed next to me, and I placed my palm on her back. I wasn't even certain what I was reassuring her of, but it felt like the right response. "That would be nice. It was good to see you," I said, motioning for her to step up to the counter ahead of us.

"Nice to meet you, Sybil—you've really got a good one here!"

Sybil returned her smile, her arm still wrapped around my waist while Erin flashed a family pass and was dragged toward the dinosaur exhibit by her kids. "High school girlfriend?"

"I had a crush on her, but I was too scared to do anything about it." I chuckled, setting down my credit card before Sybil could pull out her phone. "I wasn't the bold flirt you know today."

Sybil's laugh bubbled from her, and she slid her hand in my back pocket, the move so familiar and her hand against my butt such a strange combination of playful and sexy. "You're not a bold flirt."

"I got you, didn't I?" I felt the absence of her hand when I tucked my wallet away again, and we walked past the front desk to head into the main atrium.

"You got lucky with me," she said, immediately sweeping her gaze around the exhibit entrances on the first floor and the swirling artwork on the second level above us.

"I know," I answered, letting my hand fall to hers. "Let's start upstairs. We're not meeting your mom for thirty minutes or so." Sybil's mom had shared about the reptiles and how you could sometimes feed a snapping turtle, which seemed like something Sybil would get a kick out of.

"What did she mean about your families?" Sybil and I walked up the stairs to the second level, dodging a stream of screeching kids in matching party hats zooming by us and a couple double-teaming a stroller.

That same familiar heat moved up my neck. "Neither of our parents were around. Hers did a lot of work with relief agencies around the world. That's what she meant by being different."

Sybil nodded, and we narrowly missed another line of kids on a mission as we reached the top of the stairs and walked toward the brightly lit exhibit filled with glass cases and information about prairies. "And your mom never came back? She's still using?"

I shook my head, and we walked along the pathway, pausing to admire the snakes. "She got clean and met a guy eventually." I tried to swallow the bitterness in the words. "As far as I know, she's still sober."

"She never tried to get you guys back, though?" She looked from where she'd been admiring a sleek black snake to me.

The snake in the case nearest us tilted its head, staring out at us before slowly slithering up the glass. "The guy she met had a lot of money and could give her the support and security she wanted," I said. "But he didn't want kids, so she made her choice."

Sybil was quiet for a few beats, and then her fingers linked with mine. "She made the wrong choice, for what it's worth."

"I'm sure it's complicated," I said, unsure why I was defending my mom and her life in Colorado, or wherever they'd moved since the last time I'd heard from her.

"I'm sure it is, but I don't care about her. I care about you. Do you ever hear from her?"

I tugged her along toward the turtles in the habitats along the wall. "Once in a while. She sent a card when Lila finished high school and flowers when Granddad was in the hospital." It had been a ridiculously large arrangement, the white roses and lilies extending out over the edge of the heavy vase. A reminder of how well she was doing, how much money had probably changed things for her. I'd thrown the arrangement in the dumpster behind the shop, a flurry of white rose petals falling to the ground in the alley. "It's fine. It's in the past."

We listened to the guide talk about the turtle's feeding rituals and how they cared for it. I hadn't wanted to talk more about my mom leaving. Lila was curious sometimes, but I wasn't interested in paying attention enough to be disappointed again. My mom had chosen money and security over us, and that was how I'd filed her away in my mind. Sybil grinned at the turtle nearing her fingers resting against the glass, her face lit with the midday sun streaming in from the floor-to-ceiling windows in the exhibit. Sybil had more money than she knew what to do with, and she wasn't running. Sybil wasn't a parent or an addict and everything was different, but it felt like with all this wealth, she'd still chosen me, and I kept a hold of her hand as we moved into another room of exhibits.

"Hey." I felt a tug on my pants and looked down at Erin's son looking back at me. "You're my mom's friend. How does this work?" He pointed at a model of the human circulatory system nearby, and I crouched to get on his level. I saw Erin not far away, showing her youngest something on the wall, and looked back to the little boy. The model showed a network of blood vessels leading to a clear acrylic heart. "Well," I said, "this is how the blood moves inside our body. Pull that lever at the top"—I motioned to the device—"and you can see the blood flow." The kid very carefully pulled the lever and watched the liquid move through the vessels with wonder, his eyes widening. "Wow! Where's the machine to show how we poop?"

I coughed into my hand, my gaze flicking up to Sybil, who was covering her own giggle, though she wasn't alone. Her mom was standing next to her and watching me. "You know, I don't think they have anything to show that," I said, rising to my feet.

"That's okay," he said, holding out a palm for a high five. "I'll just look at my own the next time I go!" He ran away toward his mom, and I chuckled.

"You're good with kids." Sybil's mom wore a dinosaur hat and held a clipboard. "It's nuts today, but I want to show you two the new exhibit," she said, holding up a pen that looked like a leg bone.

Sybil inched closer to me, and I wrapped an arm around her waist. She'd said of everyone in her family, her mom would be the hardest to convince, and while touching Sybil felt beyond natural now, I was careful not to pull her too close or take the opportunity to steal a kiss. Instead, I pointed to her mom's pen. "Is that a model of the *Supersaurus*'s hind leg?"

Sybil's mom beamed. "You did your homework! Yes, it is." She gave me a rundown on the high points of the exhibit, and it was interesting, thinking about how kids learn scope and context for creatures they've never seen. "I have to show a group around, but can you come down in twenty minutes?" She grinned widely, and I saw the resemblance between Sybil and her mom. The suspicious, protective mother seemed to have faded, and she pulled me in for a hug, too. "It's a treat to get to show off my work to my kids," she said, hugging Sybil again. It was the first time I'd seen Sybil's energy and giddiness reflected in someone else in her family. She was convinced she was vastly different from them all, and I wondered if she saw it, too. I heard her mom whisper something in Sybil's ear before heading for the stairs. "Twenty minutes," she called from across the room.

"I'd say she's warmed up to you," Sybil said. "You even got a hug."

"That was unexpected. She seems excited. Kind of reminds me of you. What did she whisper to you?"

Sybil shrugged, but I saw the hint of a grin on her lips.

"And I'm begging you not to make a bone joke. Especially not a joke about your mom holding a bone."

"Give me a little more credit than that." She nudged my arm with her shoulder. "I won't make a bone joke until I see the *Supersaurus*." She lowered her voice and linked her arm with mine. "You know, when I can test if my fingers will wrap around the bone like my mom's did."

I pointed toward the IMAX theater to the left, where a sign announced the next show would be starting in a few minutes. "She actually whispered that she was wrong, and you really seem like a good one," she said as we walked into the darkened auditorium.

I felt an unexpected pride in having won over her mom. More than that, the feeling of wanting more, of wanting excuses to keep showing her family how good we were together, and how great Sybil was in general. "Your plan is working," I said, motioning for her to walk ahead of me, but she stopped abruptly and reached back to grab my hand.

Soon we found spots on the second level, spreading out on the floor to watch the show above us. "Any reason you needed my hand so suddenly?"

Sybil settled against me as we stretched out on the floor. "Your high school girlfriend was waving at us from over there," she said, flashing a smile at Erin. Sybil was right, and I gave Erin a wave. I guess we were back to pretending, though I didn't mind, because this particular pretending felt a little like Sybil being jealous. Erin didn't have a phone pointed at us and had already refocused on wrangling her kids.

"Okay." I squeezed Sybil's fingers as the announcer welcomed us to the presentation on black holes.

"You know," she said quietly, "speaking of holes . . ."

"You're better than that," I turned my head to whisper, and my lips grazed the shell of her ear. The lights lowered as the presentation began, the narration playing over the swirling vortex of space above us. "Pay attention to the stars." I ran my thumb along the edge of hers, and the way her breath hitched left my body with a reaction completely inappropriate for an explanation of astrophysics.

"I like the stars," she said, resting her head against my shoulder, the curls tickling my chin.

"Me, too," I murmured, inhaling and trying to memorize every moment we were sharing. In the dark, we weren't pretending, not even with ourselves, and I could feel my hold on control slipping, because I hadn't thought about getting back to school all day.

I leaned closer and whispered in her ear, "Do you mind no one recognized us? I mean, besides Erin?" I made circles on her shoulder.

"No," she said, looking up at me in the darkened theater. "Means we get to try again another time. I'm not sure I've ever spent this much time with a man without things getting out of hand." She slid her thumb back along mine. "I like it."

I tipped my head back and followed the moving images above us. "Me, too."

31

Sybil

THANKS FOR COMING WITH ME," I SAID. **"I PROMISED** my mom I'd at least look at places." Ahead of us, the real estate agent in her sharp blue blazer smiled over her shoulder, her silver bob shifting but somehow staying exactly in place.

"No problem," Kieran said as Carol pointed out the light pouring through the massive windows in what she called a chef's kitchen. Marcus would love it, but the space felt overwhelming to me.

I glanced down at the handout Carol had shared with me when we'd entered the home. Glossy photos showed the five bedrooms, six baths, and manicured backyard featuring a pool and hot tub.

"Now, I know this is a little bigger than you wanted," Carol said, "but I have a feeling this is what you're really looking for. Just look at the marble countertops."

"I didn't know you were interested in places like this," Kieran said quietly when the agent's back was to us again. She motioned toward the entryway, signaling us to follow her, and I leaned toward him.

"I'm not. I asked to see small one- or two-bedroom houses."

"That chandelier is a Lonenklein." She pointing to the sparkling overhead light fixture, awaiting recognition from Kieran and me.

After a beat of silence, he put on the most canned show of enthusiasm I'd ever heard. "Oh, wow. Lonenklein."

Carol beamed, and I snorted into my hand when she motioned again for us to follow her, this time up the main staircase, the wrought iron banister a sharp contrast to the white walls and cream carpet. I mouthed "Wow?" and he shrugged. "You weren't saying anything," he whispered, and I giggled.

"Now, this is the main bedroom," she said with a sweeping gesture around the room, where an immaculately made four-poster bed sat as the centerpiece, and French doors led out to a balcony arranged with flowerpots. She didn't make mention of the artwork on the walls, which looked a lot like still shots from kind of mediocre porn. She glanced down at her phone and then back at us. "I need to take this call, but let me give you two a few minutes alone to imagine how you might fill this kind of space."

"Well," Kieran said, staring at a five-by-five canvas showing two men in ball gags and nothing else at the feet of a blonde in a sexy nurse costume. The framed art over the shoulder of the nurse looked a lot like something from a Holiday Inn. "Do you think these are Lonenklein, too?"

I stood close and joined him in the examination. "Definitely, from their Pornhub period."

Kieran laughed and reached for my hand as we slowly circled the room. He'd been holding my hand a lot since that day at the Science Center, even when we were alone, and I'd come to crave the feel of it. There was another painting of a tongue against the head of what appeared to be a flaccid penis dripping with hot pink paint. "Now, this one makes you think," he said, making me giggle again.

"Is this all really expensive art and we're just classless jerks?" I pointed to a framed photo of a really well-lit group scene where a redheaded woman enthusiastically tended to the very real-looking genitalia on several headless mannequins. "This is probably invaluable."

Kieran shrugged, and we both glanced toward the doorway at the sound of Carol's voice carrying down the hall. "Probably. I don't know anything about art. Maybe we should ask Carol if there's a way to buy the art along with the house."

I pressed my hand to my mouth to stifle the giggle, and Kieran pulled me toward him to muffle the sound, the closeness calming and comfortable. "This is the fifth place she's shown me that's way bigger than I'd want." I stepped into the en suite, where a claw-foot tub sat under a picture window overlooking the backyard. "She keeps saying she's sure this is what I really want. Do you think she knows something I don't?"

Kieran leaned an elbow against the door frame. "No. I think she's not listening to you." He pointed to the shelf behind me, where four dildos sat artfully among the white towels and bottles of essential oils. The largest was about the size of my forearm, with an American flag design on the silicone. I stepped closer to see the face of a bald eagle on the head. "If she really knew what you wanted, she'd never try to sell you a room decorated with an American flag dildo."

"Yeah. Canadian, maybe. It would be more gentle." I loved making Kieran crack up like he did. It sent my heart soaring to see him laugh in an unhinged, doubled-over way. "Hey, Emi texted that they're going out tonight. Want to come?"

He nodded, still pulling out of his laughter. "Sure, if you want me to." He gave me an assessing look, his head tipped to the side. "You look surprised. Why? Where are we going?"

"I thought I'd have to talk you into it is all." I slid past him back into the bedroom, enjoying the clean scent of his aftershave. "And it's a surprise."

"Sorry about that," Carol said, breezing back into the room. "What do we think?" She stood with a hopeful expression. "The seller has the place listed at two million, but I can get them down if we act quick."

Kieran squeezed my hand, and I shook my head. "No, I'm not interested." I gave the room one more glance. "I asked to see much smaller houses than what you've shown me. You don't seem to be listening to what I want, so I'll be working with someone else." I gave her a kind smile. "But it's a lovely home." I tugged on Kieran's hand, and we excused ourselves past Carol to head toward the front entrance.

TWO HOURS LATER, I sat between Kieran and Emi, laughing at one of Deacon's stories. Marcus and Lila had shown up together at the same time Kieran and I arrived. The table was filled with the remaining fries and the last mozzarella stick amid a lot of empty glasses. The bar was loud, and it was karaoke night, so everyone was extra boisterous in their cheers, jeers, and applause, and we regaled our table with the last house showing. "The patriotic dildo might have been a selling point if the house was what I wanted! I mean, I actually love that the owners really knew who they were and weren't hiding their sexuality."

"You should have seen her tell the real estate agent she wasn't listening to her," Kieran said casually. His arm was draped over the back of my chair, and he nursed a beer, his fingers sliding against my shoulder every so often, always sending a spark of anticipation through me.

"Good for you," Emi said, raising her glass.

"But now I have to find someone else," I said. "Or maybe just look for an apartment."

Emi nodded. "You have options, and our couch is yours as long as you want it." The waiter stopped by the table then and pulled Emi's attention away from us.

"You could have warned me about the karaoke," Kieran whispered in my ear. "I would have just dropped you off."

"That's why I didn't tell you," I said, angling my head toward him so our lips almost brushed. "And why I insisted you get a few drinks." I motioned to the beer, encouraging him to finish it. He'd finally agreed when Lila showed up and promised to get his car home.

His fingers grazed my shoulder again, and he paused with our gazes locked for a second before he gulped the last of his drink. "What should I sing?"

I smacked his chest harder than I meant to. "Shut up! You're going to get onstage?"

He grinned. Kieran Anderson actually grinned, his face shifting to a completely adorable, boyish look. "You already did," he said, referencing Emi's and my rendition of "Made You Look" by Meghan Trainor from earlier in the night. We brought down the house, of course.

"I know, but I never expected you to."

Lila threw a balled-up napkin across the table at her brother, and I took in the way Marcus's arm was behind her chair the way Kieran's had been on the back of mine. "I cannot believe this is happening."

Emi cheered, almost spilling her freshly delivered drink, and I felt so much love at this table. I worried Kieran would feel awkward with my friends, but he fit in so well, it was hard to believe we weren't a real couple, that we hadn't done this a hundred times. He'd only had a few beers, so I was pretty sure the alcohol wasn't the only reason, but Kieran was more relaxed than I'd ever seen him.

"Who is going up there with me?" he asked, looking to me and then to his sister, who shook her head vehemently. He looked back to me, widening his eyes and giving me a hangdog expression.

"There *is* a song Deacon and I usually do," I said.

"But I love that song," Deacon interrupted. "It's my jam."

"Deacon and Kieran duet!" Emi clapped and announced the pairing, giggling before she finished saying it, though everyone else joined in.

Deacon looked at Kieran, holding his palms up, and Kieran shrugged. "Why not?" He pushed back in his chair and followed Deacon toward the stage to my cheers, but he paused and doubled back to the table, dipping low and pressing his lips to mine to the cheers and whoops of our friends. "For luck," he said, pulling away from the kiss, seeming to ignore the dazed expression on my face. We were a little drunk and we were in public, so I tried not to read too much into the kiss, but the feel of it still lingered on my lips as he picked up my beer and finished it.

"Hey!" I cried.

"Don't worry," he said with a wink. "I'll leave you a note letting you know I took it."

He flashed me a quick smile as the callback to the day we met hit me. I pressed two fingers to my lips as he jogged toward the stage to meet Deacon, who pointed to the song they'd be singing.

Emi and Marcus laughed at his reaction along with me, and I scooted around the table to sit by Lila and get a better view of the stage. Kieran mouthed "You owe me" from the stage as the opening chords to "Let It Go" from *Frozen* began to play.

I grinned and watched him jostle with Deacon for who would sing which part, but when he opened his mouth and sang into the mic, I was shocked. Kieran's voice was smooth and clear, and I stared at him. "He's good," I said. "He's really good."

Lila leaned toward me, laughing as Deacon played his part as Elsa while Kieran sang. "He sang all through school and earned some music scholarships before he quit."

"But he gave it up?" I leaned nearer to Lila but didn't take my eyes off Kieran, whose expression changed as he sang. He still stood ramrod straight but looked at ease with the microphone. And he smiled in a way that looked so free, I couldn't help but smile back.

"I haven't seen him sing in front of anyone since our grandma died," Lila said. "It was their thing, and when she was gone, he decided other things mattered more."

Onstage, Deacon and Kieran had shifted from just singing to putting on a whole dramatization, and I cheered at their antics, blowing a kiss to Kieran, who pretended to catch it before launching into the final verse. His voice carried through the bar, and there was a bit of a hush until everyone burst into applause and Kieran and Deacon gave deep bows to the crowd before returning to the table, arms over each other's shoulders.

Kieran fell into the seat next to me and wrapped an arm around me, pulling me against him and nudging my ear with his nose. "That was fun." There was a thin sheen of sweat on his brow from his and Deacon's performance, and he dropped a kiss on my cheek before Deacon pulled his attention, though not his touch, away to plan their next song. I wondered how I was going to feel when he went back to school, when this whole thing was over and I didn't get his touches anymore. I couldn't imagine it, though. This just felt so right.

Lila took a drink from her beer and whispered, "I think he's starting to figure out what matters again."

32

Kieran

"TOLD YOU I WOULD BOUNCE BACK," GRANDDAD said, settling on the couch in our apartment. "Doc said I'm basically back to one hundred percent."

I handed him a glass of water I'd filled in the sink. "That's not what he said." What he'd said was that, with time and continued physical therapy, Granddad would likely make close to a full recovery.

He waved me off. "Close enough. I'm just ready to not need a babysitter on the stairs. How am I supposed to date like that?"

"I don't know," I said, thumbing through the mail on the counter. "Wouldn't that give you an excuse to hold on to your date?"

He scratched his jaw and then snapped his fingers. "Hot damn! You're right. You really did get the brains in the family." He laughed at his own joke, and I smiled to myself. It was great to hear him laughing and joking again. I wondered if he'd been laughing all along. I'd been so caught up in everything, I was figuring out now that there was a lot I wasn't paying attention to. It all seemed clearer now that I was spending so much of my time with Sybil.

"You know," Granddad said, "I do plan to take the shop back over. I'm not ready to retire."

He'd told me the plan over and over again, and sometimes I wasn't sure if he was reminding me or himself. I understood more than anyone how comforting it was to turn to a plan, a prescribed path, so I let him walk me through it again. "You'll go back to school. Lila will take one of the jobs she's been offered, and I'll run things for another five or six years."

I nodded. "And then sell it?"

That was the part he never landed on, and as usual, he tipped his head side to side and did his best to dodge the question. "Time will tell, my boy. Those real estate developers have been sniffing around for ages." He sipped his water, and I looked out of the corner of my eye to see if his hand shook, but it was steady. "I'll figure it out once you kids get back to your lives, though. I know it's been hard for you to hit pause on it all. Is everything taken care of for you to go back?"

I'd kept the details from him, sharing only the basics so he didn't worry. "Just about," I said. "A few loose ends to tie up." I owed Miles a call about the apartment, and the paperwork was on my desk with the phone number to call and commit to the next semester. I wasn't someone who put things off, but I hadn't called yet, and the deadline was approaching so soon; it was right after Sybil's sister's wedding.

"When you go back to Texas, will Sybil go with you?"

"Um, I don't know," I said, stacking the envelopes so that I could avoid eye contact. I hated lying to him, but there was no choice—he'd never accept the truth, but without the money, I couldn't save the shop. "It's still pretty new, and she's been busy getting ready for her sister's bachelorette weekend, which she's just returned from, so we haven't talked about it." I'd barely seen her over the previous week, but I'd get texts and photos of the projects she was working on. My favorite was of the group all in T-shirts with "Smile, This Dentist Is Getting Married!" printed across the front. She'd sent a follow-up message including all the options she'd suggested referencing fillings, cavities, and opening wide that had been vetoed. I'd even started to miss her horrible dirty jokes. "It's probably too soon to make big decisions like that for each other," I added.

"Ah, yes, but when you know, you know." He glanced at the photo of my grandma on the side table. "And I can spot a man in love with my eyes closed."

I was saved from responding by the knock on the door. I was expecting Tom when I swung it open, but Sybil was on our welcome mat, bouncing on her heels. "Lila said you were up here," she said, leaning in to kiss my cheek, the brush of her lips soft against my stubble and her hand pressed against my chest.

"We were just talking about you," Granddad said from the couch, opening his arms for a hug.

She dropped a peck on his cheek as well, and he winked at me over her shoulder. "I told you, Joe, I won't leave him for you. You'd be too much for me sexually."

"I don't know," he said. "I haven't kept up with advancements. I imagine some things have changed."

"Oh, there are great websites," she said, a grin across her face. "You can learn everything that's new before you get back out there."

Granddad laughed, but I covered my ears dramatically. "No, thank you. Change in subject, please." This time they both laughed, and Sybil settled on the couch next to Granddad.

"He's so sensitive," she joked, resting a friendly forearm on Granddad's shoulder. "I did a thing," she said, locking eyes with me. "A big thing!" She bounced in her seat like the secret she was teasing was working its way out of her in the form of energy. "And I wanted to celebrate with you."

"Can you share what this big thing is?" I opened the fridge—the closest we had to champagne was orange juice, but I pulled it out. Giving in to Sybil's energy was easier than fighting it, and more importantly, I liked her like this.

"Not yet," she said. "But I put some of my money toward a good cause, and I want to celebrate." She looked from me to take in the room, her eyes landing on a photo on the side table, her announcement forgotten. "Joe, is this her? You said she was pretty, but she's beautiful!" She held up the framed photo of my grandmother.

"That's my Rosie," he said, a softness appearing on his face. "Great love of my life."

I pulled glasses from the cupboard, watching the two of them as Sybil handed the photo to Granddad. "Tell me about her," she said, looking over his shoulder at the photo.

"She was the one for me. Mouth like a sailor, and she had the best laugh," he said, a wistful expression taking over his face. "You remind me a little of her." He patted her knee, and my heart clenched at the affection in his touch. He was a toucher, a hugger, and our neighbors and customers all got a piece of that affection, but the way he was with Sybil was how he was with Lila and me. He was treating her like family and falling for her. "Of course," he said, "she wasn't as lucky as you!"

"I don't know," Sybil said, tracing a finger along the edge of the photo. "She had you. I think she was pretty lucky." She continued admiring the photo.

"Best I could do," I said, handing over two glasses of orange juice. "What are we toasting?"

"To your big thing?" Granddad held up his glass and raised an eyebrow at Sybil.

"You know," she said, setting the photo gingerly on the table, "that can wait. To Rosie! Sounds like she was an awesome fucking lady." She clinked her glass with Granddad's, and he beamed, his eyes a little wet.

"That's the kind of toast she'd approve of," he said, tapping his glass to mine. "To finding women who bring us joy," he said to me, his expression turning more pointed before he drank from his glass. "Now, you two leave an old man to nap," he said, shooing us from the living room with an exaggerated wink. "There must be something you can get up to in Kieran's room. Maybe some of those new advancements?"

I rolled my eyes and finished my orange juice.

"I actually did want to talk to you about something," Sybil said, sipping from her glass as if it were a crystal flute and not a scratched water glass that used to be a jelly jar. "But if that door's a rockin' . . . " she said with a sly grin to Granddad.

"If only he were so lucky," the old man said with a chuckle. "But do send me those websites!"

"Glad you and my granddad can make me so uncomfortable together," I said, sitting on the edge of the old desk once I closed the door behind me.

"You love it," she said, tapping her palm against my cheek. She had to stand close to me to do that, and I inhaled her familiar scent and pressed my hand to the desk to stop from sliding it along her hip. "And it's good he's interested in getting out and dating."

Sybil stepped back and fell to the end of my bed, crossing one leg over the other. "You made your bed?" She looked over her shoulder, as if to be sure.

"Yeah . . ."

"Did you know someone would be in here?"

"No, I just make it when I wake up."

She shook her head as if in disbelief. "We are such different people." She was right, but watching her on my bed, settling her body over the blankets, made me imagine messing it up with her. How she'd look panting and breathless against my pillows, how much I wanted to let myself lose control with her. It had seemed like a bad idea before, but now, with her stretched out before me after a week apart, I just wanted to be close to her, and I lowered myself to join her on the bed.

I stretched out next to her and rested on one elbow. "Vegas was good?"

"Amazing." She toyed with the hem of her shirt as she told me about the weekend, lifting it and dropping it repeatedly, giving flashes of her stomach every time. She finished her story and let the shirt fall with an inch of her soft skin showing, tipping her head to the side to look at me.

"I'm glad you had fun." I stroked my finger along that exposed skin and traced circles. "I missed seeing you," I admitted. "I've gotten pretty used to being around you every day."

Sybil's gaze softened at my touch, and she sank her teeth into her lower lip. "Me, too." She lowered her gaze. "Bet you never saw that coming."

"Yeah," I said. "I guess I didn't." I drew circles with my fingertip on her skin. "You know, Granddad asked about me going back to school." I'd wanted to talk to her about it, but she stiffened and then rolled away from me.

"That's what I wanted to talk to you about." She stood and then reached into her back pocket and handed me a folded piece of paper. "It was too much to Venmo, so . . ." She held it out. "Here's the money."

"Oh," I said, taking the check from her. "I thought we were waiting until the end . . ."

She paced between the door and the bed. "I know," she said, tucking hair behind her ears, "but I figured you shouldn't have to wait until the end, and you can pay down bills to take care of Joe so you're ready to go back to school. And I'm trying to spend the money in good ways, so . . ."

I studied the check, unfolding it and looking at her loopy handwriting, missing the feel of her next to me. I'd never held that much money in my hand, but it felt different than I thought it would. "So weird to imagine paying things off all at once," I said, tallying the medical bills and outstanding debt in my head. "Thanks." I stood and tucked it into my back pocket. "I guess you're almost done with me, huh?"

"The wedding is a month away," she said. "And you'll probably forget about me when you're around all those smart doctors again. What will I do without you when you go back to your real life at school?" She flashed me a grin and fell back onto the bed like we were switching places.

"Probably go back to driving like a madwoman," I said, trying not to stare at the endless curves of her figure. "And you'll be free to date someone for love instead of . . . for PR reasons."

"I've spent too much time thinking about the future today. I don't want to think about it for another minute," she said, looking toward the ceiling. And I didn't, either, because I liked seeing her on my bed, and the money in my pocket made me uncomfortable, and nothing was the way it was supposed to be. I felt calmer about that than I expected. Sybil Sweet wasn't just in my bed. She was in my head, and I had no idea how to reconcile that with what I needed to do moving forward. My mind was always swimming with what came next and how to get back on track, but somehow, with her here with me, the only thing I was overwhelmed with was *her* and how much every minute I spent with Sybil made me consider scrapping all my old plans in favor of new ones that included her.

33

Sybil

I OPENED THE DOOR FOR KIERAN, MOTIONING AROUND my hotel room. "Welcome," I said, waving toward the fireplace and the chandelier sparkling with the light from the setting sun outside. "Isn't it awesome? I went with Grace to discuss a few things for the wedding with the planner and decided to get a suite for the weekend. Swanky, huh?"

Kieran walked through the room, admiring the same things I had, and I noticed how he looked everywhere except the king-sized bed. That was probably smart. He looked good, in jeans and a white polo shirt that made his olive skin seem sun-kissed despite the weather just barely dipping its toe into spring. "And walking distance to the concert?"

Stewie had asked us to make an appearance at an event featuring local bands. When I'd asked Kieran if he wanted to go, he suggested dinner before to make a night of it. The idea of an excuse to spend time with him under the guise of our agreement was tempting, even though I expected him to balk at the whole idea of the event. I could have been knocked over with a feather when he replied that he'd make a reservation and pick me up, sending back It's a date.

"Just two blocks," I said, striding toward the bathroom to finish applying my makeup. "I want to see you a little drunk tonight."

I dug through the makeup bag on the marble counter, in search of my lipstick, when Kieran followed, resting one forearm against the door frame, showing off the lines of his stomach and chest under the shirt. He relaxed against the frame, but his eyes were intent on me. "I don't really get drunk. That night at the karaoke bar was a rarity."

"You were pretty flirty that night. I'm curious how you normally flirt." I dragged my gaze from him and slowly spread the long-lasting lipstick over my lips, enjoying the way the deep red color transformed them.

"I've flirted with you," he said. "You've seen it."

"Well, sure." I dabbed at the corner of my lip with my fingertip. "But say I was a stranger you met at a bar. What line would you use?"

"I don't hit on women in bars."

I rolled my eyes. "Okay. Pretend I'm a cute girl you met in a cadaver lab when our eyes locked over an open chest cavity. What's your line?"

"This may surprise you, but I've never hit on someone over a body, either." He ran his fingers through his hair. "But I guess . . . I don't know. I'd say 'Hi.'"

"Just hi?" I cleaned my lipstick-smudged finger with a tissue. "That kind of fits you."

"I'm boring," he said.

"No, just classic." I leaned closer to the mirror to check my work, and cut my gaze to Kieran. "And I see you looking at my butt," I added with a wiggle.

His cheeks pinked but he didn't deny it, and I liked the idea of him watching me.

He was quiet for a moment while I worked on my lashes. "You look really nice," he said, breaking the silence, and I held the wand still before the last swipe. "Not just your butt, I mean," he added, sweeping his gaze up my body.

"But my butt, too, right?" I wiggled again and grinned at his overexaggerated nod before giving myself one last once-over. "I figure if I'm in a fancy hotel and we're going on a fancy date, I should look cute, right? The dress is new." I did a twirl, feeling a bolt of heat through me as he watched me from his perch in the doorway.

"Very cute," he said, his low voice echoing off the walls of the bathroom. I walked toward him, but he didn't move, his body still filling the doorway, and he dragged two fingertips down my arm before nudging me. "Turn around." The command and the stroke of his fingers combined made goose bumps rise on my skin, and I faced away from him.

"You look beautiful." Kieran's breath grazed the back of my neck when he spoke, and my breath caught when I felt his fingers against the zipper at my back. "But there's a tag," he said, snapping it from my dress. "Now you're perfect."

I let out a nervous laugh. The sensations from the last few seconds had raised my temperature, and I squeezed my thighs together.

I slowly turned again, fixing an appreciative smile on my face when I looked up at him.

"You're up to your hero stuff again." I backed against the

door frame, resting just beneath his forearm and feeling sheltered by his body. "All chivalrous. A girl will get used to you if she's not careful. Might start to feel like a real date."

"You can get used to me." He stroked my shoulder, fingers catching on the strap of my dress, toying with the fabric. "You're stuck with me as a date, at least for a little while longer." His lips tipped up in a mischievous way, and he added, "I can't have you looking like a mess when we go out."

"Oh, so it's like that? What happened to beautiful?" I swatted his chest, trying to take a step back, but his free hand slid to my waist and he held me in place.

"Both can be true! Would you prefer I didn't tell you the tag was still on?" He was laughing, which made me laugh, and our voices bounced off the tile walls in tandem.

"I mean, you didn't have to say I was a mess." The doorway felt smaller the longer we laughed, and the cool wood pressed against my back as I looked up at Kieran.

"A very intriguing mess."

"You said that the night we met."

His laugh faded into a more sincere tone, and his hand grazed from my waist down my hip.

The way our bodies almost touched and the look on his face—it was too much, and I felt warm and safe and overwhelmed, but in a good way. My mind whirred with all the things that could happen next, with how easy it would be to kiss him and close the inches between us, and what might happen after he pressed me against the wall. Everything felt possible, and my breath caught in my throat.

He must have read my reaction a different way, though, because he took a slow step back, his arm fell from its perch against the door frame, and he gave his head an almost imperceptible shake before looking at his watch. "I guess we should get going. Our reservation is for seven."

"This feels like a real date, Kieran."

"I asked you out for dinner, so I think it *is* a real date," he said.

"Remember I told you those usually end with awkward first kisses?"

He winked. "We already had our first kiss. But I don't remember it being awkward."

I felt my cheeks heat but nodded, smoothing down my dress and moving past him to grab my bag from the bed, where I'd tossed it. "Any more messiness before we leave?"

He shook his head. "What about me?"

I rolled my eyes. "You're never messy."

He held the door for me, running a palm over his jaw. Under his breath, Kieran said, "Sometimes I really want to be."

I stepped out the door, double-checking I had my phone in my clutch, but Kieran didn't follow. He was still standing in the doorway, watching me. "What are you doing? You hate being late." I held out my hand to guide him down the hall, but he pulled me back toward him, his arm sliding around my waist.

"What if our kiss was at the start of the date?"

"That would be messy," I said, breath catching on the last syllable as his other hand cupped the side of my neck.

"Yeah." His lips slid over mine and that same sinking sensation overtook me, that feeling like I was drowning in this kiss in the best possible way. Kieran's grip was firm and his kiss insistent as he angled me toward the wall, slanting his lips to deepen the embrace, which seemed to go on for hours before we parted. His chest heaved and he guided a fingertip under my lip. "Now it's a real date."

34

Kieran

I WAITED IN THE DOORWAY AS LILA'S HANDS FLEW OVER the keyboard and she toggled between screens. "Well?"

"It's great," she said with a smile spreading across her face, looking up from the screen. She'd stopped over to report on our finances—I knew enough to do a cursory review, but Lila knew all the ins and outs, and she extended her palm for a high five. "I think we're going to make it if this keeps up, plus the money from Sybil," she said, the reference giving me a sinking feeling. It was the same feeling I'd had when I handed Lila the check to deposit.

"We can tell Granddad when Tom brings him back from the doctor's appointment. He's so ready to be back full-time." She tapped a few things out on her keyboard, and the charts and projections on the screen shifted. "The store's books will be in good shape for him when he takes back over."

I leaned against the door frame. "I still worry about him coming back to work full-time."

She shrugged. "Doctor said he should be fine, and it's what he wants. We can talk him into hiring a little more help, too."

I didn't realize I was pulling my phone from my pocket until I saw Lila's reaction.

"Sybil?" Lila looked pointedly at my phone, and heat rose on my face as I shoved it back in my pocket, because texting Sybil had been an automatic response. She was invested in this scheme, of course, but it wasn't even that. She'd be excited we were close to saving the shop, and I found a lot of comfort in her smiles and exuberant celebrations. I wanted to tell her the good news. The night at the concert had been fun—the bands were decent, and Sybil was in her element with all the people and dancing. I'd even had a few drinks with her, but my head had been in that hotel bathroom all night. She'd smelled so good, and I couldn't forget how we'd laughed. And that kiss. I'd wanted to kiss her all night. I'd wanted to kiss her all year, which was why it had been a bad idea.

"Just a notification," I lied. Lila was still convinced I was going to fall for my fake girlfriend and her infectious laugh and beautiful fingers and the curls she could never quite contain. "Is the semester going well?"

She pushed back from the desk and pulled her own phone from her pocket at the buzz of a notification. "Good. I'll take the CPA exam after I finish my master's this semester. I'll pass." She crossed her legs and rested her phone on her knee after tapping something out.

"Then you have to decide which of these job offers to accept." I was proud of her—she'd had three offers months ahead of graduation and had been balancing helping me with her schoolwork all year. Lila laughed at something on her phone and tapped out another reply.

"Sorry." She flipped her phone over. "Marcus was sending me pictures of a recipe he tried that bombed miserably." She hurried forward, knowing I'd ask about all the time she'd been spending with him lately. "I'm really leaning toward Chicago," she said, smiling once more at her phone before tucking it away. "It's the best offer, but it's far away." She looked over my shoulder at the front of the store when the chime sounded. Chad was out front at the counter. "But I haven't decided—the offer here is fine, too."

I hated that she was waffling on this out of some idea she needed to stay. She'd pointed out the irony in me worrying about that too many times to count, but I didn't care. "You should go to Chicago."

"But then who would give you shit and keep Granddad and Tom out of trouble?"

The familiar voice startled me, and I spun at Sybil's approach. She looked like she'd just come from working out, a sports bra peeking from under a T-shirt with the neck cut wide so it slipped off her shoulder. I reached to adjust it on instinct. "I think I could handle it." She flashed me an appreciative glance, but her face lacked its normal brightness.

"Hey, Sybil." My sister looked at her phone again and rose, pulling her backpack from the floor. "I gotta get to my study session, but tell her the good news, Kier!" Lila flashed a smile to Sybil before ducking out the front, her check-in with Chad barely audible from the office.

"I wasn't expecting you. What's up?" I studied her face, noticing the dark circles under her eyes that hadn't been there when I'd seen her a few days ago. When I'd kissed her at the end of the date, too, making everything even more confusing.

She smiled, but it was a fake one. "Just a weird day," she

said, walking into the office and looking around like she always did, running her hands over everything. I usually enjoyed watching her body language as she took in the now familiar surroundings. Today she seemed edgy, distracted. "Can I hang out here for a while?"

"I'm just about to head upstairs to shower. I told Granddad I'd take him to the library," I said, taking a few steps toward her. "You can stay here, though."

"Oh. Okay." She turned away from the photo she always admired, the Ferris wheel one. "No big deal." She ran her hands down the front of her shirt as if it needed smoothing, and something in her posture unsettled me.

"What's going on, Syb?" I slid my palm down her bare arm, immediately noticing the goose bumps rising on her skin. "Something is wrong." I stepped closer, taking in the crease between her brows and the way she held her mouth with a tension I'd never seen in her before. I cupped her cheek, sliding a thumb gently along that set jaw.

"I'm probably making too big a deal out of it." She looked up at me through her thick lashes, her eyes welling with tears.

"What's wrong?" I was on high alert now, my body tensed, and I let my palm slide along the side of her neck to flatten over her shoulder. "Did someone do something to you?" Anger flared in my chest at the idea of someone hurting her.

She sighed, not moving out of my touch, but a tear slid down her face. "I fucked up."

"What do you mean?"

"Remember two weeks ago when I wanted to celebrate? I made a donation to charity. A big one," she said, her voice breaking, and she swiped at her eyes before sucking in a ragged breath. "Is it stupid if I ask you to hold me for a minute?"

"Of course not." She slumped against me, and I stroked my fingers along her spine, the other hand keeping her close, unsure what I was protecting her from but knowing it wasn't an option not to. "Can you tell me what happened, Syb? Are you hurt?"

She pulled her face from my shoulder, wiping her eyes. "It's a nonprofit that works with shelters across the city. I thought, why help just one when there's a group that helps a lot?"

She shuddered, and I tightened my grip on her waist.

"That sounds like a good thing." I stroked her back again, hauling her closer to me, the feel and sound of her crying gutting me. "Baby, what's wrong?"

"I gave them half a million dollars," she added, lowering her voice and unsuccessfully holding in a sob. "I posted about it this morning. You know, maybe it would make other people want to join in and give, too." She wrapped her arms around my waist, and I tightened my hold.

I ducked my chin to meet her eyes. "Syb, that's amazing. I don't understand why you're crying."

"It's not a real charity," she said. "They seemed so legit and . . ." She ducked her face to my shoulder. "That news station called me, and the newspaper reached out, and everyone can see how I messed it up."

I saw red, felt my throat close with fear and rage, and I pulled her to me again, holding the back of her neck. She'd been trying so hard to impress everyone, and I knew from the way she clung to me, she thought she'd failed.

"I look stupid," she said, sniffling. "I am stupid. And I could have given it to a place that needed it . . . And I know it's dumb to be so upset."

"It's not." I stroked her back between her shoulder blades as she tucked her chin into the crook of my shoulder. "Of course you're upset." I kissed her forehead, wanting to shelter her from it all.

"I should have been more careful with researching that it was a legitimate charity, and I shouldn't have posted anything about the donation online, but I never thought . . ." She sniffled. "They'll see I'm the same irresponsible, worthless Sybil who can't get things right. Everyone will see."

"No," I said. I dipped my chin lower and cradled her head against my chest. The motion left my lips near her ear, and I kept stroking up her back and along her nape. "You were trying to do something good that would help people," I said, letting her cry against my shoulder. I'd never felt a sense of duty stronger than knowing I needed to comfort her and remind her what she was thinking was wrong. "The only thing you can't get right is obeying the speed limit," I said, feeling the smile I'd hoped for against my chest.

She chuckled and spoke with a teary voice. "They're guidelines."

"They're not," I said near her ear, tightening my hold at her waist. "That's why you get speeding tickets."

She laughed against me, the sound choked but a little more like the Sybil I knew. "You're supposed to be being nice to me."

"I'm sorry," I said, stroking her hair. "I'll be nice."

"You are," she said, resting her cheek against my chest, her voice clearer. "I was spinning and panicking and I ignored all the calls. I just drove and then I was here." She rested her palm over my stomach, stretching her fingers across my obliques. "Looking for you."

I flattened my hand against her spine and leaned back slightly to see her face. "Stay with me." She'd stopped crying, but I still slid my thumb over her cheek, tracing along her skin. "Or we can go somewhere."

Her eyes roamed my face, and I hated seeing worry on her features, the way it dimmed her light. "You can't just leave the store, and you have plans with your granddad."

"He won't mind. I can leave." I tucked a curl behind her ear. "For you I will."

"You don't have to worry about me, I'll just—"

I pressed my finger to her lips, interrupting her protest. They were as soft as I remembered. "Maybe this isn't real, but you're real. You're real to me. And if I can do something to help, I'm going to do it."

"Okay." She looked at me again, her lashes still wet and her eyes wide. "Can I stay with you?"

"Yeah." I pulled her in for another hug, wrapping both arms around her again. I still felt red with anger, but fear was working its way into my bloodstream—fear someone would cheat her, would make her lose belief in herself. And there was something else, too, something just as hard to ignore. She felt right in my arms—she felt perfect in my arms, actually, and I didn't want to let her go. "There's nowhere else I want you to be," I added, certain these emotions were going to lead to another moment in my life where the bottom fell out.

"Thank you," she said against my chest.

And I didn't care anymore about the guaranteed disaster the end of this was going to be.

35

Sybil

THE DOOR CLICKED BEHIND US, AND KIERAN IMME-
diately flipped the dead bolt.

"What is this place?" I'd been so exhausted, I had fallen
asleep in the small office, my head dipped to the side in the
chair. When I woke up, Kieran's palm was on my shoulder,
shaking me awake, and he told me he had an idea. We'd driven
for hours, crossing the border into Minnesota and then wind-
ing through the woods until we'd reached this cabin, tucked
into the trees along a lake and with a dock it looked as if time
had forgotten. We were far enough north that there was still
ice on the water.

"It's Tom's old fishing cabin. I know it's not much and it's
cold . . ." Kieran looked around at the tiny space. "It's not as
nice at that hotel downtown, but I can light a fire, and I know
you were so upset with all the attention, I thought being away
from everyone might be—"

I didn't give him time to finish and wrapped my arms

around him. The warmth and solidity of his body was all I needed. When his arms fell around me, a palm flat on my back, I melted into him. "It's exactly what I wanted. This place is perfect." He pulled me closer, and the pressure was like an added layer of protection. "Five stars. Highly recommend."

Kieran chuckled and rubbed my back in the cabin's stillness. The furniture was covered in sheets, and the bulb in the overhead light flickered. "But I do actually need to light a fire or we're going to freeze."

"You won't keep me warm?" I said, letting him pull away and admiring the stretch of his body as he gathered logs from the metal container near the small fireplace.

He chuckled, searching the nearby shelf for matches and kindling. "You told me we should keep things unwarmed," he said over his shoulder. "I believe you asked me to consider you unfuckable and like my cousin. And, granted, for cousins, we've shared a lot of kisses since then."

"Yeah," I said, gently unfolding the sheet from the couch and trying to avoid kicking up a mountain of dust. "But when I said to treat me like your cousin, I was probably drunk."

"You said it stone-cold sober." He looked over his shoulder, that grin I was coming to love on his face.

"I was carb drunk. Odds are good I'd had, like, three donuts." I settled on the couch, rubbing my hands over my biceps through the coat. "But you agreed."

I admired Kieran's body perched by the fireplace, bent over so he could construct a pyramid made of logs. The match took to the kindling, and the fire rolled before he stepped away, catching sight of me warming myself. Without a word, he took two long steps toward me and dropped onto the couch beside me. "It'll warm up soon," he said, pulling me against him and taking over, moving his hands up and down my back.

I let out a little sigh and settled against him, which would have been sexier if we weren't both still in our winter coats.

"And I never agreed you were unfuckable," he said, rubbing his hands together.

"Yes, you did," I protested. "We shook on it."

"I agreed with your rule that we keep things platonic," he said.

"So, unfuckable."

He chuckled. "Those two things aren't the same." He pulled his head back to study my face. "Are you warming up?"

I nodded, trying to unzip my coat but fumbling with the thick gloves Kieran had handed me when we hopped in the truck.

"Let me," he said, taking hold of the zipper and sliding it down. "Platonic means I agree it's smart to keep this fictional relationship as uncomplicated as possible and not introduce sex into the equation." He continued the zipper's path, the teeth audible against the crackling of the fire. "To me, considering you unfuckable isn't possible." He slid the coat off my shoulders, sliding his palms down my arms to free them from the sleeves. "It's just not a sentence that makes sense. You drive me to distraction. You touch your lips sometimes when you talk and you have such amazing lips, and that Joe's Donuts T-shirt is too small, but I can't take my eyes off you when you have it on. Really, I can't ever take my eyes off you. You are so incredibly fuckable."

I shivered under his slow touch, despite the growing warmth in the small room from the fire. "You've never said 'fuck' to me so much before," I said, pulling my arms from the sleeves once the gloves were off. "I kind of like it."

Kieran's eyes darkened when I reached for the zipper on his coat, copying his actions and slowly dragging it down. "You like when I say 'fuck'?"

I slid my palms over both his shoulders, pushing the jacket down his biceps. "Yeah," I said softly. "It's a good word, and when you say it, it's extra special because you don't swear often."

"Hm," he said, shrugging out of the coat. "So when I say . . . 'fuck the Denver Broncos,' you get . . ."

"Hotter than hot," I said with a chuckle.

"And it's not heat, it's the fucking humidity," he said, mingling his fingers with mine.

I fanned myself as his hand moved back to my waist.

"Or fuck the patriarchy?"

"Stop, I can only get so wet." We both laughed, and I let my hand move back to his shoulder. "I like the word when you say it."

"I'll keep that in mind," he said, his fingers still toying with mine. The wood in the fireplace began to crackle, and our fingers stroked along each other's hands as the light flickered. Kieran's voice was low and soft when he spoke again. "I like when you say most things."

The light above us flickered, and he moved a thumb over my palm. "I was glad you were there today," I said, savoring the slide of his fingers against mine. "I don't know how I would have handled it . . ."

"You would have, though." His body wrapped around me like crushed velvet. "You're stronger and more capable than you give yourself credit for."

I looked up, meeting his gaze. "That's the best compliment anyone has ever paid me." Above us, the overhead light flickered once more, drawing my eyes to the ceiling.

"It's true," he said. "But should I have added a 'fuck' to it somehow?"

I giggled, shifting so I could slide my thigh across his, resting in his lap with my knees straddling his thighs. He was solid under me, hands coming to my hips to steady me.

"Fuck," he murmured as I settled on top of him.

"That's better." I dragged a fingertip along his hairline, and he tensed under me, his thigh muscles flexing at my touch and his hips giving a subtle thrust upward. I wanted more. I wanted so much more.

I gave an experimental roll with my hips, finding him hard between us, and I moved one hand to the back of his neck, scratching his nape gently. "What if it was real?"

Kieran's hands settled at my waist, his thumbs on my waistband and then rolling in circles along my hip bone. "If you and me was real?"

"Yeah." I rolled my hips again, grinding against him through his jeans and my yoga pants, my body lighting up at the pressure, and months' worth of touches and looks and fantasies were building to a crescendo. "If we were real and you swept me off my feet to a remote cabin in the woods after I had a horrible day." I bit my lip as the promise of how good this could be tiptoed through my body. "What would you do?"

Attraction was never an issue, but I'd messed so many things up in the last week, I wasn't sure I could handle Kieran turning me down, but with the fire, and his roaming hands, I couldn't stop myself from asking. The "what if we were real?" game was the fantasy I loved to sink into at night alone. But now he was under me, looking at me, and I held my breath when he opened his mouth to speak.

"If we were real . . ." Kieran's gaze fell to my lips and then lower to the dipping neckline of my top. "I'd kiss you. I'd kiss your lips and along your throat." His palms slid up my side and under my T-shirt, moving slowly over my ribs. "Your shoulders and right here along all five freckles." He touched the space between the tops of my breasts. "And make sure you knew you were the most incredible, irresistible woman I'd ever met."

"I'd remind you that you tell me that all the time."

The tips of the fingers on his right hand grazed the underside of my bra, and I shivered. "If this were real," he said, his fingers against my sensitive skin like a slow-moving trickle of water, inching closer and closer to my nipple, "you'd know I would never stop telling you how much you mean to me." He diverted the path of his fingers to stroke up the side of my breast, but the groan of frustration I might have let out was interrupted by his lips grazing the base of my throat. "How your voice makes me smile." His nose moved along my neck as he kissed up. "How I dream of the way you taste when you come." His lips touched the corner of mine. "How lucky you make me feel."

"What if tonight it's real?" My head was spinning and my body was on fire everywhere we connected. "I don't want to stop."

"Are you sure?" His hands stilled, but he pulled his head back to meet my eyes, and his gaze was intense and searching. "That's not why I brought you here. I just wanted to get you away."

"I know." I stroked his face, the pressure between my legs

maddening. "But . . ." I rolled against him again. "It doesn't change what we both want."

His eyelids fell, the angles of his face highlighted by the flickering shadows, and he was quiet for so long, I doubted my decision until his hand began a slow slide up my back. "No photos."

"One," I said with a grin as his palm moved over my bra strap. "Don't you think our waiting public would want to know?"

"No deal." He stroked the nape of my neck. "If we're doing this, it's not for anyone else."

"Just us," I said on a gasp when he pulled my face to his and pumped his hips.

"Fuck." His lips crashed down on mine, the kiss inelegant and needy, and I was ready when he wrapped his fingers around the back of my head and pulled me in as it deepened. "I've wanted this for months," he said, running kisses down my neck, the bruising kiss of moments before now a series of teasing, soft licks.

"We deserve some fun," I said on a pant when his wide palm cupped my breast through the thin fabric of my shirt, and a moan escaped my lips. We'd spent so much time pretending, so much time pushing this thing between us to the side, that every part of me craved his touch.

"You deserve everything," he said, rolling my nipple through my bra, and I ignored the warm sensation that had nothing to do with his straining cock under me and everything to do with how those words curled around my heart. "What do you need right now?" His lips dipped to my throat again, and I rolled my hips faster, seeking more pressure and friction. "I want you to feel so good."

"I need to see what you're like when you're not worried about keeping everything under control, when you don't have to be responsible and think about other people."

"What if all I want to think about is you?"

His intense gaze was like a caress up my spine. I reached between us, stroking his length through his jeans. "Do you think about me a lot?"

"Fuck. Yes," he said against my cheek, his lips moving lower and sucking my nipple into his mouth over my shirt. "You make me want to lose control."

"Lose it," I panted, and Kieran rolled me to my back. My yelp caught against his lips when his mouth crashed down on mine again.

Kieran's fingers skated between us and under the waist of my yoga pants, sliding lower with teasing, sure fingers. "I want to taste you again like I did the first night," he said, pressing a finger in circles around my clit, the fabric between us simultaneously adding to and robbing me of the full experience. "Do you know how good you taste?"

"And then?"

The light flickered again before cutting out, leaving us in only the firelight, with flickers of shadows playing across his face as he lowered himself from the couch to the rug, tugging me to the edge of the cushion and pulling my yoga pants and underwear down my thighs. "I know some things we could try," he said, kissing my knee.

"Creativity is important," I said, letting my knees fall apart. "Fundamental." My head fell back against the couch when his breath teased my clit.

Kieran slid the flat of his tongue up my slit, and I groaned, immediately needing more, but he kept teasing me with long, languid strokes of his tongue as if in answer.

"Oh, God." I groaned again when his long, thick middle finger slid into me, curling to just the right spot and making me arch against him.

"It's been such a long day, just make me forget I made such a mess of everything." My breath stuttered when he curled his finger again while making tight, fast circles over my clit, interrupting the pattern with a diagonal flick of his tongue that had me crying out.

"You're perfect. You're mine," he said, continuing his finger's maddening pace. "The only mess you're making right now will be you coming all over my face." He swirled his tongue around my clit. "Understood?"

I nodded, my head tipping back.

"Say it," he said, adding a second finger, holding my waist, his shoulders spreading my thighs wide. "Say you're perfect." His breath teased over me, and I needed his mouth. "Admit what I already know," he said softly, meeting my eyes. He curled his fingers inside me. "Say it."

"I can't," I panted, squirming against him.

"If this was real, I'd spend hours, days, years reminding you that you're perfect. You're the perfect version of you, and you are perfect to me." He dropped a kiss next to my clit. "And I need you to know it." He teased his tongue just outside where I needed it, making every nerve ending spark in anticipation.

"I'm perfect," I mewled, pressing my hand over my face as the words left my lips, but there was no time for embarrassment, because his lips and tongue were on me, and there was nothing else in my brain other than the wave after wave of pleasure he was pulling from me. And I felt perfect.

There was something so incredibly hot about him not speaking, not taking a break from my body to offer banter or respond. His mouth was responding, and my pleasure pulled into tight coils low in my belly. His consistent swirling motion had me on the edge. The next swipe of his tongue over my clit broke me, and I bowed off the couch, crying out with the warm air on my bare skin as the rolls of pleasure moved from my center outward.

Finally, Kieran raised his head, swiping the back of his hand across his mouth.

"Fuck," I said with a slow smile.

36

Kieran

I LIKE YOU," SHE SAID DREAMILY. HER FACE WAS RE-laxed, and the crease between her brows that I'd been worried about was gone. She slid her fingers along my hairline softly. "If this were real, I'd tell you that all the time."

"I like you, too. I . . ." I kissed her thigh. "I like you more than I've ever liked anyone." The honesty felt refreshing, like I'd lifted a weight off my shoulders, even though it was this game of what-if she'd created.

"Even Hannah Carson?"

"Definitely." I chuckled and drew circles on her hip bone and then kissed her there. "If this were real, I'd be out of my mind about you and how much I want to focus on you."

"We're not done yet, are we?" She sat up straighter and looked me over.

"We've barely gotten started." I slid my palms under her top, exploring her ribs, and massaged her breasts. The shirt came off easily and ended up on the floor on the other side of the couch, and before I could start on her bra, she reached behind her back, unhooking the clasp and tossing the garment aside. She sat in front of me in the light of the fire with an impish grin on her face, and I couldn't look away.

"You've got a lot of clothes on still," she said, tugging at my hoodie and adding it to the pile on the floor. With the heat from the fire warm against my back, I pulled her in for another kiss. The pressure of her hands moving down my chest and over my stomach pushed me to deepen the kiss, needing more of her heat, more of her skin. Sybil broke the kiss, unfastening my jeans and looking at her own ministrations as she lowered my zipper and freed me from the confines.

Her strokes were unhurried and firm and already driving me wild. "Sybil," I groaned, but her lips were on mine again, her tongue meeting mine stroke for stroke, and I pushed down my pants, making a grab for my wallet.

"Condom?" she asked, pulling at my pants and boxers as I looked through my wallet.

I held up the foil packet and kicked my pants aside. Her expression was so . . . Sybil. One part wide smile and another part devious expression. I stroked her lower lip with my tongue, this time soft and slow, wanting to savor every moment before giving way to the kiss, knowing we might not get this chance again.

"Pretending to date a really organized guy has perks." She plucked the condom from my hand.

"It's real tonight, remember?" I said before kissing her again and dragging my lips down her neck. "Do you still want me to lose control, Syb?"

"God, yes." She stroked me again, her palm moving up my

length. "I need out of control. Everything lately has been too . . . ordered."

I guided her to turn toward the couch, stealing a kiss along the nape of her neck and dragging my lips lower over the curve of her spine, then back up, enjoying the way goose bumps sprang up along her spine as I kissed each spot. "I want to tease you and do all kinds of things to drive you wild, but your body, Sybil . . ." I palmed a full round cheek, earning a perfect noise from her.

"Well, what if you don't tease me now, and then we spend the rest of the night figuring out how to drive each other wild?" Her sharp intake of breath when I punctuated her question with a light smack was all the encouragement I needed. "You know I like spontaneous."

I kissed the side of her neck. "Mm, okay. I like that idea." I pressed my palm against the middle of her back, easing her down. "Bend over and spread your legs."

I watched her body curve forward and hurriedly rolled on the condom. When I stepped back to her, I pressed against her heat, sliding my length along her slit and teasing her clit. I had to close my eyes to the overload of sensation. "It's not spontaneous, though. I've been thinking about this for a long time." I moved my fingers between her thighs, finding her wet and hot, and I stroked her clit, pulling a mew from her lips.

"Kieran," she said, grinding against my fingers. "Don't make me wait."

I nudged her opening with the head of my cock, teasing her even though I'd said I wouldn't, and reveling in how it felt when she backed against me. "I know you want this," I said. "But do you want hard and fast or soft and slow?" I stroked her lower back and palmed one cheek again. "Because with you, I want both."

"Hard. Fast." She wriggled against me. "Now."

I smiled to myself at her last addition and pressed into her opening, the squeeze of her wet heat an immediate jolt to every sense as I slammed forward all the way in and she cried out. Sybil backed into me, urging me forward, and I pulled out and slammed into her again, her slick, hot body welcoming me with each powerful thrust. Each of her cries was like a shot of adrenaline, and I could already feel heat gathering at the base of my spine. "How's your balance, Syb? Can you use one hand to stroke yourself?"

"One-handed is new," she panted out when I thrust in again.

"I bet it's not new at all." I shivered at the roll of her hips against me and her own hand. "I want you to think of me, to think of us, the next time you do this."

The idea of her thighs spread wide, and her getting herself over the edge, pushed me closer, too. "Give me another one," I said, with two shallow thrusts before slamming forward again.

Her thighs shook, and I braced my hands on her waist to pull her back against me. "So good," she groaned. "Just a little more," she said between heavy breaths.

I moved a hand from her waist and swatted her cheek, soft at first, then firmer. "Like that?"

Her only response was a moan, and I smacked her cheek again while burying myself in her repeatedly, her eager body meeting mine thrust for thrust until she tensed and pulsed around me as she cried out again, my name on her lips as I crashed through my release, fingers digging into her full hips until we both came down.

"We're so good together," she said, breathless and limp under me as I helped her to slowly rise, wrapping her in my arms, needing more contact. "Why did we wait so long to do that, Kieran?" Her voice was soft, and I wanted to hear her say my name like that over and over until we fell asleep. Not just tonight but every night. I'd never felt like that about anyone. I'd never taken my focus off being a doctor to imagine who'd be next to me when I did it, but now it was hard to imagine anyone else. I squeezed her tighter, not ready to separate yet and glad she couldn't see my face, because she'd be able to tell.

A FEW HOURS later, I returned from the kitchen and set two glasses of water on the table by the bed we'd hastily made after another round on the couch.

"Cold!" Sybil curled into herself at the intrusion into her cocoon with my return.

"Sorry," I said, tucking the blankets back around us. "I brought you snacks, though."

She looked over my shoulder at the small bag of Oreos I'd picked up at a gas station on the drive up. "Cookies are my love language."

"I know." I pulled her against me, drunk on her, addicted to this effortless closeness we had found together in the cabin. I mingled my legs with hers, which earned me a yelp as she tried to pull away.

"Why are your toes like ice cubes!" She squealed and I chased her feet with my own, drinking in her giggles.

"You told me you couldn't do it again if I was still in my socks, remember?"

"Just socks is not a good look," she laughed, "but I didn't

think of the consequences!" She wriggled away from me, but I wrapped my ankle around her legs and dropped a kiss to her lips, a soft peck to steal her giggle, which deepened immediately when her lips parted, inviting me to fall into a dizzying kiss with her.

"The consequences," she said, her voice breathy as she melted against me again. She didn't finish her thought, or maybe she was as confused as I was at how a fake-dating relationship could feel so real, how pure and right it was to laugh with her and kiss her, how absolutely perfect it was to sink into her heat.

"Tell me something real about you," she said, twisting in my arms and changing the subject. "Not because—well, not to convince other people just because we're naked and warm except for your feet, and because you saved me . . ." Her voice trailed off, but I could hear the longing in her tone. I rolled to my back and looked at the ceiling, pulling her with me, taking in the way her soft curls brushed my neck, the way so often with her it felt like I'd known that sensation forever.

"I love the zoo."

Sybil rolled onto one elbow. "That is not what I expected you to say. My God, Kieran. That's practically whimsical."

"It's science, too." I chuckled and ran a finger along her spine, continuing the route around her waist and across her stomach. "When I was little, my school took all of us, and I don't know, I thought it was a magical place. All the animals, and we could just have fun like all the other kids. I haven't been there in years, but I always think of that place as . . . I don't know. Something really special."

Sybil lowered herself again, resting her arm across my stomach.

"It's stupid, but when I was there, everything weighing on me felt far away. That my mom left, that we had to work at the shop a lot, that there was all this pressure to take care of things, it was gone." I remembered trudging toward the exit, not wanting to leave. I followed the line of Sybil's spine up and down. That was the way I felt with her, like the stuff not working in my life didn't seem to matter as much, like it was far away.

Sybil's finger traced circles on my chest. "I like the otters," she said finally.

"I liked them, too." I snagged her hand as it neared my neck, kissing each fingertip while I could. "They hold hands," I said, linking our fingers, curling mine around hers. "Like this, in the water."

"And." She tightened her fingers in mine and straightened. Her movements were always so vibrant when she got excited, and she propped herself up on one elbow. "I got a little obsessed with otters a while back and found out everything there was to find on them. Did you know they're actually really smart? They can use tools, and they're apex predators, like sharks?"

I thought about my classmates, though they'd all be ahead of me when I returned. The idea that I was going back, that it was imminent, still had not fully hit me, and I still had to get in touch with the school and Miles. "Apex predators? Sounds like they'd do well in medical school."

She flopped onto her back, pulling the blankets tighter around us. "Do you miss it?"

"I miss being good at something, at moving toward something." I tucked a hand behind my head. "A lot of people are driven and motivated by the competition, but for me, it's something else."

"It's making things happen. Fixing." She toyed with the fraying edge of the old quilt. "Right?"

I nodded. "Yeah. I guess that's it."

"Were you always like that? You always liked fixing?"

I couldn't remember a time when I didn't have to take care of things, but I paused on her question, unsure how to answer. "I didn't have a lot of choice when we were with my mom. She was . . . well, usually she wasn't on top of stuff even when she was there. And Lila was still so young . . . it was I do it or it doesn't happen. Mom believed it would all just fall into place and . . . it never did. Makes you learn cause and effect early, you know?"

"Do you think you'd still want to be a doctor if your mom was more present? Like, do you think the science and the peopling would still appeal to you without that?"

I didn't know. I wasn't sure how I felt or what I really wanted, and that made my stomach flip. "Lila says I'm not good at peopling."

"You're pretty good at peopling with me."

"You're a special case." I looked at the wooden beams across the ceiling and thought about her question. "I like that there are questions that can be answered in medicine. I like finding solutions. I think even if things didn't need fixing, if I'd never had to fix things my mom left broken, I'd like that part."

She nodded and rested her head in the crook of my neck, her curls tickling the bottom of my chin. "Do I remind you of her? Your mom?"

She had, in the beginning. I'd worried I was going to fall for someone who could leave the way she had, which made me put my walls up. But with Sybil in my arms, with her languid body next to mine, I shook my head. "The good parts," I said.

"I mean, she'd forget to buy food or take us to school, but when she was present, when her attention was on us, it was amazing." I hadn't let myself remember that in years, remember the way I clamored to make her smile and feel her hug me, and how full I felt when it happened. "You make me feel like that, like everything brightens up."

She rolled her body to rest her forearms on my chest. "If this were real, I would remember to buy food. I might even have dinner waiting for you when you left the hospital."

I chuckled and tucked a curl behind her ear. "You're going to learn to cook?"

"Well, I'll have Marcus have dinner waiting for us when you leave the hospital."

"That's less romantic, and yet probably more delicious . . ." I let my gaze roam her face. "It's nice to imagine staying together, though."

"It is. But you have to go back to school." She smiled sadly and curled next to me again. "Do you regret agreeing to this whole thing? I know you needed the money, but it's kind of been a lot of trouble for you. Must have taken time away from your studying. I've barely heard you talk about school lately." The question was abrupt, but I was surprised how unjarring it was for her to ask it, how used to her questions I was.

"No," I said. "No regrets."

"Are you only saying that because I'm so fuckable?" She grinned and tickled my side with a few fingers but paused her teasing at my silence.

"No," I said, staring at the ceiling. "If this were real, I would tell you it's because you're so . . . lovable." I'd known I loved her the moment she walked into the shop upset. I couldn't say that now, though, couldn't throw a wrench into this whole thing because I'd gone and caught feelings for her. I could manage those feelings. Instead, I lifted our linked fingers over her head, rolling her to her back. She looked up at me with wide eyes, and I dropped my lips down to hers to avoid her gaze, certain she'd know in an instant that there was something I was keeping from her. I trailed kisses down her neck. "Let me show you how much I do not regret this." I unlinked our fingers, pressing her hand to the pillow over her head before I moved lower on her body, taking one perfect brown nipple against my tongue and knowing there was nothing I regretted about us. I had no doubts. I was falling in love with her, and under the warmth of the blankets and in the path of her smile, that was what I knew was true.

"Kieran," she murmured, sliding her fingers through my hair with slow, gentle strokes. "For what it's worth." She nudged my chin to get me to look up on my path down her body. "I'm really going to miss you when this is over and you go back to school."

I kissed her sternum again instead of responding, because with her voice in my ears and her body against me, those feelings felt much less manageable than I'd anticipated. It struck me just then that if I wasn't more careful, I was going to put my goals on the curb to stay like this.

37

Sybil

EMI ADJUSTED THE NECKLINE ON MY DRESS. "YOU sure about this?" The studio lights illuminated the *Good Morning, Des Moines* host talking about an upcoming basketball tournament.

I shook my head and slid my hands down my hips. "Nope. Am I about to make a fool of myself?"

Emi took both my biceps in her hands. "This is good. I'm proud of you. Did you tell your family?"

I shook my head. "Not yet. Their allergies to social media have come in handy this week." The breath I sucked in was slow, and my leg shook from nerves. Kieran and I had spent the second day at the cabin brainstorming what to do, and I'd contacted the authorities, though it was unlikely much would come from that, and he'd had the idea to use the media attention to my advantage. I looked at the set and the cameras—it didn't look much different from when Kieran and I were together, but he wasn't with me this time.

The PA leaned in close. "It will be a few minutes and then we'll get you set." She clipped the microphone to my dress and wrapped the cord around back. I held my fingers close to my palms to keep them still until Emi handed me my phone, which was illuminated with an incoming text.

KIERAN: You'll do great. I'm sorry I can't be there.

He'd had to take Joe to a doctor's appointment, and I started tapping out a reply.

KIERAN: Don't kiss anyone during this segment, though. That's our thing.

I pulled Emi toward me and planted a kiss on her cheek as I snapped a selfie to send him.

SYBIL: Too late.

KIERAN: No fair but I'm glad she's there with you. Granddad and I are watching in his doctor's office lobby. Can't wait to see you come on!

Emi rested her chin on my shoulder as the basketball segment wrapped up. "Your fake boyfriend is kind of sweet, isn't he?"

"Yeah," I said as a photo came through of him kissing Joe's

cheek. I pressed my palm over my mouth to stop the laugh, but my body relaxed as I pulled my hand away.

KIERAN: Turnabout is fair play.

"He really is." I pressed the heart button and zoomed in on the photo, looking closer at their faces side by side.

"Only you would randomly hook up with a guy, end up paying him to date you, and then have him actually be a really good guy with a fun family." She tipped her temple to mine. "You really *are* lucky."

The PA motioned for me to join the host on set, and Emi squeezed my arms again before taking her seat to watch.

Once the cameras were rolling, I thought I'd be nervous again, but it was like Kieran's text had been a drug or something.

"You may remember our next guest. We first met her along with her boyfriend of Joe's Donuts after they won the lottery. Today she's here to talk about something much less sweet: scams. Welcome back, Sybil."

"Thank you," I said, trying to ignore the camera and focus on her.

"You recently shared that you'd made a large donation to an organization helping to support local shelters and food pantries." I saw a screenshot of my post on the monitors and felt the blood rushing to my cheeks. "Tell us what happened."

"Well, I wanted to use the money for good. I've had so many people in my life who help in the community—Kieran and his family, my mom and sister . . ." I pressed my hand on my knee to stop it from shaking. "And I wanted to, too. This organization approached me and it looked great—instead of helping one organization, I could help lots, and so I gave them the money."

They'd sounded genuine on the phone and looked legit in person, and I didn't figure it out until it was too late. "It turns out, they were scamming me."

"That must have been difficult to learn." Maria nodded, her expression sympathetic.

"It was," I said. "I felt embarrassed about making such a big mistake and being tricked. I felt horrible that the local organizations that I thought I was helping wouldn't get the money. And I still feel that way. I wanted to hide out and not talk about it." I cut my gaze over the host's shoulder to where Emi was standing. She gave me a thumbs-up with one hand and in the other held my phone with the picture of Kieran and Joe on it. The sight of it, and knowing he was watching, pushed me forward. "But, with some help, I realized hiding wouldn't solve anything, and maybe this was a chance to help other people. It's embarrassing to admit you've been tricked, but I hope this helps someone feel better about coming forward. I hope they won't make the same mistakes I did."

"According to the Federal Trade Commission, two point six million people reported fraud or being scammed just in the last two years. We've asked Allison Kent from the Iowa Fraud Council to join us and share tips to avoid being scammed."

The camera switched to the brunette seated next to me, and I let out a breath as she shared five tips, things I wished I'd known sooner but definitely didn't consider. I glanced again at Emi, who still held out the photo of Kieran and Joe. "And if you're in doubt, please contact us," Allison said as the information for the IFC showed on the screen.

The host turned back to me. "Sybil, we appreciate you telling your story. What will you do next?"

I'd come up with this idea while Kieran and I sat on the floor of the cabin, with takeout from a diner in the nearest town and a bottle of wine we picked up at a gas station between us. I'd rarely seen him so relaxed, and maybe that was a little the fire and the bad wine, but I had a sense maybe it was me, too. He'd told me he thought my idea was good and helped me work out the details. I gave the host a quick smile.

"I'm in a lucky position to have more money to donate. And I know not everyone has won the lottery, but every bit helps. I'm giving to the Pennsylvania Street Shelter, but here are five great organizations that could use your help and have a great track record for service to the community." I remembered Kieran kissing me after he told me he liked the idea, not a kiss meant to lead to something, but a soft kiss in the firelight that I felt in my toes, a kiss I felt in my spine now as I sat straighter. "Please join me in supporting legitimate organizations that do so much for the people we love and the people we haven't met yet."

Emi was hopping up and down as I walked off the set a few minutes later. "You did great!" She wrapped me in a bear hug.

"Thanks," I said, hugging her back until the PA stepped up to remove my microphone pack. Emi handed me my phone, and I had a bunch of messages.

KIERAN: Granddad told everyone
in the lobby that was his future
granddaughter on TV. You did
great. Perfect.

MARCUS: Great job, Syb!

DEACON: Is Allison Kent single? I
might be into older women. Also,
you were awesome!

I beamed, sending emojis back to everyone and following
the PA through the maze of hallways to the greenroom.

"How do you feel?" Emi asked as we stepped outside, pushing through the glass double doors. "Think it will make telling
your mom easier?"

I nodded, but my phone buzzed in my hand, and I saw a
text from her.

Mom: I'm so proud of you.

Unbidden, tears filled my eyes, and I stopped walking. "I
guess she saw the segment," I said, handing Emi the phone.

MOM: Please come home so I can
hug you, and give you cookies, and
make plans to annihilate those
people who took advantage of my
baby.

MOM: But mostly, I'm proud.

"She never watches TV during the day," I said, and Emi
shrugged. Even to my best friend, I couldn't admit that I
wasn't sure of the last time my mom had been proud of me. "I
wonder how she even knew to see this."

SYBIL: I was going to tell you about
it tonight. I'm surprised you were
watching in the middle of the day.

We strolled to Emi's car. It was a used Honda CR-V with
a bumper sticker we couldn't get off that read "I'd Rather Be
F _ _ _ ing" and a sketch of a fishing pole. "It did feel good to
talk about the shelter, and I think the advice they gave was
good. I think it was maybe not a horrible idea."

"It was a good idea. Most of your ideas are good," Emi said,
walking to the driver's side. "Give yourself more credit than
'maybe not horrible.'"

I'd heard that before, but on the heels of the interview, it
was easier to believe. I paused again, climbing into the car, to
see another message from my mom.

MOM: Kieran told me you were
going to be on the show and sent
me a link to watch it. I'm so glad
he did.

My face warmed again, but it wasn't embarrassment this
time. And really, it wasn't just my face, because he had to know
what it would mean to have my mom say that to me in the
wake of this happening.

"I have another idea," I said, closing the door. "Something
I want to do for Kieran. Tell me if you think I can pull it off."

38

Kieran

THE BOWL CLATTERED TO THE GROUND, MIRACU-lously staying upright as it wobbled, though a bit of the lemon curd flung from the side and landed on the wall. I bent to silence the still-spinning bowl and then snapped a towel from off the counter but noticed both the silence in the room and my sister's stare on me. "What? It slipped."

"Were you . . ." She wiped her hands down the front of her apron and narrowed her eyes in my direction. "Humming?"

"No," I said, returning to the sweet scent of the lemon filling. We were making samples for a possible catering job for an event at the zoo, and I'd made extra to take to Sybil, but I was adding a little more lemon zest to hers, plus fresh blueberries. The dark blue fruit made a pleasant mosaic in the yellow. "I don't hum."

"You usually don't," she said, sliding the tray she was holding back into place. "It's been years since I've heard you do it. But you were just humming a Taylor Swift song."

I rolled my eyes and looked back into the bowl before she could inspect my face any longer. It was a Taylor Swift song, but that was only because Sybil had come over the night before and she'd made me watch the video with her multiple times, cuddled together on my small childhood bed. "It was just stuck in my head," I said without looking over my shoulder.

"Uh-huh." She crossed her arms over her chest and leaned a hip against the counter.

I kept folding in the blueberries. "It's catchy."

"Uh-huh."

"It feels like you want to say something." I began spooning the mixture into a piping bag, and I could already imagine the noises Sybil would make eating one of these donuts. She called them yummy noises, and I was getting bad at pretending to be annoyed, because they were really similar to the sounds she'd made once the music video was over, the ones she'd made into my pillow so we weren't too loud. A warm flush ran up my neck, and I cleared my throat, throwing my sister another glance. "Go ahead."

"About how you're humming and distracted while making Sybil special donuts using Grandma's family recipe? Why would I say anything about that?"

I gently compressed the piping bag and made a grab for the extra donuts I'd set aside. "She likes lemon curd. What's the harm?"

Lila laughed and crossed one leg over the other. "I didn't say it was a bad thing," she said. "I like you two together."

"We're not together," I reminded her, pressing the tip of the piping bag into the donut. "It's still fake, but she's nice and I want to do something . . . nice for her."

"I can guess the kinds of nice things you want to *do* for her,"

Lila said, jumping out of the way before I could snap her with the dish towel in my hand. "Hey!" she said with another laugh, returning to the sink to finish washing up. "I'm not even teasing you about getting paid for it. Give me some credit. I'm just saying . . . you seem happy."

I set the first donut aside and started filling the next. "I am," I said finally, once I'd picked up the third to fill.

"That's a good thing," Lila said over the sound of the running water in the sink. "Enjoy it!"

I nodded to myself, filling two more donuts as we worked in silence until she shut off the water.

"Are you worried about the money part?" She leaned a hip against the counter again and began constructing a box. "Because I was just kidding."

"I know," I said, that now-familiar creeping sensation at the base of my spine.

"And I'd love to say forget the money and just date her for real, but it would be a bad decision to give up on being able to get out of debt," she added, the sound of the cardboard flaps fitting into place punctuating her sentence. "Granddad's medical bills are paid and the shop is in good shape."

"Yeah, I know." The lemon dribbled down the side of the donut, and I caught it with my finger before setting the pastry next to the others. "It's amazing."

"And you used the rest of the money Sybil gave you to pay your outstanding bill for school?" Lila began setting the donuts in the box, angling them just so with the hints of yellow and purple peeking out for each one. She paused for a moment. "You paid that, too, right?"

I'd had the phone in my hands and the number typed in a hundred times over the last two weeks to call the admissions office to confirm my reentry. I'd stand in my room, finger hovering over the call button, and Sybil would text or call or show up or laugh, or she wouldn't do anything but I'd imagine the warmth of her smile, and I'd back out of the call. "I've got another week," I said, wiping down the counter.

"Yeah, but why wait when you can take care of it now?"

"If the store keeps doing well, maybe I don't have to use her money for that, is all."

Lila handed me the box. "That doesn't make any sense. Why wouldn't you use the money? You're still going, right?"

I scraped the last of the sticky, blueberry-dotted mess into the trash, eager to escape her inspection. "Of course," I said, finishing the job and placing the bowl in the sink. "I mean, I don't have a choice. I'm already two years into the program. It's what I've always worked for."

"You have a choice," she said from behind me. "But you've always been certain about being a doctor. Is this about going back or leaving her?"

"I just haven't gotten around to making the call yet." I let the water run into the bowl, using the sprayer to clear the edges of the lemon residue. "It's not like she and I could really work," I reasoned, washing the bowl. "That would just be too . . ."

Lila handed me a dry dish towel. "Lucky?"

I nudged her out of the way, set the bowl down, and tugged the apron over my head. "Unrealistic. I still don't believe in luck."

"See, I think you don't trust when good things happen."

"Don't we have reason not to?"

Lila looked at her watch, something she'd been doing all afternoon. "Maybe, but that's toxic thinking, and it can keep you from being happy."

"I'm sorry, didn't we grow up with the same parent?" I checked my own watch, and we had plenty of time to get to the meeting. "It's smart to be cautious."

"Cautious, sure, but you're humming, you're running off to Tom's cabin. Hell, you're singing karaoke and you're putting off getting back to school. Plus you're . . ." She motioned to my face with both hands. "You're smiling, a lot. Maybe you haven't called because you're not sure you want to leave."

Chad yelled for Lila from the front of the shop, and she gave me a pointed look before going out to answer his question. I pulled my phone from my pocket. I'd dialed the number for Admissions so many times, I had it memorized. Lila had it partially right. I didn't want to walk away from Sybil. We only had a little over a week left in our arrangement, and every time I imagined her not being in my daily life anymore, my shoulders tensed and the world seemed heavier. But she'd asked me at the cabin if I'd still want to be a doctor if things had been different, if I didn't have to fix things, and the question had nagged me ever since because I didn't know anymore. I'd been racked with indecision about the thing I'd been clear on my whole life. I needed time to get my head on straight, but time was running out.

My gaze kept snagging on the box of donuts I'd made to take to her after the meeting. They were sweet and kind of messy but in the best way, so they were basically just like her. If I didn't go back to school, I had no idea what I would do, but if I went back, she and I would be truly done.

I heard Lila helping a customer through the swinging door and eyed the box on the counter. I only had a few minutes, but I hit the call button and walked back into the office. The auto-response clicked on, informing me the office was closed and I could leave a message or call back during business hours. When the beep sounded, I decided to stay on the line so that maybe I could get more time to make my decision, to defer for another year. I'd been lucky lately, and maybe luck would be on my side if I gave it a chance.

If I had more time, I could figure it all out and try something real with Sybil. As the robotic voice walked through the options, I settled in the chair and hummed the same song to myself until I could click zero to leave a message.

"My name is Kieran Anderson, and I need to speak with someone about my offer of reentry for fall. I'd like to know my options for deferring it."

39

Sybil

I CAN'T BELIEVE YOU PULLED THIS OFF." DEACON turned in a circle, looking around and shoving his hands in his pockets.

"I can," Emi said, nudging my shoulder with her own. There was a bit of a chill in the air, but it was near balmy for early spring, and kids and families ran by the entry to the zoo where we stood.

"It's one hell of a surprise party," Marcus said. "Lila texted that they're almost here, and she told Kieran she was meeting with the manager about a potential catering job." He kept insisting he and Lila were just friends, but I didn't believe it.

I glanced at my watch. The sounds of kids running around the zoo surrounded us and mixed with the music from the band playing near the bald eagle exhibit.

Emi saw me looking and wrapped an arm around my waist. "They'll get here soon. And you did a great job. He's going to love it."

I nodded. After the time at the cabin, everything had shifted with Kieran. Things had really been shifting for a long time, and I didn't think we'd been really pretending since that dinner with my family. But since we'd returned, I'd been sleeping at his place, though more often than not, we weren't sleeping much. "He's not really a birthday guy," I said. "I didn't even know his birthday was coming up until Lila said something at the shop a couple weeks ago."

"He'll love this," Emi said, giving me a squeeze and pointing at the car driving toward the zoo's main entrance. "He'll love it because you planned it."

I ignored the wave of hope her words inspired and watched the two of them approach, deep in conversation. My nerves pinged again, worrying Emi was wrong and he'd hate all this attention and think I was being too over the top, like others thought of me. When they reached the door, we hid behind the main counter, listening to their conversation as the door opened.

"Surprise!" I jumped up from behind the counter along with my friends, and Lila joined us in calling out, "Happy birthday!"

"What's . . ." Kieran looked around the main lobby. "What's going on?"

"Well, when it's your birthday and people jump out at you and yell 'surprise,' that usually means it's a surprise party." Lila patted him on the back and flashed a wide smile to Marcus across the room. *Just friends? Yeah, right.* "Sybil planned it."

I stepped forward and took his hands, aware of the few families passing us. "Happy birthday," I said more quietly, kissing him on the cheek. "Are you surprised?"

"Completely." He pulled me into a hug, and it was natural

at this point, an automatic response when we were near each other.

"Oh no," Deacon joked. "They're about to start making out. I'm not into watching."

Emi punched his shoulder. "They are not, but where did you get that lemonade?" Marcus nodded toward the door, and all three of them, along with Lila, walked out the back of the entrance to find one of the snack stands positioned near the flamingo exhibit.

"You threw me a birthday party at the zoo?" He looked around to make sure no one could overhear us. "Is this . . . Are we trying to get our picture taken or something?"

I stepped back from Kieran's embrace and watched him take in the scene outside. "No. I mean, I guess I can't stop people from taking photos, but no media allowed, and I think people will mostly take pictures of their own kids." Taking his hand, I led him outside. "I bought out the zoo. Did you know you could rent out a whole zoo?"

Kieran stopped in his tracks, our hands still linked. "You can't rent out an entire zoo for me."

"Well, I can. I did," I said defensively, tugging on his hand again. "But it's not just for you. C'mon, it's almost time for cake."

We strode out into the sunshine, and this time when Kieran froze, I gave him a minute to take in his surroundings before tugging him forward again. There was a huge banner at the entrance reading "Happy Birthday," with signs pointing toward the exhibits and stations we'd arranged. There were hundreds of kids gleefully running from spot to spot and others frozen in place, captivated by the animals. To the left, the music from the carousel, along with children's giggles, filled the air.

I squeezed his fingers, linked with mine. "I remember you

said what a special place this was for you, so I thought you might be okay having a birthday party if you were sharing it with all these kids the shelter and the local Boys and Girls Club support."

I followed a group of children holding cotton candy with my eyes, but Kieran still hadn't said anything, and I turned back to him. His expression was unreadable, and he still stood stick straight. "Oh no," I said, stepping in to him and lowering my voice. "You hate it? I took it too far, didn't I? I'm sorry. I just wanted to do something special for you, and I thought if something small was nice, something big would be better. And you've been working so hard on the shop and to help me and thinking about school so much that I thought you might like an escape for a day."

His posture loosened in an instant, and he pulled me to him again, our joined hands over his heart. "This is special." He tipped my chin up and dropped a sweet kiss on my lips. "I don't even know what to say. This is . . ." He kissed me again. "You're incredible."

"Happy birthday," I repeated when we broke from the kiss. "Lila helped me out a lot with the plans, and we partnered with some other businesses, so we were able to arrange for enough food that every family can take some with them, plus a little gift for each kid. If I never see wrapping paper again, it will be too soon."

He looked over my shoulder, eyes bouncing from thing to thing, and his smile widened. It was a rare Kieran smile I didn't see very often—free and wide and lasting.

"And I made sure the otters were ready for you," I offered. "Turns out you can't pet them, but I really tried. These zoo-keepers were unbribable."

I couldn't help but return his smile, and my God, I wanted to make him look like that all the time. And when I noticed him blinking and his eyes growing wet, I joined him in that, too. "Don't cry," I said, cupping his cheek. "Then I'll start crying and I hear otters are very perceptive, so . . . there's nothing sadder than an empathizing otter."

He chuckled and pulled me into a hug. No kiss this time, just the warm embrace of his arms. "Can't have that," he said into my ear. "I love it. I love . . ." He trailed off, and my pathetic heart lurched. "Everything. I don't even know what to say."

I rested my head on his chest and enjoyed the moment, pretending that "I love" had been followed by "you." "You haven't even tried the cake yet," I joked, finally stepping out of the hug. "That's probably the most special part."

He squeezed my fingers and followed me down the hill to the massive birthday cake waiting for everyone.

"This is all really special," he said, looking at the crowd. When I didn't say anything, he squeezed my hand. "Do you not think so?"

"No, I do." Up ahead, Emi held up ten fingers, signaling there was a little time left before the cake, and I tugged Kieran through the double doors leading into the simulated Outback in the Australia section. "I'm really proud of it. Is that wrong?"

"No." He paused, and we both watched a wallaby hop by in the grassy area nearby. "You should be proud."

"There's just so much more that people need. I want to do more." I'd snagged cotton candy from the vendor on the path, and I chewed a bite thoughtfully, my gaze sweeping the area, which was free of kids and families at the moment.

"You can," he said as we paused on a bridge overlooking a

pond. A black swan glided through the water. "You can do anything. You can really make an impact if you want to, and not just because of the money."

I chuckled and rested my forearms on the wooden barrier, leaning forward to get a closer view of the swan. "Are you about to make a joke about my bad driving?"

He shifted behind me, and I smiled to myself as he settled his hands on either side of mine. "I wasn't. I must be slipping." He rested his chin on my shoulder, and I followed his gaze along the surface of the water as the swan moved past us. "You did throw me a birthday party." He brushed my curls away from my neck, and his breath caressed my ear while I relaxed against him.

"You really like it?" I tilted my head to the side and felt him brush a kiss there.

"I really do."

"Can I tell you something?"

"Of course." He settled one hand at my waist. "I want to tell you something, too."

On the other end of the pond, two wallabies jumped by, and he was right about this place seeming kind of magical. "When I was planning this and pulling everyone together, people took me seriously. Like, they listened and treated me like I was . . . I don't know, someone who had a good plan. And I actually did have one."

He nodded, and his chin bobbed against my shoulder.

"I liked it."

He traced circles against my belly with his thumb. "That's a good thing, then."

"Yeah, just kind of . . . scary. This worked out, but what if I try again and I screw it up?"

"I wish you saw yourself like I see you." He wrapped both arms around me, pulling my back against his chest. "And I promise, this is not a commentary about your driving." He spoke softly near my ear. "But you're in the driver's seat, and if you take a wrong turn or even get pulled over for speeding, you'll still be able to get where you're going because you're actually a skilled driver, even if your style isn't the same as other people's."

I bit my lower lip and felt tears well in my eyes. "You still got in a dig about my driving."

He squeezed me tighter and kissed the side of my head. "You just go so fast."

Laughing, I wriggled in his arms until I was free to drape my hands over his shoulders and meet his gaze. "Thank you."

"For making you laugh?"

I shook my head slowly from side to side and tipped my forehead to his. Our noses almost touched, and I whispered, our breaths mingling, "For believing in me. For encouraging me to believe in myself. I never really knew I needed that."

I listened to him inhale slowly before he spoke. "If this was real, would you want it to last?"

A slew of kids ran past us, making us crowd against the railing to avoid being trampled—we both laughed as they shouted that they were going to cut the cake soon. My phone buzzed in my pocket, and I was sure it was Emi tracking me down, which meant it was a matter of time before Deacon was sent on a recon mission to find me. Kieran was facing me now, his dark eyes on mine. "It already feels real to me," I admitted. "I know that's not the deal, but it . . . does. So, yes. I would."

His features relaxed and his lips crashed down on mine, the kiss bruising with his palms on either side of my face. "I want it to last," he said, pressing his forehead to mine. "I want it to be real."

"This is crazy. What does this mean?" I nodded, already fast-forwarding to agreeing with him. "We can't just decide this, can we? We're at the zoo."

"And it's time for cake," he said, linking our fingers together. "C'mon." He tugged my hand. "They'll send Deacon to find us soon, and I don't want to get on that guy's bad side. He's my *Frozen* brother now."

"But we'll talk more after cake and otters?"

He tugged me to him and dropped a soft kiss to my lips again. "I'm not letting you go."

My cheeks hurt from how wide I was smiling, and I wanted to search the ground for any lost pennies just to hedge my bets as we hurried toward the exhibit exit. Without the tree cover, the sun shone bright on us when we pushed back onto the path. I shaded my eyes against the glare with my free hand. "Wait, what did you want to tell me?"

He tugged on my hand, leading me down the hill to the waiting crowd around the cake. Emi jogged toward us along with the event manager for the zoo. "I called the school," he said. "About my reentry."

My giddy mood dipped. I knew it was coming. I knew he had to go back to school and he was so excited, but it meant him leaving, not just the state but for a whole other reality. I forced a big smile, though, because I knew what it meant to him. And maybe I could go with him. "Yeah?"

"Yeah," he said. "I told them I want to defer my reentry. I don't want to leave yet, and I don't want to leave you."

I froze mid-step, the news sinking in. He wasn't leaving. This was real. This event was going off without a hitch and had me thinking about possibilities, and Kieran wasn't leaving. I threw my arms around his neck as Emi and the event manager met us.

"This must be the birthday boy," the woman said from behind me. "The hashtag 'love and donuts' couple, clearly."

Emi chuckled. "They're always like this." She tugged on my shirt. "C'mon, lovebirds. Don't make the kids wait for cake."

"You know," the event planner said to Emi when I pulled apart from Kieran and we were ushered toward the crowd, "when I saw that video he made about her, I knew they would be. It's just really nice when those things work out in the end."

I looked at Kieran, who squeezed my hand. It seemed like everything was going to work out perfectly.

40

Kieran

THE SHOP HAD BEEN BUSIER THAN NORMAL THAT morning, and I hadn't had time to call my mentor back until after the morning rush. "Kieran," he said, his voice low and rumbling when he picked up the call. I imagined him in his office in front of the wall of textbooks, many of which he'd authored. "How is your grandfather?"

"He's doing well," I said, settling in the office chair with the bustle of the shop on the other side of the door. I heard Granddad talking to customers from his perch behind the register. "You heard I'd requested another deferral?"

"I did." He was quiet for a moment, the way he let something hang in the air, waiting for a student to fill in the open space. He was deliberative, intentional, and methodical in medicine and with people. He was the kind of doctor I wanted to be, but I did know this trick, so I waited for him to speak again. "Are you sure you want to do that? You're already a year behind. A deferral would mean two years, and we don't often approve that."

I'd known that was coming when he'd emailed asking me to call him. I'd felt good making the call to request it, and then I'd shown up to the zoo and talked to Sybil, and it all felt right. It wasn't until the email from Dr. Wagstaff that the inkling of doubt crept in, because since starting school, he was the kind of man I longed to be. Respected, settled, set financially, and a groundbreaking researcher. Through the cracked door, I heard Sybil laugh with Granddad. No matter the doubt that had crept in, that was why I was doing this. I wanted more time to get the shop successful, and I wanted more time with her. "I'm sure." I watched Sybil cut through the kitchen and held up a finger as she entered to indicate I was on the phone. "I want to be a doctor. I've been working toward it my whole life, and I think I'll be a good one."

She leaned against the door frame and gave me a supportive smile.

"I just need more time to make sure I can focus when I'm back."

Dr. Wagstaff sighed. "You will be a good physician, Kieran. I just want to make sure you know what you're risking. And to make sure this is what you really want, both the deferral and the career."

His question took me aback, and my response was knee-jerk. "I promise, that's not it at all." That same question had gnawed at me since Sybil asked me something similar at the cabin, but it was too late. I'd spent too long working too hard to change my plan now.

Sybil pulled two donuts from behind her and set one on the

desk in front of me on a napkin. They were the same ones she'd made under Granddad's supervision early that morning. She'd been too excited to wait for me to come downstairs and flagged me down while I was taking out Mrs. Nguyen's dog to show them off. I grinned and swiped a finger along the side of the donut, taking a lick of the chocolate icing. "And I know the risks of the request," I said into the phone. "I know it's not guaranteed, and if they turn it down, I'll figure it out for fall, but I think this is important. I hope you understand."

We said a friendly goodbye, and he promised to advocate for me with the committee before we hung up.

"Who was that?" Sybil slid onto my lap, a crumb from her own donut falling on her chest.

"You dropped this," I said, dipping to kiss the spot below her collarbone where the crumb had landed. "So messy sometimes."

She giggled, and I moved my hand lower down her back. "You like me messy."

"I do," I said, shifting my lips to her neck. "A beautiful mess."

"Your granddad is right on the other side of the door," she groaned when my hand slid lower and I dragged my lips across the shell of her ear.

"He was in the other room last night," I said, squeezing one of her cheeks. "You didn't mind then."

"I only came in here to bring you a donut," she said, twisting her neck to catch my lips in a quick, sweet peck. "Hold that thought for later."

I grudgingly lifted the treat to my mouth. She said she'd started looking into recipes and fallen down a rabbit hole of ideas. This one was flavored with cardamom and honey, and it was good. "Delicious," I said, kissing her again and leaving little bits of sugar on her lips.

"Who was on the phone?"

"My mentor at school. He wanted to make sure I was certain about requesting the deferral. That I knew the risks."

Sybil tensed on my lap. "What risks?"

I made circles on her lower back. "Well, deferrals are rarely approved—mine was a special case the first time, so there's a chance they could say no and I'd have to enroll this fall or drop out."

"No!" Sybil tried to slide off my lap, but I held her against me. "You can't drop out."

"I'm not," I said. "And Dr. Wagstaff will advocate for me. He has a lot of pull."

"Kieran, you never said it was that risky. You can't do this." She studied my face intently.

"I want to. I do think Granddad could use a little more time before he takes things over fully, and I don't want to leave you."

"What if I'm not worth it, though?"

The look on her face when she said it sent a pin into my heart. "You are." I kissed her but let her slide off my lap this time when we parted. She liked to move while she thought through things, and my resolve strengthened knowing I knew that about her. "And worst case, I'll have to go back to Texas in September and we do long distance, but if there's a chance for us to have more time here together, I want to take it." I held out my hand, and she dropped her fingers alongside mine. "You're rubbing off on me. It's worth taking a chance on luck, right?"

She smiled, but it didn't quite reach her eyes. "But there's a chance they could approve it, right?"

I nodded. "Definitely."

"Because you said it yourself, you want to be a doctor. That's always been your goal. You're not putting that in jeopardy for me, are you?"

"It is the goal." I kissed the tops of her fingers. "But why not push my luck? I'm a good guy . . . maybe I can have my donut and eat it, too."

"I guess," she said, watching me take a bite. When I groaned—an honest groan because the flavor combination really was good—she grinned. "You really like it?"

"I do. And I really like you." I pulled her in for another kiss and paused when our lips were a breath away. "If they say no, I'll try to bribe them with these donuts."

With a woman who tasted like sugar and honey and was choosing me, I was pretty sure luck would be on my side.

41

Sybil

THIS TRADITION IS A LITTLE STRANGE, HUH?" I helped my sister pull her satin garter up over her knee while the photographer snapped photos and Mom teared up.

Grace lowered her voice. "Mom insisted it was a family tradition. I didn't want to fight with her over it."

"What is this even symbolic of? Passing the torch from your sister putting on your underwear to your husband taking it off?" I paused as the photographer requested and looked up at Grace. Her hair was arranged loosely on top of her head. The makeup artist had made her look understated and somehow showstopping, too. Her dress hung in the window nearby, and we were both wrapped in satin robes, like the other bridesmaids. "But for the record, I'm honored to put on your underwear. You're beautiful, Grace." I studied her smile— since she was a type A overachiever with a slight God complex,

I thought she'd be pinging left and right, but she'd been relaxed all day. "You look happy."

"So do you," she said, searching my face. My hair was loose, the curls held back with a pearl headband she had given me. "You've seemed happier the last few months."

"Well," I said, standing when the photographer signaled she had what she needed. "I won the lottery." I smoothed down the front of my robe for no other reason than wanting to do something with my hands. "That helps."

"It's not that." Grace adjusted the garter above her knee, shifting it from where I'd placed it. So still somewhat my same sister. "It's him. You and him. Seems like this guy really came into your life at the right time." Grace rested her palms on my biceps. "And I love that for you." She pulled me into an embrace, the smell of her perfume surrounding me as the emotional punch of her words hit me somewhere near my solar plexus, because that was exactly how I'd felt at the zoo, though now I couldn't stop spiraling about Kieran giving up medical school to stay with me, even for a year.

"Thank you," I said, blinking back tears because I wasn't going to do this here, and also I wasn't confident in the water resistance of my makeup, despite the cosmetologist's assurances. The reality was, our three months were supposed to end today, and even though I wanted us to be Twinkies, I worried we were still more like soft cheese—a limited-time engagement.

One of Grace's bridesmaids called her over to the other side of the suite, and Mom wrapped an arm around me the moment Grace stepped away. She was already in her light blue, floor-length dress, the custom handkerchief with the extra lace from Grandma's dress in her hand. "I can't believe it," she said, tugging me close.

"That Grace is getting married?"

"No," she said, dabbing at her eyes. "That both my girls are happy and thriving and in love at the same time." She tucked the handkerchief away and dropped a kiss against the side of my head. "And she's right—you're different since you started dating Kieran."

"You mean I actually show up at your place on time for once?"

She laughed. "Well, *that* is new." She stroked a hand along the neckline of my dress, hanging on a hook near Grace's. "No, you're more . . ." She studied my face, and the familiar guilt bubbled up again. "I don't know exactly, but you're more you. More confident you can do anything. I know I've had my suspicions about him, but I think he maybe helped you see that about yourself, and for that reason alone, I'm beginning to trust his intentions."

I would never have put it in those words. I'd spent so many years hearing how I'd done things wrong that I'd stopped doing things altogether. I'd only paid attention to the habit because of Kieran.

"I had my doubts, but I think you might go the distance with that boy. And for that I'm thankful." She adjusted my headband, and I inhaled her perfume. "I was telling Janice all about the birthday party at the zoo, and she couldn't believe it. You know I had to brag about what a great job you did. I told her about how you pulled together all the community organizations and how that morning show wants you on again to talk about fundraising. We ended up being late for our spin class!"

She chuckled, and it *was* funny. I could count on one hand the number of times Mom had been late for anything.

"Those are the stories you told her?"

"Of course! What else would I tell her?"

"I don't know," I said, toying with the necklace hanging around my neck. "Maybe about how I ordered way too much cake and ended up with frosting all over me because I tried to carry it myself." Mom's expression shifted and I hurried on, not wanting her to feel bad. "That was a pretty funny story," I added. "Those are just usually the ones you like to share."

"Sybil Marie Sweet," she said, touching her fingers to her jawline, something she did when she was pushing back emotion. Some people covered their mouths or eyes, but that would ruin her carefully applied makeup, and that wasn't an option.

I braced for the lecture that usually followed the use of my full name.

But she just said, "You're right. I do tell those kinds of stories about you." Her voice fell into resignation. "Probably far too often."

"It's . . ." I started the sentence planning to end it with "not a big deal," but the words felt bitter on my tongue. "It actually really bothers me," I admitted. "I've always wanted to be someone you were . . . I don't know, someone you felt you could brag about instead of laugh about."

Tears welled in her eyes. "Oh, Sybil."

"I know you don't mean to make me feel bad, but it does. So hearing you say you were telling Janice about the good work I did . . . well, that felt good. It felt like you were proud of me."

"I'm sorry, baby." She pulled me into a hug, her arms tight around me as I blinked back tears, telling her the truth feeling like a weight being lifted. "I've always been proud of you." She hugged me again, and when we finally broke apart, she grabbed for a nearby tissue box.

Dabbing at her eyes, she motioned to Grace across the room, where Warren's sister was helping her to fasten her necklace. "Your dad sent her that, did you know that?" She touched the bracelet on her wrist, the one I'd given her. "And a nice note about how he understood why he wasn't invited, that he wants to start trying to be there more for you girls. He told me he's been getting some counseling, which has helped some things fall into place for him. I know he wants to be in your lives again. To get to know you." She smiled at Grace and then me. "I'd like that. I think you'd enjoy knowing him as an adult. You're a lot like him."

"I know," I said, "unreliable, bouncing from job to job, flighty, but—"

"No," Mom said, holding up a hand. "No. I meant creative, empathetic, charming, energetic, curious, and absolutely dogged when you believe in something. Those are the reasons I fell in love with him in the first place, the reasons I had children with him. I don't think I always appreciated those things about your father when we were together, but they were all there." She held both of my biceps. "All that is to say, the stories I should tell are ones that highlight those traits, because that is what I see in you. Those are the things I've always seen in you."

I fanned at my face as the tears welled in my eyes. "You have? I always felt like you guys thought I'd end up being like him. Absent."

"Never." She pulled me into a hug. "But you also have something your dad didn't have."

"Millions of dollars? A really fantastic ass?"

"Oh, his butt was a thing of beauty. The way that man looked in sweatpants!" Mom said with a laugh, and gave me another squeeze. "But what I meant was that you're with a partner who truly believes in you, who sees all the amazing things about you that shine and helps you see them in yourself, and I am so happy you do, because for all your father's faults, and they were many, I didn't pay enough attention to the parts that shined, and I think Kieran does with you. And I think you're two people who are going to really care for each other."

Grace approached us, concern on her face, and I dabbed at my eyes. "What's wrong?"

I accepted the tissue she handed me, blotting the corners of my eyes. "Nothing. Mom was telling me how nice dad's ass used to look in sweatpants," I said through a laugh, earning a gentle shove from my mom.

"I said 'butt,'" she added, dabbing at her own eyes. "Don't be crass."

"I . . . don't even want to know," Grace said, shooting me a curious look. "The photographer is about ready for us, Mom."

They posed together for a few photos, and I found a mirror to inspect my mascara, which still looked good, though inside I was a mess of emotions as I thought about Mom's words. Kieran did believe in me and see me, in all the ways that really mattered. I replayed all the little moments where he'd cheered me on, and I took a deep breath to try to compose myself. Despite the happy butterflies all those memories gave me, something had been eating at me since Kieran told me he'd requested to defer his reenrollment. When Mom brought up taking care of each other, it was a reminder that I'd made the right choice and hoped I'd done enough.

I looked at my phone screen, where a series of texts were waiting from Emi.

> EMI: Did you tell him you'll move to
> Texas with him yet?

I blew out a slow breath, because the idea of leaving home threatened to ruin my eye makeup, but I knew in my heart it was the right thing. I couldn't keep him from his dream, and I didn't want to give up on us. I knew she'd talk me out of the other part of my plan, the plan to ensure the committee would approve his request to defer. But if it didn't work, I'd move with him.

> EMI: Also, Marcus just asked me
> for advice on asking someone out.
> WHO IS MARCUS ASKING OUT?

> EMI: And give Grace a big hug for me.

> SYBIL: I have no idea who Marcus
> is seeing but be thankful he can get
> over you.

> SYBIL: And not yet—after the
> wedding, I think!

> SYBIL: And if you ever get married,
> can you promise I don't have to
> help you with a garter?

EMI: If I ever get married, I think I'd
want something much more interesting
under my dress.

SYBIL: Well, obviously I'd help you
with a wedding strap-on

EMI: This is why we're friends.

EMI: Know yet what you're going to
say to him?

I had no idea, but Mom was pointing to her watch from the other side of the room, her short-lived moment of chill gone, and I set my phone aside, reaching for my dress. I had a few "I dos" and Pachelbel's Canon in D to figure out what to say to Kieran when I told him he didn't need to choose between school and me.

42

Kieran

THE BEST MAN PLACED A HAND ON WARREN'S shoulder, and both men were tearing up. "Alfred, Lord Tennyson said love is the only gold. And, Warren, with Grace by your side, you, my friend, are truly rich." He wiped a tear from the corner of his eye and lifted his champagne flute. "To love."

We raised our glasses after the best man's toast, which was the opposite of a cliché and embarrassing speech. I barely knew Warren, and I felt like I'd been to war and band camp with him and would go back to both if he asked.

"How am I supposed to compete with that?" Sybil whispered near my ear, taking a sip of her champagne.

"Have any Tennyson quotes up your sleeve?"

"I could drop in some Taylor Swift." She took another sip, glancing at the handwritten notes in front of her, the loopy cursive so familiar to me now.

"You'll do great," I said, leaning in closer, my lips almost brushing her ear in that way that had become so familiar. I thought about pulling back but reminded myself it no longer had to just appear real. "The odds are good Warren's dental school buddies are Swifties, right?"

She giggled. "I don't think so, but I wouldn't guess you were, either, so . . ."

"It's just that one song," I said defensively.

"Sure." She fiddled with the strap of her dress, which was made from the same material as her sister's but with touches of teal like the other bridesmaids'. I slid a fingertip along the fabric that crossed low on her back, noticing how goose bumps rose on her skin.

"Fine. Maybe a few songs on that album," I mumbled.

"I knew it," she said.

She looked at me like I was her person, and, despite my anxiety about what the review board would decide, I knew I didn't want to be apart from her. She searched my face the way she had so many times before, and I stroked the line across her back again, the slow slide against her skin feeling far more intimate than something we should have been doing in public.

She leaned closer, her elbow grazing my stomach. "You're a certified fan now, huh?" She smelled sweet, and I began a path along the edge of the dress, from her shoulder toward her lower back, soaking in the way she reacted to my touch.

"I'm a fan of you," I said, repeating the motion in reverse. Her lips were slightly parted, the familiar deep red color inviting. "And that one song," I added. The reception buzzed around us, and across the table, her mom and stepdad chatted amiably with some friends, but Sybil captured the entirety of my attention.

"And now we'll hear from Grace's sister, maid of honor

Sybil." The DJ's voice cut through my daze, and Sybil was on her feet and away from my touch before I knew it.

"Here goes. Taylor Swift is better than Tennyson, right?" she said, downing what was left of her champagne before grabbing my untouched glass with a wink. "Do I seem nervous?"

I did my best to pretend the last few moments hadn't happened and shook my head. "Shake it off."

Sybil accepted the mic and scanned the crowd. "For those who don't know, I've had a bit of luck the last several months, and I get asked often what it feels like to be so lucky." She looked across the room to me and I smiled, recognizing the speech she'd brainstormed lying in bed with me.

"I tell them I have no idea, but I should pay someone to figure it out for me," she said with a smile, and the crowd responded with laughter. "But what I actually tell them is that I've been lucky my whole life." She looked at Grace, who leaned against Warren. "I was lucky to have Grace as my older sister—she was so well-behaved. Our mom wasn't prepared for me, so having the element of surprise on my side was a real win. I was lucky she was in my corner, no matter what. Come to think of it, I'm lucky Warren has been, too."

Warren kissed the side of Grace's head as she dabbed at her eyes.

"But most of all, I learned about luck when my sister talked about Warren." She paused and looked at the couple again. "You know my first question when she said she'd met someone was 'Is he hot?'" The room filled with laughter again, and I saw Sybil visibly relax and set her notes aside. "Warren, she said yes. But after that, she got this dreamy look in her eyes that never quite went away, and she told me about your smile and your sense of humor, and she told me how you made her feel seen and valued and loved."

Sybil paused again, waiting for the collective *aww*. "But the thing was, she continued to say those things. She told me how you were special and how she'd trust you with anything. I'd never seen my sister like that before, and one day she told me how lucky she was to be in love with you, how lucky you were to have found each other."

That was the end of her planned speech. She was about to raise her glass and call for the toast to the couple, but she looked across the room at me, eyes meeting mine, and she kept going. "That's where I learned about feeling lucky, but that's also where I learned luck wasn't enough. I've seen these two build a home together, and I was crashing in their guest room a lot, so I have *all* the dirt on their fights," she joked, earning a laugh and a playful shushing motion from Grace. "But I've also seen them share with each other, share it all—their fears, their hopes, their dreams, the things we don't tell other people because we're afraid they won't understand. I watched them go the extra mile to help each other. I saw these two realize how lucky they are to have each other and put in the time and care to build something between them. I saw the kind of partner I wanted to be someday."

She met my gaze for another moment as her words sank in, and my heart started beating faster, but she broke eye contact and looked at her sister and brother-in-law, raising her glass. "So join me in toasting Grace and Warren. To being lucky and realizing what you have."

Everyone raised their glasses—my own glass empty after one sip, since the beautiful woman onstage had stolen mine, along with every ounce of good sense and self-preservation. I wanted nothing more than to pull her into my arms and have her admit what she'd said was about us, too. A chorus of voices repeated her toast, and the applause circled the room as Sybil hugged her sister, the two sharing quiet words before Warren joined the hug. A passing server offered me a fresh glass and I accepted, eyes not leaving Sybil. "Thank you," I said, probably too late for them to hear me.

The DJ played a love song, announcing everyone was invited to join the couple on the dance floor. As Sybil stepped off the stage, I took another drink of champagne and walked toward her. "Still in my duties as a wedding date to dance with you, right?"

She gave me a small smile. "I wouldn't want to hold you in breach of contract," she said, handing her glass to a server passing by the edge of the dance floor.

"Decided to dispense with the lyrics?" I said, taking her hand to join in the slow dance in progress.

"Was it okay?" She rested her palm over my chest, and I covered her hand with mine.

"It was perfect," I said, guiding her hips as we moved to the beat of the song. "You changed the end."

A couple near us laughed, and I leaned closer to hear Sybil's response. "Yeah, it came to me on the fly," she said, resting her head on my shoulder, her fingertips grazing the nape of my neck for a split second. "Talking about just luck was too . . ."

"Insufficient?" I offered.

She nodded against me, pulling away to meet my eyes again. "Yeah. Like, if it's just luck . . . that's not enough, right?"

I shook my head, trying to read into her words enough to figure out what was next for us. "Definitely not enough."

I took her hand from behind my neck and spun her out and back, breaking the tension over the hold I was letting her have on my heart.

Coming out of the spin, she grinned widely. "Everyone is going to be jealous of how good we look out here," she said, sliding against me.

"That's the goal, right?" I spun her again as the song reached the last crescendo. I couldn't see her face as I said it, her body a blur of cream and blue lace and red, kissable lips.

Her palm slid to my neck as she spun back into me, her body pressed to mine. We held each other, moving to the closing beats of the song, and she searched my face again, lips parting as if to say something, and like a sucker I waited again, breath caught in my chest. She blinked and her expression turned playful. "Exactly the goal," she said. "Big finish?"

"Yes," I said, stepping forward to lower her into a dip. I felt like a little kid, I was so giddy about her, about this being for real. I dropped a slow, soft kiss to her lips. "Big finish." But this was just the beginning for us.

43

Sybil

OUTSIDE KIERAN'S WINDOW, RAIN PELTED THE glass, the sky dark, but I couldn't tell if it was early or the storm was just strong. As I made my way back to bed from the tiny bathroom down the hall, thunder clapped and a flash of lightning lit the sky.

"Hey," he croaked, voice full of sleep, when I slid back under the covers, warming my bare legs under one of his T-shirts. "Morning," he said.

"It's raining," I said, taking advantage of our proximity to soak in the warmth of his bed. "And cold."

"Want another blanket?"

"No." I nudged my way against him, hand on his chest, like I had so many other mornings, and his arm came around me the same way, like an instinct. "I'll just make you keep me warm."

"I already gave you my shirt," he said, his hand wandering circles on my side under the blankets.

"Thanks for helping me into bed last night." I glanced at my dress in the closet. "And hanging up my dress."

"No problem." His palm flattened and shifted from circles to long, slow sweeps up my side, over my ribs, and down to my hips. "You crashed pretty fast once we got home." His strokes paused, and he added, "Got back to my place."

"I like calling it home," I admitted, earning one of those grins I was seeing more and more of.

I'd been so close to telling him the night before, so close to kissing him and asking him to take me to Whataburger once we got to Texas. "It was a long night," he added, resuming his strokes up and down, his touch having the desired effect of warming me, but also making me want more.

"Because your date got drunk?"

He chuckled, the movement making the mattress vibrate. "Exactly. I had to make sure you didn't put someone's eye out doing the YMCA or injure yourself doing the electric slide."

"There was a rumor that song is about a vibrator," I mused, fiddling with the hair at the nape of his neck.

"Really?" His palm swept lower as another clap of thunder shook the building, his fingers toying with the hem of my shirt.

"It's not true, but there should be more songs about sex toys," I said, caving to the feel of his hands, which made me want to lean into every stroke and touch. I lifted my knee to his hip, and he immediately swept his palm lower.

"You can write one," he said, sliding his hand under the shirt and over my bare thigh. "Next career move."

"That patriotic dildo really was giving 'Proud to Be an American' vibes," I added, breath stuttering when he dragged a finger along the line of my panties over my thigh. Our voices were low in the darkened room, with only residual light from the streetlamps casting shadows over Kieran's face. I traced a finger along his jaw, the prickle of his morning stubble so familiar and the soft, hooded look of his eyes as he teased me clear on his face, when a flash of lighting filled the room with energy, and I arched against him. "Do you need to open the shop this morning?"

His lips moved along the column of my throat, and he spoke against my skin, the sleep in his voice shifting to something else. "I posted that we'd be opening late today." His hand fell away from my panties but moved over my stomach before I could complain. "I thought we might want . . ."

I sucked in a breath when he stroked a path up my stomach and the pad of his thumb brushed over my nipple.

"Time this morning."

"Kieran," I groaned as his thumb worked over my peaked flesh in the tight circles I liked, waiting to brush over the tip until I was worked into a frenzy. "We do need time," I said, knowing there were so many levels of truth to that. We needed this bed and hours to enjoy each other, but I needed more time like this, wrapped in him, wrapped in us. I guided his chin toward me, pressing my lips to his, the kiss in time with a clap of thunder, and I sank into the bruising wholeness I felt against him. "We should talk."

"Take this off," he said, tugging on the shirt. "I promise I'll keep you warm and we can talk after."

I sat and wriggled out of the shirt, tossing it aside.

"Lay back against the pillows," he directed, and I reclined, seeing his shadowed gaze move over my body in the low light before he shifted to tug my panties down my thighs, tossing them across the room. "What do you want to do with our time,

Syb?" He leaned forward, and I prepared for another kiss to take my breath, but he diverted at the last minute, his lips falling to my collarbone and his hips settling between my spread legs, the familiar hard length of him against my bare center.

"I want time for everything." I ground against him, sliding my fingernails against his scalp before guiding his chin so he looked at me. "I want everything." I repeated the words, hoping they conveyed it all, hoping he'd understand "everything" meant his sleepy voice in the mornings and his pathological need to be on time and the way his hand felt against my lower back leading me through a crowd. "Everything," I said in a lower voice as the deep rumble of distant thunder filled the room.

I kissed him, enjoying the interplay of our tongues, and the friction between my legs at the pressure of him reminded me of how lucky I had been feeling every day lately. Kieran broke the kiss and dropped his lips to the tip of my nose, the gesture so out of place in the heat of the moment that I giggled, taking in the playful expression that had crossed his face. This was us, and I didn't want to lose it.

"Relax," he said, kissing down my chest and stomach, nudging my thighs apart.

"Do I look tense?" I stretched.

"You look like you're . . ." I watched him move over my body, landing on my face, his stare intense in a way I didn't expect, and he didn't finish his sentence but dipped his mouth between my thighs, and the first touch of his tongue took me to the first night, and the last time, his lips making paths that were both familiar and shockingly effective and driving me wild. "Ready."

"Kieran," I groaned, my breaths coming fast as he worked

me toward an orgasm while the rain outside pounded against the building. "Everything," I repeated, and his thick finger slid into my heat, curling at the right pace to make it impossible to catch my breath as my thighs quaked.

The orgasm built slowly until it didn't, and I crashed along with the noise of the storm outside, Kieran coaxing the pleasure from my body and slowing to bring me to another orgasm until I pulled him forward for another kiss.

I expected this moment to be filled with long, intense eye contact, but he guided me to my stomach and raised my hips. I liked it this way—it was always so good, and I looked over my shoulder, still needing to catch his gaze in the dark, but his stare was on my back as his hand trailed between my shoulder blades, pressing my upper back lower as he teased me with his finger. "Condom," he said, his voice flustered. "Can you reach the nightstand?"

I stretched but couldn't. "I'm on birth control," I said, grinding back against his teasing finger. "And I trust you."

Kieran groaned, and the head of his thick erection pressed against me, my body eager with the promise of him inside me, of the power in our joining. "Syb . . ." His palm slid down my spine, his fingers almost deferential against each ridge of my vertebrae.

"Everything," I said, backing against him, breath escaping in a gasp when he pushed inside, us bare to each other.

His thrusts grew in intensity fast, both of us frantic for more and more of each other, more and more of this. I gripped the bedding in front of me, meeting him thrust for thrust as he hit the right spot almost immediately, knowing my body so well. I wished I could see his face, but I knew with every breath that we'd have hundreds, thousands of mornings like this, and

I smiled and cried out as he thrust against my G-spot again and again until I was on the edge, and that was when his finger slid against my clit, finding me in the dark, in the chaos. Everything felt like it made more sense with him near me like this.

I clenched around him as another series of heavy thunder and lightning shook the world, and I came hard around Kieran, who followed me over the cliff, his hand at my waist tightening. He grunted, guiding us both down to the bed, still connected, both our breath coming fast as we came down from the climax. His hand was hot against my skin, and I pressed my back to his, imagining how he'd look when I shared with him all the things I wanted to say. Working out the right words to use. "So, I was thinking," I said, linking my fingers with his. "About us."

He kissed my shoulder. "I like us."

"And Texas," I added. I wondered what it would be like to live somewhere new, to start over with new people in a new town. It was exciting and terrifying. "I was thinking—"

We both stopped short at the crash from the kitchen, and Kieran was on his feet in an instant, snatching his basketball shorts from the floor and running out. I searched the floor for his T-shirt and ran out behind him to find him hunched over Joe, who lay still on the kitchen floor.

"Call nine-one-one," Kieran shouted over his shoulder, and began pressing on Joe's chest. "He's not breathing."

44

Kieran

SYBIL'S VOICE WAS A BLUR IN THE BACKGROUND, AND I felt my body move as if on autopilot, my training taking over.

Hands centered on the chest.

Elbows locked and shoulders directly over hands.

Two inches down.

One hundred to one hundred and twenty compressions per minute.

She was crying behind me, and I felt her footsteps and her panic, but with each compression, I could block it out. I knew what to do. It was automatic. I could fix this.

Open the airway to a past-neutral position and tilt the head back.

Pinch the nose, take a normal breath, and make a seal over the patient's mouth.

Each breath lasts one second.

Repeat.

Sybil paced behind me, the rhythm of her steps, my compressions, her steps, my compressions. Breath. Breath.

I did it over and over again, focused on his chest and counting and doing everything I could to take care of him until the paramedics rushed through the door behind me, nudging me aside. I stepped away, gulping in deep breaths and feeling Sybil's palm on my back, her body at my side. I watched them work, and somehow I slid into shoes, but I didn't remember them appearing. The paramedics strapped him to the gurney, and I searched for anything to think of besides the fact that Granddad wasn't breathing on his own, because despite all my education, I couldn't wrap my head around him not making it. He would. He had to.

I needed to focus on something else—anything else. I sucked in ragged breaths and tried to still my shaking hands as we hurried out of the apartment, and I saw the magnet on the fridge, the one I'd sent him from Texas with the mascot giving a thumbs-up.

I couldn't go back. I'd have to stay to take care of the shop and Granddad. No matter the committee's decision. I would have to stay out for another year, and I'd have time to make it all work—to do things right with Sybil; to really take care of Granddad, because he was going to make it. He had to. And I needed time to figure out how to quiet the doubts in my head about medical school. I should have been panicked about that, but what I felt, what emotion stood there on the sidelines with worry and fear that Granddad wouldn't make it, was something like relief.

45

Sybil

TOM PACED BACK AND FORTH ACROSS THE WAITING room, sipping from his paper coffee cup, taking his ball cap off and then putting it back on every few minutes. Lila was thumbing at the screen of her phone, but I watched the bounce of her knee under the big hoodie she wore. When they'd arrived, the sun had just been rising, but now the waiting room was filled with sunshine. *That has to be a good sign, right? The storms have cleared.* I thought about saying it, but Tom was still pacing and Lila's knee was still bouncing, and I held it back. Kieran had been with Joe and the doctor for about ten minutes, and I took the seat across from Lila, pulling out my own phone.

> DEACON: Emi and I are at the shop and Chad is on his way. Lila called Marcus for help when she heard.

DEACON: How is their grandpa?
How's my man, K?

SYBIL: Kieran is with him. No news
yet. Is Marcus there, too?

I heard a familiar voice say "Hey," and Marcus rushed in, taking the chair next to Lila and wrapping an arm around her to pull her in. I watched the two of them, Marcus looking older than he normally did to me, and Lila softer.

"Seems I'm the only one here without a date." Tom gave Marcus a clap on the shoulder and then took a seat. "If Joe's back there charming a cute doctor, I'm really gonna feel left out." Lila laughed with her head still on Marcus's shoulder, and Marcus sent me one of those "how do I react here?" looks. But Lila chimed in first.

"I mean, some chicks dig scars, but not head wounds and cardiac problems, so I think your feelings will be safe." She and Tom laughed, and I saw the tears in both their eyes. "He'll wait to charm a doctor until he's breathing on his own, and you can be his wingman."

"That's . . . dark," Marcus said, joining them with a smile.

"You like how dark I am," Lila said, squeezing his arm.

Marcus kissed the side of her head. "I do."

Tom gave me a pointed, wide-eyed look in response to their conversation, and I shrugged but wrapped my own arm around his shoulder and squeezed. "I'll be your date until Kieran gets back."

We didn't have to wait long, because a few moments later, he pushed through the doors into the waiting room where we sat, scrubbing his face as he approached, and everyone seemed to hold their breath. He was still in basketball shorts and wore a worn hoodie. "They're running tests," he said, "but he's conscious and talking."

"Thank God," Tom said on an exhale.

"It'll be a few hours until they know anything, probably," he said, collapsing in the chair next to me. "You can go back to see him, Lila." He gave a curious look to Marcus and added, "There can be two people at a time."

She nodded and grabbed Marcus's hand without saying anything else, though she dipped to hug Kieran before they walked through the double doors.

It was quiet for only a few seconds before Tom asked, "We not gonna talk about that? That kid's a good one, right?"

I nodded. "He's a good one. No need to worry."

"I should call Chad to open up the shop. There are pickup orders this morning." Kieran pulled his phone out, and I placed a hand over it.

"He's on his way. Emi and Deacon opened up the shop, though. It's taken care of."

He gripped his phone a moment longer until I coaxed him to release it.

"We took care of it," I reassured him. "You don't have to handle anything else right now."

"Okay," he said, leaning back in the chair. He tipped his head back, resting it against the wall. "I guess it's good I asked for a deferral," he said, reaching for my other hand. I studied it as our fingers linked. Everything was so different now, but I squeezed his hand. "I have to help with the shop before I go back."

I nodded, ready to encourage him to not worry about it for

the moment. "There's nothing you can solve right now. Maybe just rest and focus on Joe."

He didn't respond, and I was about to attempt my point again, when his phone buzzed in my hand, "Dr. Charles Wagstaff" flashing across the screen. He opened one eye but jumped up when he saw it. "That's my mentor from school."

"Calling on a Sunday?" I asked.

He tapped the screen and walked across the room with it pressed to his ear. He spoke low, and I couldn't hear what he was saying.

"You think he'll go home and get some sleep at some point?" Tom asked.

My face flamed, thinking of how the morning had started, and I looked back to Kieran, who had turned away from us. "I doubt it."

"Good man to have in a storm. Lucky you two were home," he said, straightening his hat again. "Lucky indeed."

"Okay," I heard Kieran say into the phone, but I couldn't read his tone. "I understand."

"Everything okay?" Tom asked, though Kieran's back was to us still.

"Was he calling about the committee?" I asked, my own knee bouncing as Lila's had earlier. When I'd called about the donation, the school said they'd get back to me, but no one had. I'd let it slip my mind with all the wedding events and my excitement to tell Kieran I'd move with him when he went back.

Lila and Marcus pushed through the doors then, his arm still around her and Lila dabbing at her eyes with her sleeve. "They're starting their tests now," she said. "But he looks better than last time he was admitted." She motioned to Kieran. "What's going on?"

Kieran tucked his phone in his pocket, and he looked ashen when he turned.

"Did you hear me? His color is good and he's responsive. We're so lucky you were there."

He nodded, his head continuing to bob. "Yeah."

"What did your mentor say?" I asked, standing. "Did they make a decision?"

He nodded, gaze snapping to mine, but the softness and sweetness I'd gotten so used to were gone, and in their place was something I hadn't seen from him in what felt like forever. Like his walls were back up. He looked at me like I was a stranger. Like I was a stranger who was bad news. His voice was low and so neutral that I recoiled in my seat. "What did you do?"

"What're you talking about, kid? She's been here next to me the whole time," Tom said, sitting straighter in his seat.

"What's going on?" Lila repeated. "Who was on the phone?"

My stomach sank and I swallowed thickly. "What did he say?" My voice was shakier than I wanted.

He took a step toward me, close enough for me to see the shadows under his eyes and the shake in his hand. His voice was louder now, filling the space. "What did you do?"

"I wanted to help," I said, shrinking into my seat again as he approached. "I just wanted to help," I repeated, the tears falling down my cheeks. "What did he say?"

"He said my goddamn career is over. He said they were going to approve my deferral because of all my potential and hard work, and then they got a phone call." He tried to step forward, but Marcus had stepped between the two of us. "What did you fucking do?"

Marcus pushed him backward with both hands on his shoulders. "You need to back off," he said. "Calm down."

My head pounded, and it felt like the floor under me was falling away. "I just wanted to help," I whispered. "To go the extra mile. To take care of you like you take care of everyone."

"Take a breath, son," Tom said, placing hands on both Marcus's and Kieran's shoulders. "Let's just take a minute here and calm down like he said."

"I'm very calm." Kieran paced to the other side of the room. "I'm calm. But I'm not a doctor. I'm never going to be a doctor, because tomorrow I'm going to get formal notification that my request to defer reenrollment isn't just denied, the offer to return is revoked for ethical impropriety."

Lila approached him, looking over her shoulder with a wide-eyed stare. "You're the most ethical person I know. What are you talking about? What do you think Sybil did?"

Only, I knew what I'd done. I gulped a breath and wrapped my arms across my chest. I just wanted to make myself smaller. "I was just trying to help."

"Why don't you explain how you helped." I saw his chest moving up and down fast, the frenetic energy rolling off him in waves.

"I . . ." I sucked in a breath. "I would move to Texas with you if it got declined, but I thought . . ."

"You thought. But you didn't ask."

"You bullied her into talking," Marcus said. "Let her finish a damn sentence."

"I thought maybe you'd think you had to choose between school and me, and if they approved your request, we'd have time to figure it out, so I . . ." I sucked in a breath again, swiping tears from my face. "I . . ."

"Offered to donate three million dollars to the school if they decided in my favor." His voice was flat, and I looked down at my knees, not wanting to see the expression that accompanied Lila's and Tom's gasps.

"I didn't think this would happen," I tried to explain, the words tumbling from my lips. "I didn't think . . ."

Kieran's voice dropped again, and he waited to speak until I caught my breath from crying, which was so much worse because I knew he wanted me to hear him. "There are consequences. You attempted to bribe the school to approve my request, and now I don't get to be a doctor. You took away my option. You took away my chance. I can't even . . . I can't be in the same room as you."

I hugged myself tighter, but it wasn't doing any good. It wasn't protecting me from those words, and I heaved another wet sob, but Kieran didn't say anything else.

He just walked out.

46

Kieran

LILA CROSSED HER ARMS OVER HER CHEST AND stared at me over Granddad's bed.

"What?" I said, keeping my voice low to not wake him.

She crossed one leg over the other and tilted her head to the side, one eyebrow raised. Granddad had been in the hospital for four days, and since everything had blown up with Sybil, Lila's eyebrow hadn't lowered once when she directed her attention to me.

"Why the fuck are you giving me that look?"

"Why do you think?"

I cracked my knuckles, readjusting my position in the uncomfortable chair next to Granddad's bed. My lower back ached, and I desperately wanted to shower off the scent of the hospital. On top of that, I'd wanted to punch a wall for days, to break or smash something, and the anger wouldn't go away. "I don't want to talk about it and I'm not the fucking bad guy here. I'm fine."

"Okay. I see that you believe that. But why did you, who have been allergic to showing emotion for most of your life, just drop two f-bombs in thirty seconds?" She glanced at Granddad, who was still snoring softly over the beeps of the monitors. "Because Sybil isn't the bad guy, either. Last week, you said you were lucky to have her."

"I was," I said. "Turns out it was bad luck."

"Stop being so fucking overdramatic."

"I thought you were concerned about f-bombs," I said.

"Only when you use them." Lila grinned. "I say the word liberally, like a fucking lady." My sister had our mom's smile—not that I'd seen the original in years—but Lila's face was like a balm, and my shoulders lowered, easing out of the defensive stance I'd been holding for days.

"I'm angry," I admitted. "I'm so angry." I held my arms out, palms toward her. "Because my whole goddamn life just imploded at the hands of my . . ." Girlfriend. I wanted to say "girlfriend," but it was so inadequate, both for what I felt and the extent to which what she'd done was like a knife to the chest. Because it seemed like the love of my life had cut the cord holding me to my future, that the woman I'd known at my core was my soulmate had taken a torch to everything I'd worked for since childhood. And I was still relieved. Relieved the decision was made for me and I didn't have to confront how uncertain I'd been feeling lately about being a doctor, and that feeling made me angrier than anything. And I didn't know how to fix it. I didn't know how to fix anything, and I felt helpless. "At the hands of Sybil," I amended. "Granddad's heart stopped in front of me because I wasn't paying close enough attention to his health, and now I have no choice but to stay and run the shop. Am I not allowed a few 'fucks' in that situation?"

"You were really hard on her, Kier." She chewed her lower lip. "But you're right. You get seven more 'fucks.'"

"Thanks."

Granddad stirred and we both stared at him, Lila breaking first and crossing to my side of the room around the foot of the bed. Her fingers brushed over my shoulder, and she wrapped her tattooed arms around my midsection from behind. "It sucks," she admitted. "Be as angry as you want. I won't say another word."

"I don't believe you."

"That's smart," she said, giving me another squeeze and nudging my arm out of the way so she could sit on the arm of the chair. "I'm going to have a lot more to say."

"She's like her grandmother in that way," Granddad croaked from the bed, stirring from his nap.

"You're up," she said, jumping up to hand him a cup of water, angling the straw to his mouth. "How do you feel?"

"Still alive," he said, resting a palm on her hand. "So, pretty damn good, all things considered."

I studied the monitors as I'd been doing, determined not to miss anything again. "Are you in pain? We can call the nurse," I said, standing next to Lila.

"I'm okay," he said. "Why does Lila have so much to say to you? Besides saving my life—thank you for that, by the way. Don't think I've said that yet." He cleared his throat and gave me a weak smile, and I motioned for him to take another drink. "What did you do, son?"

"Nothing," I said with a wave. "Nothing that matters right now. We're just focused on you getting well."

He nodded. "And what did Sybil do to earn you being hard on her?"

"Were you listening to our whole conversation? I thought you were asleep," Lila said, settling back on the arm of the chair.

"Ah," he said with a chuckle. "Old granddad trick. I've been pretending to be asleep for years. You wouldn't believe the things you two admit when you think I'm not listening."

"Son of a bitch," Lila said with a laugh, taking his hand that hung near the side of the bed. "That's genius."

"I'm not just a pretty face." He patted her hand, seeming almost like his old self despite lying in a hospital bed hooked up to all these monitors. "Now, will you tell me why you're fighting with my future granddaughter?"

I adjusted the blanket at the foot of his bed. "It's a long story."

"Well, then," he said, kicking my hand lightly from under the blanket. "It's a good thing I'm confined to a hospital bed. And my heart might explode if I disobey doctor's orders again, so I've got plenty of time to lie here and listen." He laughed at his own joke, but I couldn't bring myself to fake a laugh.

"We broke up." Had we? I suppose it was implied in me storming out after telling her how badly she had screwed up. My stomach roiled at the memory of her expression, the way she crumpled even as she tried to pull herself into a tighter and tighter ball. She'd texted and called, all some version of an apology, but I couldn't read her messages without getting angry all over again, without being reminded how everything I thought I could stand on was turning to dust.

"No," he said. "How can that be? You two are so good together. I assumed she'd go back to Texas with you, really."

I tried again to adjust the blanket, and he pushed my hand away with his foot. "I'm not going back," I said, giving up and taking the chair Lila had been occupying. "You know you can't take the shop back over, right? I'll stay and run it."

Granddad looked at Lila with wide eyes like he hadn't heard me correctly. "How hard did I hit my head?"

"It's . . . it's a long story, but I can't go back to school, and there's no one else to run the shop." I looked down at my hands to avoid his inquisitive stare. "So I'll do it."

Lila returned to the chair and sent another raised eyebrow my way, but she didn't say anything else.

"No." Granddad pounded his fist against the bed. "Absolutely not."

"Calm down, Granddad," I said, eyeing the heart monitor. "Your heart."

"Exactly." He pointed at me, his body looking frail but that one finger steady and aimed at me. "You and your sister are my heart, and I'll be damned if you're giving up on your dreams to take care of me. Not going to happen." He let his hand fall and took a slow breath. "And if Lila offered to drop out of school and run the shop, you'd say the same fucking thing. So, no."

The room was quiet for a moment with only the beeps of the monitor and the whirring from the compression bands around his legs. "Granddad took one of your 'fucks,'" Lila said, and after a beat, Granddad laughed, I laughed, and Lila smiled, and I noticed his heart rate lower as the tension in the room seemed to dissipate.

He patted the bed and I stepped closer, taking the hand he offered. "I requested a deferral for my reenrollment," I said. "Asked the committee to allow me one more year, which they usually don't do." He nodded, letting me finish. "And Sybil called the school and offered to donate a lot of money for their new building if they approved my request."

Lila winced, despite her earlier insistence that I was over-reacting.

"They took that as a bribe, which it was, I guess. And officially rescinded my offer to reenroll for ethics violations. So it's not that I'm not going back to school. I couldn't even if I wanted to, and it's unlikely I'd get into any other medical school, not with that kind of mark on my record."

"Oh no," he said. "I'm sorry, son. I don't know what to say. And Sybil must feel awful."

"They're not really talking right now," Lila said.

"I see." Granddad squeezed my hand. "And you're mad."

I nodded, though even as I agreed, I wasn't sure whether I was mad at her or just mad at myself for not being able to fix this and forget her. Or for not having been brave enough to make my own choices sooner about medical school. If I could fix this, I could focus on something again, and maybe that would make it easier to push her smile, and the way her fingers felt against my face, and her lucky pennies out of my memory.

"You know, I love Sybil. I think she cares about people. And she loves you." He raised his bushy eyebrows for emphasis. "I think she's someone who acts on her gut, and you're a thinker, a logic guy."

"We're polar opposites." I loved her energy and creativity and how being with her felt like being in the center of a storm together, but that would never work long-term. "We're wrong for each other."

"When you come at a problem from two angles, gosh, that can be a great position to be in. But I do think she's always going to be someone who makes impulsive decisions, and yes, this time it was a really bad one and there were consequences, and I get that you're angry, and you should be angry." He squeezed my hand, and I knew he wanted to wave his arms around and pull me into a hug, but the squeeze was enough. "I'm not saying that you have to forget or forgive what she did, but I know you and I think that you want to. And don't fool yourself into thinking decisions made solely with this," he said, lifting a finger to his temple, "aren't sometimes bad decisions, too."

I shook my head, even as the rightness of what he was saying and how well he knew me landed on me. I did want to forgive it all. I didn't want to feel this way, but I couldn't picture looking at her and not seeing the uncertainty of my future, even though I hadn't been certain before this, and her question from that night in the cabin, about why I wanted to be a surgeon, came back to me. About Dr. Wagstaff's questioning whether I wanted to be a doctor. And now the only question I was left with was whether I could be with someone this impulsive. I paced the small space. I couldn't. It wasn't even a question. I couldn't, no matter how good I felt when I was with her.

Granddad kept going, pulling me back from my own spiraling thoughts. "If it means being with who you love for the rest of your life or losing her, I have to believe it's worth taking the time for a conversation."

I nodded and looked at his hand over mine, where his IV was attached. "I'll think about it."

"And we're selling the shop," he said, patting both our hands. "I can't run it, and you two have lives to lead. The card for that real estate developer is on my nightstand. Not sure what the building is worth, but give him a call."

"Granddad," I said. "We don't have to sell it. You love that place."

He nodded. "I do love it. I built it with my Rosie, but it's just a place." He patted our hands again. "Place isn't family, and neither of you love it like I do. So we sell."

"Are you sure?" Lila asked, shooting me a quick glance filled with concern.

"Absolutely." He nodded once, resolute, and rested his hands over his stomach. "Now, I'm two for two on good advice. Let's talk about this Marcus fellow." He gave Lila a sly smile, earning a groan from my sister.

"We're just friends."

Granddad laughed, and I was going to join in the teasing, though Marcus had been the one blocking me from getting to Sybil the other day, so he probably wasn't my biggest fan now, either. Before I could say anything, a woman holding a clipboard knocked on the door. I recognized the blue plastic from Granddad's last stay in the hospital and braced myself for the discussion of the bill. "Mr. Anderson? A moment?"

In the hall, she introduced herself. "I have some forms for you to sign and review," she began.

"We set up a payment plan the last time," I said. "I worked with Angela in billing and—"

"Oh," she said, holding up a small hand. "There's been some miscommunication. Your grandfather's medical expenses have been taken care of."

I stared at her while I tried to decipher what she meant. "We paid off the bills from his last stay, but—"

"No, there's a note on the file to bill a Sybil Sweet. It's all been arranged. I just need to review a few things with you as his power of attorney."

I didn't focus on anything else the woman said because I kept mentally tripping on Sybil doing this, and she must have done it after the blowup, after I screamed at her for what she'd done to try to get me back into school. My face was hot, and I nodded at the rest of the woman's explanation, relieved once she handed me the paperwork to review on my own later. When she walked away, I pulled my phone from my pocket and navigated to Sybil's number.

> KIERAN: You didn't have to pay his
> medical bills but thank you for
> being so generous to us. I don't
> know how to repay you.

I expected a quick response. Sybil always checked her texts immediately. Sometimes it drove me nuts when I was talking to her, but now, when I was on the other end of the phone, I was eager for that contact.

> KIERAN: And I'm so sorry for
> yelling at you.

Eagerness turned into anxiety as I stared at the message until it shifted to read. And then nothing. There weren't ticking clocks in the hallway of the hospital, but it felt like there were as I paced back and forth. I thumbed through the forms the hospital administrator had handed me in a half-hearted attempt to read them, but my attention was always on my phone screen until finally the dots appeared.

> SYBIL: This is Emi. I took Sybil's
> phone because she was getting so
> upset about you not responding
> and spiraling about ruining your life.

SYBIL: So, I can tell her you texted, or
you can figure out a better way to begin
this conversation because I think you
both deserve more than a text.

SYBIL: And how is your Granddad?
Lila gives Marcus updates but
Sybil's worried sick about him.

I smiled to myself at the snappy, almost leveling tone of the
first text and the care in the second. Sybil's friends were so much
like her, and I missed her so much it had become an actual ache.

KIERAN: He's doing better. Outlook
is good. Thank you and Deacon for
helping with the shop.

I thought about how much had changed in my life from
three months ago. I wouldn't have called anyone to help three
months earlier—I wouldn't have *had* anyone to call. And now
I didn't have to call—Sybil's people showed up for us, no questions asked; our neighbors showed up; we even got a nice note
and get-well-soon flowers from Maria at Channel 13. Things
were being taken care of without me orchestrating any of it,
and it was okay. Things were more than okay, actually, I
thought as I looked through the glass on the door at Lila and
Granddad laughing, and then returned to my phone.

KIERAN: And please don't tell her I
texted an apology. I'll figure out a
better way to start this conversation.

47

Sybil

"JOIN THE PARTY," DEACON SAID, LOOKING UP FROM where he was reading on the couch. He spread one arm across the back of the cushion and coaxed me forward. "Don't worry, I'll keep my numerous charms at bay."

He pulled me against him, squeezing my shoulder, and I sank into him, inhaling the scent of his soap. He was wearing his glasses, which he only did for reading. I didn't even know he needed glasses until he started classes. "What are you studying?"

"It's for my psych class." He closed the book, using his finger to mark his place. "The professor is having us read popular books in addition to the textbook."

"*ADHD for Smart Ass Women*," I said, tracing a finger over the title. I touched my pocket; it was an automatic habit to search for my phone, though Emi had confiscated it that morning. "Good book?"

"Well, it's homework," he said, pushing his glasses up on

his nose. "But, yeah, not bad. Did you know women are under-diagnosed because ADHD often looks different in them than in boys and men, and professionals haven't paid attention to the differences for years? Isn't that fucked up?"

I nodded. "But you're gonna change all that when you're Dr. Deacon?"

He laughed and opened the book again. "Nah, but I'll learn from the people already changing things." Everyone had been surprised when Deac finally shared he had started school to study psychology. I wasn't, though. He was fun and wild and unpredictable, but he always had a spark for helping people. When he talked about people he served with, his expression was different. He was planning to reenlist, but I always thought he'd make a good therapist someday. Someday. Not today, because he was currently flashing his abs and smirking. "Dr. Deacon has a nice ring to it, though. Might sound good screamed by the next woman who can't resist me, huh?"

"Never change, Deac." I laughed, something I hadn't done much of at all in the previous few days. It felt good, if a little forced, and I snuggled against him, pushing the hem of his T-shirt back down. "Just don't let me near your admissions office."

He didn't respond to that but tightened his hold on my shoulder. "You hear from him?"

I shook my head. "No, and Emi took my phone."

"Want me to distract her so you can get it back? She thinks I don't notice how she checks me out when I take my shirt off, but nothing escapes me."

I laughed again, thankful for our easy rapport. "No, she was right. I was in bad shape waiting for a reply." I must have sent fifteen texts and left a bunch of voicemails, and nothing. Then

I'd felt guilty bothering him while he was taking care of Joe, and then back to knowing I needed to apologize. When Emi had taken my phone, I was curled in a ball on her bed staring at it. "He's not going to reply. I think I ruined it."

"You meant well," he said, still looking down at the book. "How much did you offer the school, anyway?"

"Three million dollars," I mumbled into his shirt. I wasn't even sure where I'd pulled the number from, but one felt like a lot, so I figured three would guarantee they let him extend the offer to go back. "I should have asked him, or maybe he's right and I should just stop doing things. My ideas are bad, Deac."

"That's not true," he said. "Most of your ideas are pretty good. You suggested my last tattoo." He pointed to the spot on his chest where there was a tattoo of Cupcake's paw print under his cotton T-shirt. "And you're the one who made me think of psychology. You told me I was a good listener. No one ever told me that before." He flipped the page. "And you put together that whole thing at the zoo."

"But I got my fake boyfriend who'd become a real boyfriend kicked out of medical school. I ruined his chances at being a doctor."

"Yeah," he said. "That didn't work out, and I want to kick his ass for yelling at you like that. I will, you know. If you want."

I chuckled and pulled my hoodie over my knees. "Marcus was a pretty good defender, and I deserved the yelling." I toyed with the cuticle on my fingernail. "He thinks I just flit through life waiting for things to happen, that I don't think about consequences."

Deacon tensed under me.

"You think he's right. He probably is."

"No," he said, setting the book down on the table in front of us and angling toward me. "He's not right, not like that, but sometimes you do put off committing to things. You act in the moment a lot. And from what you've said about growing up, you got lectured when you failed or struggled and other people saw it, so who could blame you for waiting for things to feel lucky? I mean, you *are* a lucky person, Syb. Hell, I'm jealous."

"What's that thing where you stop being scared of something after you're around it a lot? I'm probably not scared of fucking up in front of people anymore."

"Exposure therapy," he said. "It's why you're not scared of my long, thick, and frankly impressive—"

My laugh bubbled out and cut him off. "No, no. I get it. And I was never scared of that."

He leaned forward and reached for the book, tapping the cover. "I actually thought of you while I was reading this."

"Think it'll fix me?"

The laugh fell from his voice. "There's nothing to fix, Syb." He handed me the book. "But a lot of what the author talks about in this book reminded me of you, and it's all about how brains can work differently. It's a lot about how to make the most of the brain you have, and the tools and resources available to help." He shrugged and stood, stretching his arms across his chest and leaving me with the book in my hands. "Maybe it'll give you a different perspective on yourself, because I know how dope you are and I think Kieran does, too."

Deacon leaned over the couch and dropped a friendly kiss on the side of my head. "If you knew it, too, if you had a different way to look at things, it might make talking to him easier if you get the chance. Trust your own dopeness, my friend."

It was such a Deacon thing to say, and I mulled over what he'd said as I watched him pack things into his backpack. "Are you going to work?"

"Nah." He clapped his hands to rouse Cupcake from her snoring. "A buddy of mine is deploying soon and asked me to look out for his little sister when she gets to town to take care of his dog." He cajoled Cupcake from her spot on the couch. "Taking Cup for a walk, then getting more details from him."

He led Cupcake to the backyard, and then I flipped through the book, studying the table of contents and wondering if it was possible Deacon was right. There was only one person I wanted to talk about it with, and I turned to the first page of the book, wondering if I'd ever get the chance. I read the first few pages and sank into the couch. If Deac was right, and I hadn't always been doing things wrong, just doing them differently, my whole life would look different. It wouldn't change anything with Kieran, but I thought about all the times he'd told me to believe in myself, to focus on my strengths, and I wondered if that was something I could actually do.

48

Kieran

I DROPPED THE SEVENTEENTH JUG OF PENNIES INTO
the trunk of my car with a grunt. I'd planned to just
collect my own, but people in the shop took notice and started
leaving them, and then strangers would show up with their
own containers full of pennies. The jars had to contain hundreds of dollars at this point.

"That the last one?" Lila leaned against the car. She'd been
with Granddad all morning in the apartment until the home
health aide arrived to check on him, part of what Sybil had
arranged along with the hospital bill.

"Yeah," I said, wiping my brow. We'd spent the morning
taking inventory of the shop and what would need to be done
ahead of selling. Lila and I had made a long list, from dealing
with supplies and equipment to finding out if we needed to
paint or make repairs. I thought it would be sadder, but adding
things to the list felt good. I hadn't realized how much I'd felt
like most of my life was standing still, and the list getting

longer and longer made it seem like we were building to something even though I wasn't sure what it was. "Do you think this will work?"

She shrugged one shoulder. "It's pretty romantic," she said, walking toward the open trunk. "You're going to take them out to the bridge?"

I nodded, thinking through my plan again. "It's a spot she likes, and Emi and Marcus said they'd get her there." I shifted my weight from foot to foot, nerves working through my body. "Is Marcus still pissed at me?"

"Yeah, but I asked him not to hulk out on you this time." She chuckled. "You nervous?"

I ran a hand through my hair. "A little, and . . . excited. If this works, I get her back, and that seems like the best possible outcome."

"I think it'll work. And you're ready to forgive her?"

I nodded and closed the trunk. "Staying mad means losing her, and . . . that's not worth it. So . . ." I ran the back of my hand over my forehead. "I want to talk and figure it out."

She grinned. "Then let's go," she said.

"Um, you're not invited." I pulled my keys from my pocket.

"Who else is going to stop Marcus from punching you in the jaw?"

"Will you stop him with a kiiiiiiiiss?" I teased my sister as I put the car in reverse to work my way out of the alley and earned a punch in the arm, and even that seemed like a good omen.

Lila helped me haul the jars from my trunk the short distance to the bridge. If Sybil said no, I was hoping someone would rob me so I wouldn't have to transport them again, but now they caught the sunlight as the spring breeze blew off the water, and sparkles swirled around us. Lila patted my shoulder as we saw Marcus's car approach, and he pulled into a spot on the other side of the bridge. "Good luck," she said, jogging across the street after a quick look in both directions to greet the group as they climbed out of the car. Sybil wore jeans and a pink T-shirt, and it felt like she caught the sunlight, too. She looked between her friends, confused, and then I watched as Lila wrapped her in a hug and then said something before pointing to me.

A delivery truck lumbered past as she turned, and my heart rate rose the second I lost sight of her. I hoped it wasn't a sign that my own luck had run out once I finally believed in luck and fate—when the truck came to a stop behind a line of traffic. "Shit," I muttered, starting to jog the few feet to look behind the back of the truck, but as I heard a honk from a car going the other direction, I saw Sybil jogging toward me, waving a hand in apology to the car. Her curls blew loose around her head, and she brushed them away from her face with the breeze.

"Hi," she said, scooting behind the truck to join me on the sidewalk.

"Hi," I said, holding out my hand to help her onto the curb. I'd come close to forgetting how right her hand felt in mine. "I'm . . . glad this didn't start with you getting hit by a truck."

"I told you I'm lucky," she said. She glanced over the bridge at the water. "You remembered I love this spot."

I nodded. "For making wishes."

She bit her lower lip. "I wish I hadn't made that phone call," she said. "You can't know how sorry I am. I would take it back if I could." She looked up at me through her dark lashes, and I saw the hint of tears.

"I know." I cupped her cheek, the tip of my middle finger grazing her earlobe. "I'm sorry I reacted the way I did."

"I deserved it," she said.

"You didn't." I sucked in a breath. "I thought my wish was to be a surgeon and this whole situation was lucky because it would allow me to get back to school." She opened her mouth to apologize again, but I pressed a finger gently to her lips. "But I think luck looks different than what I thought, because I don't know what my professional dream is anymore. What I do know is I can't imagine wanting any dream for myself that you're not a part of. And if I'm honest with myself, I was more upset about my plan changing than about what actually happened."

She stared at me with tears welling in her eyes, and even though I'd rehearsed this in my head over and over, it was coming out all jumbled with her in front of me. I stepped back and pointed to the ground where the jars sat. "And I don't think I would have realized that was possible before you."

Her eyes grew wide looking at the jars. "You got me lucky pennies?"

"Everyone I knew brought them to me, and then people at the shop started dropping them off." I pointed at the mason jar on the right. "That one is from Granddad and Tom. They wanted me to tell you that."

Sybil pressed a palm to her mouth and bent down, tracing her fingers over each jar.

"I can't give you much," I admitted, crouching down to join her. "I don't have a plan right now. I don't know what I'm going to do, and my sister informs me that therapy should be in my future, but I thought if I could give you this, if I could give you hundreds and hundreds of coins to wish on, well, maybe it might be a start." I took her hand again. "You made me believe in luck, and love, and wishes coming true, and I want you to have all the lucky pennies that you can because you deserve every single one of them."

The delivery truck that had been idling behind us finally rumbled past, and over her shoulder I saw Emi, Marcus, Lila, and Deacon waiting by Marcus's car and watching us. Sybil looked from me to the pennies and then over her shoulder at her friends.

"So I guess I'm asking you if we can still be real." I heard that same ticking clock I'd heard in the hospital hallway, but this time it didn't tick for long because I knew exactly what to say next. "I love you, Sybil. I'm not worried about losing control in my life anymore, because I've lost it. You're all I think about. I love you so much, I'd willingly get in your passenger seat, knowing my life was in jeopardy."

She giggled through tears. "I don't drive that fast. Maybe you just go too slow."

"Maybe," I said, realizing how much I'd missed touching her and feeling her skin under my fingers.

"Syb. I didn't trust that good things could happen to me before you. But you're my good thing, and loving you . . . having you look up at me like you are now is the best thing, and I want you for keeps." I cupped her cheek, brushing a tear away with my thumb. "You're what I'd wish for every time."

She bent to pluck a penny from the top of one of the jars. She held it between us, kissed the air in front of it, and threw it into the river. It caught the sun's light for a moment as it hung suspended in the air before falling into the water below and disappearing beneath the current.

"Will you tell me what you wished for?"

She shook her head and wrapped her arms around my neck, her soft body pressed to mine, and I knew I'd never let her go again. "If you tell, it doesn't come true," she said against my neck. "We've gone over this before."

"Okay," I said, cupping the back of her neck. "But can I get a hint?"

She sank her teeth into her lower lip and then nodded, tipping her chin up, and I didn't hesitate to press my lips to hers, drinking in the warmth and sunlight taste of her kisses.

"It's felt real to me for such a long time." She held on to me. "I wanted my family to take me seriously before I knew how to do that myself, and now I'm really trying to take myself seriously, and it's because of you." Her fingers clutched my shirt, and I felt the pressure of them over my chest. "I love you, too."

My cheeks hurt from the stretch of the smile. "Will you please tell me what you wished for?"

She shook her head but wrapped her arms around my neck. "No!" The cheers of Sybil's friends and Lila from across the street registered in the background, but when she attempted to look at them, I pulled her lips back to mine.

If I was lucky enough to kiss her again, I wasn't going to let anything stop me.

EPILOGUE

Good Morning, Des Moines
Transcript

MARIA: Viewers may remember our next guests from their
    sweet viral videos last year. A lost winning lottery ticket, a
    donut shop, and a love story we all fell for. Welcome back,
    Sybil and Kieran.

SYBIL: Thank you for having us on the show again.

MARIA: Now, it's been quite a year for you two. What's
    changed since then?

SYBIL & KIERAN: [*chuckle*]

KIERAN: Is "everything" a fair answer?

SYBIL: He's not wrong. We're still in Des Moines, but yes, a lot
    has changed!

MARIA: Sybil, you've started a nonprofit to help local
    families. Can you tell us about it?

SYBIL: The Rosie Foundation is named for Kieran's
    grandmother. It's dedicated to supporting housing and
    food insecurity for metro families. Kieran and I have seen

the impact support can have, and right now, we're working with the Pennsylvania Street Shelter to raise funds for their expansion. So far, we've raised two point six million dollars, and you can join us this weekend in getting to our goal of three and a half million.

MARIA: See the event information on the bottom of the screen. What a wonderful initiative. And so important. And, Kieran, when you're not supporting Sybil's philanthropy work, you've been busy as well?

KIERAN: Yes, I will begin a graduate program in biomedical science in a couple months.

SYBIL: He's going to be an incredible medical researcher, answering the big questions.

MARIA: Wow! You're one busy couple. And what about Joe's Donuts?

KIERAN: We sold the shop—it was time for someone else to take over.

SYBIL: It's called the M-Shop now. There's no better lunch spot in town.

KIERAN: My granddad always wants to eat there, which is high praise for Marcus, the chef and owner.

MARIA: I notice a little sparkle on your hand, Sybil. Anything else you want to share?

SYBIL: Oh, yes. We got engaged last night, actually.

MARIA: Wow! Congratulations! Want to tell us about the proposal?

SYBIL: Well . . .

KIERAN: You know . . .

SYBIL: So much of our relationship was public, I think we'd rather keep that story just for us.

MARIA: Totally understand. Well, we're glad you could join us again in the studio, and viewers can stop by the M-Shop for lunch and consider supporting the Rosie Foundation. Up next, our news team has information about a local education company that is under new leadership and a wave of people adopting hedgehogs from the West Coast to keep as pets, plus more fun things to do as we move into spring. Stay tuned.

CREW: We're clear.

MARIA: Thanks again for coming back. Sybil, you're almost a regular guest now, and we got so many calls after the interview we did with you and others about seeking an ADHD diagnosis as an adult. I read the book you mentioned that your friend gave you, the one you said helped some pieces fall into place, and women viewers especially responded so strongly to you saying what it meant to have another lens to understand yourself.

SYBIL: That segment was great. I still talk to the other three women. Jasmine and I have actually discovered a shared love of go-kart racing. We're going later this weekend.

KIERAN: [*laughs*] She's a natural speed demon. Everyone knows to watch out.

SYBIL: Hey, now. Don't be salty just because you're too scared to compete with me.

KIERAN: You're right. I couldn't keep up. Happy to cheer from the sidelines.

MARIA: [*laughs*] You're a good match.

KIERAN: We're lucky to have found each other.

SYBIL: Very lucky.

ACKNOWLEDGMENTS

Jason Mraz and Colbie Caillat sang "Lucky I'm in love with my best friend," which couldn't be truer for me. Thank you to my husband for being a constant source of encouragement, humor, absolutely awful plot ideas (seriously, why do I keep asking?), and of course, love. None of my books, especially this one, would come to life without you.

Writing lively, caring, funny family members is never a challenge because of all the real-life examples I have from my own caring, lively, hilarious, and supportive family. I love you, Williams, Jr.—you're absolutely my favorite kid. Thank you to Mom and Dad, Jay and Amanda, Mike and Melissa, Bruce and Jean, Barb, Tim, Allison, Kaitlin, all the ARFCO cousins, and the best niece and nephews anyone could hope for.

Kerry Donovan sprinkles magic onto every book we work on, and I'm so lucky to have her as an editor. Thank you to the Berkley team—working with you is like being surprised with a dozen of your favorite donuts every morning. Thank you especially to Genni Eccles, Dache' Rogers, and Kalie Barnes-Young, along with the Berkley creative, marketing, and sales teams. A huge thank-you to Kristin Dwyer and the LeoPR team—so thankful for you!

I feel like I've won the lottery with my agent, Sharon Pelletier. Thank you for always being in my corner and knowing the right mix of sugar and salt to bring to our conversations! I appreciate you. Thank you also to Lauren Abramo, Nataly Gruender, Masie Ibrahim, and Gracie Freeman Lifschutz at Dystel, Goderich & Bourret and Kristina Moore at UTA.

Liz Parkes designed the cover for this book, and I will never be over how beautiful it is. Thank you for capturing Sybil and Kieran and the energy of their love story. You're incredibly talented, and every single piece of art you create leaves me breathless—thank you for being part of this story. Thank you also to production editor Lindsey Tulloch and copy editor Angelina Krahn.

To the RFC Turtles. You inspire me. Thank you to Jen DeLuca, Rosie Danan, Alexa Martin, Suzanne Park, Nikki Payne, Ali Hazelwood, Olivia Dade, Natalie Caña, and Pris Oliveras, among so many other authors whose words make me smile and whose friendship I value dearly. In addition to being inspiring writers, thank you to Rachel Mans McKenny and Janine Amesta for your help editing and developing this story—donuts and coffee will always be on me.

For Bethany, Emily, Haley, Sarah, Jessica, Kristine, Tera, Ambre, and Suzi, just thank you. I switched careers midway through writing this book, and though the change was an excellent decision, I will be forever thankful for the colleagues who listened, mentored, cheered, and laughed with me through it all. For Jasmine, Jacki, Harun, Matt, Amanda, Sahira, Jen, Tera, Kelly, Milly, and so many others, thank you for years of friendship! For Molly, Anette, Lora Leigh, Jim, Jennifer, Dynette, Taylor, Allie, and all my other new colleagues, I'd be remiss if I didn't say how the joy and fulfillment I've found working with you has left me ready to write about love and happiness.

Finally, thank you to Juicy Readers and all the readers who choose to spend time with my books. Ten books in, it's still wildly affirming to know my words are invited into your heart. Thank you for loving my imaginary people as much as I do!

KEEP READING FOR AN EXCERPT FROM

Technically Yours

1

Cord

Five Years Earlier

WHEN SHE WALKED OUT THE DOOR, THE SCENT OF her lingered in the air like a reminder of the what-ifs burrowing into my head, and I stared at the set of house keys on my desk. The two identical cuts sat side by side, the light reflecting on the surface of the metal. Since Pearl had made her choice, I needed to let her walk away and set off on the path she'd chosen. I needed to give up on all the nights under the stars, and the feel of her skin dusted with sand, and my pathetic heart. I knew that, but I was still on my feet and halfway to the door before the sound of her heels on the tile had faded.

"Wait," I called out. The overhead lighting against the dark sky outside the office windows was like a muted spotlight making the white of her shirt that much brighter against her skin. Her gaze had traveled back down the hall toward my door, and our eyes met for an instant. "Pearl. Wait."

At my approach, she turned, giving me her back and a view

of the nape of her neck, the soft and supple skin I'd wanted to kiss a hundred times. "I don't think we have anything else to say to each other."

My instinct was to step back, to walk away and let her go. But damnit, this was Pearl. I shifted so I was close enough to feel the warmth of her body and waited for her to pull away. I was basically asking for the pain of more rejection, but then she shifted toward me, one tiny, incremental movement, and I slid my fingertips down her biceps, the contact between us like a thousand micro shock waves on my skin. "Will you look at me?" I didn't stop the slide of my fingertips over her arms. "Please."

Her eyes met mine and held when she turned to face me, resignation in her voice. "What's left to say?"

"I just want to know one thing," I said. A crease settled between her brows and I gently wrapped my hand around her wrist, raising it so we could both see her tattoo. "Your heart." I grazed my thumb across her wrist, pausing on the third star inked there. "If it spoke louder than your head, what would it say right now?"

"Cord, what does it matter?"

I lifted her wrist higher in response, breaking eye contact with her to examine the stars I'd memorized while hoping for something more between us. "It matters to me." I spoke against the tattoo, my lips brushing over her skin, and I could feel the hitch of her breath.

"It doesn't matter what my heart would say, because . . ." Pearl brushed hair off my forehead, the contact making me close my eyes for a second. This was the moment. This was *our* moment, and I didn't want to lose it. Behind her, the doors to the elevator opened, but she didn't move as we continued to search each other's faces. The words hung between us, unfinished, while she brushed the same spot again and then slid her fingers into my hair. "Because my heart is unreliable."

Our lips were a breath apart in the empty lobby, but the whole space felt full, full of everything I knew we both wanted, everything we could be. My voice was low when I spoke. "Nothing about you is unreliable." I drew her closer, and the soft way she leaned into me felt both familiar and brand-new.

"I should listen to my head." She stepped back, not letting go. "I need to listen to my head."

With her back against the wall, I inched closer, my hand now firmly at her waist. "But what would your *heart* say?" Pearl wore delicate diamond studs that gently scratched my lip when I spoke near her ear. "Because it should get a say."

"Cord . . ." She let my name hang there. I don't know if she moved first or I did, but then our mouths met, lips and tongues melding in the way I'd imagined for so long. The kiss deepened, and my whole body reacted to every move of her soft lips. The way she held me, fingers digging in, made me feel claimed in the best way.

"Don't go," I panted, breaking the kiss and then taking her mouth again, holding her lower back to pull her flush against me. When she rocked her hips, soft meeting hard, I groaned, needing more. "Stay with me." I trailed my lips down her jaw before finding her lips again, my palm at her neck to hold her to me.

Pearl deepened the kiss, her fingers in my hair like an answer, but then she stepped back, eyes wide and the pulse in her neck throbbing. "It's too risky." She fumbled behind her and pushed the down button as I regained my senses.

"What? No. I don't understand." My heart pounded, and I shook my head as if rebooting this moment.

When the doors opened behind her, I thought about reaching out, of pulling her back into the kiss, but she'd stepped out of reach on purpose. "If I could put heart first for anyone, Cord, it would have been you." She took two steps backward into the waiting car.

"But . . . but it *can* be me." I wished I had more practice fighting, because I wanted to fight for her, get her footsteps to move toward me and not away, but my head still spun from that kiss. "You can put your heart first with me right now."

"It's not what I need. I don't want . . . I can't want this. You know I can't." Pearl shook her head as the doors began to close. "But I wish I could."

By the time I lunged forward, my brain connecting with my body, the doors had shut and I was left in the empty lobby, with the imprint of her kiss on my lips and every muscle in my body poised to follow her and fight for this. But she didn't want to fight, and she was already gone. Still, I waited for the doors to open, holding my breath in hopes she'd change her mind.

I waited a long time, staring at my warped reflection in the elevator doors before deciding I would never wait like that again and never put myself in a situation where I wanted to.

2

Pearl
Present Day

As I FLIPPED OVER MY PHONE, THE THIN GOLD bracelet on my wrist caught the light, the chain cutting through the four small stars tattooed on my wrist.

SHEA: Show me the dress.

PEARL: I'm not taking a selfie. I'm in the middle of the first big social event of my career.

SHEA: I know you look bangable.

PEARL: Bangable isn't my aim. I'm working right now.

SHEA: Your aim lacks creativity. This is why I'm the fun sister.

I brushed my fingers against the smooth satin of the gold floor-length gown before slipping my phone into my clutch and closing it with a gentle, satisfying snap. The wash of the cool breeze from the air-conditioning swept over the exposed skin at my back, and I straightened at the prickling sensation. The room swirled with people, and before I stepped back into the hall, I surveyed the countless donors and supporters in formal wear.

On the far side of the room, Ellie Dawson laughed with a trio of people in their seventies. The two of us had started in our new roles a few weeks earlier, and I knew in the coming years we'd compete to secure a promotion to director when the current director retired. After five years in California, I'd come back to Chicago for the right job and to leave the wrong man. Ironic, since what I thought was the right job took me to the West Coast in the first place, even though it had been impossibly hard to leave. Now I was focused on OurCode. Taking another deep breath, I reminded myself that this was *the* job. After everything I'd gone through to get to this point, this room and these new faces were an essential part of my next steps, and I couldn't afford for anything to distract me.

I stepped inside and reviewed my game plan for the evening, particularly who I was supposed to connect with based on our pre-gala preparations. OurCode, like other programs designed to encourage kids with traditionally marginalized identities to take an interest in coding and careers in tech, had support across the industry and a solid reputation. The assembled crowd had paid a thousand dollars a head to attend and would donate more to support the program's expansion to serve more kids in more ways. That expansion was a priority for the board and my boss, Kendra, and the gala was going to be the launching pad for our new plans. I scanned the room for Kendra again. It was odd that she hadn't arrived yet.

"Pearl, a minute?" The chairperson of the OurCode board touched my elbow. Kevin wore a tux, his entire look put together, except for a deep crease between his brows. He was also the CEO of Kaleidescape, a cybersecurity company whose stock had risen fast, and he wore a harried expression on his face.

"Sure."

He waved Ellie over as well, and we walked toward a corner of the ballroom, where he waved off any pleasantries. "Kendra isn't coming tonight."

To my right, Ellie stilled, her shock seeming to register along with mine. "What?" and "Why?" came from us at the same time.

"I can't get into the details for legal reasons, but she has resigned from OurCode, effective immediately." Kevin's tone was hushed, and both of us leaned forward.

"She quit?" Ellie's voice was a hiss, and she shook her head as if trying to slot the new information into existing grooves in her brain.

The impatience that bled into his tone made it clear he wasn't planning to give us any further information. "She is no longer affiliated with the program."

I intentionally took a slow breath before speaking, the combined weight of the bodies behind us suddenly making me feel claustrophobic. "There are hundreds of people here expecting to learn about the future of the program. We arranged everything around Kendra making those announcements. What are we going to do?" In my head, I pictured the detailed plans we'd spent weeks on, the speech we'd crafted, the hours spent toiling over the right wording and how to frame the strategic goals.

"One of you will have to give the speech." He still looked like he'd rather be anywhere else.

"That will raise red flags," Ellie said. "Can you do it as chair?"

Kevin ignored her question. "Neither of you knows the speech?"

My stomach dropped, and I pulled my sweaty palms away from the fabric of my dress. "I know the speech, but . . ."

"Okay, well, Pearl, you do it. Come Monday, we'll figure the rest out. You *can* do it, right?"

I glanced to my left, expecting Ellie to step in, to take the spotlight, but she'd literally taken a step back, so I returned my gaze to Kevin. "I could, but wouldn't it be better coming from you or another board member?" *Or someone who isn't petrified by the idea of standing on a stage.*

He glanced over my shoulder, a polished expression returning to his features when he made eye contact with someone else. "I'm sure you'll be fine." He held up a hand to whoever had caught his eye. "We'll touch base afterward. Excuse me."

He left us standing in unsteady silence, and Ellie turned to me. "What the hell just happened?"

Just me volunteering to speak in front of three hundred people because our boss is mysteriously gone. I took another quick breath, knowing I didn't get to lose it, not in this space and not in this room.

Ellie's tone was doubtful, and I realized our moment of shared uncertainty was already over. "Are you sure you can give the speech?"

Even though I wasn't, her tone irked me. "I don't have a choice." *And it's not like you stepped up.* I gave her a slight smile and searched the stage for the notebook containing a printout of the speech along with reference materials. That notebook contained everything I'd need to cram before getting onstage and coming face-to-face with my fear of public speaking, and I reluctantly left Ellie to mingle with donors while I prepared.

Once I sat backstage with the binder, I let myself freak out, now that there was no one around I needed to think I was bulletproof. I'd never been one to let my guard down at work, certainly not in this new position. The only time I had was when I worked at FitMi, and even then, it was really just with one person.

Cord's face filled my mind. His sable-brown eyes and long lashes—lashes many people would kill for—and his hair that was always a little too long, falling over his face and tempting me to brush it back, the wayward strands begging for my fingers. He could have been the right man for me in a different universe. Cord told me once that he'd give me a sign if he was in the room and I had to do something hard. He'd met my eyes and told me I could speak directly to him, and he'd be smiling. I sipped from my glass of wine and grinned at the memory. He'd been so sure that if I ever had to be on a stage, he'd be there to support me. That was when the idea of us as a couple was a fantasy I only allowed myself to entertain when there was time to wrestle my heart and imagination back under control. That was before there was a real chance and then a real choice. And it was before I made that choice.

He'd been my boss, then we'd been friends, and one night, I'd given in to the urge to brush the hair off his face, and we'd almost been so much more. Now he was nothing, and we hadn't spoken in years. I let my eyes fall closed, the sounds of the hum of conversation and smatterings of laughter rising over the din of the bustling hall. They were all going to be staring at me. My neck heated, and the dress felt too small, but there was no choice—I couldn't go back to Kevin and tell him I couldn't do it or that I was scared.

I opened my eyes and read through the speech again, even though I didn't need to. I'd written it and practically had it memorized. I did not know what would happen in the organization without Kendra, but three weeks into a new job, I didn't intend to be the weak link. Ellie was hoping I'd at least stumble, giving her the upper hand.

Not today.

The lights dimmed, and the volume rose with the sounds of people moving toward seats. I imagined a sea of black tuxes spotted with colorful gowns and pastel satin moving between the tables like water, everyone full of dinner and cocktails. After a quick check-in with the student speaker I'd be introducing, I smoothed my hair, checking my edges, then rested a palm on my stomach and took another slow breath. *Okay.*

My fingers shook as I clutched the notebook, and the memory of Cord's too-long hair and baritone voice once again filled my head. *Speak to me. I'll be smiling.*

I decided I would still picture him—even though I'd made sure he would never actually be there—and I stepped out onto the stage.

Denise Williams wrote her first book in the second grade. *I Hate You* and its sequel, *I Still Hate You*, featured a tough, funny heroine; a quirky hero; witty banter; and a dragon. Minus the dragons, these are still the books she likes to write. After penning those early works, she finished second grade and eventually earned a PhD in education. When she's not writing, reading, and thinking about love stories, she spends her days working in university administration. After growing up a military brat around the world and across the country, Denise now lives in Des Moines, Iowa, with her husband, son, and a dog so quirky, she really needs to end up in a book.

VISIT DENISE WILLIAMS ONLINE

DeniseWilliamsWrites.com
X NicWillWrites
NicWillWrites
AuthorDeniseWilliams
NicWillWrites

Ready to find
your next great read?

Let us help.

Visit prh.com/nextread

Penguin
Random
House